GOOD PEOPLE

Ewart Hutton

WINDSOR
PARAGON

First published 2012
by Blue Door
This Large Print edition published 2012
by AudioGO Ltd
by arrangement with
HarperCollins*Publishers*

Hardcover   ISBN: 978 1 445 84230 1
Softcover   ISBN: 978 1 445 84231 8

British Library Cataloguing in Publication Data available

Printed and bound in Great Britain by
MPG Books Group Limited

For Annie, Mercedes and Calum

I could have gone home by a different route, I could have driven a lot slower, but it was late, the end of a long and tedious day. My inner child was nudging, so I let the self-centred little bastard slip out of his cage. It would be a distraction, and I would only be adding a couple of minor new enemies.

Boy was that going to prove to be one great big painful underestimation.

The squad car was off to the side, parked up on a stakeout for hayseed drunks, just where their radio chatter had placed them. I caught a glimpse of it in my headlights as I crested the hill. Getting on for close to midnight, and I was tramping it.

They pulled out behind me, their full light rig coming on to crank up the drama. I played with them down through a few safe bends, and then pulled over to give them at least the start of their Stormtrooper moment.

'Detective Sergeant Glyn Capaldi.' I grinned up into their torch beam and waved my warrant card.

Now they were truly regretting it. Driver and Shotgun, both of them young. They knew me by reputation. Hawked up and spat out of Cardiff, and put out to graze in the tundra. And here I was with my Jonah vibe ranged out over their rear seat. And I was drinking their coffee supply. I was no longer in a hurry. This had turned into my Saturday night. The ratshit investigation I was working on had left it too late for me to make it to The Fleece in Dinas before closing time.

The talk was desultory. They didn't quite trust me enough to bitch about the job. We stuck mainly to the safe subjects of high-performance cars we had chased, and gruesome RTA's attended.

Their call sign broke through an undercurrent of static on the radio. Shotgun picked up the handset eagerly.

I leaned forward to rest my arms on the back of his seat. 'I speak Welsh,' I warned him cheerily. It was mainly a lie—my Italian was better, and that wasn't good—but he didn't need to know that.

But he ran with the bluff and took the call in English. A minibus driver had reported being hijacked and abandoned in a lay-by.

'Been nice having your company, Sarge,' Driver said, strapping in, and starting the engine up.

I eased myself over to the door. 'I'll follow you down. It's on my way home.'

They didn't like it, but they didn't argue. Arguing would have kept me in their car.

I pulled out behind them. With their blue strobe turned off, the night had got big again. Gradations of darkness, treetops in serrated silhouette, the loom of the hills against the paler sky, dishcloth shreds of clouds trawling in from the west. Rain before morning—my newly acquired Pig Wales lore.

We found the minibus driver sheltering in a telephone booth outside the hulk of a Baptist chapel. The booth's light was the only illumination in the street of a village that looked like its occupants had packed up and retired underground for the winter.

He crossed the street towards us as we parked, stepping off the pavement without checking. He had obviously been hanging around for long enough to know the likelihood of traffic. He walked with the stride of a man who is advertising grievances.

Driver and Shotgun got out of their car with that air Traffic guys have of sloughing skin every time that they exit their vehicle. It was their call, so I hung back out of courtesy, just listening in. Catching that the minibus driver had managed to flag down a car that had dropped him here. By his estimation, we were already something like two hours into the event. You could cover a lot of Wales in two hours.

'How many passengers were there, sir?'

'Six. I was taking the bastards to Dinas.' He looked at the three of us entreatingly. 'It's not as if we'd even fucking argued about anything.'

I nodded sympathetically from the sidelines, my interest raised by the mention of Dinas.

'They were totally pissed, all of them, not one of them would have been capable of driving safely,' he protested righteously.

'Do you have the names of the passengers?' Driver asked.

'No, you'll have to get those from the office. I was just told to pick them up at Shrewsbury Station, off the train from London. They'd been at the England–Wales match at Twickenham.'

'Did you see who actually drove the minibus away, sir?'

'It was the middle of the night out there. A poxy lay-by full of puddles and junk.'

'You were outside the vehicle?' I asked, slipping into the conversation. 'Detective Sergeant Glyn Capaldi,' I introduced myself, calculating that it was

3

time to start trying to sharpen this thing to a point. Driver gave me a look, but it was a token, he knew that he was outranked.

'They tricked me,' the minibus driver protested.

'How did they manage that?'

'One of them told me someone was going to be sick. I hate that smell,' he announced vehemently. 'Beer puke on the upholstery, you can't get rid of it. So I found somewhere to pull over quickly. Two of them got out and went round the back as soon as I stopped.'

'Did you hear them being sick?'

'No. A lot of passengers get sick for one reason or another, and I don't listen out for it. I kept the engine running. Next thing one of them is at the door saying that there's something about my rear wheel that I should see. So I get out, and there's the other one crouching, kind of squinting at my nearside back tyre. "Should that be like that?" he asks me, and like a prat, I get down there trying to see what the fuck he's talking about. Next thing I know the bus takes off, and I'm left out there in the dark.'

'No build-up to this?' I asked. 'It came as a complete surprise?'

'Total. I thought they were all as happy as Larry in the back. What with the booze, their fucking rugby songs, and joking around with the girl.'

My face cracked. He looked at me, puzzled by the change. Driver and Shotgun hadn't picked up on it. 'What girl?' I demanded.

He swayed back defensively, shaking his head. 'A hitchhiker. It wasn't my idea. I didn't pick her up. I stopped for diesel at a garage this side of Newtown, and she was already inside when I got back from

4

paying. The passengers said they had offered her a ride to Dinas. I didn't argue.'

'Describe her,' I said, letting him hear the new snap in my voice.

He shook his head again, sickly smile set, wanting to help me now. 'I can't. She was stuck up in the back behind the men. I never saw her properly. I only heard her laughing back there.'

A flash: Regine Broussard.

I sometimes get a foreboding when things are about to go very, very wrong. It predicts awful possibilities from the merest of nuances. It translates as a melting feeling in the region of the kidneys. A little bit like sex. Perhaps it was my Ligurian genes? Warm loam reactions in a damp northern climate. Often it got me into trouble. I should have learned by now to run the other way, but some warped instinct always managed to spin me in the wrong direction.

And the tickle makes me wince.

Shotgun saw it. 'You all right, Sarge?' he asked, eyeing me curiously.

I ignored him. It had to be the woman. The source of the tickle. The presence of the woman added the crown of thorns.

Otherwise it was fairly typical Saturday-night bloke behaviour. Drink and testosterone fuelled. A prank with a potentially lethal edge. Sparked by impulse, opportunity—or the driver was not giving us the complete story of his relationship with his customers. Either way we had six drunks and a minibus, and a lot of different ways that they could wreck it.

How many ways did they have to wreck the woman?

5

What did I know about these men? According to the driver they were all young. They liked rugby. They supported the national team. They were country people. They had hired a minibus so that they could drink responsibly. All of that, if you discounted their age, stacked up reassuringly. Not quite nuns, but the profile was comfier than skanky-haired baby-fingerers with weighty Temazepam habits. A bunch of nice lads out on the town for the day.

So why the fuck had they turned idiotic?

There was no way to answer that yet. I left Driver and Shotgun to take the minibus driver back and deal with the procedures. Until we had a victim of some variety, or a complaint from someone other than the driver, I was redundant. I volunteered to cover the road between there and Dinas, keeping an eye out for the minibus.

With only a minor detour I let my route take me past the lay-by the driver had described. I used my high beams to light it up. Puddles and wind-blown rubbish. I got out and walked slowly. The hard light did weird things to empty crisp packets, disposable nappies and crushed drink cans. I almost missed it, floating upside-down in a puddle, the peak tipped away, looking like a miniature coracle.

It was a baseball cap. Dark blue, soaked, with an illegible logo. No telling how long it had been there. I turned it over and round in front of a headlight. No identifying labels. From its size, if could have belonged to a kid. Or a young woman with a small head. I put it in the glove compartment. I had thought about using an evidence bag, but I didn't want to tempt fate.

I saw nothing on the rest of the way home. No

skid marks, no smoking wreckage, no Indians circling the wagon train. I stopped in town and called Dispatch, gave my contact number, and asked them to log a message that I wanted to be kept up to date with the story.

Then I had no excuse. The Fleece was closed. The Chinese takeaway was closed. And a cold rain was starting, earlier than I had predicted. It was time for bed. I drove out of town. Heading for home.

The planks on the bridge rumbled under the wheels as I crossed the river into the utter blackness of Hen Felin Caravan Park. At this time of the year I was the only resident. Unit 13. I wasn't superstitious.

The site held the frost, the electricity supply was erratic, and the water that came out of the taps was the colour of weak tea, but there was an upside to the location. It kept the public away. People who might think that it was a local policeman's duty to help them out with squirrels in the attic, or neighbours playing the harmonium too loud. The site was out of town, badly lit, muddy, and in the holiday season it was full of outsiders whose brat-kids taunted the locals for speaking queerly.

Another advantage was that it was a caravan. It was temporary. It kept my impermanence tangible. Some day I would be leaving this awful place. Every time I walked in through the door, and was met by the mingled smells of condensation, plastic curtains and propane gas, I could remind myself that this was not going to last. This was the smell from family camping holidays long ago in Borth. And holidays in Borth had never lasted. Thank Christ.

The message light on the answering machine was

blinking. I hit the play button thinking that the dispatcher might have an update for me. Two messages. The first one was from a cop in Caernarfon who thought he might have some information on a stolen Kawasaki quad bike that I was investigating. I hoped that he was wrong. Caernarfon was way the hell to the north, and the geographical limits of this case were already stretching me.

The second message was even less welcome.

'Capaldi, it's Mackay, we need to talk.'

The voice was Scottish, clipped, and to the point. Mackay was ex-SAS and we went back a long way. Every time he resurfaced in my life trouble happened, albatrosses fell in flocks from the sky. Currently, he was only hopping along the fringe, having become my ex-wife's current lover.

It hadn't really upset me when he had taken up with Gina. In fact, it had had the beneficial effect of keeping both of them off my back. The trouble was that she, at this point in the orbit of our relationship, unjustifiably in my opinion, felt that I was the sack of shit in her life. Now I could start to worry. What poison had she managed to work into Mackay's system concerning me?

I double-checked the lock on the caravan before I went to bed. It was a token gesture, a fruit-juice carton would be more secure. After Mackay's call, I knew that I was going to be crediting every sound that I heard out there tonight with having army training.

I sent a flighted wish out into the night for the woman in the minibus to be safe. I didn't include the guys. They had got themselves into it, and I wanted to retain enough juju in my system to keep

8

Gina and Mackay out of my life.

*   *   *

The telephone woke me too early on Sunday morning. I registered wet windows, grey sky, and the branches of the riverside alders drooped and dripping as I lurched to the dining nook to answer it. On mornings like this I truly missed the city, where you could pretend that weather didn't exist.

'Glyn Capaldi,' I grunted.

'Sergeant, a minibus was hijacked last night over at . . .'

'I know,' I interrupted him, 'I left a message for you to keep me updated.'

He went silent for a moment. 'We've found it,' his tone changing to eager.

Overnight, the isobars had packed together and the wind was coming strong out of the northwest. And cold. The rain that stung my face as I opened the caravan door was thinking about applying for an upgrade to sleet.

I went out of town on the mountain road, climbing up to open hill country. Scrub grass, sedge and heather, with grey, lichen-splotched boulders crumbled in for texture. It was a big, scrappy geography up here.

The minibus was parked on a narrow lane beside a small arched bridge near the junction with the mountain road. There was a marked police car close by. Uniform locals. I recognized the man who was making a point of watching my approach. Sergeant Emrys Hughes. We knew each other. He didn't like me. It wasn't a complicated issue, just a matter of his boss detesting mine. The fact that I didn't like my boss either didn't seem to help.

He shouted something up at me as I parked on the splay. I ignored him. I wanted to take in an overview of the scene before I got involved in other people's perceptions.

The minibus was parked, neatly squared off, on a patch of compacted gravel. It hadn't been abandoned. Thought had gone into where and how it had been left.

Emrys turned away from me. He must have shouted something else, because two more uniforms appeared from behind the minibus, where they had been sheltering from the wind. Emrys issued an instruction, and one of them came over the bridge, and up the slight incline towards me. I smiled to myself, recognizing a troop movement.

He had his head lowered, and kept his face slanted away from me to keep the rain out of his eyes. I gestured for him to go round to the leeward side and dropped the passenger window. He lowered his face to the opening. Lanky and young, his eager expression overcompensating for his nervousness. 'Sergeant Hughes told me to tell you that we're in control of this.'

I leaned across the seat towards him and grinned. 'Sergeant Hughes told you to tell me to fuck off?'

His face dropped. 'No, Sergeant, not at all.'

'Where are the people from the minibus?' I asked before he could recompose himself. 'Have you managed to get them down off the hill?'

He looked confused, and shot an involuntary glance at Emrys. 'There weren't any people.'

'What were you doing round the back of the minibus?'

'Sheltering.'

'Had you checked for footprints, any other evidence, before you trampled the area?'

His brain mired on that one. I didn't wait for an answer. I got out of the car and fought my way into my coat, the wind whipping rebellious life into the sleeves and tail. It was even colder out here. The young cop caught up with me, trying to get my attention, but not quite daring to come abreast. I ignored him.

'Morning, Sergeant Hughes,' I called out affably.

He glared at me stonily. 'What are you doing here?'

'I got the call.'

He scowled. 'There was no call. Not for you. This isn't a CID matter, Capaldi. We're handling it.' As usual he put a heavy stress on my name. As if he had had a grandfather die on the Anzio beaches and I was somehow to blame. Emrys Hughes was a big man, with black, wavy hair, craggy features, and a mosaic of broken veins in his cheeks. His square bushy moustache and matching set of eyebrows looked like they might have been lifted from an identikit box.

I inclined my head towards the minibus. 'Have you put in a request for a SOCO team?'

'Why would I do that? This isn't a crime scene.'

'The minibus was stolen.'

He shrugged. 'And now it's here.'

'So what's your plan of action?'

'I've put a call in to contact the owner and get him to come up here with a spare set of keys.'

'You intend to move it?' I deliberately pitched my tone to needle him.

He struggled to keep his temper. 'It went missing. Now it's been found. Happy endings.'

11

'It was stolen, Sergeant.'

'I know the owner. I'm sure he won't want to press charges.'

'Someone was drunk in charge of a stolen minibus last night.'

He pulled a fat face and shrugged.

'Where are they?' I asked.

He leaned his face in towards mine, lowering his voice. 'I know these people, Capaldi.'

'If you haven't been able to make contact with the owner yet, how did you come by the passenger list?'

He flashed me a pitying smile. 'We're a small community. We know who the lucky bastards are who can get hold of tickets to a rugby international like that. And the operative word here is "community". Sometimes you have to take the sensible line. I know them all, I can vouch for them personally: they're good people. Not one of them has a criminal bone in his body.'

'It's still taking and driving away. Driving under the influence. Maybe more, if the driver decides to stay mean.'

'He won't,' Emrys announced confidently. 'And, after the rollicking I'm going to give them, none of them will be doing this again.' He spread his hands, trying me out with a reasonable-man-to-reasonable-man smile. 'Okay, they were wrong. But that would have been the drink, the excitement of having been in London. It would have been meant as a bit of fun, nothing malicious.' He shook his head. 'And they'll stick together. Even I'll never find out which one of them actually drove it away. You're not in your city now. There's a time and a place for the heavy-handed route and this isn't one of them.'

It was a big speech for Emrys. This was obviously important to him. Credibility issues, perhaps. 'Where are they?'

He tried out a grin. 'In their beds I assume. Getting ready to wake up and realize how lousy they feel.'

I recognized that he was offering me an opportunity here. The chance to play Cottage Cop, ingratiate myself into the community, show them that I didn't always have to be seen as an aloof and hard-ass outsider.

'What about the woman?'

He frowned. 'We don't know for sure that there was one. That could just have been the driver trying to make it worse for them . . .' He raised his hands to stop my protest. 'Okay, I promise you this, if there was a woman on that minibus with them last night, she'll have been treated with absolute courtesy and respect.'

'So where will she be now?'

'Wherever it is, she'll be safe. I can guarantee that. I expect she'll probably have been offered hospitality for the night. It's not like the city, women don't have to fear for their bodies or their lives.' He smiled smugly. 'We don't lose or misplace our womenfolk around here.'

Womenfolk . . . He actually used the word. As if he was describing a separate species that could be displayed in pens for admiration and grading. I used a spluttered cough to cover my astonishment.

'Are you all right?' he asked.

I nodded. 'I'll make you a deal.'

He inclined his head to listen.

'If you can convince me that everyone who was

13

on that minibus last night is safe and sound and where they're meant to be, I'll walk away and leave you to wrap it up your own way.'

He nodded. 'I'll take that deal.'

'And that includes the woman.'

He smirked. 'If she exists.'

I left him to get on the radio, and went over to take a closer look at the minibus. There was a dent in the front offside wing that could have been historic, and a new scratch on the driver's door that cut through the dust patina.

At the rear I had a hunch, and dropped to a crouch to study the exhaust. I moved in close; the uniforms had already corrupted this area, and I couldn't make it worse. Using the long serrated blade of my Swiss Army knife, I probed inside the pipe. When I pulled it out a set of vehicle keys fell on to the gravel.

This fitted in with the careful way that the minibus had been parked. The keys had been left for us to find. Emrys was right. Someone was trying to signal that there was no malicious intent in this.

I dangled the keys at Emrys as I walked round to the side door, but he was occupied with the radio and didn't see me. The two uniforms, who had been circling the minibus with me, keeping it as a shield between us, looked like they thought I was fucking Merlin when they saw the keys.

I always carry a couple of supermarket plastic bags in my coat pocket. Generally, they're for shopping, but occasionally they come in useful in situations like this. I unlocked the minibus door, and, using my handkerchief on the handle, slid it open. I put the plastic bags over my shoes before I climbed in.

14

Stale cigarette smoke was the main olfactory make-up over the background of synthetic upholstery and diesel. I sniffed selectively. No vomit. No dope. No girls' stuff either, or I just wasn't good enough to pick it up.

I trawled the interior slowly. Some rubbish on the floor, a couple of beer-bottle caps, a crumpled potato-crisps packet. This didn't look like a vehicle a bunch of drunks had stumbled out of.

I found it tucked under the seat in front of the back seat. I felt the tickle again. Bad news arriving. Regine Broussard had also been in possession of a plastic carrier bag.

I pulled it out carefully. This had been well used, creased and bearing the faded imprint of a butcher in Hereford. I looked inside. Paco Rabanne aftershave and Calvin Klein underpants both boxed in their original packaging.

'Capaldi . . .'

Emrys was at the open door.

'I'll take that.' He held his hand out.

I passed him the bag. For a moment I mistook his expression for fury. Then I realized that the torsion in his face went with anxiety.

'None of them are there . . . None of them got home last night . . .'

*　　　*　　　*

'Have you any idea what conditions are like up here?' I asked the duty officer at headquarters in Carmarthen over the radio.

'I can't authorize a helicopter search.'

'Yes, you can.'

'I need senior officer clearance.'

15

'Call DCS Galbraith.'

'It's a Sunday,' a note of panic rising in his voice at that prospect.

'And this is an emergency. I have seven people missing up here in conditions of extreme exposure. One of them is a young woman. You take the fall if any of them die or suffer serious injury.' I let that doom note resonate for a moment before pressing down on the exaggeration pedal. 'You don't know what it's like. I'm talking mountain conditions here, an enormous wind-chill factor, snow, a warren of forestry trails to be covered.' The last bit, at least, was true.

'Is a helicopter any use if it's snowing?' he asked.

'It's passing over,' I said quickly, 'but the wind's getting colder.'

'Okay,' he came to a decision, 'I'll set it up, but it's your responsibility. I am only acting on information received.'

It's only accounting, I told myself, the budget must have an allocation for such emergencies. I raised a thumb of acknowledgement to Emrys, who was down at his own car, on the radio to his boss, trying to get more people in for the search.

But where to start? I traced the course of the minor road with my eyes until it disappeared into the forest that rolled outwards and onwards for hectare after hectare. New growth, old growth, clearances, logging trails, abandoned trails, and the bastard, shape-shifting magic trails that I always ended up getting lost on. The imminent prospect of moving into that forest held no appeal.

The imminent prospect of a call from Detective Chief Superintendent Galbraith was even less appealing.

I had a lot to blame Jack Galbraith for.

For a start, he had rescued me. After my career in Cardiff had effectively gone down the tubes, he had stepped in and offered to have me in the Carmarthen Division. The Wild and Woolly West, as we used to say in Cardiff. I had thought about it when I had gone in to clean out my desk in that strangely empty squad room. After they had told me that it was safe to surface from my "emotional" leave. Why was he taking in a burned-out and redundant "hero"? Jack Galbraith did not have a reputation as a philanthropist. Had someone in high places called in a big favour? Or was he setting up an even bigger one, to be redeemed at some future date?

'I've been informed that you used to be a good cop, Capaldi,' he had told me on that first day of my official reincarnation in Carmarthen. When I had been born again as one of his men. 'That's why you're here with me instead of wearing a rinky-dink security uniform and patrolling the booze aisle in some shanty-town supermarket. I'm giving you another chance. See if you can get back some of that good judgement that you occasionally used to demonstrate.'

'Thank you, sir,' I had replied humbly.

'Look at this.' He walked across his office to the map of Wales that hung on the wall.

I looked. He tapped the map, a drummer's rhythm. I didn't have a clue what I was supposed to be looking at. He was tapping the bit in the middle, the empty bit, the bit God gave to the sheep.

'Do you know how much it's costing . . . to send men out from here . . .' he rapped the pen on each of the divisional headquarters, then came back into the middle again '. . . to here? Every time a case comes up?'

'I can imagine.' I nodded sympathetically.

'Overtime, petrol, hotel bills if they have to stay over.'

'And you're paying out for unproductive time with all that driving,' I added helpfully. I would have kept my mouth shut if I had known what was coming.

'Exactly. You've hit it right on the head there, son. Unproductive bloody time.' He sat down on the edge of the desk. A power move. Looking down at me, nodding at the question before he had even framed it. 'So what are we going to do about it?'

I didn't even pretend to think that I was being invited to advise on strategy here. 'I don't know the answer to that, sir.'

'I'm going to try an experiment, Capaldi.'

I gave him my best fresh, interested look.

'I'm going to put a man in there. A resident detective, someone who can cover the routine crap, so back-up only gets called in when it's absolutely necessary.'

Something plummeted. I felt like a specimen butterfly watching the mounting pin descend. 'You're surely not thinking of me for this, sir, are you?'

He grinned. It wasn't meant to be friendly. 'I'd have thought you would be grateful for any chance.'

'I'm straight out of the city, sir.'

'And you fucked up good there, didn't you?' He didn't embellish. Didn't remind me that I was responsible for the messy death of a man. He didn't have to; the memory still kept me on familiar terms with the Hour of the Wolf most nights.

18

'But I wouldn't know how to operate out there,' I protested, not faking my bewilderment.

'Don't fret your head about that, Capaldi. No one fucking does.'

*   *   *

We cordoned off the minibus with incident tape, and set up the command post there. With all that country to cover it was as good a place as any.

We had a mountain-rescue team on its way down from Snowdonia, volunteers from Forestry Services, and police teams with dogs already working their way into the forest. Inspector Morgan, Emrys's boss, had turned up and was now running the uniform end of things. Apart from some filthy stares, he kept away from me, and left me in charge of the communications with the helicopter. Which was ominous. Had me wondering whether perhaps there wasn't an emergency budgetary allocation after all.

My mobile rang. A number I knew only too well.

'Capaldi . . .' the voice boomed.

My stomach clenched. 'Yes, sir.'

'We're on our way.'

The wind had dropped, the rain had thinned to a fine suspension. It wasn't quite the Ice Queen blizzard that I had invoked. 'I don't think there's any need, sir. There's nothing to do but wait, you'll just get cold and wet up here.'

Jack Galbraith chuckled darkly. 'Don't think you can call up a fucking circus, Capaldi, and not invite the chief paymasters. I'm bringing DCI Jones up with me. If my Sunday's fucked I may as well spread the misery.'

19

'Yes, sir,' I replied snappily. Bryn Jones was one of the few cops in Carmarthen who hadn't treated me like an AIDS carrier when I had limped in damaged from Cardiff.

'Give me the background,' Galbraith instructed.

I laid it out for him. Emrys Hughes couldn't expect low profile now, so I nudged up the spin of the hijacking to six booze-fuelled guys and an unknown but vulnerable woman. Seven people missing in the hills. I played down the discovery of the neatly presented minibus. That didn't fit in so well with the dark-tale storyboard.

He was silent for a moment, and then I could just make out indistinct conversation at the other end of the line.

'You're wrong.' He came back on the line.

'Sir?'

'We think you're wrong. This group isn't the sort to be involved in anything truly sinister. You've been watching too much redneck massacre shit.'

'It's the woman that I'm concerned about, sir.'

'The men don't fit the gang-rape mould.'

'What do you think I should have done, sir?'

'Waited.'

'I'm sorry, sir, you're breaking-up . . .' I cut the connection.

That was an unofficial rebuke. Was it going to end up turning official? Had I overreacted? I thought hard about it. No. Even Emrys Hughes had been spooked when he realized that none of those good people of his had made it home. But where had they made it to?

The helicopter's call sign squawked over the radio. 'DS Capaldi—we think we might have a sighting for you.'

'Think?'

'You're looking for seven people?'

'Check.'

'We've only got five here.'

'What about stragglers?'

'I've circled. There's only five.'

'Is one of them a woman?'

'Sexometers aren't standard operating equipment.' I could hear the laugh in his voice. 'And from this high up I can't distinguish tits.'

Two of the party apparently missing, and this funster thinks it's a joke. I was tempted to tell him to check his mirror if he wanted to be able to distinguish a real tit.

2

I got to the location first. I needed to stay ahead before Morgan could pull rank and swamp me. I had to cheat to make sure of it. Knowing my luck with the weirdness of forestry tracks, I got the helicopter pilot to call the turns and guide me in.

I stopped the car as soon as I saw them.

Five men. Even from this distance I couldn't mistake them. I felt the bad tickle in my kidneys again. Somewhere in the night we had lost the woman. One of the men, too, by the look of it.

I let them come to me. I wanted time to observe them. They were making their way down an incline on a forest track between new-growth fir trees. All were dishevelled. Some of the faces seemed vaguely familiar. The two at the front, similar in height, had the look of brothers. The older-looking of the two had his mouth set in stock chagrin, the other one was experimenting with damping down his smirk, trying to tamp some regret in.

They both met my stare. I had the impression that they had been practising.

The three following behind were having a harder time of it. The one in the middle, an enormous guy, had his shaved head drooped, and his arms draped around the shoulders of his two companions, who were bracing themselves to keep in step with his lurching pace.

The big shaven-headed guy was wasted. The other two were using the effort of supporting him as an excuse to look anywhere but my way.

I heard vehicles pulling up behind me, car doors opening. I didn't turn round. My car was blocking the track so no one could get past. I concentrated, trying to read an explanation. The only consolation so far was that there was no spilled blood in evidence.

'Where have you been, Ken?'

I was suddenly aware of Emrys Hughes standing beside me.

Ken—Mr Chagrin, the older of the two who looked like brothers—shook his head and pulled his mouth into a tight grimace of shamed apology. 'We're really sorry to have put everyone through this, Emrys.'

'What happened to you?' Hughes asked entreatingly.

'We spent the night in Gordon's shooting hut. Up by the old dam.' He pulled a wry, regretful smile. 'We were abandoned.'

'Where are the rest of you?' I pitched in.

'Sergeant—' Emrys and I both turned

instinctively. Inspector Morgan glowered at us. 'This is not an open inquisition. I want these men to have medical attention as a priority. And then they'll be taken down to Dinas and given hot food and dry clothes before we even think about asking questions.'

'We need to know about the others, sir,' I protested. 'There could still be lost or injured people up here.'

'It's just us, Inspector. There's no one else, and no one's hurt,' Ken said penitently, then gestured back towards the big slumped guy, 'Paul just over-indulged a bit.'

'What about the woman who was with you?' I demanded.

He smiled apologetically. 'I expect she's back in Cardiff by now.'

'Where's Boon?' Emrys asked, before I could ask Ken for clarification.

'Sergeant Hughes, Sergeant Capaldi, that will do!' Morgan shouted angrily.

We stood back to let the five men shuffle past us like a file of train-wreck victims, paramedics coming up to meet them. The conscious ones gave Emrys Hughes a shamefaced smile as they passed. No one looked at me.

'When do I get to talk to them, sir?' I asked Morgan.

'You don't, Sergeant Capaldi.'

'Sir?'

'DCS Galbraith'—I could tell that it hurt him to say the name without spitting—'is diverting directly to Dinas. He will interview them himself. And he didn't request your presence,' he added, clawing back a little consolation from my expression.

23

I couldn't get over it. Suddenly no one was worried any more. By my reckoning we still had two missing persons to account for. But, since these five had turned up without any severed heads in string bags, the consensus appeared to be that everything was sorted.

I tackled Emrys about it before he joined the convoy driving back down the hill.

'Don't fret, Capaldi. It's over.'

'You don't know what's happened.'

'Not the detail. But I trust these people. If there were any kind of a problem they would tell me. I know that they wouldn't go calmly into those ambulances if there was anyone still in trouble up here.'

I couldn't share in his faith. I kept it to myself, but another thing rankled. Even scrubbed up and alert, I couldn't picture any of these guys in Calvin Klein underpants, or wearing Paco Rabanne aftershave.

So it looked as though I was the only one who had not been sprinkled with happy dust. Was the Italian side of me not seeing something that the Welsh side could embrace? Okay, I could run with it. I didn't know these men, I had been excluded from the enchanted circle, so I was allowed to be mean-spirited.

I could dig for dirt.

But first I had to find it. The groups that had made up the search party were dispersing. I homed in on a Land Rover with *Forestry Commission* on the side and two bushy-haired occupants rolling cigarettes. They looked out at me as if I was a swish who had just dropped in from a piano bar through a hole in the space-time continuum.

I buttonholed the driver. 'They said that they stayed at a shooting hut up there. Near an old dam.'

'Right.' He nodded, staring at me, waiting for something strange to happen.

'Do you know where it is?'

They shared a silent geographer communion. Then the passenger leaned forward, his finger starting to point, his visible thought process chewing through the directions he was about to give me.

'Great, I'll follow you,' I exclaimed, slapping the side of the Land Rover with macho gusto, like I was a roustabout *jefe* getting the crew rolling. I ran to my car hoping that they would assume we had just made some kind of a deal.

It worked. They blazed a convoluted trail, which may have been intended to shake me off. But I hung on behind them until the passenger flashed me a hand sign to let me know that we had arrived. I realized very quickly that it also indicated they were not stopping.

The hut was a long, low, timber-boarded affair, like a barrack, with a sagging mineral-felt roof, and plywood squares replacing some of the missing window panes. Well on its way to dereliction. It looked like the kind of place construction workers would have used. The only reason it had lasted this long was because no vandal could be bothered to take the kind of exercise required to reach it. The area in front had been cleared and levelled, but it was rutted and potholed now, and self-seeded birch and spruce saplings were collaborating with gorse

25

in an effort to take over.

They had called it a shooting hut. On the drive up here, I had imagined something with rustic pine supports and trophy antlers nailed to the walls. This was more like a stalag way past its sell-by date.

I stood outside trying to get a feel for the place. Imagining it was night. Why would they come here?

Because it was so far off the edge of the world that anything could happen, and no one would ever be any the wiser?

I buried the thought. I went back to the facts. The minibus driver had said that the men didn't seem to know the girl. So she wasn't local. This location had to be the choice of one or all of the six men. It's night, it's cold, it's late, and it's a long way into a labyrinth. Why here? And why walk? Why not use the minibus? Why park it way the hell over where we found it? Because you were all so fucked-up that it seemed like fun at the time?

Because your party was still flowing?

I opened the door and met the party. Beer bottles and cans mainly, some wine, one bottle of vodka. All empty. But all stacked neatly. Tidied up. With empty crisp and snack packets crumpled and stuffed into a supermarket carrier bag.

The place had the damp, earthy smell of fern roots. I was standing in a vestibule. To my left was a small room that would have functioned as an office or foreman's room, to the right a larger room, door hanging open: the mess quarters. In front of me, opposite the entrance, was a toilet cubicle with no door, and a cracked WC pan.

I went through the open door into the mess room. The floor had been swept. Not thoroughly; scrappy piles of old pine needles, twigs and other

26

debris that had blown in through the broken windows had been pushed back against the wall. The other homely touch was six—I counted them—sawn log rounds arranged as seating. It all implied organization.

But when? Had this been set up before they arrived? Premeditated? Or had they all piled out of the minibus and set to making an impromptu den? And why only six pixie stools for seven people?

None of the log rounds had been recently cut. I touched the nearest one. It was still damp. But in this atmosphere so was everything else. I looked out of the windows. There were no other log rounds in sight. No imprints of any in the soft ground around the hut. It was possible that they could have ranged out with torches and collected these in the dark. Or they could have had them here already. But only six? Almost but not quite knowing how many were coming to dinner.

I nearly missed it. Running a last check before I backed out of the room I caught a glimpse of white behind the door. White and clean—alien matter in this place. I picked it up carefully. It was a crumpled paper tissue, slightly damp from absorption of the moisture in the atmosphere. I took a deep sniff. A complex background of unidentifiable fragrances. Opening it out I saw black smudges. The lessons from a fractured marriage informed me that these were smears of ruined mascara. Tears of fun or tears of terror? Another thought to bury.

I had made contact. My first meeting with the woman. I sniffed the tissue again to fix the esters in my olfactory library, and then fitted it carefully into an evidence bag.

I went back to the vestibule. The door to the

small office was stuck. A clean section of arc in front of it showed where someone had tried to push it open and given up. Or had they? I put my shoulder to it and leaned in hard. It screeched horribly against the floor and opened with difficulty. The space was dark and even mustier than the mess room. Some damp Hessian sacks had been nailed over the windows. I pulled one away, grimacing at the slimy feel of it in my hand.

There was so much crud piled on the floor that I looked up reflexively, wondering whether this section had lost its roof. It hadn't. But, even if it had, dead bracken did not usually tumble out of the sky in quantities like this. This had been imported. It had been heaped against the far wall, and it looked as though it had been compacted. To make some kind of a nest?

Another thought struck me.

To make a rudimentary bed?

*   *   *

DCI Bryn Jones was smoking outside the Methodist Church Hall in Dinas when I drove up. In the absence of a police station the hall had been commandeered for the occasion.

I ran up to him. 'I'm sorry I took so long, sir. I got lost trying to find my way out of the forest.' It wasn't a lie. It was late afternoon now, almost dusk.

He just nodded, slowly exhaling smoke through his nostrils, a slightly ambivalent smile forming. 'Thanks for your contribution to my Sunday, Sergeant Capaldi.'

Bryn Jones was short, but big in breadth. With tight black curly hair, happy green eyes, and a

28

massive face that looked like it had been formed by pounding putty into place. He had a neck that seemed reluctant to narrow, and in the dark blue suit he appeared more constrained than dressed.

I gestured inside with my head. 'Is DCS Galbraith in there working on them?'

'Notice an absence?'

I looked around, puzzled. Not getting it at first. And then it hit. There was no one here.

'Wives and girlfriends, concerned family . . .' Bryn confirmed, seeing it dawn on me.

'Where are they?'

'Gone.'

'Have you taken them in?' I asked, surprised, wondering whether to start feeling vindicated. 'Is it turning out to be more serious than we thought?'

'They've gone home. All of them.'

I stared at him for a moment, perplexed. 'Even the men?'

He nodded. 'Even the men.'

I shook my head, trying to clear a path to my next question. Then the inner voice of self-preservation sideswiped me. 'DCS Galbraith—has he gone home too?' I asked, trying to conceal the hope in the question.

Bryn dropped his cigarette end, crushed it underfoot, and then shook his head. Not unkindly. 'No. I'm on lookout duty.'

I didn't have to ask who the smoke on the horizon was.

Jack Galbraith was sitting at a stacking table at the end of the hall, an empty plastic chair beside him, and an identical one opposite. He was having a cigarette under a sign that read *Please refrain from smoking under the eyes of the Lord.*

29

He looked up when I entered, closed his eyes, and steepled his fingers. I hoped that he was looking for guidance. Trying to find the strength to stop him swearing under the eyes of the Lord.

'Fuck you, Capaldi.' His eyes flicked open. 'Where do I fucking start?'

Bryn Jones slipped into the empty chair beside him.

Even seated, you could tell that Jack Galbraith was tall. He had light brown hair swept back in a swagger behind his ears, a strangely effeminate frame for the firm, square-boned face with its deep-set, incisive, brown eyes. He looked as though he had been built for stamina, for distance and endurance, and you could tell from his bearing that he thought that he still had it, just hadn't tried it out in a long time.

'My wife thinks this is a put-up job to stop me taking her to an amateur choral rendition of fucking *Elijah* . . .' All his years in Wales had hardly touched the gruff Scottish accent. He ticked the points off on his fingers: 'That supreme fucking tosser Inspector Unctuous Morgan has witnessed my ritual humiliation. And you called out a fucking helicopter.'

'No disrespect, sir, but we are in a church here,' Bryn said quietly, out of the corner of his mouth.

'No we're not,' Jack Galbraith corrected him. 'We're in a church fucking hall—there's a difference. In here, I'm allowed a few transgressions.' He paused to dump his cigarette into the residue of a mug of tea before fixing his gaze back on me. 'What have you got to say for yourself, Capaldi?'

'I thought we had a situation, sir. I had seven

30

people missing, one of them a woman, in extreme weather conditions. I made a decision that seemed to be appropriate for the circumstances as I saw them at the time.

'I was especially worried about the woman—a hitchhiker, picked up by the men. She didn't know them. And the men were drunk. In my opinion she was vulnerable. And I'm still concerned for her. Do you remember the Broussard case, sir? In Cardiff? About six years ago? A Haitian illegal immigrant?'

'There's no parallel.' Jack Galbraith shook his head and smirked. 'Tell him, Bryn,' he instructed. 'Give him the low-down on the little flower he's so concerned about.'

'She was a hooker, Sergeant.'

'A Cardiff tart,' Jack Galbraith amplified. 'Called herself Miss Danielle.'

I tried to absorb my surprise. 'They picked her up in a rural petrol station. The minibus driver said she was hitching.'

'That was the cover story,' Bryn explained.

'It was organized, Capaldi.'

'It was meant to be a stag event,' Bryn clarified. 'They were setting up a surprise for the two bachelors in the group. They were meant to believe that the girl was just an innocent hitchhiker.'

'Then, surprise, surprise, the girl drops the Young Rambler guise'—Jack Galbraith clapped his hands together—'and at least one of our two virgins gets his rocks off, courtesy of his buddies.'

I tried to get my head round it. They waited me out. 'But they took her up to a hut in a forest. That's where I've come from.'

Jack Galbraith nodded. 'We gathered that. And we also notice that you haven't returned clutching a

31

dripping axe in the evidence bag.'

'Did you see anything up there that we should be concerned about?' Bryn asked.

I thought about the crumpled tissue, the log rounds, the bracken bed. 'No, sir.' I shook my head and frowned. 'But I don't get it.'

'Where have we lost you, Capaldi?' Jack Galbraith asked.

'Why did they stay up there for the night? The men, I mean. It was cold and damp. Uncomfortable doesn't even begin to describe it. And they must have realized the furore it would cause.'

'That's where it went wrong for them,' Jack Galbraith said. 'According to the master plan they were supposed to have their party, get the virgins' cherries popped, and be back in their beds, tucked up with their loved ones, before they were missed.' He eyed me carefully. 'Tell Capaldi the story we were told, Bryn.'

I picked up on his use of the word 'story'. Jack Galbraith was very precise with his words. And instead of the savaging I'd been expecting, he was being relatively gentle with me. Was I about to discover the reason?

'They claim that they were very drunk. That, despite the conditions up there, they slept through until the morning.'

I remembered the sight of them coming down the hill. 'They did look pretty rough,' I conceded. 'One of them, the big one, was totally out of it.'

Jack Galbraith grinned. 'Paul Evans, one of the virgin bachelors. That must have been some kind of a fuck, eh?'

'It didn't look like rapture to me, sir,' I observed.

'But it wasn't just the demon drink that was their

undoing.'

'No?' I answered cautiously. He looked amused. I wondered if he had found some way to fold me into the blame for this.

He grinned. 'No, it was the Big Bad Pimp.'

'Sir?'

Jack Galbraith gestured, and Bryn took over. 'They're claiming that it was the girl's pimp who drove the minibus away.'

'A pimp . . .?' I didn't try to hide my astonishment.

He nodded. 'According to the men, he had never been part of the arrangement. They had assumed that they could persuade the minibus driver to take them up to the hut, then just give him a good bung for his waiting-around time.'

'The driver never mentioned that.'

'They never got round to negotiating it. When the girl was picked up at the service station she announced that the deal had changed. She wanted her pimp with her. Told them that she felt vulnerable out here in the boondocks without protection.'

I pondered it, seeing how the fit started to work for them. 'So the girl has it arranged that this Cardiff pimp is waiting in a lay-by in the middle of nowhere, all set to cut the minibus driver adrift, jump into the driving seat and carry them away?'

'That's more or less how the authorized version goes,' Jack Galbraith confirmed.

'Which means that there's no drinking and driving involved?'

He nodded. 'Correct. Our heroes remain unblemished.'

'And then they're abandoned by the pimp and

33

his girl.'

'Like some kind of fairy story, isn't it? Our bunch of poor foundlings left to their cruel fate in a woodsman's hut in the middle of the dark fucking forest.'

I shook my head. 'It doesn't work, sir.'

'Explain.'

'The place where we found the empty minibus this morning—if that was the rendezvous, the place where the pimp and the girl had arranged to be picked up and taken back to Cardiff—they would never have found it. Not in the dark, not in that warren of forestry tracks. Chances are, this guy's never driven in a night situation that didn't involve street lights.'

Jack Galbraith and Bryn exchanged a glance. 'It does work, Sergeant,' Bryn said.

'Why?'

Jack Galbraith pulled a face. 'Because we have five solid, upright and honest citizens who all say that that was the way it happened. And we're all so dreadfully sorry to have inconvenienced everyone.'

'They even had a whip-round while they were here to pay for the damage to the minibus,' Bryn added.

'Damage caused by the pimp, mind you. These guys are nothing if not magnanimous,' Jack Galbraith observed with an ironic chuckle. 'And it also works because I don't have any relevant reports of a missing person, or a woman claiming that she has been abducted and abused.'

'Has anyone in Cardiff been able to talk to the girl?'

They both shook their heads. Jack Galbraith frowned. 'No. And do you know why? Because the sanctimonious fucks claim that they found the number in a telephone booth. And now they've lost it.'

'Do Vice know this Miss Danielle?'

'Nothing matching the description we've been given,' Bryn replied. 'Either the girl was using a false name, or the men don't want us to trace her.'

'So they just walk? It's over?'

Jack Galbraith nodded. 'There's nowhere to take it. These bastards are too respectable for us to resort to the rubber hose, never mind the thumbscrews.'

I didn't know whether that was a coded invitation for me to opt out of their enforced inaction. I accepted it as such anyway. And then I remembered that we had another missing person. 'There were supposed to be six men. Only five came down the hill.'

'They dropped off one of their number on the way. He never went into the forest.' He looked over at Bryn for amplification.

Bryn checked his notes. 'Boon Paterson. He was on leave from the Army, going home today. He asked to be let out in Dinas.'

That fitted in with the six pixie stools that I had counted in the hut. 'What kind of a name is Boon?' I asked.

'I'm sure I wouldn't know, Sergeant Capaldi,' Jack Galbraith replied with a mean chuckle, making a drawn-out meal of my surname.

*   *   *

It was already dark when they left, the afternoon colder now and winter-killed. I felt oddly lonely watching them go, like I was the patsy who had somehow been tricked into staying behind to man the empty gulag.

The Fleece didn't exactly lift my heart with gladness. It was virtually empty. Locked into a race memory of not being able to drink on a Sunday, the old men who usually occupied the back bar stayed away.

I took a stool at the bar. David Williams, the owner, wasn't around. That suited me fine. I leaned over the counter, took my glass down from its place on the shelf, put it under the beer tap and filled it. Self-service meant I could avoid the inclusion in my drink of stuff from the black plastic bilge bucket that stood under the pump, collecting everything from drips through pork-pie particles to the common cold virus.

David popped his head round from the serving area of the front bar. He came over, picking up his drink as he passed it. The two separate bars were a godsend to him. He could keep a drink active in each one, and work on the mistaken belief that his customers were only seeing the half of what he was actually consuming.

'Scandal?' he asked with a great big eager grin.

'What have you heard?' I closed the beer tap.

He pretended to look crestfallen. 'You mean you're not going to tell me?'

'I want to hear your version.'

He checked to see who might be listening, then leaned forward and lowered his voice. 'The story is that they picked up a couple of hitchhikers on their way back from the match, supposedly without realizing that they were working girls.' He raised his eyebrows, waiting to see if I would respond.

36

'One hitchhiker.'

'Just one?' He sounded disappointed.

'Go on,' I prompted.

'Whoever it was turned out to have a boyfriend with her. They tried on some sort of a shakedown, and then they took the transport and abandoned our boys up in the forest.' He leered salaciously. 'What we're all wondering is, what went on up there that the boys wouldn't want their loved ones to know about?'

He stood back and waited for my reaction.

I just nodded, noncommittal. It was a raggedy version, maybe deliberately so, but it was interesting that the group had managed to get their spin working for them so quickly.

'You're not going to tell me?' he asked, disappointed.

'I couldn't improve on that, David.'

David and Sandra Williams were Dinas's version of the Golden Couple. That status was still current only because any contenders to their throne had opted for a Bronze future in a bigger place.

David was also the nearest thing I had to a friend in Dinas.

'I've seen some of those guys around,' I said. 'Tell me about them. Two of them looked like brothers.'

He didn't have to think about it. 'That's Ken and Gordon McGuire. Ken's the oldest. He got the family farm, Rhos-goch. A big holding out on the Penygarreg road, some hill country, but a lot of good river land.'

'Good farmer?'

'Yes, but you wouldn't have to be on that land. A walking stick would sprout if you left it in the dirt long enough.'

'The brother?'

'Gordon's an auctioneer with Payne, Dyke and Thomas.'

'A lush?' I asked, knowing the occupational hazard.

David shrugged. 'Not as bad as some. Good at his job, though. He got a nice Victorian farmhouse when Ken got the farm.'

'Who's the big guy? Shaven head.'

'Paul Evans. Works for his father, a builder up at Treffnant. He's a really good rugby player. Awesome tackler.'

'He looks like a dumbfuck.'

'Paul's okay until he gets a drink in him, then you want to keep away.'

'Boon Paterson?'

'Boon hasn't been around for a while. He joined the Army.' He looked at me, interested, picking up on a new twist. 'I'd heard he wasn't there. Was he?'

I shook my head. 'Who are the other two?' I had no real picture of them, just props swaying under Paul Evans's weight.

'Trevor Vaughan and Les Tucker. Trevor farms up in the hills, and Les has a pretty successful timber-felling business.'

'Which ones are married?'

'Ken and Gordon—the McGuires. Les has a long-term girlfriend though. Sara Harris, she's a hairdresser in Dinas. You'd probably know her if you saw her.'

So Trevor Vaughan was the other bachelor. 'Paul and Trevor, have they got girlfriends?'

He shook his head. 'I wouldn't know. All I do know is that they both still live at home.'

'What keeps them together as a group?'

'Ken and Gordon, probably. Trevor was Ken's best mate, Les was Gordon's. They've just kept together from school. Paul and Boon got to tag along.'

I hadn't seen Boon Paterson, so I had to exclude him from the mental line-up. Four of them fitted there, worked as a loose match. I could imagine them pictured in a local newspaper, a group shot of young Rotarians handing over a large-format cheque to a good cause. But Paul Evans stayed out of the shot. Why were they associating with a lunk like that? What would a bunch of young countryfolk require muscle for?

I moved my hands in front of him as if I was drawing open a concertina. 'In a range that spans monsters to saints, where would you place them?'

He smiled, not needing to think about it. 'Customers.'

I returned the smile dutifully. But I couldn't shake Paul Evans from my mind. Performing a function. Pinning down the shoulders of a woman whose face I couldn't see. Her legs thrashing wildly. For the enjoyment of the others.

*   *   *

'Capaldi, we still need to talk.'

Back at the caravan, and another message from Mackay. I reset the answering machine. I was almost tempted to call him. Get this thing over with.

I picked up the receiver. Then gently put it back down again when it occurred to me that my wife might answer it.

I picked it up again, dialling the Dispatch number, just remembering what Emrys Hughes had said about the embargo he had put on the news of the minibus discovery. The news that I was supposed not to hear.

'This is DS Capaldi.'

'Yes, Sergeant.'

'Did Sergeant Hughes instruct you not to call me with an update on the hijacked minibus?'

'No, Sarge—that was Inspector Morgan.'

I heard the laughter in the background. I smiled as I put the receiver down. It was good to know that I had support in lowly places.

3

Torches . . .

The thought of torches brought me out of a fitful sleep. They had to have had light.

I called headquarters in Carmarthen after breakfast. Bryn wasn't around, but I got someone to check the transcripts of the group's statements. Torches were mentioned. The story was that the pimp and the girl had made off with them when they did their runner.

But, according to Bryn, there had been no confrontation with the pimp. They had paid over the agreed fee up front when they arrived at the hut, and waited for the good times to roll. The girl had said that she was just going outside to use the minibus to prepare herself. Next thing they knew, both girl and pimp had managed to sneak off in the minibus.

Sneak off? I couldn't see it. The guy could hardly have gathered up the torches without declaring some sort of intention. No matter how smashed you were, you would know the party was finishing when the lights went out.

It was like the parked minibus, the neatly stacked rubbish in the hut, the tart's missing telephone number . . . Disturbances in the details. Their story was frayed at the edges. But the smell coming off it wasn't bad enough for Jack Galbraith to keep it open. I recalled his parting admonition, warning me off any direct approach to the members of the group.

The upside of having to investigate crap cases in the boondocks that no one else wants to touch is that it gives you the autonomy to invent leads that will take you to wherever you want to be.

Which, on this Monday morning, was the service station outside Newtown where the minibus had filled up with diesel. And where they had managed to add Miss Danielle to the roster.

I showed the manager my warrant card and told him that I wanted to see the security CCTV coverage for Saturday night.

He looked at me warily, and for a moment I thought he was going to tell me that it had already been erased, or that the cameras were only there for show. 'You people have already been to look at it.'

'When?'

'Last night.'

'Two big guys? One wide, one Scottish and grumpy?'

'Yes.'

So Jack Galbraith and Bryn had diverted here on

41

their way home. Taking this seriously. But they hadn't called me. If there had been anything on the tapes to justify action, they would surely have contacted me.

I persuaded the manager to run the tape for me, and settled down in front of the dirty monitor in the cleaner's cupboard that he called an office.

I felt a small flutter of anxiety below my sternum. Crazy. I didn't know this woman. She hadn't existed for me thirty-six hours ago. And she was probably some junkie hag, back in Cardiff now, just where the story placed her. But we had made the same sort of mistake with Regine Broussard. I wasn't going to let it happen twice.

There was no denying I was nervous. I was about to get my first sighting of her, and I couldn't shake off a sense of something that shifted between romance and doom.

I fast-forwarded through the tapes to get to the point where the minibus arrived at the service station. Business was slow. The forecourt was empty when it pulled in, the CCTV image grainy and stuttering. The driver got out and proceeded to fill the tank. No one else got out of the minibus. No other cars there either, so no witnesses to trace through the DVLA computer.

It happened too quickly. She was there just after the driver screwed the fuel cap back on and walked out of shot to go and pay. I rewound and watched again. I hadn't missed anything. She just appeared, no approach. It was as if the tape had jumped or stalled, editing that segment out.

I peered at the screen. It didn't help. The picture quality was terrible. A baseball cap. Blonde hair bunched through the gap at the back. I moved in as

42

close as I could, but couldn't tell if it was the cap that I had found. Her facial features were a blurred soup of pinkish pixels over a knotted scarf tucked into a puffy, red, down-filled jacket. About a hundred and sixty-two centimetres, I gauged from the relation of her shoulders to the roof of the minibus. A large rucksack sagging one shoulder.

She was on the far side of the minibus from the camera. Head bent, as if she was in conversation with someone through the sliding door on the side. She tossed her head back, her face turning into the camera, the smile pronounced enough to register as a big, happy smudge. Then she slid her rucksack off, handed it into the minibus and climbed in after it.

I knew the rest of the story. She didn't escape.

I had just witnessed a transaction. Something had been negotiated between the woman and some of the men in the minibus. But what? A lift or a fuck?

*　　　*　　　*

I went back to the counter. The young cashier glanced up from a magazine. She seemed tired, dark circles under her eyes, bad complexion, the mix of colours in her hair making it look like she had fallen into a chemistry set.

'Were you working Saturday night?'

'Some of it,' she said, an edge of suspicion in her tone and eyes.

'Can you have a look at this?' I moved to the side to create enough room for her to get into the room and see the image that I had paused on the screen.

She stared at it blankly.

43

'This is at half past nine. Did you see this woman getting into that minibus?'

She shook her head. 'No. I was clocked off by then.'

'Who was on duty?'

'Him.' She cocked her head towards the manager, who was stacking shelves.

I pulled a face in frustration. The manager had already told me that he hadn't seen her.

'Helly Hansen . . .'

'You know her?'

'No. Her jacket—it was a Helly Hansen.' The covetousness in her voice surprised me.

'I thought you hadn't seen her?'

'I saw her earlier, when she arrived. I've always fancied a jacket like that.'

I kept my excitement down. 'You saw her arrive?'

'It was busy. Something like half past seven, seven o'clock. People going into town for Saturday night, people coming home from a day out shopping. It got dead quiet after that.'

'Are you sure about that?'

'Positive. If that's the one you're looking for, that's when I saw her.'

At least two hours. What was she doing there two hours before the minibus picked her up? It was a blow. It tied in with the group's story. That it had all been pre-arranged, that the girl had been there waiting for them.

Or did it?

If a pimp had brought her up from Cardiff, why had he arrived so early? Even a deep-city hustler would have to realize that a service station whack in the middle of Baptist nowhere was no place to drop one of his girls off to trawl for casual trade.

'You should ask Tony Griffiths.'

'What?' I did an auditory double take.

'You want to know about her, you should ask Tony. He was the one what brought her in.'

*   *   *

'Bryn, she was carrying a rucksack . . .' I could hear the plea in my own voice. *Sanction this. Please make it so I can take this forward with an official blessing.*

There was no response at the other end of the line. I was used to it. Where Bryn Jones was concerned, silence was a communications tool. He was a born moderator, always giving you the chance to reconsider what you had just said to him.

'A rucksack, Bryn.'

'I know. We watched the footage.'

'Hookers don't carry rucksacks.'

'DCS Galbraith and I discussed that.'

'She was hitchhiking.'

'That's an assumption. You've no evidence to support it.'

'What would a tart be doing with a backpack?' I asked, and immediately sensed the flaw in the question.

'Sex toys, fantasy outfits, sleazy underwear, unguents, cosmetics, spermicidal jelly, Mace, condoms,' Bryn enumerated, 'and a big woolly jumper and nice warm tights, because she's coming out into the cold night air.'

'Bryn, she looked like a hitchhiker.'

'That's an emotive reaction, and you should know better. Face it, on that screen she just looks fuzzy.'

'Those bastards are lying.'

'Probably,' he admitted calmly.

'You can say that and just walk away from it?'

'Yes, because we have no evidence of a crime having been committed. And yes, they probably are lying, because it's normal behaviour when white middle-class males get discovered in flagrante delicto with a prostitute. It's a function of the squirm reaction.'

'Did Emrys Hughes hand in a bag?'

'What kind of a bag?'

'A carrier bag. I found it in the minibus. It had some aftershave and designer underpants in it.'

'I expect he gave it back to whichever of the men had left it behind.'

'Bryn, the bag was from Hereford.'

'So? People travel to Hereford to shop.'

'None of those bastards that I saw walking down that hill would have bought those things. They don't fit.'

'You're speculating again.'

I paused, bringing myself back under control. 'What if I could find the person who gave her the lift to the service station?'

He was silent for a moment. 'Are we talking about a pimp?'

'No.'

'We would be interested in that.' He paused. 'DCS Galbraith has asked me to pass a message on to you.'

Which meant that Jack Galbraith knew that I would be calling Bryn. 'And what would that be, sir?' I asked, switching to formal.

'Don't blow this up into something it isn't in an attempt to climb back on board the big ship.'

46

'No, sir.' I had a sudden flash of my fingertips clutching the gunnels with Jack Galbraith's polished brown brogues poised over them. 'I have to go, sir,' I said, catching sight of the truck in my rear-view mirror. I cut the connection and got out of the car as it approached, weaving to avoid the worst of the potholes in the lay-by. A small truck with a standard cab, but an unusually high-sided, open-topped rear.

The driver's window rolled down. I assumed that the head that poked out belonged to Tony Griffiths. 'I got a call from the office to meet someone here.'

I held up my warrant card. 'They said that this was the best place to intercept you on your route.'

He looked at me suspiciously. 'I don't know you.' He glanced down at my warrant card and scowled. 'What kind of a name is that?'

I beamed up at him. 'My parents embraced the spirit of Europe.'

He wasn't impressed. 'I don't remember being the witness to any incident.'

'I'll come up,' I said, swinging round the front of the truck before he had a chance to say that we were fine the way we were. I climbed into the passenger's side of the cab. It was overheated, despite the open window, and smelled of something stale and bad that I couldn't put my finger on.

His look of suspicion shaded off into new knowledge. He pointed a finger at me, pleased with himself. 'I heard about you. You're the city cop they shifted up here. What did they catch you doing?' He grinned wickedly. 'Kiddy-fiddling, was it—with a name like that?'

I overcame the urge to tip his face into the steering-wheel boss. I needed him.

'What's this about?' he asked, still grinning,

47

cranking the window back up. He was wearing a high-visibility yellow tabard over stained and crumpled blue overalls. He had dark oily hair swept back behind his ears, small but smart brown eyes, and a dark complexion that was accentuated by a heavy shadow of beard growth. The way he sat hunched over the steering wheel gave him the appearance of a small man, but the shirt and overall sleeves rolled up past his elbows revealed hairy and powerful forearms.

'You're not in any trouble, Tony. I just need your help,' I said reassuringly, forcing a smile, keeping it friendly. 'Saturday night, someone tells me that you might have dropped a female hitchhiker off at a service station on the Llanidloes road outside Newtown.'

'I don't pick up hitchhikers,' he came back at me, deadpan. 'We're told not to. It's against company policy.'

I smiled at him. 'Don't worry, I'm not going to tell anyone.'

'And my last drop was eleven o'clock Saturday morning. Bachdre Kennels, half an hour away from my place.'

'You were seen, Tony. Seven, half past seven, Saturday night.'

He shrugged. 'I've got a motorbike. A trials bike, it doesn't take passengers.'

He was lying. But why? He didn't look like a man who would give a toss for company rules.

'My only concern is for the woman.'

He held my gaze and shook his head.

'You were seen with her.'

He just shrugged; he knew that he didn't have to give me any more. But he didn't smile. That was important. He wasn't cocky about it. I looked for the natural line of leverage.

'I'm worried about her, Tony. She got into a minibus with six drunk guys, and she hasn't been seen since.'

He shook his head and dropped eye contact. 'I've nothing more to say.'

He wasn't going to tell me. What had he been doing on Saturday that he did not want me to know about?

I spat on my palm and laid it flat on the seat between us. An old Ligurian trick of my father's. Sometimes it worked, impressing strangers with the deep scope and breadth of my ouvrier honesty. 'This goes no further, I promise you. Anything you tell me stays here. Stays strictly between us.'

He glanced down at my hand, and then up at me with a look that told me he had been around too many gypsies in his time to fall for that one. 'You're a cop,' he stated simply.

'I can be trusted,' I replied earnestly.

A knowing smile split his lips.

'What can I do to prove that?' I asked, still hoping that rhetoric and persuasion were going to carry me. Not quite catching the shift in his concentration. Not realizing that the bastard had actually started to think about it.

'Are you serious?'

'Of course I'm serious. I promise—you can trust me.'

'No. About proving it?'

'Does that mean you did give the woman a lift?'

He grinned. 'You haven't earned my trust yet.'

'How do I do that?'

He held up a mobile phone. 'You know what this

is?'

'It's a mobile phone.'

'It's also a camera.' He smiled as my expression turned puzzled, and inclined his head towards the rear of the truck. 'Do you know what I carry in the back there?'

*　　　*　　　*

He lowered the tailgate. I understood then why the sides of the truck were so high. To stop people seeing the dead meat.

'Farm casualties,' he explained. 'We get paid to pick them up and dispose of them.'

The components of the pile in the back of the truck were small in number, but they made a big gruesome bundle. Two dead sheep tangled on top of a black-and-white cow, which lay on its side, legs splayed out, as stiff as driftwood. The harness and wire cables from a winch curled over the grouping. The smell was noxious. An ammoniacal reek from stale urine, combined with lanolin, and the start of decomposition. The sawdust that had been used to cover the truck bed had absorbed unimaginable fluids and turned to gelatinous slurry.

'Jesus . . .' I gagged involuntarily.

He laughed. 'You get used to it. These ones are fresh.'

I had no intention of getting used to it. 'Why are you showing me this?'

'This is the deal.'

I shook my head. 'I don't get it.'

'You've got to shag the cow.'

I waited for the punchline. It took me a minute to realize that it had already arrived. He was serious. 'You can't really expect me to . . .' The line was too absurd to finish.

'I don't expect you to do anything. You want something from me. You need to pay a price.' He pointed at the rear end of the cow with his mobile phone. 'I want a shot on this which makes it look like you're fucking that thing.'

'Are you some kind of pervert?'

'No, I just want to be safe. I need a cast-iron guarantee that if I tell you things you have a real good reason not to spread them. I can't think of a better reason than a picture like that.'

'I couldn't do it.'

'That's your choice. It's all voluntary, Sergeant Capaldi.'

Oh fuck . . . We had stopped pretending. We now both knew that he had a story to tell me. 'Why are you making me this offer?'

He thought about it for a moment. 'I want to help the girl.'

'Do it for her then,' I entreated.

'No. I need to keep myself covered.'

'You want win–win?'

'Fucking right I do.'

I shook my head slowly. It had to stop here. She was a stranger. She would have moved on, totally oblivious of my search for her. She didn't need any kind of sacrifice. Bryn Jones was right, no crime had been reported, no one was missing. She would be back in Cardiff by now. Where I should really be, instead of discussing necrophilic bestiality with a twisted hayseed under a too big sky. It was time to let go.

He lifted the tailgate tentatively. 'Okay?' he asked. 'I drive off now and you leave me alone?'

51

I started to nod. 'Tell me,' I blurted. 'One thing
. . .'
He stared at me.
'Was she a prostitute?'
I thought that he wasn't going to answer.
'No.'
Another flash on Regine Broussard.
Oh fuck . . .

*   *   *

I drew the line at dropping my trousers. We had a brief, heated, artistic disagreement over that, until I persuaded him that it could all be done by inference. By posture, camera angle, and the loose ends of my belt drooping free.

He had the grace to lend me a pair of heavy-soled rubber boots. The kind that abattoir workers wear when they hose the crud off the floor. Crouched there, arms splayed, trying to get into position while he shouted directions, I must have looked like some monumental fool.

Fool . . .? I was kidding myself. Substituting vanity for the bigger picture. Which had me flying way off the outer scale of foolishness by simulating penetrative sex on the rear end of a dead sideways cow.

Back in the truck cab, trying to warm up, he wanted to show me the images.

I shook my head. 'If those pictures ever see the light of anyone else's day, I will arrange it so you have your balls cut off. And believe me, I can do it. I have the contacts. I'm a cop, and I'm half Italian.'

'Don't worry, they're just my insurance.'

I held a Bad Cop stare on him for a moment to

underscore the threat. 'So, what were you doing wrong on Saturday afternoon?'

He braced himself for it, still not comfortable with confessing to me, despite the huge security deposit he had just obtained. 'I was using the truck to run some deer carcasses for a couple of mates.'

'Poached?'

He shrugged. 'I was just doing the delivering.'

'You bastard!' I exploded. 'You put me through that depraved fucking charade to cover up a bit of poaching.'

He shot me an aggrieved pout. 'My mates take trust very seriously. The man whose land the deer came from is a vindictive bastard. *And* I was using the company's truck.'

'Poaching.' I snorted dismissively.

'You seemed to think it was worth it at the time.'

He was right. I had accepted the price. I calmed myself down. 'Where to?'

'A butcher down on the Radnor, Herefordshire border.'

'Where did you pick the woman up?'

He looked at me, surprised that I didn't want more detail on the butcher. 'On my way home. Near Painscastle. I was sticking to the back roads.'

'Show me.' I flicked through his road atlas to get to the right page. He pointed. It was a minor road that strung a line of nondescript villages together. 'Is this where she had started from?'

'No, she'd come from somewhere outside Hereford. She'd got sidetracked, a lift from a farmer who'd left her there. The road was quiet, she was lucky that I came along.'

Hereford again. I tucked the reference away.

'Where did she want to go?'

53

He grinned. 'Would you believe Ireland?'

I contained my surprise. 'Was she Irish?'

'No, she was foreign.'

'What kind of foreign?'

He pulled a face. 'She told me, but I didn't get it. I didn't want to keep asking in case she thought I was thick. It wasn't a common foreign country though. I would have got something like France, or Germany, or Poland.'

'How well did she speak English?'

'A bit of an accent and a few words the wrong way round, but pretty good really.'

'Did she tell you her name?'

He pulled his contrite face again. 'She told me, but I didn't really get that either. It was something foreign, beginning with an "M".'

'Can you describe her?'

He nodded. 'She was a real smiler. Big high cheeks that puffed out when she grinned. Her face was small but kind of chubby. Not fat or anything. Just . . .' He searched for the description. 'Just nice.'

She sounded Slavic. Or Scandinavian with the blonde hair? 'Did she say why she was going to Ireland?'

'To meet up with her boyfriend. I don't know whether she was talking about an Irish lad, or a boy from her own country who was working over there. She knew that she had to get a ferry to Dublin, and she would be met there.'

A boyfriend. The fit went in. The carrier bag from Hereford with the aftershave and the underpants. Presents for the beloved. The worry was that she would not have left those behind lightly.

'Not quite the straight-arrow run to Holyhead where you dropped her, was it, Tony?' I said, smiling to soften the accusation.

He looked hurt. 'That wasn't my fault. I even suggested taking her into Newtown to catch a train. It was already dark by then. But she didn't like that idea.'

'Too expensive?'

'I don't think that was it. She had already asked me if I knew how strict the Immigration people were at the ferry port. I got the impression that she thought there might be too many people asking questions on a train.'

'The service station was her choice?' I asked, letting him hear my doubt.

'Yes. We checked the map. She wanted to stick to the country roads, she said.'

'You liked her?' I asked.

The question puzzled him. He looked at me warily, wondering where I was going with this. 'I liked what I saw of her,' he answered guardedly.

'Weren't you concerned for her? It's night now. The dead of winter. She's a stranger, and you've left her in the middle of nowhere.'

He bristled. 'It wasn't the middle of nowhere. I left her where it was light, and where she could buy stuff if she needed it. I even bought her chocolate. And water. I've never bought a bottle of fucking water in my life before. And I went back.'

'You went back?'

'Everyone was coming into town at that time of night. I reckoned she wouldn't be able to get a lift. So I gave her about half an hour to get fed up, and then I went back to see if she wanted somewhere to stay for the night.' He held up his hands as if anticipating a protest. 'Just a bed, mind you. I didn't have any other intentions.'

'But she turned you down?'

'No. She wasn't there. She'd already gone.'

This rocked me. 'Tell me, Tony, what time would this be?' I asked very carefully.

He thought about it. His head moving slightly with the enumeration process. 'About eight o'clock. No later than quarter past. I hung around for a while to make sure that she hadn't just gone for a bit of a wander.'

It made no sense. Her destiny lay with that minibus one and a half hours later. So where had she disappeared to?

'Sure you don't want to have a look?'

I turned round. He was holding the phone up tauntingly, a big grin on his face. I had counted on him not being able to resist it.

I snatched the phone out of his hand.

A split second of jaw-dropped surprise, and then he wailed, 'You bastard—' Making a lunge for it.

I held him back with my forearm, the other hand holding the phone up out of his reach.

'Give that back to me, you fucker!' He was snarling now, pushing hard, trying to snatch at the phone in my hand. He was straining, twisted out of balance. I dipped the forearm I was using to restrain him, and used my elbow to chop him hard in the groin.

A huge gasp of air fused into a groan and he went slack. For a moment all he could do was stare at me reproachfully, mouth wide open like a betrayed carp.

He shook his head. 'I should have known better than to trust a fucking cop.'

'You didn't trust me,' I corrected him. 'You tried using extortion. I gave you my word, and that's all you need.' I opened the door and backed out of the cab holding up the phone. 'I'm impounding this on suspicion that it's been used to take pornographic images.'

4

I christened her Magda. I was getting closer. Most likely East European. A student or a migrant worker, probably running in the wrong direction from an expired work permit.

Not a prostitute from Cardiff.

I had been vindicated. I had my own proof that the group had been lying. Now I had to face the scary edge of that triumph. What had really happened in the hut on Saturday night? Where was the girl now?

I spent the next two and a half hours back at the service station watching the CCTV footage in real time. I saw Tony Griffiths walk across the forecourt to buy the chocolate and water. He had been careful, he'd kept his truck out of surveillance range. But I didn't see Magda. Not until the minibus.

I called Bryn Jones in Carmarthen.

'Sir, I have uncorroborated evidence that the woman might have been an East European student.'

'How uncorroborated?'

'No one is going to speak up.'

'Can you be any more specific than East

European?' he asked.

'No, sir, sorry.'

'Okay, we'll spread the word informally. See if we have any reports of missing persons that match out there in migrant-worker land.'

'Thank you, sir.'

I sat in my car and put in enough calls about the other cases I was working on to log that I was still on the planet. Just. I even called the guy in Caernarfon about the Kawasaki quad bike. Now that Tony Griffiths had told me that Magda had been making for the ferry in Holyhead, I wanted to keep an excuse to visit North Wales active.

I leaned back, closed my eyes, and tried to recall the image of the group coming down the hill on that cold Sunday morning. The two brothers in front, the other three staggering behind them.

Who to brace?

I could probably forget the three with partners. The McGuire brothers and Les Tucker. They would now have backtracked with enough explanations and excuses to make them as virtuous as Mother Teresa. Paul Evans, the big one, would either be dumb or belligerent. I didn't relish tackling either persona.

I called David Williams at The Fleece.

'Trevor Vaughan, the hill farmer. How do I find him?' I asked.

I wrote down the directions. As usual I marvelled at how complicated it was trying to find anywhere in the countryside.

'Anything else you can give me on him?'

'Quiet. Nice man. Inoffensive.' He went silent.

'Am I hearing hesitation?'

'I don't like spreading unsubstantiated rumours.'

58

'Yes, you do—so give.'

'There's talk that he's done this before. Visited prostitutes.'

'Am I missing something in Dinas? Is there a local knocking shop?'

He laughed. 'No, Sandra wouldn't let me set it up. I'm not talking about Dinas; it's trips away, to London or Cardiff, rugby games, agricultural shows, stuff like that.'

I thanked him and hung up. So the talk was that Trevor Vaughan wasn't a virgin. So why did the rest of the group use him and Paul as an excuse for the presence of the girl? Probably to wrap themselves in sanctity, and preserve them from the wrath of their partners. Or was it their intention to test the truth of the rumours?

Some friends.

*   *   *

The road to Trevor Vaughan's farm followed a small river, which had receded to an alder-lined brook by the time it arrived. The hills were steeper here, the land poorer; sessile oaks, birch, and hazel clumps in the tight dingles, monoculture green pasture on the slopes where the bracken had been defeated, and glimpses of the wilder heather topknot on the open hill above.

A rough, potholed drive led off the road past an empty bungalow and a large new lambing shed to the farmhouse. No dogs barked. An old timber-framed barn formed a courtyard with an unloved, two-storey, whitewashed stone house, raised above the yard. Its slate roof was covered with lichen, and the old-fashioned metal windows were in need of painting.

I'd been around these parts long enough to know not to let the air of neglect fool me. These people could probably have bought a small suburban street in Cardiff outright. They just didn't waste it on front, or what they regarded as frippery. They saved it for the important things in life: livestock and land.

I parked in the courtyard and got out of the car. Still no dogs. Just the sound of cattle lowing in one of the outbuildings. A woman appeared from around the side of the house wiping her hands on an apron. Small-framed, short grey hair, spectacles, and an expression that didn't qualify as welcoming.

'We don't see representatives without an appointment,' she announced in a surprisingly firm voice.

'I'm not a rep,' I said, opening my warrant card. 'I'm a policeman—Detective Sergeant Glyn Capaldi. Are you Mrs Vaughan?'

'Yes.'

'Is Trevor around?'

She scowled. 'I thought we were finished with that business. Emrys Hughes told Trevor that it was over.'

I smiled. 'I just need to ask a couple more questions.'

'You'll have to come back another time.' She inclined her head at the hill behind the house. 'He's busy up there with the sheep.'

'I could go up and see him.'

She gave my car a sceptical appraisal. 'You won't get up there in that.'

'I could walk.' She looked askance at my shoes. 'It's all right, I keep some boots in the car,' I told her. She sucked in her cheeks, her face tightening into mean little lines as she suppressed her natural inclination to tell me to get off their land. I was glad that she wasn't my mother.

Following her instructions, I took a diagonal line across the contours, steadily rising towards the open hill, making a point of shutting all the gates behind me. I came to a collapsed stone field shelter with an ash tree growing through the middle of it. According to the woman's directions I was spot on track.

And I would have kept on going like a naïve and trusting pilgrim, onwards and upwards to the open moor, if a fluke of the wind hadn't brought the sound of sheep to me. From the wrong direction. I followed the sound to the crest of a rise. The ground dropped into a cwm, and, where it levelled out, I saw a Land Rover in a field beside a pen of sheep. The old crone had deliberately misdirected me.

The dogs were the first to see me traversing down the steep side of the cwm. Two of them. Black-and-white sheepdogs circling out at a scuttling run to flank me, practising dropping to their bellies, preparing to effect optimum ankle damage. The sheep, sensing the dogs on the move, started to make a racket.

Trevor Vaughan, in the pen, looked up from the ewe he was inspecting. He raised his voice and called the dogs in. I waved. He watched me descending for a moment, and then waved back, any welcome in the gesture held in reserve.

He was wearing a grey tweed flat cap, an old waxed jacket worn through at the creases, and green waterproof overtrousers. I had checked, he was twenty-four, but he looked older. A mournful, triangular-shaped face, which, for a man who spent his life outdoors, was remarkably pale.

'Mr Vaughan,' I shouted, as I got closer, 'I'm Detective Sergeant Capaldi.'

'I know who you are, Sergeant. Emrys Hughes told us.'

The dogs, sensing a distraction, made a move towards me again. He checked them with a series of short whistles, and with a couple of clucks and a gesture he got them on to the open tailgate and into the back of the Land Rover. I was impressed.

'I have nothing more to say about Saturday night.'

'I'm not here to ask about that.'

He looked surprised. 'You aren't?'

'No, I want to know where—what's her name? Magda?—where is she now?'

He wasn't a good actor. He shook his head and feigned surprise, but he wasn't used to it. 'I don't know anyone called Magda. I don't know who you're talking about.'

I gave him a con cop smile. 'Who decided to call her Miss Danielle?'

'That's what she called herself.'

'You're lying, Mr Vaughan.'

He didn't protest. He looked away from me. I thought I had him. And then I heard it too. I followed his line of sight. A late model, grey Land Rover Discovery was coming up the cwm towards us. I stuck myself in front of him. 'I need to know, Trevor. Has anything happened to that woman?'

He shook his head. Almost imperceptibly. It was aimed at me. As if he didn't want whoever was driving the Discovery to see that he had communicated.

'Trevor . . .' The yell came out of the open window as the Discovery pulled up. The driver pretended to only then recognize me. 'What are you doing here?' his voice registering surprise. Ken McGuire was a better actor than Trevor Vaughan. The old crone had not just misdirected me, she had call in reinforcements.

'Afternoon, Mr McGuire,' I said cheerily. I sensed that I had got close to something with Trevor Vaughan, but instinct warned me not to let Ken McGuire suspect it.

He got out of the Discovery playing it puzzled, looking between the both of us. 'I came over to borrow a raddle harness, Trevor. You're Sergeant Capaldi, aren't you? I've seen you in The Fleece.'

'I was out for a walk, Mr McGuire.'

'He was asking about Miss Danielle, Ken,' Trevor volunteered.

I pulled a weak grin and resisted shooting a reproving glance at Trevor.

Ken winced theatrically. 'Please, Sergeant, we're trying to forget that episode.'

I couldn't resist it. 'Like you've forgotten her telephone number?'

He didn't break a sweat. 'That's right. And just as well, eh?' He chuckled. 'No more temptation down that road. We've learned a hard lesson. That right, Trevor?'

'That's right.'

'You didn't mention that she was foreign.'

'What makes you say that, Sergeant?' Ken came back just a bit too quickly.

I shrugged. 'A rumour I picked up. That the girl was from Eastern Europe. Trying to hitchhike to

Ireland.'

'She didn't try that story on us, did she, Trevor?'

Trevor shook his head.

'And as for her being foreign—who knows? We're hicks up here, Sergeant. Ladies of the night from Cardiff are as exotic as the label gets. We're not good with accents.'

'Where is she now, Mr McGuire?' It was a long shot, but I was up close to him, and I wanted to see if anything flecked his composure.

'In Cardiff, I imagine,' he replied without hesitating, without a flicker. He grinned at me wickedly. 'I'm just sorry I can't pass on her telephone number, Sergeant—you seem so interested.'

The patronizing bastard actually winked at me.

*   *   *

Emrys Hughes and a uniformed sidekick flagged me down before I got back to Dinas.

I was impressed. It had happened quicker than I had expected. Someone was carrying more clout than I had realized.

'Afternoon, Sergeant Hughes,' I said pleasantly, lowering the window.

He gave me a measured dose of silence before he slowly leaned down towards me. 'Your own boss warned you, Sergeant.'

'And what would that warning have been about?'

'Harassing my people.'

I played perplexed. 'Harassing . . .?'

'Don't get cute,' he growled. 'You know exactly what I mean. You were specifically told to lay off the men from the minibus.'

'Questions, Sergeant. That wasn't harassment. I was only following up on some discrepancies in their testimony.'

'There is no case. This has nothing to do with you. You were told not to contact them.'

I bluffed. 'Detective Chief Superintendent Galbraith is not entirely happy with all the answers we've had.'

He called it. Leaning in closer and lowering his voice to keep his sidekick out of earshot. 'Yes, he fucking is, or this thing would still be live.'

I acted hurt. 'Why do you think I'm asking these questions?'

'Because you're playing the lone fucking vigilante. You've got no authorization and you know it.' He glared, challenging me to refute him.

I just nodded, suppressing my frustration. If I made it worse I would have his boss, Inspector Morgan, on my back too.

He grinned, savouring his moment of triumph. 'Back to work, eh, Sergeant?' he suggested smugly, straightening up.

I ignored him and drove off. We both knew that I had to take the warning seriously. Morgan and his men could make my life in these parts even more difficult than it already was. But another message was coming in over the horizon. Ken McGuire really did not want me talking to Trevor Vaughan. I sighed inwardly. Revelations like that can corrupt the best intentions.

*   *   *

It had been a bad day, which, I soon discovered, had the potential to get worse.

'You've had a visitor,' David Williams called out when he saw me walk into The Fleece.

'Who's that?' I asked absently. I was distracted by the prospect of a proper bath and a hot meal. I had temporarily forgotten that people did not come to visit me in Dinas.

'He was Scottish.'

I stopped rummaging in the drawer of the reception desk where I kept the shampoo and flannel I used at The Fleece. 'Did he leave a name?' I asked, already knowing the answer.

He glanced down at a notepad. 'Graham Mackay.'

Why did he want me? One possible answer to that question disturbed me. Really disturbed me. Knowing what he was capable of, both on and off the field of battle.

How deeply had Gina got into him? Could he now be the besotted instrument of my wife's intense rage?

She blamed me for everything that had gone sour in her life. She blamed me for her weight gain. For the first crow's feet in the corners of her eyes, the advent of grey hairs, and the back pains that she never used to suffer from. The increase in traffic on the streets of Cardiff was down to me, as was the dogshit on the pavements.

But most of all she blamed me for the *Merulius lacrymans*. As if I could really be held responsible for the dry rot that had been discovered in the house after she had bought me out of my share. I had laughed when she first accused me. That had been a mistake.

'Was he on his own?' I asked.

'Yes. He said he was on his way to Aberystwyth

and that he'd call in again on his way back through.'

'No,' I said to David as he started to pull my pint.

He looked surprised. 'Sun's over the yardarm.'

'I haven't finished work yet.'

'Someone you don't want to meet?' His question followed me as I left the bar.

*   *   *

I got away fast. It was precautionary. It would have been messy enough tangling with one of Gina's run-of-the-mill lovers, but mixing it with the one who had been trained in the precise arts of close-range warfare would have made the mess too one-sided.

Trevor Vaughan was still a temptation. But, after my visit this afternoon, he would now be well and truly buffered. So I decided to shift my interest to the one member of the group that I could currently tackle with impunity. Mostly because he was no longer around.

And I still couldn't get a handle on the name. *Boon* Paterson?

It was virtually dark now, with a vague wash of blue-grey light high in the west, the sky clear, promising a cold night. I crawled slowly along the frontage of the few houses that comprised the hamlet. Low cottages with a terrace of ugly brick houses, and a corrugated-iron chapel surrounded by metal railings.

Boon Paterson's house was the one I would have chosen. A freshly painted stone cottage with its first-floor windows hunkered down under low eaves. The soft light through the curtained windows promised the warmth of a proper fire, and an

67

imagined smell of baking. All safe and well inside, with the cold and cheerless night shut out.

The woman who answered the door was wearing a faded yellow dressing gown and a frown.

'Mrs Paterson?' I asked.

'Yes,' she replied guardedly, pulling the dressing gown tighter around her.

I held out my warrant card. She leant forward to read it before I could introduce myself. 'What is this about, Sergeant?' She wasn't local. English. Slow, flat vowels, a south or southwest accent.

'Have I come to the right address for Boon Paterson?'

She blanched. 'Yes. Is anything the matter?' Her voice rose anxiously.

I smiled reassuringly. 'No. There's nothing to worry about. I'm just trying to get in contact with him.'

She shook her head, watching me carefully, as if she was trying to work out whether I was about to spring something awful on her. 'I'm his mother, Sally Paterson. He's not here.'

'I was aware of that.'

'Well, why turn up here in that case?' she snapped, visibly annoyed.

'Does he have a mobile phone number?' I asked quickly, before she could close the door in my face.

'I'm letting all the heat out here.'

'I could come inside?' I suggested.

'Is Boon in any kind of trouble?'

'No, I just need his help on something I'm working on.'

She relented. I caught a glimpse of sandwich preparation on the kitchen table as she led me through to the living room. A portable gas heater stood on the hearth in place of my imagined open fire. The furniture was old, chunky, and looked comfortable, and there were some classy touches of understatement in the arrangements and the decoration. I would have moved into the place as it stood and only changed the fire.

'Does this have anything to do with Saturday night's shenanigans?' she asked.

'You heard about them?'

She smiled for the first time. 'It would have been hard not to, round here.'

'My interest is in the young woman that was in the minibus.'

'Boon wasn't there.'

'He was when she was first picked up. He could give me a description. Perhaps help me identify her.'

She looked surprised. 'I didn't think there was any mystery. I thought that she was supposed to be a prostitute from Cardiff?'

'That's what I'd like to establish.'

'Is there some sort of doubt?'

I decided to trust her. 'I'm concerned that she might still be missing.'

She cocked her head to look at me. 'Capaldi? I think I've heard your name mentioned, but I haven't seen you before, have I?'

'Probably not. I haven't been here long. I used to be in Cardiff. I'm here on a secondment.'

'You must have done something very bad to deserve that,' she said, deadpan.

I smiled wanly. She hadn't realized how close to the mark she was.

'And young ladies don't go missing in these parts, Sergeant.'

'I've already had something along those lines explained to me.'

She laughed, it softened her features. 'Well, a word of advice: don't believe everything that the sanctimonious buggers tell you.'

'Can you elaborate on that?' I asked, trying to keep a lid on the flash of interest that she had just sparked.

She shook her head, shrugging it off, moving on to look at me quizzically. She had an intelligent set to her face, but there was a carelessness about the way she projected herself. Without too much effort she could have shifted to attractive. This evening's projection, however, was tiredness. 'Do the McGuires know that you're asking me these questions?'

'Your son's friends?'

She nodded.

I decided on honesty. 'I think they thought Boon's absence kept him safe from me.'

She laughed. I sensed that it was private amusement.

'Did Boon mention anything to you about Saturday night?'

'I haven't seen him.'

It was my turn to show surprise.

'I'm a care assistant at the Sychnant Nursing Home. I'm working nights at the moment.' She touched the collar of her dressing gown, explaining it. 'Boon must have left in the small hours on Sunday morning. He had packed up and gone by the time I got home.' She frowned. 'I don't know why he left so early, he wasn't due to catch his flight until very late last night.'

'He's posted abroad?'

'Cyprus. He's with the Signals Regiment.'

'Where was he flying from?'

'Brize Norton, Oxfordshire. It's not really that far.'

'Perhaps he had other people to say goodbye to?'

She pulled a face. It made her look older and even more tired. 'More like he couldn't stand spending any more time with his mother.' She tried it out as a joke, but a tiny crease of pain blistered the surface.

Her emotion was palpable. I smiled sympathetically. She started to respond, and then remembered that I was a cop, that I was trained to entice people into the confessional. She shook her head, pulling herself out of it. 'Testosterone. It turns young men into monsters.'

She moved forward and reached out to the mantelpiece behind me. For an irrational instant I felt myself thrill at the possibility of physical contact. 'Here,' she said, stepping back, handing me a framed photograph, 'that's Boon.' I hid my disappointment as she retracted.

But I couldn't conceal my surprise.

'You didn't know?' she asked, amusement showing in her eyes.

I shook my head. Boon Paterson was a handsome, sturdy, not too tall, young black man. He was standing in khaki fatigues besides a camouflaged Land Rover, a wide smile on his face, and a radio with a long whip antenna strapped to his back.

'His father?' I asked, hoping that it didn't sound too crass.

'His father's a shit,' she said vehemently. But she had understood the question. 'Boon's adopted,' she

71

explained in a softer voice. 'His birth mother was sixteen years old, and no one was volunteering as the father. She gave him his name. Kind of ironic, isn't it? You call your child Boon, and then decide that you can't cope with the reality of it.' She was pensive for a moment. 'My husband left me,' she said, explaining the outburst.

'I'm sorry,' I said.

'So was I.' She smiled wryly. 'Now I have to spend my nights at the Sychnant Nursing Home.'

I looked down at the photograph again. Trying to understand what it must have been like. To be black and grow up in a place like this.

She read my mind and shook her head. 'I'm sorry, Sergeant, that's it, time's up. I'm running behind now. I've still got to shower, and I've got stuff to prepare to sustain me through another long night.'

She shook hands under the front porch. Her parting smile was warmer. I walked to the car thinking about her. We shared the same polarity. We were both outsiders, both damaged goods. By the laws of magnetism I should have been repelled. I wasn't.

*   *   *

As soon as I was clear of the house, I tried calling Boon on the mobile phone number that Sally Paterson had given me.

I got an unable-to-connect message. No answering service. I tried again, with the same result. He could still have been in transit. On a plane with his phone switched off. Or, if he had returned, he could be catching up on sleep, or already on duty.

To try to go through official channels would require clearances that no one was going to give me.

On the drive home I rotated through the other information that she had supplied. Wondering what she had meant when she told me not to believe what I had heard about young women not going missing in these parts? Was Boon being black just a surprising fact? Did it have any relevance to Magda?

Why had they dropped him off in Dinas? His mother had been surprised that he had left so early. She had been hurt that he hadn't seen fit to say goodbye to her. Even if he had been part of that group that had lurched down off the hill on Sunday morning, he would still have had plenty of time to report in at Brize Norton.

I started to develop a scenario. I put Boon back on the minibus. They have now picked up Magda, and have dumped the driver. Sod the pimp story, one of the group is driving. But that's immaterial. They are heading towards the hills to continue the party.

With an attractive white girl on board.

And one black guy.

What if Magda was turned on by Boon? She wouldn't know the social pecking order here. Her first impressions are of a busload of rednecks and an attractive young black kid. Where's the choice? So is this what gets Boon booted off the bus in Dinas? And, more importantly, what does it do to the group's perception of Magda? Does it change the dynamic? Angel to slut?

The telephone woke me in the early morning.

'It's Sally Paterson . . .' A woman's voice trying to contain urgency.

'Sorry . . .?' I said groggily.

'Boon's mother. You gave me your number, I didn't know who else to call.'

I straightened up, adrenalin kicking in. 'What's happened?'

'I've just got in from work. There's a message on the answering machine from Brize Norton. Boon never reported in for his flight back to Cyprus. No one knows where he is.'

5

Sally Paterson opened the door before I managed to knock. She had been watching for my arrival. Her hair, which had been pinned into a loose bun, was escaping in straggling wisps, and she was still wearing the sickly pink polyester housecoat that doubled as a uniform at the Sychnant Nursing Home. I followed her through to the kitchen, her handbag gaping open on the table where she had dropped it before checking the answering machine. She had shadows of fatigue under her eyes from her night's work, and was speedy with worry, her heels working like castors, seeking solace from motion.

'Did you make the calls I suggested?' I asked.

She nodded distractedly, and I guessed that she hadn't picked up much comfort. 'I went back to the Transport Officer at Brize Norton. No change there. Boon's about to be officially classified as absent without leave.'

'What about his base in Cyprus? It could be a simple case of army SNAFU.'

She shook her head. 'He never arrived. And he's not on the way. There were no alternative travel arrangements. He was expected on the Brize Norton flight.'

'Did you get in touch with the taxi company?'

'I rang the one he usually uses. They didn't get a call to pick him up on Saturday night.'

'We'll ring round,' I said soothingly. 'They may have been too busy.'

'They would still have known if he had called,' she snapped. She threw her head back and screwed her eyes closed tightly. 'I'm sorry,' she sighed. 'I mustn't take this out on you.'

'That's okay.' I persuaded her to sit down. She was frayed from trying to contain the arcing sparks of her anxiety. The night shift hadn't helped. I made a pot of tea and sat down opposite her. 'How did he get home?' I asked.

'Home?' she replied, eyeing me blankly.

'The minibus dropped him off in Dinas. That's at least five miles away. How did he get back from there?'

She shook her head while she was thinking about it. 'I don't know.' She looked at me wanly. 'Is it important?'

'I don't know.'

'What do I do?' she asked, trying hard not to let helplessness in.

'The first thing you ought to do is try and get some sleep.'

She shook her head in a vague protest.

'Is there anyone you can get to come over? Family? Any friends you would like me to contact?'

'My mother's in Dorchester, but I wouldn't want to worry her.'

'Any special friends?'

She smiled weakly. 'You're very tactful, Sergeant Capaldi. No. No special friends. Boyfriend. Or girlfriend.'

'You can call me Glyn, if it helps.'

'Glyn . . .' She tasted it. Then nodded. She looked up, eyes suddenly alert now, as if she had reached a decision. 'Do you know why he doesn't talk to me any more?'

'You don't have to say anything,' I said quietly.

'No, I want to. I have to keep trying to understand this myself.' She arranged the words in her head for a moment. 'It's because he blames me. Blames us, I should say, but his father's not around any more to take his share. He blames us for bringing him out here. For depriving him of his culture, he tells me. His heritage. You see, now that he's in the Army and teamed up with other Afro-Caribbean men, he's accusing us of dragging him away from his natural background.' She laughed self-mockingly. 'And to think that we deliberately brought him as far away as we could from that background. To keep him safe, we thought.'

I glanced out of the window. Cold slate roofs, grazing sheep and slanting rain. About as far away from life on the Street as you could get. 'Why Wales?' I asked.

'It wasn't meant to be Wales. We just wanted to get out of the city. Boon was six months old; we wanted to be in the countryside. I thought we could try somewhere like Oxfordshire or

Northamptonshire. Somewhere not too far from town. But Malcolm was offered a good job here in Mid Wales.' She shrugged. 'Housing was cheap, we could buy a nice place, and still be relatively well off.'

'What kind of a job?'

'History teacher. Head of a small department. And then he ran away.' She smiled, punishing herself. 'It looks like that pattern's repeating itself.'

'How did Boon get on?' I asked quickly, to stop her dwelling on it. 'Socially? As a boy growing up here?'

She looked at me, and for a moment a sparkle came back into her eyes. She had recognized the question that I had been waiting to ask. 'This brings it round to the others, doesn't it?'

I nodded. 'Do you like them?'

She was silent for a moment. 'In their own way they were kind to Boon, I suppose.'

'In their own way?'

'It's not their fault, they were children, but there is a certain endemic ignorance in country people. When I say "ignorance", I probably mean intolerance. They don't like change. They're not used to things being different. Somehow it's not quite right.'

'They gave Boon a hard time?'

'Let's just say that they made him aware of his difference.' She pulled a face. 'I'm being unfair to them. They did become his friends. And they stayed that way.'

'But . . .?' I prompted.

She smiled weakly. 'I think that he was always made aware that that friendship was a gift. I remember one time he came home after a football

77

match. He must have been about ten. They had been playing a team from another school who started giving him a hard time, calling him names. But what he was so pleased about was how his friends had stood up for him. "Mum," he said to me, ever so excited, "Mum, and do you know what Gordon said back to them? Gordon said, 'He may be a bloody Coon, but he's our bloody Coon.'"

Neither of us laughed.

'He broke the bond?' I asked. 'He went away to join the Army?'

'That was another difference. They all had farms or family businesses to move into.'

'And he liked the Army?'

'Yes. He was a bit overawed at first. A bit scared, although he wouldn't admit it. You know, out there in the bigger world, and the regimentation, and the discipline. And then he discovered his Soul Mates, and I turned into the cruel bitch who had deprived him of the funky upbringing that they had all shared. Boys and the Hood, or whatever the hell it is.'

'Why would he not turn up at Brize Norton?'

It was a question she had been torturing herself with. She shook her head. 'I don't know. I told you, he didn't talk to me any more.'

'Was there a girlfriend?'

'If there was a current one, I hadn't been told about her.'

'Current?'

'He had quite a serious affair with a Czech girl he met in Germany when he was stationed there. Then he was posted to Cyprus. As far as I know, he hasn't had a long-term relationship since then.'

She tried to smile to cover her distress, but her

hands came up to her face, and she gave in to her tears. 'I just hope something awful hasn't happened to him,' she wailed.

I went round to her and put my hands on her shoulders. It had been a long time since I had tried to comfort a woman. I felt awkward and unpractised. I kept my hands light and unthreatening, and felt her muscles relax slightly. The touch began to feel both intimate and sanctioned.

'Please,' I said, 'you mustn't worry. Let me put the word out, so that we can at least discount the worst of your fears.'

She reached a hand up to lightly cover mine. It was damp from her tears. 'Thank you.'

She walked me to the front door. I hesitated to ask, given the state she was in, but I had to keep the momentum going for Magda's sake. I turned to her on the threshold. 'You mentioned, when we first met, that I shouldn't believe them when they said that young women didn't disappear around here.'

It took her by surprise. She nodded hesitantly. Then she surprised me by smiling. 'How about a girl going on for eighteen who leaves for school one morning and is never seen again?'

I took my notebook out. 'Can you give me details?'

She put two restraining fingers on the notebook. 'I'm sorry, I'm being selfish at your expense. There is no mystery. I told you that my husband left me?'

I nodded, watching her.

'He went out that morning too. They left together. Him and the schoolgirl.'

*   *   *

79

Okay, I could sympathize with Sally Paterson. The anxiety that her missing son was causing her, coupled with the other kicks in the teeth that life had dealt. But I couldn't pretend that I wasn't experiencing a lift of professional elation over the gift that had just been handed to me. Now I had legitimate questions to ask the group about the disappearance of their buddy Boon.

Bryn Jones didn't quite share my enthusiasm.

'It's an Army matter,' he stated drily, when I called him in Carmarthen. 'Let them clean up their own mess.' In that terse sentence I realized that Bryn and the military shared a history.

'It could be germane, sir.'

'There is nothing for it to be germane *to*, Glyn. And don't even think about mentioning a missing woman.'

'The people on the minibus were the last people to see him, sir.'

'The last people that we know of,' he corrected me.

'Don't we have a duty to his mother, sir? To try and get close to what was on his mind that last night. In case it has some sort of bearing on why he didn't turn up for his flight to Cyprus.'

'What's she like?'

'Distraught, sir.'

'You're a sly bastard, Capaldi.' I heard the contained laugh under his voice.

'Is that a yes, sir?'

'You know it's not a yes. But I'm not in control of your actions until I get a chance to confer with DCS Galbraith on how we should instruct you.'

'Thank you, sir.' I disconnected quickly before he

could remember his beef with the Army and rein me back in.

Trevor Vaughan was my obvious choice. But going to his farm would be pointless; it would just end up as a stand-off between me, him, and whoever had been appointed as minder for that day.

*   *   *

Even in the sad dead grip of winter an amateur like me, who was still trying out for his country-boy badge, could tell that Rhosgoch was a prosperous farm. The hedges were tidy and the drive was smooth, lined with beech trees that someone had had the unselfish foresight to plant a few generations ago.

Ken McGuire's grey Discovery was parked in front of the house along with a red Audi A3 and a low-slung, black, two-door BMW 3 Series. All swanky machinery for these latitudes.

The house was a big architectural hybrid; a Victorian copy of a Georgian façade in stone, with a two-storey yellow-brick side extension. It was all in good shape and, I was glad to see, the dogs were kept locked up.

The woman who answered the door disappointed me though. She didn't go with the house or the cars on the drive. A myopic woman in an apron, who peered at me as if she had forgotten that opening front doors sometimes revealed people standing there.

'Is Mr McGuire in?'

'No, he's out in the cattle shed, checking the bedding.'

'Can I wait for him?'

'I don't know about that.'

'Birdie . . .?'

The woman at the door cocked her head at the sound of the voice down the corridor.

'Who is it?' the voice asked, coming into view. She was in her mid-twenties, loosely styled brown hair, outdoor cheeks, a slight build, and the natural confidence of a woman who had learned to master horses and brothers at an early age.

'Detective Sergeant Capaldi.' I held up my warrant card. 'Mrs McGuire?'

She nodded, an all-purpose smile masking her scrutiny and curiosity. Taking just a little bit longer over it than she needed, to fit me into place. 'It's all right, Birdie, I'll take care of the sergeant. I'm Sheila McGuire. Please, come in.' She used the act of opening the door wider as an excuse not to shake my hand. 'Ken isn't around at the moment. Assuming that it's him you're here to see?'

'Would you mind me waiting?'

'Not at all. We're in the kitchen. I'll put the kettle back on.'

I followed her. She was wearing a baggy sweater, and swung a good bum in a pair of tight-fitting, navy blue riding breeches that were stained at the contact points with something that I assumed was equestrian.

When I walked into the big kitchen, the other woman sitting at the long refectory table, with a cigarette and a mug of coffee, made no pretence of welcoming me into the tent. She looked at me as if I was something that had turned up on her plate that she hadn't ordered.

'This is Zoë McGuire, my sister-in-law.' Sheila

82

introduced us. Zoë raised her eyebrows in mock surprise, and then deigned to incline her head at me, still watching, as if she had been tipped off that I was about to do something really stupid.

So, this was Gordon's wife. The younger brother, the auctioneer. I marked her down for the black BMW. I was in the presence of both the McGuire ladies and had not prepared myself for the eventuality.

Zoë was wearing make-up and showing cleavage. Both were artfully presented. Her hair was blonde and cut short, gamine style, setting off the sculptural forms of the long neck, chin and cheekbones. She had played it wild with the make-up around her eyes, making them hard to read.

'I hope that you're here to arrest the bastards,' Zoë declaimed. I thought that the accent might be Shropshire or Cheshire.

Sheila laughed.

'What reason would I have to arrest them?'

'They've reneged on the deal, the cheapskates.'

'Zoë . . .' Sheila protested amiably.

'What deal would that be?' I asked, playing it slightly dumb and nervous in the presence of glory.

'You tell him,' Zoë instructed Sheila. 'You're pissed off about it too.'

Sheila smiled, apologizing for her sister-in-law. 'Our husbands have cried off taking us to the rugby in Dublin.'

'It's a bloody institution, the Dublin trip,' Zoë wailed.

'They're not going?'

'Oh, they're going all right, they just don't want the WAGs with them this time. Selfish buggers,'

83

Zoë snarled.

'Ah.' I grinned, pretending that I had only just seen the light. 'I thought you meant arrest them for what happened on Saturday night.' I segued into a big, dopey cop smile, and waited for the reactions.

Sheila had the grace to look uncomfortable. Zoë just shrugged and pulled a face. 'Bloody schoolboys,' she hissed.

'It was a silly stunt that went wrong, Sergeant, and now the episode is closed,' Sheila said firmly.

'And they learnt a lesson,' Zoë added.

'What lesson was that, Mrs McGuire?'

'Getting ripped off by that dirty bitch, and spending a freezing night out in the forest. And then having to pay for the repairs to that minibus.'

'Zoë, Sergeant Capaldi isn't here to talk about Saturday night,' Sheila said, and from the look she gave me, I realized that I was meant to recognize that as an instruction.

'What are you here for?' Zoë asked.

'Do you know Boon Paterson?'

'Of course,' Zoë answered.

Sheila just nodded, but I thought that I picked up a small surge in the current of her concentration.

'He didn't turn up for his flight back to his unit in Cyprus.'

'Has there been an accident?' Sheila asked, and this time it was Zoë's attention that seemed to be nailed.

'Not that we're aware of.'

The back door opened and Ken McGuire walked through in socks and a pair of faded blue overalls, a light dusting of chopped straw in his hair and on his shoulders. The air of slightly preoccupied contentment that he had carried from the cattle

84

shed was wiped into a big, puzzled, angry frown as soon as he saw me. This time he wasn't faking the surprise.

'You . . .' he spluttered angrily. 'What the hell are you doing here?'

'He's here about Boon, Ken,' Sheila explained, cutting in over the erupting tirade.

'Boon?' It took a moment for it to register; he was still so affronted at the sight of me in his kitchen. 'What's Boon got to do with anything?'

I explained, taking it as far as I had got with Sheila and Zoë. He looked thoughtful as he listened.

'Did he mention anything on Saturday night that might have made you think that he didn't want to go back to his unit in Cyprus?' I asked. 'Did any conversation or discussion like that come up while he was home on leave?'

Ken shook his head. 'Not in front of me. None of the others mentioned it either. If he had said anything, it's something we would have talked about, believe me.'

'He was drunk, wasn't he?'

Ken frowned and looked at me sharply. 'Why do you say that?'

I smiled pleasantly. 'I would have thought that it might have loosened him up. If it was on his mind, that's when he would talk about it.'

He relaxed. 'I take your point. And I suppose we all had a pretty good skinful that night.' He smiled mock-ruefully at the ladies, and then shook his head. 'But the subject didn't come up. Only the inevitable fact that his leave was over.'

I nodded understandingly. 'How did he get home?'

'Pardon?'

'You dropped him off in Dinas. It was late, it was cold, and, you said it yourself, he was very drunk. So how did he get home?'

'You didn't abandon poor old Boon, did you,' Zoë protested, 'in your rush to get that dirty bitch up into the hills?'

'Zoë!' Sheila hushed.

Ken smiled to include me in the conspiracy that we shouldn't take his sister-in-law too seriously. 'We dropped him at his house. He asked us to. He was supposed to be travelling in the morning.'

I stared him out for a moment, giving him the opportunity to retract. 'DCI Jones told me that you said in your statement that Boon Paterson asked to be dropped off in Dinas.'

He shook his head. 'No, sorry, he's got it wrong. He must have misheard us. Boon asked to be dropped off at home. Your Inspector Jones must have heard us saying that we drove through Dinas on the way out to Boon's.'

'He was okay with that?'

'Who was okay with what?' Ken asked, puzzled by the question.

'The pimp who was doing the driving. He didn't mind running a taxi service?' I asked, deadpan.

His eyes drilled into me, trying to find what level of belief I was working on. 'He didn't have a choice. We were the paymasters.' He flicked a glance of apology at the ladies.

'Why did Boon want to be dropped off?'

'I told you. His leave was over. He was travelling the next day.'

'But not flying out until the evening. This was his last night, I would have thought that he'd have

86

wanted to stay on with his friends for as long as possible. Continue the party.'

'We tried to persuade him.' He shrugged. 'I'm afraid you'll have to ask him why he wanted to be dropped off early, Sergeant.'

'It wasn't a case of imposing apartheid?'

Ken's lower jaw dropped as if he had been sucker-punched. I heard the women's gasps of indignation, but I didn't turn, I was locked on him. Letting him see that in my belief system he was full of bullshit.

'I want you to explain exactly what you mean by that,' he said slowly and coldly.

'You told Boon to get off the minibus because you didn't want him playing with a white girl.'

'Sergeant, that is totally unfair!' Sheila protested behind me.

Ken went rigid, his fists balled, and his eyes screwed tightly shut, and I realized that I had made a bad misjudgement. This man was seriously outraged. I had seen it before, fury on the way to manifestation, and I prepared myself for an onslaught. But the moment passed. He opened his mouth; there was a slight gurgle before he spoke. 'I'm not going to dignify that with an answer. I want you out of my house now. And I am going to report you for making that disgraceful accusation.'

I smiled at him, and shrugged just flippantly enough so that he couldn't take it for an apology. Okay, I may have been wrong with the racist slant, but, in my book, the guy was still a liar. 'Mrs McGuire?' I turned to Zoë, pulling out my mobile phone. 'What's your husband's work number?'

She gave me a puzzled scowl, but called out the number. I watched Ken as I tapped the digits in. He tensed when he realized my intention. I nodded slightly, the gesture just for him, thanking him for sharing his discomfort with me.

Sheila had seen it. 'What do you want to talk to Gordon about?' she asked, questioning Ken with her eyes.

'I assume that he wants him to verify something,' Ken told her.

I smiled happily at them both as my call was answered. 'Good morning, Payne, Dyke and Thomas.' The receptionist's voice was chirpy.

'Gordon McGuire, please.'

'Who shall I say is calling?'

'Detective Sergeant Capaldi.'

'Please hold, I'll see if he's available.'

Ken smiled at me. It was the wrong sort of smile. Suddenly he wasn't nervous any more. I wheeled round. Zoë was holding her mobile phone.

Texting is silent.

'Sergeant Capaldi?' the receptionist came back on the line. 'I'm afraid that Mr McGuire is in a meeting, but if you would like to leave a number he'll call you back.'

'Thank you very much, I'll try again later.' I cut the connection.

'If there is some misunderstanding with our statement, Sergeant, I'll get the others together and we can get in touch with Inspector Jones to rectify it,' Ken offered helpfully, not a trace of malice or recrimination in the bastard's understanding expression.

Zoë hunched her shoulder at me in lazy apology. For being part of a conspiracy? Or for just providing unconditional protection?

88

*   *   *

The bastards were playing a game with me. Ken McGuire had changed their story on the spur of the moment. Because he could. He had that power. He just had to call round the group with the amended version. The revised consensus became the new truth.

Where was Magda?

Where was Boon Paterson?

Did they connect?

Slamming Ken McGuire's composure had been gratifying, but self-indulgent. Now I was going to pay for it. Because he was going to use his influence to get Inspector Morgan to cripple me. I was going to have to do something fast. To either find something concrete I could take to Jack Galbraith to get the investigation sanctioned, or to convince myself that I had been pursuing phantoms. What I didn't have was time.

Trevor Vaughan was their soft spot. I needed to brace him hard. But they knew that he was their weakness; the defensive block would be in place. I had to try to persuade them that it was no longer required.

I found the Evans family builders team at work on a loft conversion in Dinas. Three men crammed into the cab of a white Ford Transit van drinking tea from thermos flasks. They stared at me as I approached. Paul in the passenger's seat, with a skinny guy wedged between him and the driver, who shared the family likeness, older, but a little more hair, and marginally less bulk.

The driver got out of the van. I held up my warrant card and introduced myself pleasantly.

89

'I know who you are. What do you want?' he asked truculently.

'I want to speak to Paul,' I said, nodding towards the van.

'I'm his father. He's got nothing to say to you.'

'It's important.'

'You're wasting our time.'

'I'm trying to help Paul.'

He shook his head. 'Paul's done nothing to need your help. So why don't you just piss off now and leave us alone.'

'I disagree.' I took his sleeve between my fingers. The move surprised him, but he let me lead him away from the van. I lowered my voice. 'It's psychology, Mr Evans. Perception. It's unfair, but it's the way the world rolls.'

He screwed his face up at me. 'What the fuck are you talking about?'

'Imagine the line-up: the McGuire brothers, Trevor Vaughan, Les Tucker . . .' I paused. 'And Paul. The public make snap judgements, Mr Evans. Based on perception and prejudice. When the first hints of rape start to leak out, guess who they're going to be looking at?'

'What are you trying to say?' he snapped belligerently. 'Nothing happened. There was no rape.'

'Are you absolutely sure about that?'

'Fucking right, I am.' But he couldn't help it: his head shot round to take another look at his son in the van.

I scribbled my mobile phone number down on a card. 'Think about it. Talk to Paul again. I've got to go up to Caernarfon now for a couple of days on another case. If you feel like you want to talk to me,

90

use this number.' I handed him the card and walked away, trying to project rebuffed sincerity.

6

I set my phone to vibrate mode. I was meant to be in my ninja persona, an integral part of the night and the quiet earth, a ringing phone would have completely screwed my credibility. A real ninja would have ditched the telephone, been content with only a sharp knife and a prayer scarf, but then he wouldn't have been born in Cardiff, and he didn't have to keep in touch with the pub.

The text message from David Williams came through at eight o'clock. Emrys Hughes had been into The Fleece looking for me. As instructed, David had told him that I had gone up to North Wales for a couple of days.

I had dressed for the vigil, but by now the chill had seeped in through all the layers. I had been rooted here for long enough to imagine fungal spores sending out emissaries in my direction, trying to bring me into the family. I was hidden in a stand of spindly fir trees that had been planted as a windbreak beside the empty bungalow at Trevor Vaughan's farm. Far enough away from the main house and outbuildings to keep the dogs quiet.

Les Tucker's crew-cab pickup truck had been parked outside the farmhouse when I had arrived. I had driven past and parked out of sight to wait for him to leave. I used binoculars on the farmyard. When Les left, he took Trevor with him.

I moved down into my position in the fir trees. I

wasn't looking forward to this. Trevor Vaughan was probably the nicest and most sensitive one of the bunch. But that was his downfall. As in life, it was the meek and tender ones who got shafted.

The pickup returned before pub closing time. For a moment I thought that Les was going to drive Trevor up to the house and continue playing bodyguard, but he just swung into the entrance of the drive to get a better angle to turn around. Trevor got out, and the pickup sped off the way it had come.

'Trevor . . .' I stood up and called his name out quietly.

He froze. There was no moon, but enough residual light for me to make him out on the drive. With the fir trees as a backdrop, he couldn't see me.

'You're not meant to be here.' He aimed his voice out in my general direction, the surprise in it ebbing.

'They thought it was safe to let you out?'

The dogs, locked up in a shed by the house, picked up on my voice and started barking. He moved towards the house.

I came out on to the drive in front of him. 'We have to talk.'

He stared at me for a moment. It was too dark to make out his expression. He dropped his head. 'All right,' he said quietly, 'but I've got to get the dogs quiet first.'

We turned the bend in the drive and the door of the house opened. 'Trevor?' his mother's voice called out enquiringly.

He pushed in front of me. I was about to grab him, thinking that he was trying to make a run for the house, and then realized that he was using his body to shield me. 'It's all right,' he called out. 'I'm just going to check what's disturbed the dogs.'

He waited until the door closed before he moved to the small shed where the dogs were still barking. He slammed a wall with his hand and called out a command. The dogs went quiet for a moment, and then started to growl. A low, deep and threatening primal sound. 'They know you're here,' he observed, looking back over his shoulder at me. It struck me then: all he had to do was take out the old screwdriver that secured the hasp on the door, and the dogs would run me off. I still couldn't make out his expression, but I knew that he was letting me know that he shared that knowledge. He tapped the wall again, and the dogs went quiet.

He took me into a section of a barn that doubled as a workshop. A bare, low-wattage light bulb illuminated a dusty workbench and a mixed collection of tools hanging from nails hammered randomly into the plank walls.

'You look cold,' he said.

'It's been a long wait.'

'You're very determined.'

I nodded. 'I'm glad you've recognized that, Trevor. Hopefully, that means I don't have to threaten you. Believe me, I would like to keep this civilized.'

He looked at me searchingly. His face was drawn and pale. I had to remind myself that this was a young man. 'What if I promised you that nothing bad happened up there on Saturday night? To the woman.'

I caught the hesitation before the qualifier phrase. It puzzled me. I shook my head. 'Too

93

general, Trevor. I need to know facts.'

'I'm sorry, but I can't tell you any more than that.'

'Who are you protecting?'

He shook his head.

'I've got all night, Trevor. I'm not leaving here until I know.'

'My mother will be out to see what's taking me so long.'

'Fine. So we do this in front of her. Do you want that? Do you want her to hear what you did to that girl?'

'I did nothing to her,' he insisted.

'Explain what you mean by "nothing".'

'Nothing.' His voice rose. 'Nothing, nothing—I didn't touch her, I promise you.' He looked at me entreatingly, begging me to believe him.

'Why not?' I grinned at him salaciously. 'She was there for you and Paul. A gift from your mates. To get your cherries popped. Although, from the rumours I hear, yours went some time ago.' I went in close to him, still grinning. 'And here it is: effortless pussy, brought to you on a plate. A gift. And you're trying to tell me you didn't take up the opportunity? Come on, Trevor.'

He tried to draw away, but he was backed up against the workbench. 'I was too tired. I had had too much to drink. I didn't want a girl, I just wanted to sleep. I went to bed and left the others to have their party.'

I pictured the pile of bracken on the floor. 'In the other room? Is that where you went to sleep?'

He nodded. I saw it then. In his eyes. What I had missed before. The pain and the evasion. He saw my recognition. I held his upper arms to stop him

94

squirming away. He leaned back over the bench, twisting his head away. 'Look at me, Trevor.' He shook his head, resisting. 'Look at me . . .'

Slowly, he stopped shaking his head. His body stiffened in my hands. When he finally looked at me his face had collapsed.

'Trevor,' I said his name quietly, searching for the right words, 'were you trying to escape?'

He nodded.

'Trevor, are you gay?'

He tensed. 'No.' He shook his head vehemently. 'No . . . I don't know,' he wailed with real anguish.

'It's no big deal,' I said soothingly. 'Not any more. Not in this day and age.'

Anger flashed under his film of tears. 'It is round here.'

*   *   *

I gave him time to get over the enormity of almost pouring his heart out to another man. Not quite voicing something that he had managed to keep between his id and his naked reflection in his bedroom mirror. Something still deniable, the safety catch still half switched on.

'Do the others know?' I asked.

'What is there to know?' His voice had a rasp to it. 'I told you, I don't even know myself,' he insisted, retreating back under protective cover. The guy dreamt of cock, but was waiting in despair for a visitation from Saint Vagina to sprinkle desire dust. Who was I to tell him that she was never going to arrive?

'I heard a rumour that you were in the habit of visiting prostitutes.'

95

He managed a half-smile. 'I heard that one myself.'

'And it seemed like a good idea not to protest too much?'

He shrugged that off. 'They meant well,' he said.

'Who did?'

'My friends. Trying to set us up with the prostitute.'

Did they? I wondered. Or was there something infinitely crueller behind it? But we had got there. We were back with Magda without me having to force the issue.

'Tell me about her. I call her Magda. What was her real name?'

'I don't really know.'

'She wasn't Miss Danielle, was she? She wasn't a prostitute from Cardiff.'

'I don't know.'

'Trevor, you were supposed to fuck this woman, and you're trying to tell me that you don't know anything about her?'

He shot me a hurt look. He still wanted me to be his friend. 'I was asleep. I was really tired. I had had too much to drink and it had been a long day. I woke up at the petrol station and she was already in the back of the minibus. I heard Gordon tell the driver that we were giving her a lift as far as Dinas. That seemed reasonable; I didn't think any more about it.'

'That was the first time you'd seen her, or heard anything about this being organized?'

'Yes, but that doesn't mean that Gordon or Les hadn't arranged it,' he said protectively.

'There was no pimp, was there?'

He thought about that. He shook his head, but

96

looked at me defiantly.

'I don't give a fuck who was driving, Trevor,' I said, guessing the reason for his stance. 'I'm not even going to ask. I just want you to keep answering me as truthfully as possible.'

He nodded.

'You dropped Boon Paterson off?'

'Yes.'

'Where?'

He frowned. He had a dilemma. He shouldn't have. He was supposed to be telling me the truth now. There should only have been one possible answer. He came to a decision. 'We dropped him off at his house. He was drunk, and it was cold—we couldn't leave him to walk all that way home.'

Those were the reasons that I had given Ken McGuire, I noted, but let it pass. I didn't want to interrupt this flow. 'So you get up to the hut . . .' I prompted.

'Yes, and everyone was cheerful. It was like a party. We still had beer and stuff, and music. And everyone was happy. She was enjoying herself.'

'And lights?'

'Yes.' He thought about it. 'Gas lanterns. They were already there.'

'And then suddenly you weren't so happy?'

He shook his head. 'Not when it was suggested that Paul or I should team up with the girl.'

'What did she think of that idea?'

'I don't know, it wasn't said in front of her.'

'What about Paul?'

'You saw what he looked like in the morning? He was even worse then. He was completely out of it, totally wrecked.'

'And you went and hid in the other room?'

'I did need to sleep. I told you: I was tired.'

'And when you wake up, the party is over. Magda, Miss Danielle, whatever she's called has gone safely on her way. The minibus has been returned. And, apart from your hangovers, everything is all right with the world?'

He nodded, eager to confirm my summation. 'Something like that. I don't know how they managed to organize it, though. And it wasn't quite as straightforward as you suggest. We had to face our families. They'd been worried stiff about us.'

'Well, that's a real fucking shame, Trevor,' I hissed, letting him hear real venom.

His head jerked, taken aback by my new tone. 'It's the truth,' he protested.

'No, it's not. You're covering for them. Something bad happened up there, and you know it.'

He shook his head frantically.

'What was it, Trevor? Dancing, bit of light smooching, everyone having a good time . . . until one of the guys tries to take it just a bit too far?'

'No. It wasn't like that.'

'The girl doesn't like it. This is not fun any more. The guys try to persuade her to loosen up.' I spread my arms, jiggling, looming towards him, playing the drunk. 'But this is just scary. The girl is frightened now. Only the boys can't smell that fear. Or if they can, they mistake it for sex. They want to continue to party. She's being unreasonable. Fucking slag, after all. A foreigner. She wants this really. What else did she think was going to happen?'

'Nothing like that happened.'

'Was she raped, Trevor? Was she slapped around? Was she held down? Or was she just so

98

terrified by that time that she acquiesced and you bastards put the conquest down to your fucking charm and social skills?'

'No one was hurt!' he yelled. 'No one was abused or assaulted. Why won't you believe me?'

I went up into his face and yelled back, 'Because you weren't fucking there—you said that you were asleep.'

He dropped his face into his hands. 'You don't understand,' he shrieked. 'This has nothing to do with that woman, this has to do with Boon.'

*　　　*　　　*

He shook his head frantically, retracting even before I had had a chance to ask him for confirmation.

'Boon Paterson was there?' I asked, not concealing my surprise.

He backtracked fast, stammering, 'No . . . No . . . We dropped him off . . . I just told you that . . .'

'You're lying, Trevor. What did you mean when you said that this had to do with Boon?'

'Nothing. You confused me. It was a slip of the tongue.'

I tried to run some sense into it. If Boon had been there, why had the group decided to cover it up? And why hadn't he turned up with the others the following morning? I had thought that I had two separate instances of missing people. Was it possible that they might both be in the same basket? Magda and Boon?

Jesus, had my apartheid crack been closer to the mark than I could have realized?

'Was Boon hurt?'

'No.' He replied sharply. But there was another tiny time-lag here that I picked up on. The response and some kind of a memory association ever so slightly out of synch. 'Boon wasn't there. How could he have been hurt?'

'You said no one was hurt up there. You used the plural.'

He shook his head sharply. 'You got me confused. I meant her. The woman wasn't hurt.'

'Trevor, no one knows I'm here.'

'What do you mean?' He shrank away from me, and his eyebrows rose as he sensed the beginnings of a threat.

And it had crossed my mind. To shock it out of him. A short right jab to the nose to let blood, pain and ratcheted sinew unlock the vault. But could I take the risk that, in his current state, pain wasn't what he wanted? The catharsis of punishment?

'Everyone thinks I'm in North Wales. No one would ever know that you told me anything.'

'There's nothing to tell you.'

'You can stop it here, Trevor. You can get me off all of your backs. And it stays just between us, I promise. No one else ever knows.'

He stared at me. 'How?' he said it more as a breath than a word.

'I trust you. If you can tell me that Magda is safe and well, I will believe you. I'll accept it, and that will be the end of it.'

He searched for the catch. 'All I have to do is tell you that?'

I smiled. 'Not quite. You need to convince me.'

He was getting close. But guilt and fear were still rippling like humps in a rug, threatening to trip him. 'They're my best friends,' he said apologetically.

'So do them a favour. Get me out of their lives.'

'You promise?' His look was gaunt. He was telling me that his entire faith in the future of the human race was relying on my answer.

I nodded. 'I promise.'

He stared at me for a moment, still teetering. He closed his eyes, the decision made. 'Ken and Les drove the minibus over to Ponterwyd to pick up the first bus through to Aberystwyth in the morning. From there they were going to make their way to Holyhead. For the ferry to Dublin.'

'That was very kind of Ken and Les.'

'It wasn't a rash decision, they all talked about it through the night.'

'I thought you were asleep?'

'They told me about it in the morning.'

'And you believe them?'

He looked hurt. 'They're my friends. Why would they lie to me?'

'You used the plural again, Trevor. You said *they* were going to Holyhead.'

He looked at me, surprised that I hadn't got it.

'Boon went with her.'

*   *   *

It made a certain crooked kind of sense. If the explanation had been flawless I wouldn't have believed it. But I was halfway there to giving this a chance.

I drove the back roads slowly, thinking about what Trevor had told me. Everything he told me, *he* had been told. Second-hand news, I reminded myself.

The girl was a hitchhiker. It had all started when she was offered a lift, and told them that she was on the way to Ireland. Except, of course, for Boon Paterson it had started long before that. A nagging and escalating dissatisfaction with his life in the Army. The prospect of a posting to Afghanistan looming. Nevertheless, until that point, he had managed to resign himself to seeing his term out.

But in that minibus, Boon had had a eureka moment. Ireland . . . Ireland, and then on to Amsterdam, to pick up with some people in the music scene there. People that he had got close to when he had been stationed in Germany. He kept it to himself at first. The suggestion to Gordon that he help him ditch the minibus driver was, ostensibly, just to keep the party going and to keep it private. Keep his last day with them running. Boon drove. This was his trip now, and he was staying in charge of it. He kept them singing, while Les guided him up into the forest.

He dropped it on them in the hut. The possibility that had been sparked by the arrival of the girl, the state of his mind, and all of them being together at the catalytic moment. Because none of it would work without them being prepared to stretch their friendship. To lie for him. He missed out the other element. Booze. How it might never have crossed his mind, and how the others would never have agreed to it, if it hadn't happened at the tail end of a long day's drinking.

But they did. After arguments, reasoning and pleas, when they realized that he was serious, they agreed to lie for him. Not just that, but to face up to a degree of shame and humiliation. To concoct a story of a Cardiff prostitute to give him time to get clear. Les and Ken drove the minibus to his house to pick up his belongings, and then to Ponterwyd for the bus to Aberystwyth. They then drove back, stopping so Les could get one of his quad bikes, which they used to return to the hut after they had dropped off the minibus.

True friendship.

It tied in with Tony Griffiths's version. The truck driver had said that Magda was on her way to Ireland, but she didn't want to use public transport. Maybe that had changed when an escort became available. Perhaps with Boon she felt less exposed. Travelling with a native.

A bird, an owl probably, flew in a low, swooping glide through my headlight beams. I swerved instinctively, and almost put myself into a ditch. I stopped, turned the lights and the engine off, and let the dark and the silence blanket me.

What was I really doing, driving around in the dead hours of the night?

I didn't want to go home. I didn't want to go to sleep and wake up knowing that Magda had passed out of my life and I was back in a realm of stolen quad bikes and rustled sheep. I didn't want to rumble over the bridge into Hen Felin Caravan Park with an instinct lifting the hairs on the back of my neck, telling me that Mackay might be staking out my home.

Or was it really because I wanted to stay out so late that only people working a night shift were eligible to visit?

*   *   *

The Sychnant Nursing Home was a large

mock-gothic pile, which, in the dark, looked like it should have had a crooked-back lunatic dancing on the rooftop in monumental rain, backlit by forked lightening.

Instead it was just dark. Which was disturbing. The excuse I was using for visiting wasn't strong enough to warrant waking the place up. I drove towards the front of the house, conscious of the sound of my wheels on the gravel drive. The closer I got, the quieter the place looked.

I made a wide turn in front of the house, preparing to roll back out to the road, when I caught sight of a lighted window. It was in a single-storey wing that ran back from the main house. I parked. An ultra-bright security light popped on as I approached the door nearest the lighted window.

The door opened on a security chain after I knocked. The glare from the light was too bright for me to make out who was standing in the gap watching me.

I held up my warrant card like a talisman. 'Sergeant Capaldi—I'm sorry about the time, but I'd like to speak to Mrs Paterson, if she's available.'

The silence and the watching held for a few more beats.

'It's all right, Latifa . . .' Sally Paterson's voice approached. The security chain clattered and the door opened. Sally Paterson stood there backlit. 'Sergeant Capaldi.' She didn't sound surprised to see me. I felt a little twinge at the formality of the greeting, and wondered whether I wasn't being a bit foolish. 'Please, come in.'

I entered a large, commercially equipped kitchen, banks of huge pans, ranges of stainless-steel equipment, and the smell of heavy-duty cleaning products, grease, and over-boiled green vegetables.

'We'll stay in here, if that's all right with you.' She turned to the other woman, a short, dark-skinned Asian of indeterminate age, wearing the same pink polyester housecoat as Sally. 'Are you okay keeping an eye on things, Latifa, while I speak to the sergeant?'

'Okay.' Latifa nodded and left the room, giving me a look that could have been baleful or sympathetic.

I sat down at a long refectory table while Sally made tea. 'You don't seem very surprised to see me.'

'I've had time to adjust. We watched your arrival on the CCTV monitors.' She turned her head and smiled. 'You made a change from the foxes and the deer.'

'You didn't answer the door?'

'I'm teaching Latifa the social niceties.'

'I don't think she's picking them up.'

'She might have been a bit intimidated by your policeman's stance.'

'You saw that?'

'At this time of night, we watch everything that's going.'

The kettle boiled, breaking the flow. She turned away to make the tea. It was one of those awkward silences when you both realize that you have been prancing ahead of yourselves.

'So, what brings you here at this hour?' she asked, bringing our tea over and sitting down opposite me. I got the feeling that she had been rehearsing building confidence into the expression that went with the question.

105

'I've got some nonattributable news about Boon.'

'Which is good news.' It wasn't a question.

'You've heard already?' I asked, surprised.

She laughed softly at my expression. 'No, it's just that I don't see you as the kind of cruel bastard who would turn up at . . .' she glanced up at the wall clock '. . . ten past two in the morning to deliver bad news to a lady.'

'It's also unverifiable.'

'Enough with the riders. The news, please?'

'He may be on his way to Amsterdam, via Ireland.'

She frowned, taking a few moments to think about it. 'He's okay?'

'As far as I'm aware.'

'Has he deserted?'

I shrugged. 'I can't answer that. I don't know any of the background.'

'The daft bugger!' she exclaimed crossly, but I caught a waft of relief under it.

'Would Amsterdam fit?' I asked.

She nodded. 'He spent a lot of time there when he was stationed in Germany.' Then another thought struck her. 'Does the Army know this?'

'I haven't told them. And I won't be telling them, either. I've had to take a vow of silence.'

'You're telling me,' she pointed out.

'I'm allowing myself a dispensation in your case.'

She smiled, acknowledging the favour. She shook her head exasperatedly. 'Via Ireland? Why on earth didn't he just get on a train or a plane and go there directly? If he had made up his mind, why faff about going the long way round?'

'It happens sometimes. People running away, they need the subterfuge. They have a false idea of how visible they are.'

She went silent. I winced inwardly, wishing that I hadn't used the words *running away*. She pulled a philosophical smile. 'Ah well . . . At least I now know that he's not in a car wreck. Which is something. Which is a lot.' She underscored the relief of it with a sharp nod of her head. 'I suppose all I can do now is wait until he decides to grace me with contact.' She smiled wistfully, and screwed up her face at me. 'You know, I've been thinking about you . . .'

The change in direction took me unawares. 'You have?' I blurted, feeling my face reddening.

'Yes. I got to thinking about missing girls.'

I realized my mistake and notched my expression down from the boudoir and back into the hallway. Curiosity cushioned the let-down. 'I thought we had agreed that it didn't happen here.'

'That's just it. I thought about it again. And then realized that it might have happened.'

'Might?'

'Yes. Two that I know of. They used to work here. Not at the same time. But they both walked out without any warning. Packed their bags and were gone in the morning.'

'Were they reported?'

'I think so. You'd have to ask Joan Harvey about that. She runs the place. It's terrible though, isn't it?' She smiled sheepishly. 'Because of who they were, we never actually worried that anything might have happened to them. That's why I never put this together when you asked that time.'

'Because of who they were?' I turned it into a question.

She hunched her shoulders apologetically. 'How

107

to put it nicely? Townies? Roll-throughs?

'Roll-throughs?'

She laughed. 'It's one of the names locals use for incomers. They expect us to move on.'

'So these girls weren't locals?'

'No, that's my point. They came from Manchester, I think. They were tough. We assumed that they could look after themselves. That's why we never considered them as "missing" per se. We just thought that they'd got fed up. Had enough of the quiet life and the dark nights, and moved on.'

'Can you remember their names?' I asked, taking my notebook out.

'Colette something, and Donna . . . Gallagher, I think. You'd have to check with Joan Harvey.'

'What sort of age were they?'

She didn't answer. She stood up, a resigned and practised smile forming that wasn't meant for me. I turned round on the bench. A tiny old woman in a pale green flannel nightgown stood in the doorway. A sparse puff of white hair over a face and neck creviced with wrinkles.

Sally moved towards her. 'You need to go, do you, Mary?'

It was too late. She had already been. I noticed the damp-dark hem of her nightgown and the trail of urine that was now pooling on the vinyl floor below her. I stood up. 'I think it's time I got out of your way.'

She smiled at me resignedly. 'Duty calls.' She put her hands gently on Mary's shoulders, feeling for the steering mechanism.

'Glyn . . .' I was at the door when she called out. I turned. She was smiling. 'You know, someday I'd really like you to see me in something a bit more flattering than an old dressing gown and this.' She dropped her chin to indicate the polyester housecoat.

There was a devastatingly urbane and romantic response to that somewhere. I didn't find it. Instead I blushed for the second time that night. 'Sure . . .' I stammered.

'Call me,' she instructed, rescuing me. 'I don't work every night.'

I crossed the gravel to the car, shaking off my ineptitude and beginning to feel jaunty. I had a date to arrange. It was then that the irony hit me. Sally had laid the possibility of two new missing girls on me just when I had almost reached the point of waving Magda off into her Irish sunset.

*   *   *

I was still meant to be in Caernarfon, so I stayed in Unit 13 the next day, kept my head down, and caught up with a backlog of paperwork. My telephone rang a few times but I just monitored the answerphone. No more calls from Mackay; Emrys Hughes rang twice, and Bryn Jones once. Both left messages asking me to call them back. Being in pretend North Wales, a land where the mountains screwed communications even more than here, I ignored them.

I could guess the reasons. Hughes would be calling to berate me for going to see Ken McGuire and Paul Evans. Bryn was probably calling because Emrys Hughes had got his boss Morgan to lean on Jack Galbraith to clap the restrainers on me.

Donna and Colette.

I wrote the names in my notebook again and

109

underlined them. Sally had called them Townies. Tough street kids who could look after themselves. I tried to shut it out, but the stereotype dropped down through the trapdoor. Cigarettes and chewing gum, unfit and overweight. Tattoos. But no kid called Dwayne or Britney in a pushchair—yet.

Or perhaps there was now. Maybe that was the future that they had run away into.

I made a note to go and see Joan Harvey at the Sychnant Nursing Home. What intrigued me was how a couple of girls from a background like that had independently found their way into the boondocks in the first place. How had the prospect of Ursa Major in the night sky ever managed to supplant the One-Stop Shop and neon lighting?

It was one of those drab and listless days at this time of year when daylight had given up trying to lead an independent existence by two o'clock in the afternoon. It was time to shut down the office. Time to return from North Wales.

I walked into The Fleece with my car keys conspicuous, the echt traveller, stretching the ricks of the journey out of my neck.

David Williams interpreted the sign language and brought a coffee over to the bar. 'Emrys Hughes wants you to call him,' he informed me.

'How was he?'

'Agitated.'

'Happy agitated or mean agitated?'

'He looked pleased with himself.'

Which probably meant that he had been given permission to tell me that I was in deep trouble.

'What do you know about the Sychnant Nursing Home?' I asked.

He looked at me for a moment, trying to work

out the angle. 'It processes the elderly. Not much trade for you there, I would have thought. Unless . . .' He leaned forward over the bar, his voice dropping to conspiratorial: 'Unless you're going to start issuing exhumation warrants?'

'Don't be so ghoulish. I'm just asking. What's its reputation?'

He shrugged. 'I don't know too much about it. It's not Rolls-Royce, but it's not the sort of place that chains the residents to the radiators either.'

'Do you know of any young girls who have gone missing around here?' I tried to keep it matter-of-fact.

He laughed. 'No, but I've got a lot of customers who are still wondering where the hot spring chicken they married disappeared to.' He looked up over my shoulder, his eyes flicking a warning at me. 'Afternoon, Emrys.'

I turned slowly. David had been right: Emrys Hughes did look pleased with himself. 'You're a hard man to contact,' he told me.

'I've been away, in Caernarfon. I thought you knew.' I waited for him to contradict me.

He smirked. 'You've missed the news then.'

'What news is that?'

'The news that means you can stop harassing my citizens.'

I looked at him, trying to fathom it. Was this a secret society thing? Was he a party to the version that Trevor Vaughan had told me? That the whole thing was a cover-up to get Boon Paterson running free. 'Amsterdam?' I probed.

He stared at me distrustfully, wondering whether I was trying to work some cruel urban wind-up on him. Then the cockiness sprang back. 'The

111

prostitute from Cardiff—she's verified the story. They found the telephone number they thought they'd lost. Gordon McGuire got me to call her, and she's corroborated their story.'

I couldn't believe it. My mouth hung open. I must have looked like a guy miming the involuntary inhalation moment after being kicked in the balls.

He flashed me a big fuck-you grin. He had mistaken my expression for chagrin. It wasn't. It was amazement. I already knew that the prostitute story was pure hokum. Tony Griffiths had told me about Magda. Trevor Vaughan had confirmed it.

Why had someone felt the need to reinforce the lie?

7

Bryn Jones confirmed it when I called him from my car. Her name, real or acquired, was Monica Trent. A thirty-two-year-old white female working out of a walk-up flat over a bookmaker's in a street off the road from Llantrisant into Cardiff. Strictly by appointment. No kerb crawlers, no random johns on street corners. It was a suburban operation, she kept it tidy and discreet, and didn't get bothered by Vice.

She disturbed me.

Not her personally—I didn't know her. But the fact that someone had felt the need to spend money or call in a favour to bolster a story that no one but me had been questioning.

Were they playing with me? Did they know that Trevor Vaughan had confirmed my suspicions that the prostitute story was a fabrication? Were they pushing Monica Trent across the board to counter any attack that I was preparing? But that's where it went screwy. They had to know that I had nothing to attack them with.

So why go to all that trouble?

Unless they were shoring-up against the possibility of something really nasty oozing out between the seams. Was Monica Trent a caulking agent?

I smiled to myself at the unintended pun. I closed my eyes and leaned my forehead against the rim of the steering wheel. Why do this when Trevor Vaughan's explanation had virtually reassured me? My head shot back. Because Trevor hadn't been there . . . He had been asleep. Completely out of it. He had given me the story that had been reported to him. He only knew what he had been told.

Or was that not quite true? He had seemed more than just uncomfortable when he had been talking to me about that night. A couple of times he had shown definite signs of disturbance. Manifestations of evasion or anxiety? I hadn't probed deeper at the time because I thought that they were resonations of his sexual distress. Could it have been more than that? Had Trevor found out something up there that he wasn't meant to know? Something that he had kept from me? Something that had disturbed him?

Too many questions and only one person to answer them.

'Yes . . .' His mother's voice was snappy and curt. Still answering the telephone with a suspicion for the instrument that she must have picked up from her parents about fifty years ago.

'Mr Trevor Vaughan please?' I asked in a smooth, plump voice. I had already checked that his father's name was Harold.

'Who's that?'

'Irfon Machinery Supplies—we've got a promotion on a new range of hedgecutters,' I said breezily.

'We don't need one.'

'We're offering a free, no obligation demonstration on your farm. Totally free.' I repeated the magic word that usually captured a farmer's interest.

'Wait a minute.'

I heard a muffled conversation. She was probably instructing him to get me to commit to a decent length of hedge trimming for their free, no obligation demonstration. 'Hello?' Trevor Vaughan came on the line.

'Hello, Trevor, it's Glyn Capaldi . . .' I waited out the silence for a moment. 'Don't hang up,' I warned into the void.

'What do you want now?' He had lowered his voice.

'Who's minding you tonight?'

'No one's minding me.'

If that was true, they were probably relying on his parents to stick close and raise the alarm if I appeared.

'Make some excuse that you have to go out. I'll pick you up at the end of your drive in half an hour. And don't call anyone,' I instructed.

'I don't want to see you. I've already told you more than enough.'

'Half an hour,' I repeated.

'Didn't you hear me? I won't be there.'

114

'If you're not, you're fucked, Trevor.'

He was silent again for a moment. 'Are you threatening me?' he asked, trying to hike some strength into his tone.

'Yes.'

It wasn't the answer he was expecting. He had to re-string his approach. 'If you hit me, I'll sue you.'

'I'm not going to hit you.' I waited for a beat. 'I'm going to let the world know that you're a fairy.'

'That's a lie!' he spluttered.

'I'll bet a lot of people may have their suspicions confirmed.'

'That's malicious slander,' he retorted furiously, but it didn't quite carry the conviction, as he had to pitch it in a whisper.

'Half an hour,' I said, snapping my phone shut dynamically, and crossing my fingers.

*   *   *

He was alone in the bad light. A forlorn figure with his thin hair drifting, wearing an old fawn duffel, a drooped and baggy pair of jeans, and work boots with the metal toecaps shining through. I heard a bunch of rooks cawing when I leaned over and pushed the passenger's door open for him.

He stared at me sullenly, but got in. 'You're a bastard. You know that? A mean and vindictive bastard.'

I ignored him and drove off.

'Where are you taking me?' he asked, looking out mystified, as if the view from my car had caused him to shift dimensions.

I continued to ignore him. It was easier to play it hard and heartless without speaking. He got the message and retreated back into his sulk. I headed confidently for the forest.

'Where are you taking me?'

His voice startled me. I had got used to our silence. We were on a track winding up the hill and deeper into the trees. He was looking out of the window with a curious interest now.

'We're going up to the hut,' I said, deciding that I could afford to ease back on the tough-cop pedal a touch.

'That's where I originally thought you were going.'

Something in his inflexion sparked a doubt. 'What do you mean, *originally*?' I asked.

'You took a wrong turn a while back,' he said, inclining his head behind us.

I let him direct me from there. It took some of the edge off of my power, but not as much as turning us into Hansel and fucking Gretel, lost in the woods, would have.

The darkness was near total at the hut, only a spooky half-light that gave the treetops, listing into the wind, an otherworldly dimension. No birds. Just that wind soughing through the gorse and the young birches.

He stood outside, his hands rammed into the pockets of his duffel coat. 'Where is this supposed to lead us?' he asked.

'Down memory lane.'

He shrugged.

'Do you know Monica Trent?' I asked.

He dropped his eyes. 'I hadn't told them that I told you about Boon,' he said, without looking up.

'And that I knew that Monica Trent wasn't their Miss Danielle?'

116

He nodded.

'Why did they do it? Why have they backed up the lie?'

'I don't know. They didn't tell me until after they'd done it. I couldn't then say that I'd already told you what I had.'

'I think it's time to tell me a bit more, Trevor.'

His eyes shot at me, a flash glance crossed between startled and calculating.

'Let's start with the lights that were here. What can you tell me about that bit of prior preparation?'

'Gordon organizes vermin shoots in the woods. It's a sort of corporate hospitality thing, for some of the people who use Payne, Dyke and Thomas.' I caught a note of disapproval. 'They crash around up here, blasting at squirrels, crows and pigeons, and then they use the hut for boozing afterwards.'

So, it didn't have to have been premeditated. They could have just met Magda at the filling station. They already had the infrastructure in place here. But someone had disappeared the lights.

'What happened to the lights? Why weren't they around in the morning?'

He shook his head. He hadn't thought about it, and it still didn't interest him. 'I don't know. Maybe Gordon has somewhere he stores them.'

I didn't pursue it. 'Talk me through it,' I said. 'You arrive here—then what?'

He thought for a moment. 'Gordon went in first with a torch. We unloaded the beer, and then we went inside when he turned the gas lights on.'

'Go on.' I nodded towards the door.

He pushed it open. I followed him through with a big flashlight. Things had changed since I had last been here. Both doors leading off the vestibule were open at a different angle. It could have been forestry workers. It could have been another one of Gordon McGuire's shooting parties. Or it could have been people looking to clear up something that they might have left behind. I thought of the crumpled tissue that I had found. Had there been something else that I'd missed?

'The girl threw a fit when she saw the state of the place,' Trevor commented over his shoulder as I followed him into the larger room, the torch beam providing him with a looming shadow. 'It wasn't really serious, she was still laughing, but I got the impression that things didn't seem quite as much fun now as they had on the minibus.'

I squared the room. Looking for omissions. But nothing seemed to have been removed.

'Gordon found a broom, and told her that if it offended her so much she could do something about it. It was a joke,' he added quickly. 'He wasn't being mean. But she took him up on it and swept the floor. As best she could, anyway.' He went thoughtful, turning slowly, trying to locate the memory. He pointed into a corner. I shone the light, illuminating nothing but dirt and the hut's geometry. 'Paul crashed out over there. That was when Gordon came up to me and said that it looked like I was the only unattached male still left standing.'

'So you made your excuses and went to bed?'

'More or less. I went exploring and found the other room.'

'Did you take the bracken in?'

'No, it was already there. A big pile of it. That was one of the attractions.'

I didn't comment. I didn't want to block his flow.

But I did make a mental note to continue to wonder what Gordon's clients, wired up for a drinking session after shooting squirrels, would want with a big bracken bed?

'I said that I was too drunk and tired, and that I was going to try and get some sleep.'

'And when you woke up in the morning, they told you that Boon and the girl had run off into the sunrise?'

'More or less. But it wasn't like they had run away. Everyone helped with it.'

I nodded. I walked round the room again slowly, raking the skirting board with the torch beam, conscious of him watching me.

'Are you satisfied now?' he asked, breaking the silence.

I pivoted and shone the torch at him. 'No.'

'What more can I say?' he implored, squinting at the light.

'Something went sour.'

He shook his head. Too fast. 'No . . .' He took a breath. 'They would have told me.'

I spread my arms, taking in the room. 'You have five drunk guys at the end of a long day. Okay, discount Paul Evans. Four guys in a highly charged and unpredictable state. You also have an attractive young female.' I made a stirring motion with a big imaginary spoon. 'This is not good chemistry. There is no natural law that says it has to go wrong. But oh so often it does.' I looked hard at him. 'And I think you saw or heard something, Trevor.'

He couldn't hold my eyes. He shook his head and turned away, walking for the door. I let him go. He had a crisis of conscience to resolve.

Outside, in front of the hut, the transitional light

119

had sucked the detail out of him. He was just a dark column. The wind now included a distinctly damp chill in its composition. I let him hear me approach behind him.

He turned slowly, his head down. 'I wanted to believe them when they told me that everything was all right.'

'What made you think it might not be, Trevor?' I asked softly.

He looked at me directly, something going beyond sadness in his expression. 'I am not a disloyal person.'

'I know that.'

'I woke up when I heard the arguing. It was louder than the music. A CD player of Paul's that we'd taken with us,' he explained.

'Who was arguing?' I prompted.

'I couldn't tell. Just raised voices. The girl was in there too. Sounding upset.'

'As if she was being hurt?' I asked, trying to keep my tone clinical.

'No. More like she was trying to reason or restrain.'

'Could you make out what they were arguing about?'

'No. It was just noise.'

'Did you go and see what it was about?'

He shook his head guiltily. 'I wanted to pretend that it wasn't happening.' He looked at me sheepishly, his words struggling out hesitantly. 'Did you ever do that? In bed at night as a child, when you heard your parents arguing?'

I nodded. 'You just want to be able to fix whatever has gone wrong between them.'

He smiled, grateful for the empathy. 'That's

right. It was like that. I just lay there and willed them to stop. And, eventually, they did. It all wound down, went below the level of the music again.'

'You went back to sleep?'

He nodded. 'I didn't think I would. Then it was the absence of noise that woke me. Everything was quiet. I thought that everyone must have fallen asleep. I had to go outside to the toilet. After all that beer. It was so quiet that it felt safe again.'

I smiled at him. 'The family restored?'

He nodded. 'But it wasn't. Paul was still crashed out in the same place. The girl was in another corner, fast asleep in her sleeping bag. But the others weren't there.'

'The minibus?'

'Still parked where we'd left it. I saw it when I went outside. It was really cold now, starting to sleet, it wasn't a night to be out walking in the woods.'

'Is that what you thought they were doing?'

'I didn't know. I didn't know where they were. Then, it was one of those flukes of sound: I heard them. It wasn't voices, just a sense that . . .' He searched for an explanation. 'That there were some people filling a space out there. I followed the hunch, and eventually caught up with them.'

'They were all together?'

He thought hard about that. 'I don't know. I keep going over that. And I still don't know. They were always set against a darker background, just a cluster, a group. They never shifted into individuals. At no point was I able to count them off.'

'You didn't join them?' I asked.

'I was going to,' he said, distress shifting into his voice. 'But something made me hold back.' He

121

looked at me intently. 'Something told me that I was not meant to be there. I was not meant to be a part of this.'

'What were they doing?' I asked, registering his despair.

I had to strain to catch his reply. 'I think they were digging.'

*   *   *

Poor bastard . . . He had been torturing himself. On top of the lousy price of sheep, and his deep baseline sexual anxiety, he now had to contend with the possibility that he had been excluded and lied to by his very best friends. Who might also, either by accident or design, have done something terrible to Boon Paterson.

He had stood out there alone in the dark and passed beyond the moment when he could have called out to them and had his answer. Because he wasn't entirely sure that he really wanted the answer. Just in case. So he had sneaked back to the hut and into his bracken burrow without anyone knowing he had been out. He had lain there, straining for sounds that would reassure him. He had heard them return from the woods, but no voices to let him count off the register.

And then he heard the minibus starting up. By the time he got outside it had gone. He could see the light wash from its headlights descending through the trees. Gordon had been left behind to give him the news that Ken and Les were helping Boon secure his new future.

'Did I believe them?' He phrased the question for me before I could ask it. 'I willed myself to.

Anything else was too awful to contemplate.' He closed his eyes tight shut. I could picture the image that was gripping him. Those men, fused together in the dark, standing over a hole in the ground.

'If it was that dark, how could you tell that they were digging?' I asked. The question had been troubling me.

'It was the sound of it. I've dug enough holes for fence posts in my time to know that sound.'

'Could you find the place again?'

He looked at me with what could have been horror. 'Are you serious?'

'Don't you want that doubt dispelled?'

'I can live with it.'

'It will get worse.'

'It's dark now.'

'It was dark then,' I reminded him.

He shivered visibly and pulled his coat tightly around him. He swivelled, and without a word he set off across the clearing to a disused logging trail with scrub grass growing in the central ridge. We passed through the stand of trees at the edge of the clearing and into an area that had been clear-felled on either side. The lack of trees gave us a lighter backdrop, and I followed a few paces behind his silhouette.

He stopped. We were on the lip of a ridge, the track dropping obliquely away in front of us, curving down into a dark stand of young spruce trees.

'Are we here?' I looked around the featureless spot, wondering what he had homed in on.

'Down there. This is about as far as I came.' He pointed down the track. 'There's a big indentation in the bank where they've dug stone out for the roadways. That's where I saw them.'

It was even darker down there. My torch was useless for picking out detail. We couldn't take this any further without more light. We went back for my car. I drove cautiously, conscious of the bottom scraping on the ridge of the track. I didn't want to rip out the sump and end up on the receiving end of another rescue mission.

I left the engine running after I had the car's headlights facing into the depression in the bank made by the small quarry. The lights put everything into ultra-high relief: the soupy lichen film on the puddles, individual boulders, last season's foxglove stumps, and the roots and bracken tubers breaking through the dirt at the top of the bank.

But what was highlighted for us was the roughly circular area, about seventy-five centimetres in diameter, of recently disturbed ground.

'That's too small for anything big to be in there, isn't it?' Trevor asked hopefully.

By anything big, I knew that he meant a body. I had been thinking the same thing. But it would take a head comfortably. Or a head and a pair of hands if identity erasure had been the intention. I didn't share these speculations with Trevor.

'What do we do now?' he asked in a hushed whisper, paying homage to the psychology of the setting. With our shadows cast starkly against the earth bank, we looked to be in a fulcrum scene from an early German Expressionist film.

I had already been juggling with the consequences behind the same question. I was aware that we could be tramping over a crime scene. But, in order to establish that, I was going to have to notch the disruption up to another level.

'We dig it up.'

I heard him suck his breath in. 'We can't do that . . .'

'Why not?'

'What if you find something?'

'That's the intention, Trevor.'

The headlights had bleached the colour from his face, but it was the tone of his voice that made me realize that he had turned even paler. 'Don't these things have to be done officially? Don't you need some sort of paperwork? Just in case . . .?' He left the possibilities hanging.

'We can make it official. Believe me, Trevor, I would like nothing better. It just needs you to make a statement. Confirm everything that you've already told me.'

He looked at me sadly and shook his head. I went to the car and got the spade I kept in the boot for digging myself out of the Nanook of the North situation that I was still waiting to encounter.

It wasn't so much a case of digging as flicking out an amalgam of loose stone and mud. It got more difficult to see as I got deeper, the light shooting over the top of the excavation, making the inside of the hole seem even darker. I had to progress gingerly, probing gently with the spade, trying to anticipate how the connection with soft tissue or bone would translate on the end of the blade. In the end the tension got too much and I dropped to my knees and used my Swiss Army knife to scoop the stony gunk out.

'Stop!' Trevor yelled excitedly.

He was crouched down behind me, his hand in the pile of loose spoil from the hole. I swivelled round. 'Look—' He thrust a handful of the stuff that I had just excavated at me.

It didn't register. I shook my head at him.

'Don't you see?' he exclaimed happily. 'This is new dirt. It's not the same. This hasn't been disturbed before. You've gone past the bottom of the hole.'

I reached my arm down into the hole. He was right. The bottom was more compacted. 'It's empty.' I said it out loud to clarify it for myself.

'There's nothing here!' His relief was palpable.

'What the fuck did they dig this for?' It was another question for myself.

Trevor wasn't listening anyway. 'Nothing happened here,' he stated happily, getting up, wiping his hands on his jeans. 'Do you believe me now? About Boon?'

'Do you believe it yourself?' I countered.

'I do now.'

'But you did doubt them?'

His face scrunched up in contrition. 'I should have known better, given them the benefit . . .' He looked at me, hesitant, a question poised.

'What?'

'I've told you everything I know. Will you stop bothering us all now?'

I gave it a beat before I replied, to establish gravitas. 'Yes, Trevor,' I lied.

I drove him down the hill, still wondering what the purpose of an empty hole was. Trevor didn't seem to have a problem with this abstraction. He had had the proof that he hadn't dared push for before, and now he seemed more at ease than at any previous time in our acquaintance.

'Who supplied Monica Trent's telephone number to Emrys Hughes?' I asked when we cleared the forestry tracks and I was able to relax into normal driving.

'They did that just to doubly make sure that Boon was covered.'

'I'm sure they did. But who supplied the number?'

He frowned. 'I'm not sure. It might have been Gordon or it might have been Les.'

He went quiet for a while, gazing out the side window. 'Can I ask you something?'

'Sure.'

'You're from the city . . .'

'That's right, Cardiff.'

'Can you recognize . . . I mean, is there a type? Without having to be flamboyant or showy or anything?'

I glanced at him. He looked worried, concerned now about my reaction to the question that he had dared to ask. I flashed him a reassuring smile. 'You should just be yourself. What does it really matter to anyone else? In this day and age?'

He shook his head. 'Not here. Not one of their own.'

*   *   *

Find the Hooker. It was a bit like a treasure hunt. For clues, I had the Llantrisant road into Cardiff, and a walk-up flat over a bookie's. I had to hope that it was enough information. Because no one was going to let me do it the easy way and give me Monica Trent's telephone number. I had already tried Directory Enquiries, but, as I had suspected, the number was unlisted.

I had got up early and revisited the hole in the

127

forest. Nothing was very different in the daylight. It was still an empty hole. No blood spoor or rent garments in evidence. I knelt down beside it. It exuded the damp, coppery smell of recently dug dirt.

Why an empty hole?

Could it have had a spiritual meaning? Had they all ceremoniously pissed, spat, or jerked off into it to seal their friendship? Or to magically secure Boon's future?

Or had something been removed?

The thought struck me suddenly. If someone had removed whatever had been buried, they had obviously felt that it was important to fill it back in again. To cover their tracks. I decided to let them keep their secret. I backfilled the hole, keeping it as close as I could to the semblance of the way that I had found it. It was a small piece of private knowledge, but possessing it meant that there was always the possibility that I might just find a fit for it.

It was a long drive back to my beginnings. South down through Mid Wales to the Heads of the Valleys, feeling like a truant. At Merthyr, I picked up the expressway down the Taff Valley, past Abercynon, coming off at Pontypridd and heading for Llantrisant for the drive into Cardiff through steep-sided valleys belling out into the coastal plain, and the tendrils of the commuter suburbs snaking their way deeper into the countryside.

I should have been excited. But this didn't feel like coming home. This was more like sneaking in.

I worked with a picture that I had fixed in my mind. The description of a walk-up flat over a shop read like sixties architecture. An unornamented block, two or three storeys with a flat roof, over a row of shopfronts on the ground floor.

I had a couple of false starts. Streets off the main road with shabby blocks that fitted the template, but without a bookie's shop. I found the one I was looking for as I drove deeper into the Cardiff suburbs, part of the later urban sprawl before it morphed into the older Victorian and Edwardian outskirts.

This was a drab concrete block of two-storey maisonettes over a row of shops. A concrete stair tower at the end of the block led up to a walkway at first-floor level that ran along the rear, giving access to the flats.

The stair tower was daubed with graffiti on the outside, but the inside was surprisingly clean and free of rubbish. As was the walkway. The bookie's was the fourth in the row from the end. On the walkway I counted off four doors.

The door was painted a contemporary shade of blue-grey. A professionally printed notice covered the small section that would normally have been glazed.

THIS DOOR WILL NOT BE ANSWERED.
THESE PREMISES ARE ALARMED.
BE AWARE THAT YOUR PRESENCE IS
BEING MONITORED.

I looked up, just as I was supposed to. Just like everyone else would have done after they'd read that notice. And I joined them all on the CCTV camera that was bracketed off the wall and angled down on me.

Monica Trent was not taking any chances.

129

I knocked a couple of times, but, as the label on the door promised, no one answered. I was going to have to wait it out.

It was about an hour before an Asian man appeared at the top of the walkway. I was out of the car and at the foot of the stairs before he was halfway down. He smiled at me shyly.

'Excuse me . . .' I started.

'I am supposed to give you this,' he interrupted, and handed me a small card. It had a telephone number hand-printed on it. I turned the card over. *If you mention that you are a policeman I shall hang up*, was written in a neat script that matched the printing.

'How did you know to give this to me?' I asked.

He smiled cautiously, showing me two distinctly yellow dog-teeth. 'I saw you on the television.'

The CCTV camera. I let him sidestep past. He nodded his thanks and accelerated away from me.

I went back to the car and called the number. An answering machine kicked in, one of those neutral professional recordings that came with the service. I heard the message out, preparing my spiel, remembering the admonition that I had been given. 'Hello, my name is Glyn Capaldi, I would very much like the opportunity to speak to you. If you would like to call me back, my number is—'

'What do you want to speak to me about?' The voice was confident, cutting in over the machine, straight to the point without preamble.

'I would like to talk to you face to face, if that's possible.'

'What would the nature of this conversation be?'

'It would be about some mutual acquaintances.'

'Who are . . .?'

'I would rather discuss that in private.'

'Hold on.' The line went quiet for a while. 'Okay,' she announced, some kind of a decision made. 'I can offer you a consultation at three o'clock next Thursday afternoon. Or ten o'clock on the following Friday morning, if that's preferable.'

'I can't wait 'til next week,' I blurted.

'That's the earliest I can offer you.'

'I've travelled more than halfway down Wales especially to see you.' I tried my best to keep the wail out of my voice.

'That is not my problem.' She went quiet for a moment—I could hear a page turned—her voice relenting when she came back on the line. 'Okay, I should be able to do something for you in a couple of hours. Go away now, and come back then.'

'Don't worry about me, I'll be quite happy sitting in the car.'

'I'm not worried about you,' she said firmly. 'I just don't want you out there disturbing my clients.'

8

I was back two hours later, standing in front of the door. The electronic latch opened before I could knock. I pushed the door open. Monica Trent was standing in the brightly lit hall waiting for me.

Rushed to give an impression, I would have described her as small. But that would have been misleading. Petite is the word the guidebooks would have used. Petite, shapely, and perfectly groomed. Hard to tell which side of thirty she was orbiting.

131

About one hundred and fifty-seven centimetres in a pencil-thin grey skirt, a crisp, white, short-sleeved blouse, and a string of fat pearls at the open neck. Her hair was shiny, bobbed and blonde, framing a clever maquillage that was toned to accentuate her green eyes, and all the possibilities that were mirrored in the curve of her cheeks.

I tried a mental exercise. Pulling my focus way back, I put her into a red, down-filled jacket, mashed-up the pixels . . . She could have passed for the image of Magda that I had seen on the service station CCTV video. Mind you, given the quality of that image, I could have put Goofy into the same jacket and not been unconvinced.

'Yes?'

I realized that I had been staring. I felt like a crude hulk in front of her. She stared back at me unselfconsciously. 'I know you,' she said to herself, frowning, struggling to get a memory snap on me.

I had never seen her before in my life.

'You haven't always been in the boondocks?'

I shook my head.

She shut the door behind me, staring at me as she circled. 'Uniform or CID?'

'Detective Sergeant.'

She nodded, satisfied with her diagnosis, and led me through into the front room.

'How did you know?' I asked.

'I watched you.' She nodded up at a monitor on the wall, its screen showing the walkway.

'You could tell that I was a policeman just by watching me on a CCTV screen?'

'Not definitely, not until you knocked on the door.' She clicked her fingers, finishing the gesture with a forefinger pointed at me. 'Capaldi . . . I know

132

you now.'

I waited for it.

'You were involved in that thing that got Nick Bessant killed. In Cardiff . . .' She screwed her face up, trying to string timelines and detail together. 'You were the hostage. They made you out to be some sort of hero at the end of it, didn't they?'

I nodded modestly. 'It was a PR job,' I said wryly, recalling Jack Galbraith's assessment: *'And you fucked up good there, didn't you?'*

'You weren't ever attached to Vice though, were you?' she asked, frowning.

'No.'

'So, how did you get involved with a toerag like Nick Bessant?'

'It's a complicated story.'

She looked hard at me for a moment, trying to penetrate my reluctance. 'Okay.' She nodded, dropping it. 'Take a seat.'

I sank into the maw of a deep, expensive, cream leather sofa. She sat down at the far end and pulled her legs up, letting the cushion settle under her like a nest. She fitted herself into the corner and watched me with just a faintly enticing smile.

I was expected to start something.

'Why did you warn me not to say that I was a policeman?'

'I recorded our telephone conversation.'

I looked at her blankly.

'If you try to pull any police stuff now, I can claim entrapment.'

'I promise you this is off the record.'

She smiled like we were sharing an intimate secret. 'It usually is. So what is it that you want me to do for you?' she asked soothingly, a woman used to dealing with nervous men.

'I want to ask you some things.'

'A consultation will be a hundred and fifty pounds.'

I tried not to gasp. 'I only want to talk.'

'That's your choice, what we do with the time. It's still a hundred and fifty pounds.'

'I haven't got that kind of cash.'

She smiled reassuringly. 'Don't worry, I take all major credit cards.' She leaned across, opened a drawer in the low table in front of us, and produced the gizmo that processed them.

I passed her my credit card. 'This is my own money,' I moaned.

'And this is my own time.' She smiled back at me sweetly.

A hundred and fifty pounds . . . For a consultation . . . I felt the pain of it. So how much would those bastards have had to pay for a fucking alibi?

'What do the names McGuire and Tucker mean to you?' I asked when she passed my credit card back.

She nodded, fingering the string of pearls at her neck. 'You tell me.'

'You claimed that you were with them last Saturday night. Six of them. At a hut in the forest.'

'Five of them,' she corrected me without even a hint of calculation. 'Ken and Gordon, Les, Trevor, and Paul. Five people, not six.'

'You've got a good memory for names.'

She shook her head. 'It's a professional trait. It reassures people if you can call them by their first name. Just don't ask me for their surnames.'

'And you had a minder up there with you?'

'That's right. Winston.'

'But he didn't go to the police station with you to confirm the story?'

'No, he's not in town at the moment.' She looked at me languidly. 'Look, I don't want to tell you how to spend your money, but you're going over old ground. This is all out in the open.'

'Humour me.'

She dropped the pearls on to her cleavage, and spread her hands invitingly.

'A bit of a strange and uncomfortable gig, wasn't it?' I asked, spreading my own hands to take in the expensive cut of the room. 'Compared to what you're used to.'

She shrugged. 'I've known a lot worse, and believe me, you really don't want to ask about that.' She grinned suddenly and bobbed her head forward, leading my eyes into her cleavage. 'Or is this where you're heading? Are you a man who gets off on the descriptive, Sergeant Capaldi?'

'I thought first names were meant to be reassuring?'

She grinned. 'You're not a normal john.'

'Tell me about what happened on Saturday night.'

'If you want this dirty, I'm going to have to turn to invention.'

'Just stick to the truth.'

'The arrangement was for me to pair up with two of them: Trevor and Paul. But in the end nothing happened. Paul was too drunk, and Trevor . . .' She shrugged. 'Trevor preferred to keep his own company.'

'Why do you think that was?'

She studied me for a moment to see whether

there was an agenda behind the question. 'Because he's a closet gay. He didn't want his friends to see that he couldn't cope with the attention.'

'So did the friends take over the gift vouchers?'

'They could have done. But they all decided to remain faithful to their partners.'

I nodded understandingly. 'You know, that's almost exactly what the guys themselves told me.'

She smiled, picking up on my shift into ironic nuance. 'Well, I hope you think it was worth it to have it corroborated. Although you could have saved the money and just read my statement.'

'I wouldn't have had the pleasure of meeting you then.'

'Thank you.' She dipped her head coquettishly.

'And telling you to your face that I know you're a fucking liar, Monica.'

She didn't flinch. Just smiled into the cold moment. 'Tch!' she clucked a reprimand. 'Language please, Sergeant Capaldi.'

'Those bastards paid you to spout that story. And now I've paid you good money to have the fabrication repeated. You score twice on this invention.' She watched me impassively. 'So tell me, how much would I have had to overbid for the truth?'

'That was the truth,' she said reproachfully, without attempting to hide her amusement.

'Bullshit. I know it's a lie.'

'Why so certain?'

'Because I know who really was there that night.'

She shook her head patiently, but I thought I caught the first flicker in her composure. 'I'm sorry, but there are seven citizens backing up this truth.'

'One of them, Winston, is a total figment,' I

136

protested. 'And you, the only real one, weren't there either.'

She smiled sympathetically. 'Drop it, Sergeant. This is the story that's out in the marketplace. This is the one that the money is on.'

'What did they tell you? That the girl had gone on to Ireland along with the so-called friend that they've supposedly faked this up for? I assume that even you would want to know that you weren't covering damage?'

'Leave it,' she said soothingly.

'I'm here because I'm worried. I'm worried about the girl who really was there that night. I'm getting all this bullshit, but no one can convince me that she's all right. So give me something for my money. Give me something real. Tell me something that I don't know about those men. Reassure me that they're harmless. Stop me worrying, Monica.'

She looked at me steadily. Balancing something. She was a businesswoman, she didn't have to give me zilch. I just had to hope that she had some fair-trade genes in her make-up.

'I work from referrals. And, before I start, the ground rule is that I am not going to do names.' She adjusted her position on the cushions, the gesture letting me know that she was offering me the favour. 'No one gets my number, no one gets to come here unless they have been recommended by someone I know and trust. It might be an uncle, business associate, dentist . . . A client tells me that they know someone who would like to meet me, and asks would it be all right for them to contact me.'

'What are you trying to tell me?'

'These people are filtered. I trust them. It's in my

own interest—I will not deal with anyone that I think could have problems . . . could be unstable.'

'How many of the men had you met before?'

'Two of them.'

Trevor had mentioned Les and Gordon as the probable furnishers of Monica's number. 'Together?' I asked. I had a picture of them here, slightly pissed, cash rich, and pretending to be worldly.

She nodded. 'They were usually down in Cardiff together. After rugby games. But we did the business separately.'

I caught the sense of a past tense. 'Do you still see them?'

She smiled. 'I saw them last Saturday, Sergeant.'

I had forgotten that the lie was still bolted to the floor. We weren't going to shift that. 'Before then. When was the last time they came here?'

She thought about it. 'Not recently.' The reply was careful.

'Why is that, Monica?'

She shrugged.

'Did they get virtue?'

She smiled out of the corner of her mouth. Shook her head, hesitated a moment before she replied, thinking about it. 'Let's just say that their tastes shifted beyond what I was prepared to offer.'

'Shifted?'

'Sorry, Sergeant, your time is up.'

My face fell. 'I've only just got here.'

'I don't go by time, I go by effort, and you've proved to be hard work.' She smiled to show that there were no hard feelings.

She walked me to the hall and clicked the door latch open. She touched my wrist on the threshold.

'They're not dangerous, Sergeant. We're not talking bullwhips and sharps.'

'But you dropped them? Is that because you saw that they had the makings of problems?'

'They moved on. It happens.'

'What's your limit, Monica? Where do you draw the line?'

She reached her hand up and patted me playfully on the cheek. 'You're clean out of credit now, Sergeant.'

'Monica, help me here,' I pleaded. 'That girl could be messed up, dead or dying. Do it for her.'

Her smile didn't waver as she closed the door on me.

I thought about it, walking back to the car. What had Monica meant? How heavy or how weird did sex have to get before she declined the transaction? And she was a professional, she was supposed to be able to handle strangeness. What kind of twisted fucks were in that minibus that Magda had climbed into?

I turned my phone on to an announcement that I had four missed calls. All from Carmarthen headquarters. In ascending order of doom. Two from the dispatcher, one from Bryn Jones, and the final one from Jack Galbraith himself.

'Fucking call us . . .'

I was in Cardiff. I was way off the Reservation. Had they found out that I hadn't let this drop? That I was in dereliction of my proper duties? I went straight to the top; there was no point in stretching out the pain.

'It's Glyn Capaldi, sir. I've only just picked up your message.'

'Where the fuck are you?' he growled.

I watched a guy in the window of a coin-operated laundry trying to fold a sheet with two hands and his teeth. 'I'm up a big hill, sir, I've only just found a signal.' I kept my fingers crossed round the lie.

'We've been trying your radio for the last half-hour.'

'I'm not in the car. I had to leave it behind and walk up to . . .'

He cut in over me. 'I don't want to know. I just want you to turn round and get back to Dinas fucking pronto.'

'Yes, sir.' I heard the charged tension in his voice and felt an adrenalin surge kicking in. 'What am I specifically going back for, sir?'

'One of that group of idiots is dead. I want you to get up there and tell me that this is benign, that we are not witnessing the start of a slaughter season.'

'Who's died, sir?'

'One of the farmers. Vaughan. Trevor Vaughan.'

*   *   *

From calls I put into Emrys Hughes and the police doctor, I sketched in as much detail as I could. His parents had found him hanging in a barn this afternoon. A neighbouring farmer had cut him down. The doctor who had been called out had pronounced him dead at the scene. The body had been taken to the local cottage hospital for preliminary investigation prior to the post-mortem. Emrys Hughes was waiting for me at the farm.

The news stunned me. I had decided that I liked Trevor Vaughan. He had been troubled and melancholic, but, at his core, he had been a decent man. And what made no sense was that last night he had actually seemed happy. Well, relieved was probably closer to the correct tuning. Discovering that the hole in the forest was empty seemed to have taken a great weight off his mind. Brought him back into conjunction with his buddies.

So what had gone wrong? What had happened between then and now to totally fuck him up? Had there always been something darker lurking?

Or was I driving towards a suicide composed of smoke and mirrors?

A uniform with a squad car was stationed at the bottom of the farm drive to deter the curious. He waved me past. Emrys Hughes came out of the barn as I drove up. He looked grim and drawn. It was the same barn where Trevor and I had had our first real conversation.

'You took your time,' Emrys said angrily as I got out of the car.

'I got here as quickly as I could.'

'Do you know what it's like, waiting at a scene like this that involves someone you knew well, and having to be totally fucking inactive?' I held my hand out to him. He looked at it in surprise. 'What's this for?' he asked suspiciously, the bluster knocked out of him.

'A truce. We need to be professional here, act in concord.'

He took my hand reluctantly. 'Okay,' he said, not quite able to relinquish suspicion.

'Good.' I smiled at him. 'Now don't say anything to me until I ask you to.'

I walked into the barn. It was timber-framed and crooked with a rammed-dirt floor, the rickety central doors of the threshing bay wide open and letting plenty of light in. My eyes went straight to the long ladder propped up against the bottom tie beam of an oak truss about three metres off the floor. Was it too obvious? I looked away and carefully scanned the interior before my perceptions could jump to conclusions.

I quartered the building carefully until I was satisfied that there was nowhere else to go but back to the ladder. This time I let myself look at the green plastic baler twine tied around the same tie beam, a length hanging down and drifting into a shallow parabola from the draught coming through the open doors. I stood under it. Three strands of twine twisted together to give it strength, unravelling now, the ends frayed.

'They cut this?' I asked.

'Yes. Mick Jones from Pentre Nant, the nearest neighbour. Trevor's parents couldn't bring themselves to do it.'

'The rest of it?' I looked at him carefully. 'Did you see the knot?'

'His neck was swollen, the doctor couldn't loosen it.'

The knot was important, but I didn't push it, I didn't want him thinking that I was macabre. 'Did the twine come from here?'

'Yes. There's a big hank of it in the next building.'

I looked at the ladder. 'Mr Jones went up this to cut him down?'

'Yes, but he didn't put it there, it was up when . . .'

'I know.' I interrupted him. There were no alternative ladder indentations on the floor. Trevor Vaughan had climbed up this. Or had he been forced to climb up? The floor's surface was too

142

disturbed now to isolate individual footprints.

He had climbed up the ladder, attached the baler twine to the beam, put his head into the pre-prepared noose, leaned over past the point of balance, and . . . goodbye cruel world. I pictured the swing. He hadn't kicked over the ladder, either deliberately or inadvertently. He was probably rotating, definitely choking, but his initial momentum would have brought him back to the ladder. A last opportunity. He could have climbed back on board Mother Earth. He didn't. So, he was either very determined, or someone had prevented his return.

'How long before they found him?' I asked, dipping my head imperceptibly, saying adieu to Trevor Vaughan.

'No more than half an hour. His father came out and found him after the dogs started making a racket.'

'He had the dogs with him?' I asked, surprised.

'No, they were shut up. They must have sensed something. Not quickly enough though. He was just hanging there when his father found him.'

'Was there any sign of anyone else being here?' I asked, wondering if the dogs could have picked up on something.

He shook his head. 'No.'

'Has he left a note?'

'Not here. No one from the hospital has called to say they've found anything.'

I looked around again. Old stale hay in the loft, rusty sickles hung from nails, junk stored in the corners against the day they might find a use for it. It all looked mean and tawdry. I reminded myself that these people didn't work with frills. 'Did he

143

have money problems?'

Emrys shrugged. 'I don't know. Things have been tight generally in farming, but I wouldn't have thought that the Vaughans would have been hurt worse than anyone else. The word is that they would be able to manage better than most. Always been known as careful.'

'How about personal life?' I asked it lightly, wanting him to keep believing that we were still confidantes. I didn't want him going constituent defensive on me.

'He worked hard. He liked his sports, the odd night out with the boys. He didn't have a drink problem.' He grinned conspiratorially. 'And he wasn't married, so he didn't have women problems.'

'How about men problems?'

His smile wavered into a frown, not grasping it. He shook his head, puzzled.

Was he acting? Had shrine mentality kicked in? Had they already started to preserve Trevor's memory? 'Did Trevor have boyfriend trouble?'

His mouth opened in slow motion. 'Fuck off . . .' He said it half bluster, half shock. The incredulous smile on his face willing me to admit that I was joking. He wasn't acting, I decided. He hadn't seen it in Trevor. I was up against the denial of the Chapelheads.

'I take it that this is news to you?'

'That isn't news, that's slander.' He shook his head again. 'You can't mean it. That's some sick idea of a joke.' He pointed out towards the house. 'His parents are up there being comforted. They've lost their son, and you are standing on their property, under the very spot where he lost his life, spreading filthy lies. Trevor Vaughan was a good

144

person.'

'There's nothing that says homosexuals can't be good people,' I suggested reasonably.

'Show some respect . . .' He choked. 'The man's dead, for God's sake . . .' He lost it then. The red mist descended, and I wasn't quick enough to see it coming. He came at me, both outstretched arms slamming into my chest. Taken by surprise, I lost balance, and my back hit the wall of the barn. I felt a sharp stab of pain in my right shoulder, but my priority was to stay upright. I knew that if I fell he would come in close and kick the shit out of me.

Still standing though, I became his dilemma. He was stalled. Blood rage was tugging one way, reason and consequence the other. He was rigid in front of me, fists balled, breathing hard, head down into his neck like a paused bull, waiting for me to do something to trigger his next action.

I was almost tempted to lamp him. To turn surprise to my advantage and put a fist between his eyes. But he was much the heavier man, and charged with the anger that would stop him feeling pain. He would probably just surge over me. And I would end up with a broken hand before the next round of carnage even started.

We were so intent on the moment that neither of us recognized the noise.

I dropped back into the world first. 'That's your radio,' I shouted at him.

It took him a moment to come back down and join me. His hand went automatically to the radio, then he remembered the stand-off and glared at me malevolently, and turned away before he answered, walking out through the open barn doors to keep the call to himself.

I didn't have time to investigate my injuries. He swivelled in the yard. 'It's the hospital,' he announced, his voice aggrieved. 'The doctor wants you there. There's something he thinks you should see before he finishes his preliminary examination.'

*　　*　　*

Dinas cottage hospital was another example of the architectural legacy that some particularly joyless Victorians had left scattered about the area. The drear, dark, Gothic stone building had once been a refuge for fallen women.

The porter who covered mortuary duties was called to come and pick me up from the shabby reception hall. I recognized him when he appeared. A member of one of the drinking cadres in The Fleece, who I knew to nod to simply as Gary. I hadn't known his occupation.

Gary led me through a series of corridors that made the reception hall seem jaunty by comparison. He didn't talk, just kept turning his head from time to time to make sure that I hadn't been spirited away.

Dr Christy Samuels was waiting for me. A big man with white hair and a craggy red face, he unravelled himself out of his chair and stood up when I came into the room.

'Good to see you again, Sergeant Capaldi,' he said, shaking my hand.

I reciprocated. I had worked with him professionally a couple of times in my past life in Cardiff. He had practised in the Valleys as a GP and a police doctor. After retiring to the Dinas area, he had kept up the role of police doctor on

146

the sporadic, part-time basis that the level of crime here engendered.

'We've bagged his stuff for your forensic people, should you decide that you're going down that route.' He led me over to a table where a couple of clear-plastic evidence bags held Trevor Vaughan's clothes and items from his pockets. Another one held a length of green baler twine, the three strands spliced, looped and knotted. I picked up the bag. The noose had been severed.

'There was too much swelling, I had to cut it to get it off,' Dr Samuels explained.

The noose had been tied with a series of running clove hitches. A simple slip knot. It would have tightened round his neck as soon as the pressure of his weight was applied. Effective, and unsophisticated. A farmer's knot.

'What's the verdict from your preliminary investigation?' I asked.

'We're shipping him off for post-mortem by the forensic pathologist. But, I haven't seen anything to surprise me.'

'Death is consistent with hanging?'

'Totally.' He glanced down at his notes. 'Characteristic oedema of the neck with associated bruising. Presence of petechiae under the conjunctivae and around the preorbital region. Involuntary defecation and urination.'

'Remind me about the significance of petechiae?'

'Ruptured capillaries.'

'Any bruising?'

He smiled knowingly. He had seen his share of the results of violent encounters in the Valleys. 'I had a good look. Some minor, healing, scar traces, similarly old bruising, the sort of thing you'd expect from someone who worked on a farm. Nothing that would indicate that there had been any sort of struggle.'

'You checked his fingernails?'

'Of course. Grime from various sources, probably lanolin, but no traces of human skin.'

'Could he have been strangled, and then the hanging simulated?'

He frowned, thinking about it, already starting to shake his head slowly. 'It's doubtful. Apart from the lack of bruising, there was no sign of subconjunctival haemorrhaging, which is an indicator of violent ligature strangulation. The post-mortem could determine if the hyoid bone has been fractured, which is another indicator, but don't pin anything on that, he was too young for the two halves of the hyoid to have fused.'

'You would be prepared to write this up as a suicide then?' I asked.

'Experience tells me yes. But . . .' He hesitated.

'Go on,' I prompted.

'This doesn't change my opinion, but I think there's something that you should see.'

I winced. 'The body?'

He smiled sympathetically. 'I'm afraid so.'

*   *   *

Grey and stiff. I had seen too many corpses. They went with the smell of bad chemicals and the cold dank room that he led me into. Trevor was stretched out almost naked on the stainless-steel table. A mass of swollen and discoloured tissue rose from his neck to his ears like a mock horse collar. But he wasn't Trevor any more. He was an absence, something useless now.

'Well?' Dr Samuels asked gently.

I collected myself. What was I meant to be seeing?

Almost naked . . .

I went closer. I had thought that he had been wearing a pair of incredibly brief swimming trunks. Now I wasn't so sure. They were light purple and wet and would probably dry to lilac, with a small, repeating flower pattern in white. His flesh was swollen around the waistband and the legs of the briefs.

'Is there any medical significance to the swelling?' I asked.

'No, they're just way too tight,' Dr Samuels explained.

'These aren't men's pants.'

'No, I didn't think so either, that's why I wanted you to see them.'

'Jesus, they must have been uncomfortable,' I said, thinking out loud. Starting to wonder what the true significance of this was. 'Can we get them off of him?'

'Not without cutting them.'

Would I be destroying a set-up that we might need to study carefully later?

He read my mind. 'I've already taken photographs.'

'Okay.' I stepped away to let him at the body. He used a pair of surgical scissors and eased the briefs off, releasing a waft of trapped faeces.

'Can we wash them?' I asked.

He grinned at my discomfort. He scraped the bulk of the faeces into a sterile bag. 'Just in case they don't find enough of the stuff inside him when they come to do the post-mortem,' he explained, turning on a pillar tap.

Young girl's pants. They would have been brief on a sixteen-year-old. It was unthinkable that Trevor could have filched or borrowed them from a mother like his. Even a thin guy like him would have struggled to put these on. And why today of all days? Or had this been a regular secret kink? Suddenly I had to know if this was special. Had Trevor Vaughan worn these today specifically to send me a message from the grave?

I went back to the anteroom and called Emrys Hughes.

His voice registered a sulk when he realized who was calling. 'I hope you're calling to apologize,' he grunted balefully.

'No, Sergeant Hughes,' I said coldly. 'I'm calling to get you to do your fucking job properly and stop acting like an emotional dwarf.'

'You can't talk to me like that . . .'

'Yes, I can,' I said, cutting in over him. 'You are in major trouble if I decide to report you for assault and obstruction. I'm giving you one chance to act professionally and redeem yourself.'

'What's that?' he asked suspiciously. I was grateful to hear cowed in his tone.

'Go up to the house. I need you to check Trevor's room carefully. As quickly as you can. I need to know if you find any women's underwear.'

'You have to be fucking joking . . .' His voice swelled ominously.

'Act professionally, for God's sake,' I yelled at him. 'That is an instruction, not a fucking whim. I am talking imperative here, this is information that is vital.' I snapped the connection closed, hoping that it punctuated my urgency and impatience.

He called back five minutes later. His tone was still sullen, but, under it, I was grateful to hear a grudging hint of submission. 'I've checked. I didn't find anything other than men's stuff.'

'Good.'

He cleared his throat. 'I'm sorry I pushed you.'

'Loyalty will fuck you over, Sergeant.'

'Not something you'll ever have to worry about,' he replied snidely.

I ignored it. 'I want one more favour, and then we'll forget about this.'

'What favour?'

'I'll let you know,' I said, hanging up on him, not realizing that I was going to be calling it in far sooner than I had expected.

Unless he had destroyed the others, or had a hidden cache, these were Trevor's one pair of special pants. It had to be significant that he had worn them today. It wouldn't have been his way to go out in one brief flare of controversy. He would have known that I would be called into this. Had this been his message to me? If so, what had he been trying to tell me?

As a sad aside, the pants convinced me that Trevor had been the only one responsible for his death. The jump off the ladder had to have been his own doing. But who had been out there, pushing at his psyche?

When I got back into the mortuary, the pants had been spread out, two halves hinged at the crotch, the deconstruction looking like a strange, textile Rorschach test. The doctor and Gary looked at me expectantly. There was something I was meant to notice.

It was on the label, in what was probably ballpoint pen, faded after repeated washing. But still recognizable as the letter 'W'.

'Who labels their underpants?' I said, thinking out loud.

The other two looked at each other, wondering whether they were meant to contribute.

'Someone with sisters,' I said, starting to complete the thought process, 'or a mother they want to keep away from their things. Or someone who's simply proud of the act of possessing . . . "W"? Winifred? Wanda?' I looked at the others questioningly.

'Wendy?' the doctor volunteered.

'Wilma?' I threw in. 'Willow?'

Gary shook his head, concentrating hard, but unable to contribute.

'Gary, you live here, do any of these names ring any bells with you?' I asked, playing on his one strength as a local.

He thought hard about it. 'Wendy,' he said at last, looking at me, pleased with himself. 'Wendy Evans. Bill Evans the builder's daughter.'

It locked into place. 'Paul Evans's sister?'

'That's right.'

'Does she still live at home?'

He shook his head. 'Not any more. Not since she ran away with her history teacher.'

Oh Jesus . . .

More planets swung into spooky conjunction.

Malcolm Paterson, Sally's husband, Boon's adoptive father, had run away with Wendy, Paul Evans's sister. And somewhere down the line Trevor Vaughan had acquired a pair of her pants.

Why?

152

9

Emrys Hughes's expression was a compound of embarrassment, perplexity and hostility. 'Why me?' he pleaded again, looking despairingly at the flimsy lilac pants in the sealed evidence bag that he was holding with the same reluctance as he would a live eel.

'Because, as you keep insisting, you know these people.'

'Dirty stuff like this doesn't happen here,' he protested miserably. 'I don't want to have to ask the Evanses if these were Wendy's pants. I don't want to have to explain to them where we found them.'

'It's upsetting for everyone. But they'll talk to you. They trust you.' The look on his face made me doubly glad that I was delegating the task. The Evanses were big, slow bastards with smalltown mores. I knew the mentality: any stranger turning up with a message connecting their little girl with the whiff of pederasty and cross-dressing was likely to be treated as a carrier of the same infections. And I had already virtually accused their son of rape. Emrys was in for a hard time, but their enraged virtue would probably not turn physical on him.

'We also need to talk to Wendy. Ask the family if they have any contact details.'

He shook his head. 'It's common knowledge, no one's heard from either of them since she ran off with Malcolm Paterson.'

'I'll get Carmarthen to put out a bulletin on her. Call me as soon as you know anything,' I said, leaving him with a fatherly pat on the back.

*   *   *

Sally answered the door in her dressing gown again. She stared at me for a moment, her lips clenched tight, beginning to shake her head before she spoke. 'Oh, Glyn, what a terrible, terrible thing . . .'

I nodded in concurrence, and walked into the hall. She closed the door behind me. 'Oh God, give me a hug,' she cried, holding her arms open. I went into them. 'Poor, poor Trevor,' she intoned mournfully.

'I know, I know . . .' I soothed, putting a light rocking motion into our connection, the slowest of shared, sad dances.

She broke away gradually, and dabbed at her wayward hair, but didn't adjust the opened neck of her dressing gown. 'Thank you,' she said softly. 'I needed that.'

'Any time.'

We let the moment hover.

'Any word from Boon?' I asked.

She shook her head, giving me a brave, practised smile. 'Did you find him? Trevor?' she whispered.

'No. He'd already been taken to the hospital when I was called in.'

'Could it have been an accident?'

I shrugged. 'We have to wait for the coroner to determine that.' I wondered how stiffly that had come out. 'I'm sorry, I'm not trying to be evasive.'

'That's all right, I understand. I shouldn't pry.' She touched my elbow. 'Go through to the kitchen, I'll make us a drink.'

I went down the corridor in front of her.

'Oh God, Glyn—' I heard her concern in the intake of breath.

'What's the matter?' I asked, turning.

She steered me quickly to a chair at the kitchen table and made me sit. 'There's blood on your jacket—on your shoulder.' She went to the sink and turned on the hot tap. 'Take it off, and your shirt,' she instructed over her shoulder.

I took off my jacket. By craning my neck I could make out the blood on the back of my shirt. It had dried into the wound, and I felt it tugging painfully as I tried to ease my shirtsleeve off.

'Whoa . . .' She stopped me, placing cotton wool, a bowl of hot water, and a bottle of antiseptic on to the table. 'You'll just start it bleeding again if you do that.' She dipped cotton wool into the bowl and started sponging round the wound, slipping out a mischievous little laugh when I winced. 'This is nasty. What happened?'

I recalled the pain I had felt when Emrys Hughes had pushed me against the barn wall. I must have hit one of the rusty nails they used to hang stuff from. I gave her a stoic grin and shook my head. 'I don't know. I must have bumped into something in Trevor Vaughan's barn.'

She looked at me sceptically. 'You should really have a tetanus shot for this.'

I winced again as she freed the cloth from the wound. Deftly, she pulled the shirt off and tossed it in the direction of the washing machine.

'I need that,' I protested.

'Not in that state. I'll lend you something. Now just sit still while I try and clean this up.'

The irony was not lost on me that I had just come from a hospital where no one had noticed the injury. I sat as still as I could, conscious of her fingers working on my back, and the moist warmth of her breath on my neck. I felt self-conscious and exposed, aware of my body as something white, lumpy and exuding musk, but, at the same time, appreciating the intimacy that had been created.

'You've got good skin,' she said, stretching her fingers across to the base of my neck.

'For a man my age?'

'I didn't introduce any qualifiers.'

I looked round at her. She smiled down and blushed. I saw the nervousness there, but also a spark, pheromones stirring, her own curiosity rekindled. The smell, the taste, and the fit of the other. I realized that it had probably been a long time for her as well. She gently smoothed out the dressing, and, almost imperceptibly, I felt her filling up the space behind, me, the back of my head almost nestling between her breasts.

I swore inwardly. Because I was going to have to spoil it.

'Sally?'

'Mm . . .' she murmured behind me.

'I have to ask you about Wendy Evans.'

The moment snapped. It was like an anvil dropping on to a picnic table, shocking the partygoers into the memory that there was real weight in the world. She walked around the table to face me, her expression grim. 'What does *she* have to do with anything?'

'She's Paul Evans's sister. I've only just found out that it was her your husband went away with.'

'What does she have to do with anything?' she repeated coldly.

'I'm sorry, I wouldn't be asking this if I didn't

156

think it was important.'

She turned and left the kitchen. She returned carrying a sweatshirt. It was pink. She was punishing me. She threw it across the table. 'Cover yourself.'

I struggled into the sweatshirt. It was tight on me. I had an image of how ridiculous I must look. She didn't smile. She stared hard, challenging me to see how much longer I dared to continue sitting there abusing her hospitality and care.

I owed her the truth. Some version of it was going to be out there shocking the community before too long anyway.

I faced into her stare. 'Sally, when we found Trevor Vaughan he was wearing a pair of Wendy Evans's pants.'

The thought was too left-field; her face crumpled, trying to get a grasp on it.

'There are connections I need to know about.'

She pulled a chair out clumsily and slumped on to it, facing me. She shook her head, demonstrating her incomprehension. 'I don't understand . . . Was he dressed up as a woman?'

'No, only the pants.'

She frowned. 'How do you know . . .? That they're hers?'

'Her mother's identified them. They were part of a set she bought on a school trip to London. She took the others with her when she . . .' I paused, trying to come up with a softer way to put it.

'When she ran away with my husband,' she finished it for me bitterly. 'Okay, so what are these connections you need to know about?'

'Do you have any contact information for your husband or Wendy Evans?'

'No.'

I nodded, accepting the finality of her answer and moved on. 'Did you know that Trevor Vaughan was probably homosexual?'

'I haven't seen Trevor for a long time. And we were never that close. He was just one of the people my son hung around with. As a parent I wasn't introduced into the workings of the circle.'

'Boon never mentioned anything?'

'I doubt that he would have said anything to me, even if he had suspected.' She went back into memory. 'Trevor was the quietest one. He was always in the background when they were together. Very polite, very nice. Quite awkward too.'

'Were he and Paul Evans close?'

She looked at me questioningly.

'I'm wondering how Trevor got the opportunity to get close enough to Wendy's things to steal a pair of pants. I'm assuming here that she didn't give them to him herself.'

She shook her head. 'Trevor and Paul were two extremes when it came to personality. I don't see them socializing together outside the group.' She closed her eyes tight and winced audibly.

'Are you all right?'

'It's such a tragic image. Why? Why wear her pants?'

'I think that he might have been trying to tell me something.'

She looked hard at me. She didn't smile. Okay, she wasn't in the mood for smiling, but she didn't pull any other face to ridicule the suggestion. She was taking me seriously. 'Such as . . .?'

I shook my head. 'I don't know. It may have nothing to do with Wendy. She may just have been a random provider of underwear. But to get there, I need to know something about her. And I don't know who else to ask.'

'The Evans family?'

'I want to continue living as a whole person.'

It wasn't much of a laugh, but it was progress. She stood up. 'We can talk in the car.'

'Where are we going?'

'You can drive me to work. You haven't spoken to Joan Harvey yet, have you?'

'I haven't had a chance.'

'The poor woman's getting more and more upset. Ever since I told her that I'd mentioned Donna and Colette to you, she's been worrying that perhaps she didn't make enough of the right noises at the time. I think you should talk to her and put her out of her misery.'

I shook my head. 'I can't.'

She scowled. 'Why not?'

I stood up. 'This particular shade of pink doesn't work for me.'

She nodded, and allowed herself a small smile. 'I think I see what you mean.'

*   *   *

We settled for a charcoal-grey wool sweater, which, under my jacket, wouldn't raise too many eyebrows. She was in a better mood when we got into the car. A shower had calmed her.

'If I drive you there, how are you going to get back in the morning?' I asked.

'You're going to pick me up and buy me breakfast,' she stated matter-of-factly.

I must have frowned involuntarily. Already

159

worrying about where I was going to find somewhere suitable at that time in the morning in this culinarily bereft part of the world.

She smiled and touched a finger lightly and briefly to my lips, as if removing a shred of tobacco. It felt like I had been brushed with a nettle. 'Don't be such a literalist, Glyn. We'll take it where we find it.'

'Breakfast?'

The smile expanded. 'What else?'

I shook my head inwardly. I would never understand the bounce of a woman's moods.

I started the car. 'You're going to tell me about Wendy Evans?'

A frown fluttered her forehead. 'God, you sure know how to smooth-talk a girl, don't you?' I pulled away, leaving the timing of the silence up to her. 'I know that I look like the obvious choice for this—the abandoned woman. But I really don't think that I'm going to be much help.'

I glanced round at her questioningly.

'I never actually met Wendy Evans, in the sense of being introduced to her. I saw her. I knew who she was. Malcolm always pointed out the kids he taught. And he talked about her.' She thought about it and laughed mirthlessly. 'I never once thought, *Look out for that one, there's a threat in the making there.* She was short, still baby plump then. I have a memory of her smoking a cigarette in that challenging way kids do, daring you to say something about it. She was probably trying to get Malcolm to think that she was exciting.'

'It came completely out of the blue?' I asked.

'My husband left for work one morning and never returned. Separations don't come much more

160

sudden than that.'

'You had no idea that a relationship had developed?'

She shook her head. 'Not that kind of a relationship. As I said, he used to talk about her. She was one of the kids that he felt sorry for. He told me that she was damaged.' She eased out a brave smile. 'You never worry about the damaged ones. Pity's supposed to make you feel emotionally superior.'

'How was she damaged?'

'I don't know precisely. I don't even know if Malcolm knew in detail. It was a school thing, teacher/pupil confidentiality. I didn't like to pry too much. I just remember him telling me once that he thought she was carrying a lot of weird emotional stuff around for her age.'

'When did Malcolm go?' I asked.

'Just over two years ago.'

'So, Trevor Vaughan had been storing those pants for at least that long.'

She looked puzzled.

'She took the rest of the set with her,' I explained. 'They were obviously special, she wouldn't have left that one pair behind if she still had them.'

'So, had Trevor been wearing them all this time?'

'Impossible.' I flashed on how the elastic had cut into his waist and thighs. 'They were too small for him. He would have ruined them after the first couple of times. He had to have been saving them for something.'

She pulled a face and shuddered. 'That's creepy.'

Another thought hit me. If Trevor had been gay, a young girl's pants would have been no kind of a turn-on. So, what if he had been hiding them rather than savouring them? To cover for someone? But why bring them out now to figure so prominently in his death?

Because, where he was going, he no longer had to worry about the person he'd been protecting?

*   *   *

Sally took me to the top storey of the Sychnant Nursing Home where Joan Harvey had her private quarters. 'Seven o'clock tomorrow morning,' she said quietly in the corridor. 'I'll see you in the car park.'

'I'll be there.'

'You'd better be.' She knocked on the door.

I half expected a parting kiss. I must have shown my disappointment, because she grinned at me knowingly as the door opened.

'Joan, this is Detective Sergeant Capaldi—the one I was telling you about.'

Joan looked to be in her early sixties, with fine lines fanning out at the corners of her mouth and eyes, slightly puffy cheeks, and a tired, intelligent expression.

She shook my hand. 'Please come in, Sergeant.' A soft South Wales accent.

We both watched Sally go down the corridor. 'She's a good person,' Joan said. 'I wish I could get her to take on more responsibility.'

'She won't?'

'She doesn't want it. She wants to feel that she's only here temporarily. That there's something better waiting just round the corner.'

I didn't say anything to Joan, but that was

another thing Sally and I had in common.

She led me into a spacious room in the slope of the roof, which managed to contain some big period pieces of furniture and a baby grand piano without feeling cluttered. I sat where she pointed me, in one of the armchairs.

She sat on the sofa to one side of me and poured tea. 'Sally has told me of your interest in missing persons.' She passed me a bone-china cup and saucer that felt as fragile as wren's bones.

'She said that potentially you may have two?'

She grimaced. 'We didn't think about it at the time, but I'm now wondering whether I might have been remiss in my responsibilities.'

'Two girls who left suddenly?' I prompted.

'"Suddenly" implies a mystery, Sergeant. It didn't seem like one at the time. It was just that we weren't expecting them to leave. They didn't give notice. They left sometime in the night or early morning. They did pack all their belongings, and it was the day after they had been paid. I'm trying to give you reasons why their departures didn't concern us more.'

'I understand. But weren't they paid in arrears? Wouldn't they still have been owed money in hand?'

'Yes, that's right, and one of them more than made up for the value of that in what she took with her.'

'Who was that?'

'Colette Fletcher. I've put some things together for you.' She leaned forward and took a photograph out of a file folder on the table. 'That's Colette,' she said, passing it to me.

It had probably been taken on the lawn outside

163

the home. An unsmiling girl, in the pink Sychnant housecoat, with straight brown hair pulled back off a wide, pale forehead, propping up an elderly woman who was smiling into a distance only she could connect with.

She passed me another picture. 'This is Donna. Donna Gallagher.' The same housecoat. But indoors this time, a shorter, plumper girl, fair hair in a ponytail, managing a smile, but self-conscious in front of the camera.

'Did you report them missing?' I tried not to sound accusatory. I was only interested in knowing if they had been logged somewhere.

She grimaced. 'I feel slightly awkward about that, Sergeant. I did contact the police in Colette's case, to report the things that she had taken with her. I needed a case number, or whatever it is, for the insurance claim. As for reporting them missing, I have to say no. You see, as far as we were concerned, they weren't missing. They had simply left our employment. They had exercised their right to go whenever and wherever they chose.'

'You didn't get in touch with the families?'

She looked at me remonstratingly. 'Of course I did. The nearest thing that they had to a family, at any rate: the children's home that they had both come from.'

I felt the tug. Unexpected information sliding home. New pathways of possibilities opening. 'The same home?' I asked, keeping my tone neutral.

'Yes, but not at the same time. It's in Manchester. I've put the details in the folder, in case you want to contact them.'

'How far apart were they, time-wise?'

She thought about it. 'Off the top of my head,

Colette was with us roughly five years ago for three or four months over the summer. Donna came about three years ago, again in the summer, and stayed till just after Christmas, if I remember correctly. The dates are in the folder.'

'Could they have been running away from something?' I asked.

'When they left here, or to come here in the first place?'

'Either.'

She shook her head slowly. 'I really have no idea, I'm afraid. They came here because they needed the work. I'm not aware of any problems with either of them that could have caused them to want to run away.' She shrugged. 'But then I didn't know the intimate details of their private lives.'

'Is there anyone here who might?'

'I doubt that very much. We have quite a high rate of staff turnover. Apart from that, Colette kept herself to herself. Donna was slightly more sociable, but not much.'

'What kind of girls were they?'

She smiled wryly. 'They came from a tough background, Sergeant. They had had to acquire the appropriate survival skills. They were much wiser in the ways of the world than the local girls. That's why I was not unduly concerned when they left. I felt that it was voluntary, and that they were more than capable of looking after themselves.'

'Would they have gone back to the city?'

'Almost certainly.' She smiled at the memory. 'I wouldn't have said that either of those girls had been filled with the joys of Nature.'

'So, why come here in the first place?'

'For the work,' she replied, looking surprised by

165

the question.

'No, to Mid Wales. To Dinas. To the country. This is such a far cry, both geographically and culturally, from the streets of Manchester.'

'There must have been something about it that appealed. To bring them back.'

I shook my head. 'I don't understand.'

'In both cases, they had spent the previous school summer holiday in Dinas. It was something that Sara Harris had been doing for a few years. She had some sort of connection with the children's home. Every summer, she had a girl from Manchester to help in the salon, to get them out of that grim environment, and hopefully, spark some interest in them.'

Sara Harris? The name meant something. 'So, what you're saying is that both girls had done a summer-holiday stint at the hairdressing salon, about three years apart?' She nodded. 'Then they go back to Manchester, and the following summer they both come back? And get jobs here?'

'That's right. Despite their apparent lack of enthusiasm for rural life, there must have been some attraction.'

But what? And then it locked into place. Sara Harris . . . David Williams telling me: Sara Harris ran the hairdressing salon in Dinas. Sara Harris was Les Tucker's long-term girlfriend.

Les Tucker was Gordon McGuire's best friend.

Les and Gordon paid to fuck Monica Trent until her services got too mundane for them.

Magda, Donna, Colette. I now had three young women in the chain of connection.

And Boon Paterson?

*　　　*　　　*

I preferred to use the back bar in The Fleece. Where the older men congregated. It was quieter, I could mope peacefully, or talk to David or Sandra without straining. The front bar was the reserve of the energy crowds, the young farmers, the rugby aficionados; shoal culture in all its deafening and jostling glory.

I should have been warned when I walked in that evening and the old guys turned their backs on me and shuffled a portentous half-step away from their usual positions. But I was too preoccupied with what Joan Harvey had told me. Wondering what the best approach to Sara Harris would be. Bearing in mind who her boyfriend was.

David, serving at the front bar, turned and saw me. His face dropped visibly. I smiled mock wearily, and waited for him to come over and explain the joke. But another signal interrupted. Hairs pricking on the back of my neck. An alarm response.

I was aware of the entire raucous mass in the front bar turning silent. Sound snuffing out on a ragged wave of curtailed laughs and shouts, glasses and bottles being put down with an unheard of delicacy.

And I knew that I was the cause.

Even before I saw Gordon McGuire, Les Tucker and Paul Evans in the opening that connected the two bars. The crowd behind them shuffling quietly for vantage points.

Not having a glass to raise, I just nodded at them.

'You're not wanted here, Sergeant,' Gordon stated.

'It's a public house, Mr McGuire.'

167

'Tell him, Dave,' Les prompted David Williams.

David shook his head uncomfortably. 'Perhaps it would be better, Glyn.'

I let them see me ponder it. Using the moment to prevent my fear response from showing, keep the adrenalin surge under control. Smelling the animosity in that crowd, there was nothing that I would rather have done than get up off the stool and walk out. But I had to live with these people, and if I was going to be railroaded, it would not be without anger.

'I'll have the usual please, David.'

'Don't do it, Dave—not if you want to keep the rest of us as customers,' Les warned. A rumble from the crowd backed him.

David looked at me imploringly.

'What's your problem, Mr Tucker?' I asked, trying to keep my voice reasonable, not let them hear the tremble in it.

'You're a fucking shit,' Paul Evans snarled, a small rumble of assent running through the crowd behind him.

Gordon raised his hand slightly to control him. 'We don't like to hear rumours being spread about our friends. Especially from people who don't know them.'

'Be specific, please.'

'You concocted a story about Trevor Vaughan being queer, and then you threatened him with exposing it.'

'Which probably drove him to do what he did,' Les chipped in.

'Are you accusing me of causing Trevor Vaughan's death?' I asked.

'Yes!' Paul Evans shouted.

Gordon shook his head. 'You can see the mood here, Sergeant. I suggest that you get out now. I'd also recommend that you apply for a transfer, anywhere well away from here.'

'Oh, believe me, Mr McGuire, there is nothing I would like better,' I said wholeheartedly. 'But tell me something: did any of you think that Trevor Vaughan was gay?'

The shouts and abuse turned on like a tap. Paul Evans actually spat at me. Gordon and Les calmed the crowd before Gordon turned back to me. 'Of course not. He was our friend, we knew him. We don't have the same bent, malicious streak as you.'

Oh shit, I had missed it . . .

'You bastards!' I screamed. The unexpectedness of it, the suddenness, the speed with which I stood up, stunning them all. For a moment I was a shockwave. They swayed back en masse, as if they were nailed to the floor. Then I was out of the door.

I had missed it. I berated myself again. I had let myself be tripped up by illusion and reality. I had confused truth with invention when Monica had been telling her tale. I had actually accused her of not being there, and then not picked up on the crucial point of her story.

Monica had told me that Trevor Vaughan was homosexual. But Monica had not been there. Everything in her story had been told to her. She didn't know Trevor Vaughan from Adam. But she knew Gordon and Les.

Why had she been instructed to push Trevor Vaughan out of the closet?

10

I worked on the assumption that Monica wouldn't live at the walk-up. She would have another life. A house in a nice suburb, or a swanky apartment in a new complex in the regenerated Docklands. If I got to Cardiff early enough I could catch her before she reached sanctuary in her fortress.

It was after one o'clock in the morning, I was belting round the Brecon bypass, when I remembered Sally. Our appointment for breakfast. All the possibilities that rippled out from there. I groaned out loud, and pulled into a lay-by.

'Sally, it's Glyn . . .'

'You're calling to ask me if I like champagne because you've booked us into a place that does smoked salmon and New York bagels?'

'I wish I was, but I'm not going to be able to make it. I'm out chasing the bad guys.'

'Where are you?'

'I can't tell you.'

'Can't tell me or won't tell me?'

'Can't tell you.'

I felt the silence and pictured her sitting in that kitchen surrounded by cold stainless steel.

'Sally . . .?'

'I'm still here.'

'I'm really sorry.'

'We haven't got very far, have we, Glyn?'

'I'll make it up to you.' I suddenly knew that I had to be decisive. 'Take tonight off, I'll take you out to dinner.'

She laughed. 'Okay.'

I remembered my confrontation in The Fleece. 'I'd better warn you, I'm not very popular in town at the moment.'

She laughed again. 'From what I've heard on the grapevine, you never were.'

I was parked outside Monica's by two thirty. It was a grey, sluggish night, not quite drizzling, and no wind disturbing the discarded fast-food packaging in the gutters and on the pavements. I set the alarm on my mobile phone and tipped my seat back, reckoning I was safe sleeping until five o'clock.

I was awakened by a tapping on the window. I opened my eyes into the harsh beam of a torch. I squinted away from the glare. 'Would you put your window down please, sir?' asked the uniform cop holding it.

I complied. 'Good evening, officer,' I said politely.

He ignored me and ran the torch over my face and the inside of the car.

'I was just trying to catch up on some sleep.'

'Have you been drinking, sir?'

'No,' I answered truthfully. I didn't bother explaining that I had been prevented by a vigilante pack.

'Is this your car?'

Bang . . . There goes incognito. I opened my warrant card. He peered down to inspect it. 'Sergeant Capaldi?'

'Can we keep this between ourselves?'

'You're a long way from your new home, Sarge.' He had recognized my name, and obviously knew my history.

'I don't want to blow a surveillance gig here.'

He took out his notebook. 'You're a celebrity, Sergeant. We've had a request from Carmarthen to log and report if you ever show up in Cardiff.'

I smiled winningly up at him. 'You don't have to do everything they tell you, do you?'

He leered back maliciously. 'Is that how you got to be where you are today, Sarge?'

The only consolation was that they were not going to wake Jack Galbraith up at four thirty in the morning to tell him that I was on the loose in Cardiff. I could tuck it away into my malfeasance sack and forget about it until the time came to invent excuses.

*   *   *

When I woke, the early risers were on the move, heading off to work, a couple of crazy people jogging, dogs being walked, a milk float gliding past. The street lights and the grey pre-dawn light combined to make the place feel even grubbier. This was my town, I reminded myself; I should feel happy to be back. Instead, I felt tired and gritty, with a taste like raw soot in the back of my throat.

I was parked outside the stair tower that led up to Monica's flat. No one was going to get up those stairs without me seeing them first. Even if she recognized my car, there wasn't much evasive action that she could take. I was fairly certain that this was the only access, and I was in control of the pass.

She turned up just after seven, earlier than I had expected, in a silver Mercedes. The driver double-parked on the opposite side of the road from me, and she got out of the passenger's side. A blue wool scarf was wrapped and knotted around her neck over an expensive camel coat with the collar turned up at the back. Her eyes locked on to me.

Was the guy in the car just a cab driver?

She ducked her head down and said something into the car. I had my answer. I should have realized. Whether he was a lover or a professional minder, she wouldn't have taken the chance of running the gauntlet of potential stalkers or deranged former clients without protection.

We got out of our cars together, the driver and I, fixing Mexican stand-off stares on each other. He was young, but a big guy, with a dirty blond ponytail and heavy stubble on his face, black jeans and a loose light jacket that would be useful for concealing tools without encumbering his movements.

I held up my warrant card. 'I'm a cop,' I shouted across the road at him.

He glanced at Monica. She had obviously neglected to tell him that. He turned back to face me down. 'Miss Trent wants to get into her place.'

I smiled affably. 'And Miss Trent shall. I just need to speak to her.' I gestured towards the stairs. 'It won't take long. Up there, or in my car, whatever suits her.'

'Miss Trent only sees people by appointment.'

'You'll be obstructing a police investigation,' I warned him pleasantly.

'There is no investigation.' Monica spoke for the first time.

A man in a bus driver's uniform walked past, eyeing us curiously, smelling a situation. 'I'll talk to you in your car,' I offered another compromise.

Monica came round to the driver and put her

hand through his left arm. He took it as a cue, and they started crossing the street towards me. I backed away from them to block the entrance to the stairs. They stopped in front of me.

'You'll be done for assaulting a cop,' I told the driver. 'There's a special kind of pain that goes with that.'

Monica shook her head. 'I know people in this town. Lloyd will be defending me from an off-duty policeman, off his patch, who was trying to extort a free fuck.'

I let my deflation show.

'I'll pay you again,' I said despairingly.

'There's nothing more to tell you.'

'Please think about it,' I wheedled, moving dejectedly to the side to let them past, showing them the equivalent of baboon-ass submission. But making sure to give them not quite enough room. Making Lloyd have to nudge me contemptuously to the side to clear the space. I shuffled abjectly, and he let his guard come down in the conquest moment.

I swung for his ponytail with both hands. He read it coming, but I was too quick to leave him with any other reaction than shock and surprise. I grabbed the ponytail and ran with it, turning to spin him, feeling the live weight as he gyred off balance, the scream as his scalp took the strain of momentum and bodyweight. Somewhere in the moment, I heard Monica scream as well.

'Don't ever push me out of the fucking way again!' I yelled down into his face as I dragged him across the pavement. I was travelling beyond reason, high with it, a feeling that was arcing between elation and terror. At last I was doing

174

something real for the cause that was figure-headed by Magda, and bolstered by my frustration.

I punched down hard into his solar plexus to give him something else to think about while I shook my handcuffs out of their pocket. He doubled up with a grunt that tailed off into a gargle as his breakfast returned to his tonsils. I snapped the cuffs shut around one of his wrists, wrapped them round a post that carried a WAITING LIMITED sign, and let go of his hair as I secured his other wrist.

I backed away, bent at the waist, sucking in air. I felt light-headed and fought down nausea. A large drop of blood appeared on the pavement. I touched my cheek and my fingers came away wet. I straightened up. Monica was glaring at me, breathing hard, her hands still locked into claws. I hadn't felt her rake me.

I knew that I had to run with the crazy-man dynamic before sanity returned.

I pointed at her. 'I just wanted to talk to you,' I yelled, still breathless. 'I just wanted the explanation that you owe me. And now look at it—' I pointed at Lloyd, slumped up against the pole, gagging into the gutter, and the small circle of onlookers. 'This is not good for business, Monica. Your boyfriend cuffed to a pole, his car double-parked, causing an obstruction . . .'

'Turn him loose,' she said, catching her breath, still defiant.

'Fuck it, Monica, I've had enough. I'm leaving you to deal with this shit.' I walked away from her. 'Call your friends in high places to sort it out.'

I was checking my cheek in the vanity mirror, staunching the blood from the two rents her fingernails had made, when she tapped on my side window. She just nodded when she caught my attention, her face harsh. I gestured for her to come round to the passenger's seat.

'You were nice to me before,' I said as she climbed in.

'You were a paying customer then.'

'You've got a problem, Monica.' She didn't flicker. 'You backed up the alibi because you thought that it couldn't be safer. Five honky farm boys, as straight as they come. As safe as vouching for Jesus.'

'Get to the point.'

'It's four honky farm boys now, Monica.'

She turned her head and looked at me coldly.

'Trevor Vaughan, the one you told me you thought was gay, is dead.'

'How?'

'He hung himself.'

She looked away and shook her head. I let her finish her internal dialogue.

'Who told you to bring up the gay thing?'

She looked back at me. 'They both did.'

She still wasn't doing names. I didn't push it. 'They gave you the story?'

She nodded slowly. 'They gave me the names. I was to mention that Paul was out of it, and that Trevor didn't want to play. If they pressed me on that point, I was to say that I thought he was gay.'

'Did anyone press?'

She shook her head. 'No one was particularly interested.'

'What about the rest of them? How were you supposed to describe their behaviour?'

'Uncomplicatedly pissed.'

'Did they tell you why you were supposed to use

176

those particular details?'

'No. I didn't ask. I just assumed they wanted me to drop in something that was off-the-wall, but verifiable.' We were both silent for a moment. 'Have you got what you want now?' she asked.

'Not quite.'

She glanced into the rear-view mirror. Checking out Lloyd. 'What more?'

'I want information on who they moved on to. After you.'

She nodded, digesting this. She took a chunky address book out of her handbag, and turned her back on me. When she swung round again she handed me a loose leaf of paper. A name and address.

'Understand this: it didn't come from me.' She opened the door, but then stopped and turned back towards me. 'I want one favour from you in return.'

'What's that?'

'If you ever manage to turn this thing around, I want prior warning. I want to be able to walk in and retract my statement before people come knocking.'

'You could always do it now.'

What she gave me then was as close to a smile as we came to that day. 'Fuck off, Sergeant Capaldi.'

*   *   *

I gave Monica the key to the handcuffs. Weighing it up, I reckoned that taking the flak for their loss was preferable to trying to release an angry Lloyd. He looked like the kind of guy who might just be ready for another round of testosterone-crazed diplomacy. I couldn't face it. I had had my

177

berserker moment, and now I was just knackered.

I drove for a couple of blocks and stopped to recuperate. I was shaking. The reaction to the quick-release hormone surge was making me shivery, and my insides felt like they were twisted into an irresolvable cat's-cradle web.

I waited out the shakes and the dizziness before I checked out the piece of paper that Monica had given me.

Alexandrina Borgia.

As a professional name it was corny but effective. It cut straight to the promise of exotica and cruelty. I got my road map out to check the address. It surprised me. I had expected somewhere closer to civilization. Instead, it was a hamlet up in the hills between Monmouth and Chepstow. No telephone number.

I tried to get a hook on Alexandrina Borgia. If she was prepared to do the things that Monica had put off limits, the chances were that she had slipped most of the way down the hill. Too old for the select trade? A junkie?

I was out of practice. I had spent too much time sucking the same air as the Women's Institute. How was I going to charm a depraved, junkie hooker into my confidence?

The call from Jack Galbraith came through early enough for me to realize that he had made it one of his priorities.

'Where are you, Capaldi?' The absence of a profanity made the question even more ominous.

I was heading for the Usk turn-off. 'Almost in Dinas, sir,' I lied.

'What were you doing in Cardiff last night?'

'I was on my own time, sir.'

'I didn't ask that.'

I let the silence swell. There was nothing lighting up on my excuses board.

'Capaldi, I asked you a fucking question.'

I decided to take a chance and see where the truth led me. 'I was seeing a prostitute, sir.'

This time it was Galbraith who went silent. 'Why?' he asked after the pause, his tone an octave lower.

So far the truth was working. I decided not to push it. 'For some relief, sir.'

'I didn't mean that. I meant, why Cardiff?' I heard it then; he sounded flustered. Had I actually got Jack Galbraith embarrassed?

'I don't know where else to go, sir. I haven't found any outlets up here for . . .' I played out the hesitation '. . . you know . . . release.'

'For Christ's sake, Capaldi! That was a long way to go for some fucking relief,' he boomed, and it sounded like I had just used up this year's quota of sympathy and understanding. 'Isn't there anything a bit closer? A shepherdess or something like that?'

'Shepherdesses are pretty thin on the ground, sir, and they tend to end up with shepherds.'

He grunted. 'Okay, whatever. But in future keep out of Cardiff—they're still embarrassed to see you around there. I'm supposed to have you safely corralled. I don't want them on my back telling me that you've slipped your leash.'

'No, sir,' I concurred meekly. 'I promise you it won't happen again. In future, I'll—'

'Capaldi, I don't want to know about your sex life,' he cut in over me.

'No, sir.'

'While you're on: we've had the pathologist's

179

report on this farmer, Vaughan, and he seems to be okay with suicide. Is that your take on it?'

'I don't think there's any doubt that he did the act himself, sir.'

He groaned. 'Why do I always hear a "but" with you, Capaldi?'

'There's no suicide note. No message to his parents. I don't know him or his friends well enough, but, from what I can gather, there were no prior attempts and no talk of suicide. He was also wearing a pair of young girl's panties.'

'I saw that in the report.'

'I think that there could be something significant in that, sir.'

'You're still talking hunch, aren't you, Capaldi?'

'There's something not right in his death, sir. Coming so soon after the incident with the girl. And another one of the group has gone AWOL from the Army.'

'Hunch?' He repeated the question.

'Yes, sir.' I sighed.

'Talk to the women.'

'Sir?' I didn't hide my surprise.

'I didn't tell you that. You're on Morgan's patch—you stretch this too far and I can't protect you. But push the wives and the girlfriends, they're the ones who usually have to tidy away the smelly stuff.'

'Thank you, sir,' I said.

But he had gone. His advice already nonattributable.

*　　　*　　　*

This was good grass country, richer than anything

180

around Dinas: rolling hilltops, thorn hedges and beech trees. A big sky, high cumulus clouds blowing up from the Bristol Channel. A cold, clear winter's day, with long shadows, and a sense, in a dog's muted bark, that sound in this season could travel a lot further than it should be capable of.

The hamlet was little more than a bend in the road that had accumulated a few houses and a defunct chapel. No pub, no Post Office to ask directions in. No people. No red-light district.

Had Monica set me up?

I drove on and got lucky. A row of bungalows with a WRVS van parked outside. The driver, a woman in her late forties, was returning from one of the bungalows with an empty tray. She looked at me suspiciously.

I showed her the address that Monica had given me. She squinted at it. 'That's Mrs Morris's place.'

'Will I find Alexandrina Borgia there as well?' I asked casually, testing to see whether her trade name was known locally.

She smiled, and it wasn't entirely friendly. 'I think someone's been having you on.' But she did give me directions.

The tarmac drive to the house was a new creation, lined with horse-chestnut saplings, with paddocks to either side, behind post-and-rail ranch-style fencing. I drove into a circular area in front of a stone-barn conversion. A fenced yard fronted a stable block on the far side of the barn.

I parked and walked up to the central glazed threshing bay and rang the doorbell. I glanced around. The CCTV camera here was tucked in under the eaves, more discreet than Monica's. Through the glass I took in a big double-height space with oak-plank floors, a nice Persian rug, and the back of a big, colourful, but tastefully upholstered, chesterfield sofa. This place was definitely more *House & Garden* than ill repute.

No one was answering. I went over to the fence by the stable yard. A notice, BEWARE OF THE DOGS, was posted prominently on the gate. 'Hello?' I shouted, staying on the drive side of the fence. I took these warnings seriously.

A young woman carrying a rake came out of an open stable door. She blinked at the light, and then registered my presence. 'I'm sorry, I didn't hear you arrive, I had the radio on.' She propped the rake against the wall and came across the yard towards me.

I put her in her early thirties. Country pretty, bright green eyes, apple cheeks, loose curled blonde hair piled up on top of her head, strands drifting. She was wearing a quilted red plaid jacket, worn through to the stuffing in places, over a white Aran sweater, tight blue jeans and fitted Wellington boots.

Something in her expression as she looked at me made me aware of Monica's claw marks on my face. But she smiled. 'How can I help you?' she asked pleasantly, an English accent, but no regional shape to it that I could place.

'I'm looking for Alexandrina Borgia.'

She pulled an amusedly puzzled face. 'I'm sorry, not here.'

'I was given this address.'

'I'm Lisa Morris. I'm the only person who lives here.' She smiled sympathetically. 'And you are . . .?'

'I'm Glyn Capaldi. I'm a Detective Sergeant.' I

started to go for my warrant card, but an instinct told me to keep it in my pocket. 'But this is a private matter.'

'Sounds intriguing. Just hold on a moment, would you?' She went over to a solid timber gate that separated the yard from the walled area behind the barn conversion, and opened it. Two large, tan-brown dogs bounded in. Big muscled things with heavy faces and serious momentum. They loped around her as she came back over to me.

'These are my boys, Jason and Junior. Rhodesian Ridgebacks.'

'They didn't bark.'

She patted one of the dogs fondly. 'They knew I was listening to the radio.'

The display of her protection was for my benefit. But she wasn't exactly telling me to fuck off yet. 'Why would someone give me this address?' I asked.

She smiled mischievously. 'You're new at this, aren't you?'

'New at what?'

'Looking for Alexandrina.'

'You do know her?' I challenged.

'Only on Wednesdays and Thursdays.'

I smiled then, my suspicion confirmed. This lady was not a gatekeeper. 'And this is a Lisa Morris day?'

She returned my smile. 'Alexandrina doesn't exist any other time.' She bent down and pulled a big dog's face into hers, jiggling it. 'Does she, Junior?'

'It's important that I speak to her.'

She stood up and studied me for a moment, absently rubbing the dog's ear between her finger

183

and thumb. 'Why would she want to speak to you?'

I was being offered a chance to pitch. 'I'm concerned for the past, current and future welfare of a young woman who may have been abducted.'

She frowned and cocked her head. 'If you are a policeman and you're concerned that some young woman has been abducted, it wouldn't be a private matter, surely?' she asked, playing it mock simple.

'It wouldn't be, if the men involved hadn't managed to persuade the powers that be that they are beyond reproach.'

'And you're not persuaded?'

'No. As I said, I'm worried.'

'And what has Alexandrina got to do with this?'

'I think she might know the men concerned.'

She nodded slowly. 'And you want to see what she can do to de-persuade the powers that be?'

'No. I wouldn't ask something like that. I just need to add to my own knowledge of these men. Try to understand what they might be capable of.'

She dropped the ingénue pose and looked at me carefully. 'Why are you doing this?'

'Because I would feel so much worse knowing about it and not doing something. I once didn't, and a woman died.' I decided to offer this woman real trust. 'This hasn't been easy.' I turned my cheek towards her and gingerly touched Monica's scratch marks. 'This is one of my rewards. And part of the bride price I've had to pay to get this far is to let a creep take a photograph of me simulating sex with a dead cow.'

A small smile flickered. 'Did you enjoy that experience?'

'No. I felt totally and utterly humiliated by it.'

'Some people long to achieve a state like that.' It

184

was a statement, no trace of bitterness or sadness in it. Just flat knowledge. Up close like this, I could make out the milky pale freckles under her eyes. Jesus, she looked so young, so innocent, so pure.

'Can you help me?'

She had already decided before she nodded. 'Come through here. Jason, Junior, back off!' she yelled, opening the gate into the yard for me.

The dogs spiralled backwards, playfully leaping for each other's throats. I watched them warily as I came through the gate. 'They'll stay back there?' I asked.

'As long as I tell them to.' She didn't try to persuade me that they were essentially soft and harmless.

She led me through the gate into a paved area at the rear of the barn. A path led through a small, formal knot garden with low, neatly clipped box borders, to a single-storey stone building that ran at right angles from the barn. I followed her to a wide, weathered oak door.

She turned in front of the door. 'I'm trusting you with this. If you turn holy or judgemental on me, you walk.' She smiled, but her look was penetrating. 'Understood?'

'Absolutely.'

The door opened grudgingly. She switched on some low-level lighting and closed the door behind us. The room had the damp, chalky smell of limewash. My eyes adjusted. It was a small lobby, a corridor to the barn conversion, and two closed doors led off the space. A pair of off-white cotton-covered sofas faced each other, framing an abstract tapestry on the wall.

'Sit down,' she said, pointing to one of the sofas

185

while she took the other, the dogs flopping down at her feet.

I glanced at the tapestry again as I sat down. It wasn't an abstract. It was a representation in graduated pinks of a huge, flared vulva. In both bottom corners, symmetrically placed, two penises were drooping out of tumescence under the weight of barbed crowns.

She saw my recognition. 'It was a commission.'

'Alexandrina's?'

She bowed her head in acknowledgement. 'Definitely Alexandrina's.'

'Are you a dominatrix?'

She shrugged. 'If that's what the occasion calls for. I can also be a Sweet Mistress.'

'What does that mean?'

'I take shit.' She grinned elfishly. 'Sometimes literally.'

'They hurt you?'

'We agree on the level of pain allowed beforehand.'

'Why?'

She raised her eyebrows warningly.

'I'm not judging. I'm just curious. You look like you could have so much else going for you.'

She smiled sagaciously, spreading her hands, 'Which would give me this place, my dogs, my horses? Working two days a week?'

'What about your husband?'

'I'm not married.'

'I was told that you were Mrs Morris.'

'I don't discourage it. The title makes me safe in the locals' eyes. I think the story has it that I'm a young widow in retreat up here to get over my grief.' She laughed at the irony behind it.

I shook my head. I was still hearing neither regret nor rancour. 'Doesn't it get to you? The things you must have to do?'

'What's the worst thing you've ever had to do in your job?'

I didn't have to think about it. 'I was there when we recovered the body of a child who had been raped, murdered and stuffed into a sewer pipe.'

She shook her head in sympathy. 'Terrible . . . Terrible . . . But you're still functioning. You compartmentalize. You learn to stuff it all in the jar called necessary evil and screw the lid down tight. Despite what you may think, I don't have to deal with anything as bad as you must encounter. I'm playing a game. I can leave it behind.' She grinned. 'Honest. I'm very focused and selfish, I'm totally reward driven.'

I believed her. But I knew that it wasn't going to stop me walking away from here and worrying about her in the future. I leaned forward to pat one of the dogs on its flank. It twisted its head to look round at me. I didn't know whether I was communing with Jason or Junior. *Stay vigilant*, I willed the dog. Lisa looked amused, as if she had just read my mind. 'Tell me the story.'

I explained about Magda. How the group had used a prostitute as an alibi, but I didn't elaborate on Monica. I told her about Trevor Vaughan hanging himself, Boon disappearing, but not about the possibility of the escape to Ireland. I wanted to keep the tension in the air.

'Which of these men should I know?' she asked.

'Gordon McGuire and Les Tucker.'

She shook her head apologetically. 'For everyone's protection, I don't do real names.'

I described them.

She chewed on her bottom lip while she thought about it. Giving me a pained look. 'No. It's too wide. Fits too many people. Can you narrow it down?'

'I think that they would have been together.'

She nodded encouragingly. 'That helps.'

But it didn't eliminate the competition. I stopped myself from speculating about the possible range of her group activity, and concentrated on trying to come up with an individual signature for Gordon or Les. 'One of them works in the forest,' I offered. Perhaps, in intimacy, he smelled of sap or resin, or chainsaw lubricant.

She nodded slowly. Something arriving. 'I think I've got him. Most of my players are sedentary, business types. His face was red. His arms were tanned up to his biceps, and every time I saw him he would have fresh cuts and gashes on them. Describe the other one again,' she instructed.

I described Gordon.

'Yes. They used to always arrive together in one car.'

I picked up on her use of the past tense. 'Used to?'

'I don't see them any more. I haven't for a while now.'

'What did they want from you? Dominatrix or Sweet Mistress?'

'Neither. They wanted to humiliate me.' She smiled at my expression. 'It's not uncommon.'

'Can you explain please?'

'Basically, they wanted me to be an inferior species. Very rarely did we ever have straight sex. If it was penetrative, they were always behind, and it was invariably anal. Usually, they preferred me to masturbate them and they'd aim to ejaculate into my face or hair. Then they would urinate and defecate on me.' She saw me wince. 'Are you okay with this?'

'Is there more?'

'The other one, not the lumberjack, was into coprophilia.'

'What's that?'

'He had a thing about his own shit. He would try to manage a hard enough stool to penetrate me while it was still inside him.'

'Oh, for fuck's sake . . .' I groaned.

'I warned you.'

'I'm sorry. I really am grateful for this.'

'Is it helping you?'

'I think so.' I closed my eyes to clear the grime from my head, to try to return to analytical. 'Why do you think they wanted to treat you like this?'

She shook her head. 'I make a point of avoiding the psychology.'

'When they came here . . . These sessions. Did they take part in them together or separately?'

'Separately. To start with. One would wait out here while the other was with me.' She inclined her head towards a door. 'But they were both into the same things. I knew they would be discussing them, sharing notes. So I was eventually able to persuade them to join up and do the session together. They took a bit of convincing, but in the end they realized that they got bonus voyeur's perks out of it.'

'You were happy with that?'

'Of course. It shortened the session. I'm not paid by the hour. And, if I'm going to be pissed on it makes sense to have only one set of sheets to wash.'

She thought about something. 'I never did get them to touch each other though.'

'You tried?'

She grinned. 'Why not? I'm a crusader. If I could have given them the taste for screwing each other it would have eased my laundry bills.'

'You would have lost the trade.'

'I did anyway.'

'How long ago was that?'

She thought about it. 'They probably started tailing off about three, three and a half years ago.'

I thought about it. I would have to check, but I was pretty sure that Gordon had been married for longer than that, and Les's relationship with Sara had been described as long term. 'Do you think that their partners could have started substituting for you?' I asked, voicing my thoughts.

She laughed. 'Darling,' she mimicked, 'let's do it differently tonight. Let me squat over your face and I'll share my curry.'

It was an awful image, but I laughed as well. She was infectious. 'Could they just have lost the taste for it?' I ventured.

She shrugged. 'It happens. Usually, it's a partner finding out. Shaming them. But both of them . . .?' She trumpeted a note of scepticism.

Why had they left Alexandrina? They had moved on from Monica for something more extreme. What new line of momentum were they following here?

'Can I ask you something?'

She smiled at me expectantly. 'For the right price, I can always find a vacancy.'

I felt myself colouring. 'Lisa's more my type.'

She leaned across a recumbent dog and touched

my knee gently. 'That's kind. But Lisa's not available.'

I nodded. 'Can you tell me what you called them?'

'My players come up with their own pseudonyms. The lumberjack wanted to be called Shaft, and the other one was Sim. I didn't understand the reference.'

I wouldn't have either, before they turned me into Country Boy. 'Simmental,' I explained, 'it's a breed of bull.'

11

The hairdressing salon was closed for lunch when I got back to Dinas. It was small, a converted double shopfront with a central door, both windows taken up with product ads and display shots of the shiny heads of sultry models who had probably never breathed the air west of Chiswick, never mind Dinas. Over the front, a sign in purple cursive script against a white background read A CUT ABOVE.

I parked diagonally opposite, where I could monitor the comings and goings without being obvious.

On my way from Lisa Morris's, I had put a call in to the children's home in Manchester to see if they had any information on the whereabouts of Donna and Colette. They stonewalled me. They informed me that they could do nothing over the telephone and that any request for information on any of their charges, past or present, should be sent in writing on official notepaper with a verifiable contact name, telephone number and a personal endorsement from God. Laudable, I suppose, given the present climate, but a bitch so far as sleuthing and spontaneity were concerned.

'Do you still send kids to Dinas?' I had asked after this exchange, pretending it was a jaunty afterthought.

'We don't send kids anywhere. We're not a mail-order service.'

I chuckled, even though the guy had not meant it as a joke. I was trying to build bridges, show them that I was harmless. 'They used to come here in the summer holidays. To train to be hairdressers.'

'We don't have placements there any more,' he had said, putting the phone down. Forthcoming bastard.

So, what had happened to sour A Cut Above?

As a cop I already knew that Friday afternoons were high season for betting shops and pubs. I hadn't realized the same went for hairdressing salons in the sticks. When the CLOSED sign was removed at two o'clock, a procession of older ladies arrived from all corners, converging on the place.

I gave them time to settle before I walked over. The bell that the door was fitted with was totally redundant, as all eyes were on me even before I had turned the handle. Ladies on seats flicking through magazines, ladies under hair driers, even the lady with her head dripping over a basin managed to sneak a look in.

Three younger women in purple tabards were standing behind the cutting and styling chairs. Also staring at me. I nodded and smiled, zapping the room with charm. 'Good afternoon, ladies. I'm Detective Sergeant Capaldi, and I'm looking for

192

Sara Harris?'

'I'm Sara Harris,' the woman behind the middle chair announced, tone and expression making it plain that she was not pleased to see me. She was short, with slickly cut, dyed-red hair, and enough make-up to service the entire cast of a kabuki production.

'I'm sorry to disturb you, this is purely routine, but I do need to ask you some questions.'

'Can't you see how busy we are?' she snapped crossly, flourishing a pair of scissors to demonstrate the point.

'I know, I'm sorry, but it's quotas . . .' I shrugged and beamed at all the ladies. They at least were dying to hear my business.

Sara leaned forward. 'Sorry, Mrs Good, I won't be a minute.' She turned, already moving, flinging the instruction at me: 'This way.'

She took me into a back room that smelled of shampoo and sharp chemicals. It was stacked with boxes, and a younger girl in the same tabard was washing cups out in a sink. 'Go out and see who wants coffee, Kylie—and don't come back in here until I tell you.'

Kylie scurried out, giving me a look that made me feel like a guy who clubs baby seals for a living.

'Les warned me that you might come round here to harass me,' Sara said, her back to a barred window, the light giving her head a magenta-tinged penumbra.

'This has nothing to do with Mr Tucker, and I promise I have no intention of harassing you. As I explained, this is just a routine inquiry. We have been asked by colleagues in Nottingham to see if we can help with information.'

193

'Nottingham?' she asked, bewildered.

'Donna Gallagher used to work here, didn't she?'

'Donna . . .?' She turned the question back on me, apparently genuinely confused.

'Donna Gallagher, she was one of the girls from the children's home in Manchester.'

'Oh, Donna . . . That Donna . . .' She shook her head, frowning. 'That was a long time ago. I gave up taking those kids two years ago.' She calculated. 'We're going back at least three, four years? How am I expected to know anything about her now?'

'They thought that she might have kept in touch. Or you'd know where she went after she left here?'

'She went back to Manchester. Back to the home.'

'What about the second time?'

She frowned. 'What second time?' Her surprise sounded genuine.

'The following summer. When she had to work at the Sychnant Nursing Home because you didn't have any vacancies.'

She shook her head, another layer of annoyance showing. But she was also puzzled. 'I don't know who told you that. Donna never came back here looking for work. She would have known better.'

'Why is that?'

'Because she was a lazy, deceitful little tart, and she knew exactly what I thought of her. So, if she's what you're wasting my time for, I want to get back to my clients.'

Was I hearing jealousy?

'How did Donna get on with Mr Tucker?'

The question didn't faze her. She smiled cattily. 'Donna thought that we were all redneck hillbillies. She made no bones about demonstrating how

194

backward she thought we all were. The only person she did get on with was Wendy Evans, but I wouldn't get too excited about interrogating her, 'cos she's hightailed it as well.'

'How did she get to know Wendy Evans?' I tried to keep it casual, shield the spark from her.

'Wendy was helping out that summer too.' She moved towards the door and held it open for me, activating the drone of conversations from the salon. 'So, sorry I can't be of any help, Sergeant, but I've got a business to run.'

'What about Colette Fletcher?'

She partially closed the door. 'What about her?'

'You remember her?'

'Vaguely. Now that you've brought Donna up. But she was even longer ago.' Suspicion formed. 'Are the Nottingham police meant to be looking for her as well?'

'No, just curious. She came back to work at the Sychnant Nursing Home too. After you didn't have a vacancy for her.'

'Is that a fact?' Her expression didn't flicker. She opened the door again. 'Will you please go now?'

I headed for the front door, a generic public servant's smile fixed for all the ladies, aware of Sara's eyes locked on my back.

'Glyn . . .'

I spun just as I was reaching for the door handle. Sally was sitting looking up at me, a magazine on her lap. 'You weren't here . . .?' I stumbled, wondering whether I had walked past her without noticing on my way in.

'No, I've only just arrived.'

She was such a fresh contrast from the farmers' wives and the Townswomen's Guild types that

195

made up the rest of the clientele. 'You come here?' I blurted, tailing off before I put my foot in it.

She smiled, picking up my meaning, and lowered her voice: 'Believe me, it's the only place in town. Literally.' She cocked her head and looked at me mock appraisingly. 'You shouldn't have bothered, though.'

'Bothered?' I asked, puzzled.

'Making yourself look beautiful for me.' The ladies on either side of her chuckled.

Once again, Sally Paterson had caused me to redden. 'I'll see you later,' I whispered. I caught a glimpse of Sara watching us. Registering that this was more than just casual. I had wanted her to report back on my interest in Donna and Colette to see if that raised any smoke in the hills.

But Sally I had wanted to keep private.

*   *   *

I went into The Fleece through the back yard. A few brace of pheasants were hanging by their necks, heads hunched, from a hook beside the back door. I sniffed instinctively as I went through. Sandra Williams hated the task of plucking these things so much that she often deliberately left them to slide past the point of no return.

She was where I had expected to find her. Sitting at the kitchen table with a mug of coffee, a paperback, and a cigarette stretched out towards the extractor fan over the range cooker. She looked up when she sensed my presence. She just nodded. Nothing looked like it could surprise Sandra any more. 'David's gone to the cash-and-carry.'

'It's you I wanted to see.'

She squinted up at me and frowned. 'What have you done to your face?'

I touched my cheek reflexively. I had forgotten about Monica's scratches. No wonder all the ladies in the salon had shown such an interest in me. Nothing to do with my natural charm after all, just that I looked like I was on the damaged end of a juicy tale of romantic entanglement.

'I got on the wrong side of an angry woman. Professionally,' I added.

Her eyebrows formed the essence of a shrug. 'I thought the vigilantes might have caught up with you already.' She used her forearm to clear a space at the table for me while I made some coffee. 'If I were you, I would to stick to using the back door for a while.'

'*Persona non grata*?' I asked, sitting down opposite her.

'I'm serious, Glyn, it's getting ugly now. They're really getting worked up about you and Trevor Vaughan.'

'Who's doing the stirring?'

'Paul Evans. David's had a few quiet words with Les Tucker and the McGuires, but they either can't or won't control him.'

'What's he saying?'

'It's a load of nonsense, but you know what people here are like.'

'Specifically, Sandra.'

She flushed and turned away to flick her ash. 'He's saying that it's you who's really the homosexual. That you tried it on with Trevor Vaughan, and when he spurned you, you started spreading the stories against him.'

I raised my eyebrows sceptically. 'Spurned?'

She smiled back weakly. 'We're old-fashioned people.'

'I know only too well.'

'It may be absurd and pathetic to you, but they take it seriously. You can't just laugh it off, it could easily turn nasty.'

'Dracula's villagers?'

She frowned. 'What?'

'Nothing. I just had an image of a crowd in smocks, with pitchforks and flaming torches, getting ready to attack Dracula's castle.'

'It's not funny.'

'I know, and thanks for the warning.'

So they were using Paul Evans as the front man. The angry mouthpiece. Was that a piece of strategy that he was aware of? Were they setting up their fall guy in case the thing backfired and I ended up in hospital, or worse? Could anyone predict what sort of a bad momentum this might have? Sandra was right, it wasn't funny.

'Well?' she asked.

I pulled a blank face, wondering if I had missed a question.

'You wanted to see me?' she prompted.

'Right.' I pulled my notebook out. 'How well do you know Sara Harris?'

'We're not intimates. We'll say hello in the street. She'll come in here for a drink and a meal with Les Tucker. Occasionally, she'll have a bit of a do with some of her girls.'

'You don't use her?'

'No, I always go to the same girl in Newtown.'

'So you didn't know the girls from Manchester she used to have working for her over the summer holidays?'

'I didn't know them personally. I'd see them in the town.' She smiled teasingly. 'You wait; when you start to notice strangers you'll know that you've really become one of us.'

I ignored that grim prognosis. 'Anything distinguish them?'

She thought about it. 'Not really. They were all young, some were a bit brash, some were a bit loud, but that was probably defensive, being away from what they knew.'

'Did you know that at least two of them came back to Dinas the following year?'

She shook her head. 'No.'

'Neither did Sara,' I said, reminding myself, underscoring it.

'Is that significant?'

'I don't know. Why didn't Sara have a girl last summer?'

'Shouldn't you be asking her that?'

'Something tells me I've managed to blow myself out there.'

She smiled. 'I don't remember it ever coming up as an issue.' She thought about it, a memory rising. 'I tell a lie. There was some talk, actually. The last girl who came to work for her was black.' She grinned. 'Now, she really did stand out in Dinas. The rumour was that Sara didn't want another coloured one, and that the home wouldn't let her pick and choose.'

'Do you remember the girl's name? Or the one from the summer before?'

'Pass.'

'Zoë McGuire?'

She cocked her head at the change of subject. 'What about her?'

'Where would I find her during the day?'

'The auctioneers.'

'She works with Gordon?'

'She's on the accounts side.'

It was still the lion's den. I swallowed my coffee and stood to leave. An afterthought arriving. 'Where did they stay?' I asked.

'Where did who stay?'

'The Manchester girls.'

She frowned, retrieving the memory. 'That's right . . . we used to talk about Sara being a bit mean where that was concerned. All that space she had at her place, and she got them to stay in a run-down old caravan of Les's.'

*   *   *

The light was going when I left The Fleece. Street lights in their first half-hearted, sad-orange flare-up. Low cloud ceiling, the poison-tar smell from coal fires and fuel-oil boilers dropping to pavement level.

I caught a flash of the head behind my car just as it ducked down.

'Hey . . .' I yelled, starting to run. Caught in the moment, not thinking that this could be planted there to pull me into something less avoidable. That thought only arrived when the boy stood up and tore off down the street. I looked across and saw the two pre-teen girls that he had been hiding from.

Just to be on the safe side, I checked the car for damage. No tyres deflated, and no nails wedged, waiting for me to move off. Nothing rammed up the exhaust pipe.

I was going to have to remember to be careful

where I parked in future.

In the car I lay back against the seat and waited for stillness to let my recently acquired history coalesce. Somewhere in the centrifuge that was spinning all that information a lump was forming. I worked at it with mental butter pats. Shaping it slowly.

Gordon and Les get the taste for sex from a prostitute.

Nothing too unusual in that. They are young when they start. Country kids. Monica is city, part of a whole strange Wonderland experience. They get to sow their wild oats with an experienced lady who doesn't laugh at their clumsiness.

Somewhere down the line, Gordon marries Zoë, and Les takes up with Sara. But they keep up the visits to Monica. The bit of illicit on the side. More unusual now, but still within the broad spectrum of bozo male behaviour.

Enter Alexandrina.

Goodbye, Monica, who is not providing the level of variety and satisfaction that they now demand. Or need? Is it an addictive degeneration? To get your rocks off voiding yourself on a woman? Or are they just upping the ante for the entertainment value? Either way, they have now narrowed the behaviour band down into deviant.

They are now officially, in my book, sad sick fucks.

But this is where the shape starts to get really interesting.

Why did they eventually stop their visits to Alexandrina?

I had two answers to that. Actually, I had three, but the one in which they saw the error of their ways and renounced Sodom for eternity wasn't worth the waste of mental activity.

The other two answers had one thing in common. They no longer needed Alexandrina.

Because Zoë and Sara had stepped in as substitutes?

Or because they had managed to find a replacement?

I tried to picture a scenario where I could get Zoë McGuire to tell me if she let her husband piss on her or sodomize her. But, short of a hospital bed, restraining straps and scopolamine, I could see no clever way into extracting that information. I had already realized that Sara Harris was not even a starter on that circuit.

So I concentrated on the other premise. Beginning with Colette Fletcher. Who had arrived in Dinas to work at A Cut Above six years ago. And had then returned, without Sara's knowledge, the following summer.

So, what brought her back?

According to Monica, Gordon and Les had switched to Alexandrina six years ago. At roughly the same time Colette arrives in Dinas to work for Les's girlfriend, and to stay in his caravan. With those connections and with a town this size, Colette and Les have to meet. And Gordon is Les's best buddy. They share stuff. So here we have the boys starting out on the learning curve of the copro-deviant syllabus. Did they also start using Colette for the practical side of their homework?

There was a glitch built into that that I couldn't resolve. If Colette was being used as a sexual toilet, why the fuck did she come back for more the next year?

This was where I needed Colette to still be around. Installed in a fuck-pad that the boys had provided. But she had run away from the Sychnant Nursing Home after that second summer. Had the boys tried to push her a bit too hard?

It was a question I couldn't answer. But I had the pattern repeating itself with Donna Gallagher. The first summer in Dinas to work with Sara and stay in Les's caravan. Meet the boys. And then return the following summer without telling Sara.

And then run away.

About two and a half years ago, according to Joan Harvey. How had the boys managed to contain their urges since then? Or hadn't they? Was that the reason Sara wasn't having girls to work the summer shift any more?

Meanwhile, our boys are getting more and more pent-up.

Until Magda drops like manna into their laps. An East European girl in transit. No one keeping tabs on her whereabouts or welfare.

A sudden terrible thought leapt in. Had Trevor Vaughan seen something so awful in the hut that night that it had caused him to take the third way out between his conscience and his loyalty to his friends?

I jumped in another direction. Les's caravan: the original fuck-pad. Sandra had given me the location so I headed over there. When I got out of the car there was a chill in the damp air. It was light enough that I could see immediately this was a nonstarter.

Too much light, that was the problem. The caravan was sited alongside the one section of road improvements that had occurred in Dinas in the last ten years: a new roundabout, complete with a bank of high-intensity sodium lighting.

The caravan perched, slightly askew, on crumbling breeze blocks, between a tyre-fitting unit, and a blank spur off the roundabout that patiently awaited the arrival of backers and takers for Dinas's first business park.

Day and night, the comings and goings to that caravan would have been under the scrutiny of everyone who drove past. And it would have been worse at night: any deviant passion bathed in streetlight, and strafed by the headlights of vehicles sweeping into and out of town.

I drove home disappointed, but not too disillusioned. I now had a working hypothesis that tied all of my missing girls together. Maybe Boon, too, if what really happened at the hut that night was bad enough to have caused Trevor to top himself.

Now I just had to find some way to prove it. Also, perversely, I had to hope that I might be wrong. Otherwise, I had to live with the prospect of Magda being out there somewhere under the patronage of a couple of perverts.

* * *

'Do you like Indian?' I asked as I walked Sally to the taxi.

'Indian!' she exclaimed, more mirthful than ironic. 'Gosh, Sergeant Capaldi, you sure know how to spoil a girl.'

But in Dinas, if you wanted more than Chinese takeaway or microwaved pub fayre, Indian was what you got. And the Golden Mogul was where you got it. It was located out of town in what had formerly been a big roadhouse pub called the Owen Glendower.

The waiter took Sally's coat, and I immediately felt the guilt over Magda dissipating, corroded by possibility and attraction. Her hair was plumped and sleek with a discreet tinge of red through it. The bone weariness from our first encounters was replaced by an expression of amusement and expectation. She was wearing a short, low-cut, tight-waisted black dress, with black tights. A double row of pearls looped down to the moan-inducing lift of her breasts.

'You look great,' I said, meaning it.

'Thank you.' She dipped her head, pleased. 'And now I can ask: what happened to you?' She brought two fingers up over the scratches on my cheek like a faith healer.

'Line of duty.'

'Cop-out.' She grinned.

'Why didn't you comment before?'

'You were working. It wasn't my place.' Very briefly, she let her fingers touch the scratches.

We kept the talk light. Stayed in the froth that floated over the darker stuff. We skirted round our marriages. Places we had been, places we would like to go to. But I could sense that she was homing in on biography.

'Do you speak Italian?' she asked.

'Not very well.'

'With a name like Capaldi?'

'My father came over from Italy to help his uncle who'd been a prisoner of war and stayed on and started a business in Cardiff. It wasn't meant to be permanent, but he met my mother and turned into a born-again Welshman.'

'He wasn't a policeman?'

'No, a wine and olive-oil importer.'

'Sounds glamorous.'

'It was hard work. Making the sales. You have to remember that this was in the days before universal wine drinking, and olive oil was something you bought in tiny bottles from the chemist to rub into babies' bums.'

'You didn't want to go into the business?'

I shook my head, skipping over it. Then realized that if this lady and I were going anywhere, she deserved frankness. 'I didn't have the choice,' I said, offering her the opening.

'No?'

'When I was younger, a friend and I got busted in Spain on our way home from Morocco. We were charged with possession of marijuana.'

She smiled conspiratorially. 'Guilty?'

I returned the smile and shrugged. 'Whatever. It was potentially quite serious though. There had been an increase in the rumblings over Gibraltar, so there was political stuff mixed in. I had to call my father to see if he could bail us out. He had a friend in Cardiff, a retired senior cop with connections. My father made me a deal: if he got us out of Spain, I would join the police force.'

She looked puzzled. 'Why?'

'To turn me into a serious citizen.'

'Would he have left you there?'

'Let's just say that this was not my first misdemeanour. Hence the pressure.'

'So, not exactly a crusading ambition since early childhood?'

'Not quite. I enjoy the work though. And I think

my father saw that I would.'

'Dinas?'

'Pardon?' But I was stalling, I knew what she meant.

'You told me that you used to be in Cardiff.'

She had remembered well. She met my eyes. Her expression was the equivalent of squeezing my hand.

I bowed my head into it. 'I met a farmer. I shouldn't have, the case was nothing to do with me. He was down in Cardiff trying to persuade his daughter to come home. Vice had found her working for a pimp called Nick Bessant. Underage but with a grown-up crack habit. What none of us knew at the time was that Bessant already had the farmer's son working for him. Gay extortion tricks and porn films in return for feeding his junk habit. This little shit had gone home and told his baby sister about the Life. Turned her head. The farmer loses his other kid.'

'I think that I may have read about this. What's coming?'

I nodded. 'We had something to charge Bessant with. Something unrelated. By this time I'd been running around Cardiff with the farmer, on my own time, trying to track down the daughter, who had run away from him again. Mind you, he hadn't said a word to me about the grief he was holding for his son. Anyway, someone comes up with an address for Bessant and I get the call. I agree to take the farmer along with me, thinking he'll get some small consolation from Bessant's arrest.'

I had missed it at first, in the back of his beat-up Land Rover, my eyes on the two dark dogs with white chest flashes, cowering from too much urban-weird information. The shotgun was empty then. When he broke it open, I had sighted through the barrels, seen a street light's cataract penumbra through the two oiled, empty holes.

'I let the farmer keep the gun.'

'You thought it was empty.'

I shook my head. Had I honestly believed that my fucking goodness was touching everything with safety? That an empty gun would stay empty because I refused to believe that there could be any other possibility?

'I missed it. We were standing there in that squalid room, the farmer and Bessant staring each other down. They both knew, though. It was only when the farmer told me he'd swear that he forced me to bring him here at gunpoint that I realized, too late, this was too sophisticated for the man. And then Bessant sang.'

'Sang?'

'"Farmer John", a Neil Young song. He only got as far as the first line.' I shrugged, trying not to recall the pink miasma of blood and brain matter. 'They put a spin on it. I was the briefly celebrated survivor of a hostage situation.'

She nodded. 'That's what I remember. Just the event. I didn't remember your name to put to it.'

'You probably also missed the little item that came later, announcing my breakdown. Then they quietly shipped me off to the Gulag.'

She leaned across and covered my hand with hers. 'Welcome, Comrade.'

We both laughed.

We were lighter and happier with each other after that. It was a shame it couldn't last.

It was Friday night, the pubs hadn't turned out,

so it was too early for it to be busy. But it went even quieter when they walked in. Sally picked up on it first. I followed her look towards the entrance. Three of them. Obviously rugby players. The prop-and-block variety. *No-neck monsters*, to quote Tennessee Williams, although in his case he had been describing children. These guys were far removed from childhood.

The biggest one was Paul Evans.

The head waiter approached them, smiling deferentially. Evans nodded curtly without looking at him, and made a beeline for us. The other two stayed at the entrance with the head waiter, who was now looking distinctly apprehensive.

Evans nodded slowly, and gave us a big, sloppy smile. 'I'd watch out if I were you, Mrs Paterson, or he'll try and drill you from behind.'

'Go away, Paul,' Sally said wearily. She knew that our night was now broken.

'Out under false pretences are you, Sergeant? Pretending that you really like women?'

I felt Sally's hand clutch my knee under the table. After the first shock, I realized that it was restraining. It was also unnecessary. Paul Evans was a slob and a bully, but also huge, which meant that in this unfair world he could get away with it.

But I could still play bravado. 'Don't get jealous, Paul. Wait for me in the car park, I've got enough left in me to shag the three of you.'

'Glyn,' Sally warned.

'Fucking queer,' he snarled under his breath, balling his fists.

'People, Paul . . .' I circled my hands, checking him '. . . witnesses. You'll be up for assault.'

'We'll see you in the car park.' He wheeled away,

209

back to his friends.

'Good,' I called after him.

'You shouldn't have aggravated him,' Sally said, leaning forward.

'He was already primed,' I told her, taking out my mobile phone.

'Who are you calling?'

'First the taxi.' I smiled at her reassuringly. 'And then the guard of honour.'

*   *   *

Emrys Hughes didn't like it. His professional duty was compromising his impulse, which was to join the three sulking rugby players into beating me into a mousse. Instead, he had to escort Sally and me across the Golden Mogul's car park to the waiting taxi.

'I had none of these problems before you arrived here, Capaldi,' he moaned.

'No, you just had your good people,' I said, nodding across at the three glowering men. 'Keep them away from me, Sergeant Hughes. They're big, but they're stupid, and I will make sure that they get real time in a bad jail if they pursue this.'

'Goodnight, Mrs Paterson,' he said, ignoring me, slamming the taxi door shut on us.

'What's going to happen, Glyn?' Sally asked anxiously.

'They'll tire of it.' I glanced back through the rear window at the receding light of the Golden Mogul. 'No one really believes it, anyway. They just have to find an outsider to blame for an event that doesn't fit their experience.'

She reached her hand into mine, lacing our

210

fingers. She let her head drop on to my shoulder. 'I'm not going to sleep with you tonight,' she whispered. She saw my face fall flat. 'Sorry,' she added with amused commiseration.

'Couldn't you give a guy a little hope?' I asked.

'I'm probably not going to sleep with you tonight.'

'That's better.'

We squeezed our hands together. This was fine. The big bad boys behind us. Driving through the night with her head on my shoulder. Night clouds and the tops of trees scudding past my eyeline. 'Did Boon ever know the young black girl from Manchester who worked for Sara Harris two summers ago?' I asked casually.

She stiffened. She unlocked her hand from mine, whipped her head off my shoulder before I had finished the question.

'What's the matter?' I asked, bewildered.

'You don't know?' she challenged.

'It was just a casual question . . . not business,' I lied.

'You have no idea how that grates. The crap I have had to put up with around here. I had hoped that you were above it.'

'How what grates?'

'Racial stereotyping. Assuming that because the girl was black, Boon would be drawn to her.'

Oh shit . . . I winced internally. 'I wasn't stereotyping,' I protested, back-pedalling. 'Or if I was, it's because they were both young, not because they were black.' Which, of course, had been my first thought. I had forgotten how sensitive women can be. How quickly romance could turn precarious.

211

'Boon wasn't here when she was around,' she explained, slightly mollified. 'You should have asked me.'

'You knew her?'

'Yes, she used to wash my hair at Sara's. A nice kid.'

'Called?'

'Flower.'

'Fleur?'

'No, Flower, the proper English spelling. Flower Robinson. Why did you want to know?'

'She came up in conversation. Any idea what happened to her?'

She shook her head. I didn't press it.

I got out of the taxi at Sally's. I glanced at her. She wouldn't meet my eyes. I told the driver to wait. She didn't protest. I walked her to her door.

'I'm sorry, I didn't mean to spoil things,' I said.

She smiled at me wanly. 'I overreacted. I think I was nervous. I haven't done this for a while.'

'Neither have I.'

'Good.'

We laughed silently, breaking the clot, and we both realized then that we could have stood there for a long time, slowly moving in closer to each other, not necessarily taking it anywhere.

But sadly we were adults now. The night was cold. And I had a taxi waiting.

12

Bryn Jones called me the following morning. When I had finished the call I remembered that it was Saturday. He shouldn't have been at work.

'We hear that you've run into a little local difficulty.'

'Who told you that, sir?'

'Concerned colleagues.'

That meant Morgan and Hughes. Concerned only because I was complicating their lives.

'We can pull you out of there.'

I groaned inwardly. Not so long ago that would have been music to my ears. 'No thanks, sir.'

'O-U-T,' he spelled it, 'you've been begging us for this.'

'It's what they want, sir.'

'What who wants?'

'A certain section of the community is holding me responsible for the death of Trevor Vaughan.'

'You don't think that was kosher?' he asked, a note of cautious tension rising into his voice.

'I'm pretty sure that he did it to himself. It's why he did it that intrigues me.'

'We could order you out,' he warned.

'I'd rather stay. I'd like to try and find out what's behind this reaction.'

'Just don't leave it too late to jump.'

'I won't. Thank you, sir.'

'Use my mobile number if you need anything.'

'There is one thing that would be useful . . .'

'What's that?' he asked warily.

I gave him the details of the children's home in

Manchester, and asked if he could set it up so that they would receive a call from me as one of the good guys. I sensed the pause on the line. He would be debating with himself whether to ask me what I wanted this for. Knowing that my answer would probably make him refuse the request.

He didn't ask, just said that he would see what he could do. 'Take care of yourself and behave responsibly,' he finished gruffly.

I pondered the nature of the call. Morgan had obviously advised Carmarthen about the situation here. Jack Galbraith had had to offer to pull me out to cover his arse. By refusing, I was being the obstinate one.

But why hadn't they just ordered me out? Since when had Jack Galbraith ever offered me a choice that he hadn't loaded? So either he felt some deep instinctual rumbling that I might be on to something, or he just wanted to irritate the shit out of Inspector Morgan.

The phone rang again. It was too soon for Bryn to have organized the call to the children's home.

'Glyn?'

'Sally. How are you?' I let her hear my surprise morph into pleasure.

'I'm fine. I'm calling to apologize for last night.'

'You've nothing to apologize for.'

'Yes, I have. I went all stiff and snotty on you. I want to make up for it.'

'There's no need.'

'Yes, there is. I want to show you that I can be fun to be with. So, it's Saturday, let's do something together today.'

I winced. There was nothing I would have liked better, but I had already allocated this as too

214

opportune a day to miss. 'I'd really love to, Sally, but I can't, I've got to work,' I explained, hoping that she was catching my genuine disappointment.

'Okay.'

'We could go out again tonight,' I offered.

'I don't think I want to.'

'Ah, right,' I replied, trapping my regret manfully.

'I think we should stay in,' she announced brightly, amused at having caught me out. 'I'll cook you a meal. Tell me, what would you like?'

'Surprise me,' I said gaily, lifted again.

I hung up, regretting the fact that I had already scheduled the day. But I had to try to talk to Zoë McGuire alone. And as it was a Saturday in winter it would be a safe bet that a red-blooded country boy like Gordon was either going to be watching or playing rugby, or else shooting the shit out of pheasants. Hopefully leaving the lady of the house free to receive interrogators.

Shooting would go on all day, but, to be on the safe side, in case rugby was involved, I would have to leave my visiting until the afternoon.

As it was, I had a piece of business that I'd been putting off while I'd been chasing my tail over Magda. The body of a Montagu's harrier had been found on moorland about twenty miles away. A Schedule 1 protected species. It had been poisoned. The RSPB had been clamouring for a report. The uniforms up there had been doing what they could, now it was time to show my face in the wilds. At least it would stop me from being spat on in the street.

*   *   *

215

On the way over, a call came in from Bryn. The children's home had, with some persuading, agreed to take a call from me. I pulled over before I got deeper into the hills and lost reception. The day manager was a woman this time, and not the dour bastard I had spoken to before. I gave her my name and the cipher phrase that had been agreed on to convince her that I wasn't Captain Hook trawling for Lost Boys.

'We're taping this conversation our end,' she warned me.

'I'm okay with that.'

'Just remember it,' she warned, giving me an insight into their relations with the local cops. A war footing.

'Colette Fletcher and Donna Gallagher—do you have any information you can give me on current or last-known addresses.'

'I can't give out that information.'

'I don't want it. Not the details. I just want to be reassured that someone knows where they are. That they are safe.'

That seemed to mollify her. 'The names aren't familiar. Probably before my time. I'm going to have to go into the computer.'

I watched a buzzard circling on a thermal while I waited. What would be outside her window in Manchester? Different worlds. Why had Donna and Colette opted to come back into this one?

'You did know that these girls left here two years apart?' she asked, coming back to me.

'Yes. Have you got contact details?'

'No. Both of them dropped off our radar when they left.'

'Is that unusual?'

'No, unfortunately. They're legally adults when they finish here, and, even though we've been the nearest thing they've had to a family, a lot of them don't give us another thought.'

'What about Flower Robinson?'

'What about her?' Her voice went wary.

'Has she dropped off your radar?'

'What do you want with Flower?' There was a protective edge to the question.

'The same as Donna and Colette. I want to know that she's safe.'

'Are you suggesting that there could be a reason why she might not be?' she asked guardedly.

'Do you know where she is? Yes or no?' I demanded abruptly, throwing command into my tone.

It startled her. 'Yes. But—'

'Good,' I cut in over her, gliding back down to gentle. 'And now I need to speak to her.'

'I told you, I can't give that information out.'

'Okay, I appreciate that, but what if I give you my number? That way she can call me. I'd like you to tell her that it's very important. Tell her I need to talk to her about the summer she spent in Dinas.'

'Where?'

'Just say Mid Wales. She'll remember.'

She expanded on Flower after I gave her my number. She was one of their success stories. They were proud of her. Reading Sociology at the University of Manchester. Living independently in a hall of residence, but still helping out as a volunteer at the home. Turning into a rounded and socially aware human being.

But would she call me?

I couldn't hang around to find out. I had to drive further up into the hills, out of telephone range, where I had a cop to meet.

Constable Huw Davies was waiting for me in his marked Land Rover. We had spoken over the telephone a few times, but we hadn't met before. He was a tall, rangy man with thin fair hair and a pointed chin. He was wearing a nonissue yellow anorak over his uniform.

'I'll take you up there,' he said in a local accent, breaking the handshake quicker than was necessary.

'Where are we going?' I asked, raising my voice as he walked round to the driver's side of the vehicle. I was supposed to be in charge here, I wanted to implant a bit of control.

'Up there,' he said, opening his door, pointing to a rutted track that led to an amorphous rise of moorland.

He stayed as taciturn on the drive up. Responding to my attempts at conversation with a quizzical frown, which he usually accompanied with a clever flick on the steering wheel that precipitated a slew of violent lurches. I took the hint and kept quiet.

We stopped at a spot that would have made a great backdrop for a postapocalyptic film. Any actors playing survivors would not have had to search too far to find the motivation to play their future grim and hopeless.

It was a damp, spongy depression of mossy tumps and spiky reeds, fringed with burned heather. A flat, lifeless place. The sense of vertical was mocked by one bent, stunted and wind-whipped hawthorn. The breeze, as if it had read the

218

script, wafted over a ruined cathedral smell from the charred heather.

I walked away from the Land Rover with the thin file containing the case notes. Pretending to consult them, I lifted my head to study random points on the horizon. I was aware of Huw Davies watching me. He didn't know it, but this show was for his benefit. After a while I called him over.

'Two holidaymakers from Kent reported it?' I asked.

'That's right, hillwalkers.'

'Busybodies?'

He cocked his head slightly, but his expression didn't shift out of neutral. 'I don't get your meaning, Sergeant.'

I smiled pleasantly at him, tapped the file. 'We both know that this wouldn't have seen the light of day if a local had discovered it.'

He bristled. 'Do we?'

'Yes, we do. The bird's carcass would have ended up in an incinerator or a lime pit. The ornithologists would have eventually noticed its absence, but no story to tell. Just a disappearance. A mystery.'

'You don't think this is a mystery?'

'No, I know who did it.'

For the first time, he smiled. It made him younger. 'That's pretty impressive. Considering you haven't been up here before.'

I shook the file. 'Someone on this list did it.'

'List?'

'The list of names you provided. People with a relevant interest that I asked you to question.'

'Didn't you read my summary? No one we talked to had any knowledge of this.'

'We can probably discount the farmers.'

'We can?'

'Yes, they'd only have had a motive if it was lambing time. So, that narrows it down to the gamekeepers.'

He looked at me searchingly for a moment before he nodded. 'They're not going to say anything.'

'The toxin's been analysed. Strychnine-based.'

'You won't find it.'

'Private stock?'

He shrugged. 'Off the record?' he asked.

'Okay.'

'I can't name names because I don't have one. This is what's come down to me. Basically it was an accident. The bird wasn't targeted. Someone had baited a rabbit to get a fox that was going for his birds. The harrier took the rabbit.' He opened his hands indicating end of story.

'How do you feel about that?'

He looked at me appraisingly. 'I feel pretty confident in telling you that it isn't going to happen again. From now on, if someone's worried about a fox taking his pheasants, he does it the hard way: he waits up and tries to shoot the bugger.'

'Is that enforceable?'

He smiled wryly. 'Ever see a Montagu's harrier?'

I shook my head.

'I used to watch that bird. It gave me a lot of pleasure. Let's just say that word of my distress has got around.'

'Okay.' I nodded, letting him know that it was understood. I was getting good at this frontier justice. He offered his hand, and I shook it. I realized that I had passed some test.

'I've been asked to ask you something,' he said.

'Me?' I was intrigued. I didn't think that anyone over this way knew me.

'Yes, when word got around that I was meeting the detective from Dinas.'

'Go on,' I prompted, no longer surprised at the extent of the bush telegraph in these parts.

'The farmer who died there recently . . . Trevor Vaughan?' He waited for a sign of recognition. I nodded, not giving anything away. 'He wondered if you knew anything about the funeral arrangements.'

'Who wants to know?'

'Bill Ferguson.'

'Who's Bill Ferguson?'

He nodded down at the file in my hand. 'He's on the list.'

I scanned the paper. 'A gamekeeper?' I asked, letting him hear significance.

'An assistant keeper. For the Coyle Estate. He's new this season. He's not allowed to make the kind of decisions we're talking about up here.'

'How did he know Trevor Vaughan?'

'I didn't know he did until he asked me to ask you about the funeral.'

I told myself not to read too much into it. The guy might just be some kind of freak who made a habit of attending the funerals of suicides. For all I knew it could be a common gamekeeper's pastime. But why hadn't he approached the obvious sources? Why come to me rather than Trevor's family or close buddies?

Did Bill Ferguson want to pay his last respects from a distance?

*　　　*　　　*

221

Huw gave me directions to the Coyle Estate. I couldn't pass up a chance to find out what linked Bill Ferguson and Trevor Vaughan. I calculated I could get there, and still be back in time to see Zoë McGuire with a safe margin, assuming that Gordon was cooperating by following his own manly pursuits.

It was a big spread. The current owner was a fancy-price-tag London barrister. The house was a copy of a Palladian mansion with fucked-up proportions, set beside a river where they fished for salmon and trout. They shot pheasants, partridge and woodcock on the surrounding parkland and farms. Up on their moors they killed grouse. A veritable pleasure dome.

The shooters were returning to lunch when I arrived. A bunch of prats seated on straw bales on a flat-bed trailer being drawn by a tractor towards a big marquee that had been set up near the house. To a man they scowled at me suspiciously as I drove past.

I was headed off at the pass before I reached the heartland. A big man with a florid complexion in a waxed jacket and the sort of Wellington boots you need a mortgage to buy climbed out of a parked Range Rover and flagged me down.

'I'm afraid this is a private shoot, old son,' he announced with bluff, insincere, affability, standing above my open window.

I flashed him my warrant card. 'I'm investigating the poisoning of a Schedule 1 protected bird.'

He wasn't impressed. 'Your people have already talked to our lads. Can't help any more, I'm afraid. Nothing has changed.' He gestured to the activity going on behind him. 'And this is really bad timing. If you do have to talk to the boys again, call the estate office and make an appointment. Okay?' he beamed at me dismissively.

My phone rang. I glanced at the display. A Manchester code.

His face clouded. 'Turn that bloody thing off, will you? Show some consideration—we ask our guests not to bring mobile phones.'

'Don't want to spoil the sound of the guns, do you?' I asked, turning away before he could answer. 'Hello?'

'Is that Sergeant Capaldi?' A young woman, Manchester accent, the tone tentative.

'Flower?'

'Yes.'

'Hold on a moment . . .' I covered the mouthpiece. The man was glaring at me now, his face even redder. I shouted, 'Fuck off, this is a private conversation.' He started to remonstrate, but I drove away on to the grass. Another complaint going out to Inspector Morgan.

'Flower, thanks for calling me.'

'What's this about?'

'Your summer in Dinas.'

'What about it?'

'What stands out in your memory?'

I sensed a hesitation down the line. But didn't push.

'I thought it was what I wanted to do,' she said eventually, 'to be a beauty therapist. I thought working in Sara's would be good experience. I didn't realize it would be washing old people's crinkly hair, and fetching them cups of coffee. And staying in that cruddy caravan. And hearing things

223

outside making noises all night.'

'What about the people you worked with?'

'There was no one really to get on with. To tell you the truth, I missed my friends and the life here.' She thought about it, trying to answer my question. 'Sara was the boss—we didn't mix too much. The other girls in the salon were okay, but they had boyfriends. I kept pretty much to myself.'

'You didn't make friends with Wendy Evans?'

'I didn't meet anyone called that.'

'What about Les Tucker, Sara's boyfriend?' I asked lightly, taking it there at last.

'What do you think of him?' she asked warily, after a pause.

'He doesn't like me.'

'He was creepy.' I waited for elaboration. 'He really fancied himself. Used to wear his sleeves rolled right up his arms as if it was some kind of a turn-on. His shirt unbuttoned. Ugh . . .' She made a gagging sound down the line.

'Flower, this is in total confidence, but I need to know if Les Tucker ever propositioned you?'

'Like in touched me up, do you mean?'

'Not necessarily physical. Improper suggestions. Anything like that.'

'He'd left some nasty stuff in the caravan when I got there.'

'Nasty stuff?'

'Porno shots. He came back to pick them up. You know, like pretending he was sorry that he'd left them there for me to see. Asking what I thought of them. Making like he was joking, but trying to see if they'd turned me on. As if I didn't know the way guys play that silly shit.'

'What kind of pictures, Flower?'

224

'I don't want to say.'

'Did he keep coming round?'

'Only once more. Not long after that. With a creepy friend. They were both a bit pissed. They asked me if I wanted to come to a party with them. A place they had up in the woods somewhere. Lots of booze, and music. Like a place in the woods is supposed to be some kind of temptation?' she asked rhetorically, her voice rising incredulously.

'He wasn't any more specific? Just "a place in the woods"?' I kept my excitement level down.

'I didn't ask for a description.'

'What did you tell them?'

'I told them I wasn't interested. I told them if they didn't go away I was going to call Sara. They went. But I called her anyway. I didn't want it getting twisted, her thinking that I might have encouraged them.'

'And that worked?'

'He kept away from me after that.'

I asked Flower for a description of the creepy friend, but the memory was too blurred by now. The one strong impression I got was that nothing would have dragged her back to Dinas the following summer.

So there it was again: what had made Donna and Colette's experience so different?

The place in the woods?

I had assumed, when Flower mentioned it, that they had meant the hut they had gone to in the minibus. But the more I thought about it, the more I realized that the hut was too public. That was where they took outsiders to shoot vermin.

No, their place in the woods would be special. A private place. A venue that was solely for their own pleasure.

*   *   *

Zoë's BMW was parked outside the house. David Williams had been right, Gordon McGuire had done well out of the inheritance deal. A desirable, early Victorian brick farmhouse, with a new, purpose-built stable block to the side.

I had been forced to abandon any hope of speaking to Bill Ferguson that afternoon. He was out there in the woods somewhere, in charge of a group of beaters, and the shoot wouldn't be winding down until the light went. I had to compromise by dropping my card off at the cottage he rented, with a note on the back asking him to call me if he still wanted details of Trevor Vaughan's funeral arrangements.

Zoë opened the door. She had toned down her make-up and outfit since our previous meeting in Ken McGuire's kitchen, but she had still managed to fix herself so that she would make an impression on anyone she answered the door to. Watching her reaction, I could tell that I hadn't quite managed to make an equivalent impression.

'Sergeant Capaldi. This is a surprise,' she observed coolly, without sounding surprised.

'Hello, Mrs McGuire. Is your husband in?'

'Gordon helps run the family shoot, Sergeant. Saturdays are a particularly busy day for him. Or didn't you know that?' Her tone was amused accusation.

'It was you that I wanted to see.'

She nodded at that. 'Let me see if I understand the procedures correctly. You're standing there,

226

looking kind of sheepish, so I'm assuming you don't have a warrant of any sort. So, unless I actually invite you in, I can shut the door in your face and there's not a thing you can do about it.'

'Something like that,' I agreed, trying to shift up from sheepish.

'So, sell yourself.'

It was a difficult product to promote. Accusing her husband of degradation and grand depravity. Possible abduction. White slavery.

'Want to buy a ticket to the Police Ball?'

She laughed. Zoë was no fool. Like all intelligent people she was curious, which is what I had been counting on. Also, she was confident enough to feel in charge of whatever situation she chose to subscribe to.

'Come in . . .' She led me through a hall with the original encaustic tiles on the floor, through to a kitchen that had a rear wall of glass, with black slate on the floor, a pink granite worktop and zinc-faced units.

'Nice place,' I observed, seeing nearly my annual salary in this one room.

'We don't have children,' she replied, as if that answered a lot of questions.

'Going to have any?'

Her look told me that it was none of my business. We were not here to be friends. She waved me to a seat at the oiled oak table and reinforced that message by not offering me a drink.

She sat down opposite me, propped her elbows on the table, laced her fingers, and faced me like an interrogator. 'Things have gone weird around here, Sergeant. Boon goes missing. Trevor commits suicide. And it all seems to have happened since you turned up on Sheila's doorstep. Our husbands get twitchy when the talk comes round to you. Which it seems to do more and more frequently. So, I see you as a catalyst. I don't know what for, but now I've got you sitting down in front of me, perhaps we can find out. Whatever this is, how do we clear it up?'

'Let's take it back to another beginning,' I suggested.

'Wherever . . .' She spread her hands, inviting me to continue.

'The so-called prostitute that your husband and the others claimed to have procured last Saturday night.'

'For Paul and Trevor's benefit,' she qualified.

'You're not picking up on what I'm telling you.'

'What did I miss?'

'I said "so-called" prostitute. I think that the woman they picked up was actually an East European hitchhiker.'

She shook her head dismissively. 'Sorry, but that prostitute in Cardiff confirmed that she was there. With a black man as a bodyguard. I'm not trying to excuse my husband for that ridiculous episode, but her admission backs up what they told you.'

We were circling round Monica Trent now. I decided to pull back slightly. I didn't want the welcome mat whipped away too prematurely. 'Do the names Colette Fletcher and Donna Gallagher mean anything to you?'

She thought about it. Shook her head. 'No. Should they?'

I believed her. 'Not necessarily.'

'You're going mysterious on me, Sergeant.'

I braced myself. 'Can I ask you a very personal

question, Mrs McGuire?'

'You can ask. I might not answer.'

'How good is your sex life?'

She held back her immediate angry reaction, thinking about it. She frowned. 'Is this pertinent?'

'Very.'

She considered it some more. 'Has this anything to do with me telling you that we didn't have children?'

'No.'

She frowned again, trying to analyse my motives. 'This has something to do with Gordon?'

'Yes.'

She shook her head. 'I can't believe that I'm even considering answering that question.'

'You don't have to tell me anything, Mrs McGuire.'

'But my silence might incriminate me?'

I remained silent.

'Oh shit, what can it matter? It's good,' she blurted. 'Gordon and I have what I would consider a very normal and healthy sex life.' She coloured, shrugging elaborately to cover her embarrassment. 'So, what does that tell you?'

I rehearsed it. *Mrs McGuire, does your husband urinate or defecate on you as part of this normal and healthy sex life?* I crumpled. I couldn't ask it.

She saw it in my face. 'Sergeant Capaldi?'

I invoked Magda, Donna and Colette. Flower, for her near-miss. Regine Broussard, for the memory. 'Mrs McGuire, did you know that your husband's sexual preferences had become so extreme that even a seasoned prostitute had to refuse them?'

She stared at me blankly for a moment. 'Who

229

told you that?' Her voice coming out as a hoarse whisper.

'The prostitute that your husband and Les Tucker used to visit in Cardiff. The same prostitute that they paid to give them their alibi.'

'Gordon and Les Tucker?'

'Yes.' Her reaction was surprising me. I had prepared myself for anger, shock or violence, or any combination of the three. Instead, she seemed to be in deep, almost amused reflection. 'Mrs McGuire, I think that Gordon and Les have a place in the forest that they take women to. I desperately need to find that place.'

She looked up at me. 'You've got it wrong, Sergeant. Gordon doesn't use prostitutes. He never has done.'

'I'm sorry, Mrs McGuire. I know it's painful, but I need to get to the truth.'

She shook her head. 'That is the truth. Believe me.' She reached across and grabbed my hand and squeezed it tightly, her nails tucked into the ball of my thumb. It wasn't a demonstration of affection; pain was involved. 'If you breathe a word of this to another living soul, I swear to you that I will rake your eyes out.'

I nodded, believing her, accepting the condition.

'Gordon suffers from pseudohermaphroditism. Do you know what that is?'

I shook my head. But I was beginning to believe her certainty.

'Look it up. Let's just say that he is not going to be exposing himself to prostitutes.'

'Your sex life . . .?'

'Has fuck-all to do with you.' But she wasn't angry. She actually smiled at me. 'We have adapted,

230

we have our procedures. I wasn't lying, Sergeant.'

'But Les is Gordon's best friend.'

'So?'

It dawned on us both at the same instant. I had the wrong brother. Zoë grinned, a new and malicious knowledge suddenly coming into her possession. I couldn't share her Schadenfreude. I was too busy wondering what else I had got wrong.

*   *   *

Ken and Les . . .

I parked up to reflect on it. Dusk was already grading itself in, but the added gloom helped the meditative process. Ken and Les, not Gordon and Les. Did it change anything? Was it just a name substitution, or could this new knowledge lead me somewhere?

I went back over the territory. A suitably chastened-looking Ken had led the gang down off of the hill. It was Ken who ran the intercept when I first tried to interview Trevor Vaughan. It was Ken who changed the story midstream about where they had dropped off Boon.

Why hadn't I seen it? It made sense this way. He had to be at the very root of this. Ken was in charge of this game.

What did I have? What was eluding me? What wasn't I fitting into place properly?

What was I missing?

It wouldn't come. I couldn't make the cognitive leaps. I was too netted into the image of Ken and Les performing unspeakable acts. And I had a new problem. It was the wrong word to use, but I had been almost comfortable with Gordon as the other

231

half of the duo. He came across as smug and predictable. Okay, he had a temper and an old-fashioned sense of outrage, but I couldn't envisage him being too imaginative. Ken, on the other hand, was analytical and wary. His precision, in association with Les's more prosaic mean streak, made for a more worrying combination.

I gave up and drove home to prepare for my night out with Sally. My night in with Sally, I corrected myself. Would I have to worry about contraception? Would it be presumptuous to secrete a toothbrush? I rumbled over the wooden bridge into the caravan park. The callous inner youth that I thought I had packed away and forgotten about managed to sneak out a salacious little smirk before I could suppress him.

I drove around to Unit 13 the long way again, keeping an eye out for sneakily parked cars. I raked the aisles down both sides of my caravan with my headlights before I stopped the car. I crouched down and shone my flashlight under it.

The blinking LED display on the answering machine in the dining nook caught my eye as I opened the door. I switched on the light in the living area, and caught myself reflected in the large rear window that overlooked the river. And, for a weird, absurdist moment, I used my reflection to look at the stranger's reflection in the same window.

Holding fractional time between us before I had to acknowledge his existence. The stranger sitting comfortably and casually in my armchair. Who was not actually a stranger.

Graham Mackay had found me.

13

'Hello, Glyn.'

'Mac . . .' I acknowledged him warily.

'It's been a while.'

'Bruges.'

'I'm still sorry about that.'

I shrugged. 'I recovered.' From a broken arm, and a near deportation, while he'd used a military channel to get whisked out of the country unblemished. And he'd been the one who started the fight in the first place. 'Why are you here, Mac?'

'Your wife has left me.'

'Ex-wife,' I reminded him. His tone had sounded accusatory. Was he labouring under some crazy notion that she might have run back to me? 'I don't know where she is,' I offered placatingly.

'I do.'

'You do?'

'Yes. She's in Devon. Somewhere near Tavistock, shacked up with a child.'

'A child?' Repetition looked like it might be a good way to get through this.

'Okay, not quite the school-cap-and-short-trousers version,' he admitted grudgingly. 'But he has to be ten, fifteen years younger than her. An itinerant Australian wine maker she met in a vegetarian café in Hereford. That paints a picture, doesn't it? You can just see that moment. Love over the tofu,' he pronounced bitterly.

'If you know where she is, why come here?' I asked, trying to keep it friendly.

'Because I want her back.'

Oh shit . . . Was I the blood price? Was I her troublesome priest? Damage me and she would let him lick her boots again? I tried backing away and stumbled into the sharp end of the dining nook. 'It's not worth it,' I said soothingly. 'If you hurt me you'll be in real trouble.'

He looked at me incredulously. 'I don't want to hurt you, I want advice.'

I returned to repetition, it seemed safer. 'Advice?'

'What do I do? How do I get her back?'

I almost laughed. 'I'm the last person to ask. I'm the one she left first, remember.'

'The two of you were together for a long time. You understand her ways. What should I change in my personality? Should I hurt Grape Boy?' He shook his head, closed his eyes, and winced painfully. 'Man, I still love her.'

He had fixed on the bond that he imagined the shared knowledge of her gave us. We were united in loss, we had become the Brotherhood of the Dumped.

What could I do? My encounters with Mackay were inevitably painful, but we went back too far, and he was hurting. I couldn't throw him out.

And then, just as I welcomed him into my tent, I realized the immediate consequence that the law of hospitality demanded. I was going to have to take him with me to Sally's. And bring him back. God or Karma, the only entities who could have witnessed that salacious little smirk when I crossed the bridge, had fitted me up for it.

I called Sally and she was okay with including Mackay in the party. I checked the answering machine after that. Amongst the routine dross and a snarled message from Inspector Morgan was one from Bill Ferguson. He would be at home tomorrow if I wanted to call him with the details of Trevor Vaughan's funeral.

We passed Mackay's parked car in the taxi on the way to Sally's. It had to be almost two miles away. The crazy bastard had put his shoes, socks and trousers into a haversack, and hiked all that way up my freezing river. In the dark.

'Why this far away?' I asked.

'I got the impression that you might be trying to avoid me. I thought I'd use a bit of subterfuge,' he explained, smiling apologetically.

*　　　　*　　　　*

It was a strange evening. Sally's house, Sally's meal, Sally as the sparkling and attentive hostess, and then we spend the time discussing my ex-wife. It was obviously cathartic for Mackay, and Sally encouraged the flow. At first I thought that she was only being kind, but gradually I realized that she was using the information to get some kind of proxy measure on me. Judge a man by the tackle that he straps on to his life. When she noticed that I had wised up to her agenda, she winked cheekily at me.

I kissed her on the doorstep. Our first proper kiss. Mackay waiting diplomatically in the taxi. Savouring that first licit, full taste and smell of the other.

'Mmm . . .' she moaned luxuriantly, her eyes closed.

'I could let the taxi take him home,' I whispered.

'You could, but you won't.'

235

'Is that an order?'

'He was the one you were jailed in Spain with, wasn't he?'

'How did you know?'

She pulled back, opened her eyes, and popped a round-mouthed kiss full on to mine. I recognized it as a dismissal. 'He needs the company tonight.'

Mackay and I were silent in the taxi home. It wasn't strained, it was just that we both had our own areas of reflection to retreat into.

Back in the caravan, I broke out the Scotch.

'Nice lady,' he observed, as he held up his glass to be filled.

'I think so.'

'You should have stayed.'

I shrugged. 'I've got work to do tomorrow.'

'It's Sunday,' he observed, slightly curious.

And this, I suddenly recalled, was Saturday night. A week had passed. I made a silent toast to Magda. Hoping she was in Ireland. To Boon in Holland. And to Donna and Colette. Wherever.

'Are you okay?' Mackay was watching me over the rim of his glass.

I dropped into the banquette seat, feeling the damp coolness through the big window on the back of my neck. 'You've been trained for situations, haven't you?'

He looked at me obliquely. 'What kind of situations?'

'Ever see any of the Dracula films?'

'Sure.' He nodded, waiting for the relevance to be explained.

'What would you do if you were Dracula, and you saw the angry villagers coming to attack the castle?'

'I'd leave by the back door. As soon as I saw the torchlight procession.'

Bruges? I didn't voice it. 'What if you don't have a back door?'

It took him a moment to realize that I was talking about the caravan. 'Are you in some kind of trouble?'

I nodded. 'Possibly.'

'Anything to do with the marks on your face?'

'No, that was a different kind of trouble.'

He laughed. 'And Gina thought you were boring!'

'Gina's character-sieve only caught my defects.'

He smiled painfully. Newly discovered empathy. He studied me for a moment. 'This is more than just about Sally's son, isn't it?'

I thought about it. This was a strange confessor to have. 'A woman made an absurd mistake once.'

'Such as?'

'Stowing away on a boat that docked in Cardiff.'

He smiled, getting my meaning. 'Of all the exotic places.'

'Her name was Regine Broussard. She was Haitian. She went to ground in the city, living rough. We took a call that a black woman with a big bright headscarf had been seen getting into a white Transit van.'

He picked up on my reticence. 'You must get calls like that all the time.'

I winced. 'That's why I ignored it at first. Then I got to thinking. Hookers didn't operate in that neighbourhood. This lady was too exotic not to have been picked up on the radar if she was a working girl. By the time I got myself into fucking gear it was too late. Two scumbags from the Valleys had panicked when she started screaming at them in French that she didn't want them to touch her.'

'You got them?'

I nodded and closed my eyes. 'And the saddest thing of all? Everything she had in the world was in a plastic carrier bag.'

'Need any help with this one?' he offered.

I opened my eyes. 'What about your business?'

'I have staff. They take care of things. And I owe you.'

I told him about the mood in the village. I kept it general, explaining it as a natural result of collective grief that had found some sort of relief by channelling its focus on the outsider. If he recognized it as bullshit, he had the grace not to let on. But I didn't want him knowing about the group. Or too much about Magda. Not yet. I didn't want him reading me as an obsessive. Apart from the security that his presence afforded, some instinct was telling me that I was going to need Mackay. What for, I didn't know yet.

I was going to find out soon enough.

*   *   *

It was a semi-detached, estate cottage in the shadow of a massive wellingtonia tree. The next-door neighbour's net curtains twitched as I walked up to the front door. Bill Ferguson had no net curtains to worry about, just what appeared to be a pair of old sheets drooping from plastic-coated wire in the front bay window.

He opened the door and presented me with a friendly, quizzically embryonic expression that was poised to shift to fit the emerging encounter.

'Mr Ferguson?' I held up my warrant card.

He nodded, showing surprise but at the same time something fitting into place. 'I thought you'd telephone me.'

'I was in the area.' I gave him the Friendly Plod smile to cover the lie.

'It's Sunday.'

'We never rest.' I grinned to show him that it was a joke.

'Come in,' he said, opening the door and stepping back to let me through.

He was a tall man, lean, with a shaved head and trimmed beard. The exposed parts of him—scalp, face and forearms—were heavily tanned. I put him in his early forties, the dry skin and the lines on his face down to the weather he worked in. His eyes showed intelligence. I had been expecting someone coarser.

I followed him into the living room. The furniture was mismatched and threadbare, the only shiny things being a CD player and four, high stacks of discs. No television, I noticed.

'Thank you for seeing me, Mr Ferguson.'

'Bill. Please, call me Bill. And excuse the state of things. This crappy furniture comes with the place. It's just too daunting to even start thinking about making improvements.' Was I catching a pinch of self-mockery? Was this guy being ever so slightly camp?

'Firstly, I am sorry about what happened to Trevor Vaughan.'

He pulled a face and gestured me into a chair, sitting down himself. 'Me too. Can you tell me about the arrangements for the funeral?'

'I will, when I know them.'

239

He looked at me sharply. 'I thought that was why you were here.'

'How did you know Trevor?' I asked. 'Through shooting?'

'No, I don't like shooting. Neither did Trevor.'

'But it's what you do?' I prompted.

He shrugged. 'It's a sport to the people I'm employed to help. But it's not my sport. Do you chase criminals when you're not at your work?' he asked with a polite smile.

'Point taken.'

'I first met Trevor at a concert.' He thought about it. 'Perhaps five months ago. At the chapel here. A male-voice choir from South Wales. He brought his mother and a friend of hers over to hear it.'

'You like male-voice choirs?'

An amused look flickered until he realized that I had pitched it as a straight question. 'I like all music. Especially choral. I got talking to Trevor in the interval. He told me that he was interested in classical music, but ignorant about it.' He gestured towards the pile of CDs. 'I told him that he was welcome to listen to my collection. I started him off on Handel, and Bach cantatas.' He smiled wryly. 'I was about to introduce him to Janáček's *Glagolitic* Mass.'

'He borrowed your CDs?'

'I offered, but he said that he would rather come over here and listen. He said the atmosphere was more conducive.'

'Did you ever meet in Dinas? Trevor's home?'

'No.'

'You were never invited?'

He took his time answering. 'He was honest with

me. He explained that his parents and his friends wouldn't understand this interest we shared.' He smiled. 'He didn't have to elaborate that they would find this friendship strange. With another man.'

'Was there anything more to your friendship?'

He smiled wanly. 'I'm getting over a ruined relationship, Sergeant. I'm not currently in the marketplace. I just enjoyed his company.'

'Did Trevor want anything more from it?'

'Why are you asking me these questions?'

'I am trying to find out what drove him to do what he did.'

He nodded slowly, considering it. 'I think that maybe he was attracted to me. But he was also frightened of sex. It was one of his problems. And he was a mild manic-depressive.' He moved a hand to describe a sine wave. 'Up, down, up, down . . .' He let his hand tail off.

'Did he ever give you the impression that he might have considered taking his own life?'

'I was surprised and saddened to hear the news.'

'But not shocked?'

'No. Not shocked. As I said, his fear of sex was only one of his problems.'

'Other contributory factors?'

'I'm not a psychologist.'

I nodded. 'I understand that.'

He frowned, trying to organize his thought process. 'There was something tearing at him. Some inner conflict going on that he couldn't resolve. He once asked me where I thought the line between betrayal and duty should be drawn.'

'Betrayal of what, duty to whom?'

'That's what I asked him. He wouldn't clarify; he just gave me one of his sheepish looks and dropped the subject. He should have been a Catholic. If anyone needed the release of the confessional, it was Trevor.'

'When did you last see him?'

He thought about it. 'Perhaps . . . Nearly two weeks ago.'

'Did you notice any change in him?'

'No. Same old Trevor.' He jiggled his fanned fingers. 'A little bit happy with the music and our talk, a little bit sad with his burdens.'

Another dead end.

'But I did speak to him earlier this week. Over the phone. To arrange to meet tomorrow.' He shrugged and pulled a melancholic expression at the futility of that arrangement now.

'How did he sound?'

'That's the strange thing. He was happy. It was so obvious that I made a joke of it. I asked if he'd won the lottery. He had had some good news, he told me.'

And Trevor was happy the last time I saw him. 'When was this?' I asked, starting to see a seam opening. 'When did he call you?'

He thought about it. 'Wednesday night, I think.'

Wednesday night was the last time I saw Trevor Vaughan. We had investigated the hole in the forest, and found it empty. He had just realized that his suspicions about his friends had been unfounded. He must have called Bill Ferguson after I had left him. Spreading his joy.

So what happened to change all that? And so quickly? What causes him to squeeze himself into Wendy Evans's panties on the following day and hang himself?

Oh fuck . . .

He saw my expression change. 'What's the matter?'

But I was already on my way out of there.

*   *   *

I called Mackay and arranged a place to meet.

Wendy Evans.

It had been staring me in the face all this time. I just hadn't connected it. It was the flag that Trevor Vaughan had been waving at me. He had worn Wendy's panties to specifically draw attention to Wendy, not to a suppressed gay guy in young girl's underwear. I had been so busy trying to probe Donna and Colette's time at the salon that I had overlooked the significance of Wendy also working there.

And Sally had mentioned that her husband had told her Wendy had been a damaged child. *Carrying a lot of weird emotional stuff around for her age.* And no fucking wonder. If I was right about this, at an age when her peers were obsessing over boy bands, she was being coached by Ken McGuire and Les Tucker in the class-A black art of sexual abuse and humiliation.

How had Trevor got possession of the panties? Wendy ran off with Malcolm Paterson about two years ago. Trevor had to have been holding on to them for at least that long. Had he found them? Had he been given them?

I could only speculate as I drove. Does he find them during a guys' night at one of the fuck-pads? Stuck down the side of a seat? He knows what Ken and Les are like. Does the sums. He protects them by not voicing his suspicions. But he holds on to the evidence.

I tried to streamline it. Donna and Colette may have been groomed into sex toys by Ken and Les, but they were essentially holiday romances. Both returned voluntarily the following summer, which must have been down to a cash incentive. But Wendy was the local connection. Wendy had roots and permanence. She was the one who would have kept the boys satisfied during the long winter months.

How had they managed it? How had they turned her? How had she borne the degradation all that time? Why hadn't she told anyone? Her family? Sara?

Malcolm Paterson must have known. She couldn't have kept something like that a secret from the man she was running away with. An older man, a teacher. Someone she would have regarded as a protector. So why hadn't he come to us? Why hadn't he turned those bastards in? Or had he thought that it was enough to pluck her from the morass and ride off into the healing sunset?

At least Wendy had gotten out of it. What had become of Donna and Colette? And the thing that was really spooking me: what were they doing with Magda?

It was that speculation that had driven me to direct action.

I met up with Mackay and transferred to his car, a muddy and well-worked Range Rover. It wasn't known around these parts, it would give us a degree of anonymity.

'Where are we going?' he asked.

This was the awkward bit. We were already rolling, but I hadn't actually told him what he was supposed to be helping me with. 'We're out to fuck up a bunch of child molesters.'

He grinned. 'Sounds good to me.'

'We're not exactly official,' I warned. 'And it could get physical. Someone might get hurt.'

He shook his head mock wearily. 'Now you're overelaborating. I liked it better when you said that we were out to fuck up a bunch of child molesters. That's all I need to know.'

'You sure?'

'Let's drive.'

I directed him to Dinas and briefed him on the bad guys.

David Williams had told me that he thought the group used Dinas Rugby Club for their pre-Sunday-lunch drinking session. We tucked ourselves in at the back of the car park. I identified Les's crew-cab pickup, and the cars I had seen outside Ken' and Gordon's houses. The white Transit van, the only vehicle I could associate Paul Evans with, wasn't parked here.

After one o'clock, the drinkers started to emerge. The group came out together. They were all wearing black armbands. I pointed Ken and Les out to Mackay.

'Which one are we after?' he asked.

I indicated Paul Evans.

He sucked breath in through his teeth. 'He's a big mother, isn't he?'

'The bigger they are the harder they fall?' I suggested hopefully.

He grinned at me. 'It's implementing the falling process that's the tricky bit.'

The group threw banter around and dispersed to their vehicles. We watched Paul cross the car park to a blue Subaru Impreza with gold alloy wheels and an enormous rear spoiler. It wasn't new, but it was still a lot of motor for a young man like Paul Evans to have as a toy.

'That's his weakness—' I suddenly realized, voicing it, seeing the deep, loving shine on the car '—that's how we get to him.'

Mackay wasn't so positive. 'We have to catch him first. And that's going to be virtually impossible with him in that machine.'

'We know where he's going.'

'Right, to Sunday lunch amid the bosom of his family. And once he gets there, he's safe. With us trailing uselessly behind.'

I watched the line of cars in front of us shuffle forward to the junction with the main road. Turning mainly to the right. I had a hunch. 'He won't go straight home. I'd stake what's left of my reputation on it.' The Subaru was two cars in front of us. 'The direct way to his place is left out of the car park,' I explained, 'but I think he'll take a longer way round.'

The Subaru turned right.

'How did you know that?' Mackay asked, impressed.

'If he turns left he's driving through countryside, his car only gets admired by sheep. Turn right and he gets to go through town. That car is his pride and joy. That's his balls on display. He's going to flaunt it every chance he gets.'

'So, we don't follow him?' Mackay asked.

'No, we turn left and head him off at the pass.'

Mackay turned left. 'There is another possibility,' he offered.

'What's that?'

'He may not be going home.'

'It's Sunday, he's been to the pub, now he eats. It's Dinas, it's bred in the bone. Like everyone else here, he runs on motor functions.'

I felt charged. Exhilarated I was moving again instead of floundering. And I had back-up. That felt unusual, and good.

I outlined the tactics as we drove to the Evanses' place.

*　　　*　　　*

We stopped on the lane that Paul Evans would have to use to get home. It was lined with untrimmed hedges and narrow verges, a ditch on one side, making it a tight fit for two cars to pass.

Mackay had parked at an angle, with his nose into a gateway, and the rear partially obstructing the lane. He was standing on the dropped tailgate with a pair of binoculars, making a show of watching something over the hedge. I was crouched on the far side, using the front wheel to mask my legs from the view of anyone approaching.

'He's coming,' Mackay announced sotto voce, without changing anything in his stance.

I heard the Subaru as it rounded the corner, the engine note overamplified by the straight-through exhaust. He throttled down, and started pumping his horn when he saw the Range Rover blocking the lane.

'Sorry, sorry . . .' Mackay mouthed, jumping down off the tailgate and gesturing his apologies as the Subaru approached. 'I'll just pull in a bit more and let you pass.' He slammed the tailgate closed. 'Lapwings in the field over there,' he shouted by

247

way of explanation.

He moved the Range Rover slowly, clearing the lane. I moved round with the car to remain hidden. The Subaru nudged forward into the narrow gap that Mackay had created, keeping it slow to avoid scratching the nearside paintwork on the thorn hedge. It was halfway through when Mackay let the clutch out sharply in reverse. The noise as the Range Rover hit the Subaru was startling.

So was the effect on Paul. He heaved himself out of the seat belt and bucket seat with a speed and dexterity that belied his size, emitting an animalistic cross between a squeal and a wail as he climbed out of the car. His expression was glassy, his eyes half shut, like a gas-blinded man, not wanting to confront the awful information that his senses had just given him.

Mackay eased forward, leaving a small gap for Paul to get past to inspect the damage. Leaving his driver's door wide open, Paul stared at the dent the Range Rover's tow bar had made in his flared rear wheel arch, shaking his head, his mouth working soundlessly.

'I'm so sorry, I must have had mud on my shoe. My foot slipped on the clutch,' Mackay explained through the driver's window. He threw in a conciliatory smile to test the waters.

'You stupid fucker,' Paul snarled, whipping round to the Range Rover, shifting out of stupor and into anger. He strode towards Mackay's door.

It was the conjunction I had been waiting for. I kept low and duck-walked to the Subaru, sidled in through the open door. I took the keys from the ignition and straddled the front seat to get the mobile phone that was lying amongst a pile of loose

248

change and empty sweet wrappers in a small well by the gear lever.

'Get the fuck out!' Paul was screaming, pounding his fist on Mackay's window.

He was too enraged to see me jump out of the Subaru. 'Look, Paul—' I yelled enticingly, moving to the front of his car. I dangled his car keys over my head like a sprig of mistletoe.

His head snapped round. The popping synapses were almost audible as his brain tried to unravel this new horror. He stared at me, mouth agape, trying to fit me into the equation. I was just too much additional bad news for one session. 'What the fuck . . .?' he mouthed.

I shook the car keys. 'You're going to have to catch me if you still want that shag you missed the other night.'

'Give me those,' he demanded in a low growl. He had given up trying to make sense of my presence, and had decided to just run with instinct and testosterone and go for the repossession of his property.

He puffed up threateningly and started towards me. But Mackay slickly closed the gap between us, with just enough of a little metallic clunk on the Subaru to remind Paul that his baby was still under threat.

Paul slammed the flat of his hand uselessly against the Range Rover. 'What do you want?' he demanded, choking on his frustration.

'I want you to take me to the Rumpus Room.'

He shook his head. 'I don't know what the fuck you're talking about.'

'Les Tucker's place in the woods that you use to party in.'

He started to shake his head again, but slower, and I knew that I had made a connection. Then I saw another thought intrude. A happier one. He had just realized that I was on the wrong side of his car, and he knew that Mackay couldn't take him on his own. There was nothing to stop him running off. He smiled. He thought that we had screwed up. He started backing away.

I let him have his moment on the hope curve before I called out: 'Haven't you realized what the deal is, Paul?'

He didn't stop.

'If you run, we trash your car.'

He stopped. I gestured to Mackay. The Range Rover reversed slowly. There was a grinding sound, and the driver's side of the Subaru began to lift on a skewed axis.

'Stop!' Paul ran back to his wounded car involuntarily. He caught my eyes pleadingly. 'I haven't been to the Den in years.'

Mackay let the Subaru drop down gently. Paul stroked the damage. 'If I tell you where it is, you let me go?' he asked calculatingly.

I shook my head. 'No—you take us.'

I had already strung a pair of handcuffs through the grab handle on the front passenger's side of the Range Rover. Mackay got out. 'Put the handcuffs on,' I instructed. Paul stared back at me defiantly. I gave the Subaru a backwards stomp with my heel. He got in, climbed over to the passenger's seat, and put the cuffs on.

Mackay and I exchanged car keys. I climbed into the driver's seat of the Range Rover. I showed Paul his mobile phone. 'Time to call home?' I suggested.

'Fuck off.'

I leapfrogged abruptly in first gear, scraping the hedge, pretending to make a meal of trying to find reverse. 'I'm not as skilful as him,' I warned cheerily, 'this thing will probably take off into your car.'

'Okay, okay—' He grimaced.

I found his home number and held the phone up in front of him, ready to cut it off if I heard any cry for help. He stuck to the script that I had given him, apologizing to his mother for not getting home for lunch. He told her that he had met up with a friend with a new Impreza, and they were going to take it up into the forest to try it out. I cut the connection when his mother began to complain.

Paul watched anxiously as Mackay drove the Subaru clear. 'He's not insured for that.'

'Well, let's hope he doesn't have an accident then,' I observed.

We set off in tight convoy. Paul craned round in his seat to watch his car being driven up close to the Range Rover's tow bar. He had grasped the set-up: as long as he kept the directions running, I wouldn't be touching the brakes sharply to test Mackay's reactions. Or Paul's anguish.

*   *   *

'Tell me about the Den,' I asked when we turned off into the forest.

He swivelled round, glowering. 'I'm taking you up there, but, afterwards, I'm going to sue the shit out of you.' His confidence was returning.

'For what?' I asked pleasantly.

'For what you've done to my car. For fucking kidnapping me.'

I smiled at him. 'Says who?'

He gestured backwards with a toss of his head. 'Says that bent rear fucking panel. Which is going to cost you plenty.'

'A bit careless that, wasn't it, Paul?'

He frowned. 'What the fuck are you talking about?'

'My friend back there, he's a soldier.' I decided to keep Mackay's military credentials current.

'So what? I'm suing him as well.'

'You haven't got it yet, have you?' I asked cheerfully.

'Got what?' he replied, suspicious.

'It's my turn to have the alibi. Good people to back me up.' He shook his head, puzzled. 'I'm not here, Paul. My friend and I are somewhere completely different. If we need to, we can get his entire regiment to confirm that. But I don't think we'll have to. You've already told your mother you're out horsing around in your car with a friend. And . . .' I leaned over and sniffed the air exaggeratedly. 'Have you been drinking? A dangerous combination that, Paul: fast cars and booze. Cause of many an accident.'

He stared at me. Running it through his head. Seeing the dead-ends shutting themselves off. His lower lip started to quiver at the unfairness of it all. 'We don't go there any more.'

I realized that he was talking about the Den. Offering me conciliation. 'Why not?'

He shrugged. 'We sort of gave it up after Ken and Gordon got married.'

'What is it?'

'It's a shack that Les's dad and uncles built when they were young. Les got to take it over. They used to take bottles of cider and fags and spend the weekends playing at being wild boys in the woods.'

'Take girls there?' I asked casually.

'No,' he replied, too earnestly. I had already caught the slight hesitation. 'It was strictly boys-only territory.' He pointed ahead. 'Take the left fork here.'

I stopped. The track he was indicating was mossy and overgrown. 'It's all right,' he urged, 'this thing will go anywhere.'

I got out and walked over to where the track branched off and curved away between gorse thickets and self-seeded birch saplings. A jay's angry screech startled me; catching a glimpse of blue and tan. I looked at the track again. A narrow set of fat wheel ruts ran the visible length.

I was suddenly conscious of Mackay standing beside me. 'The Range Rover will get down that.'

'So I've been told.' I pointed to the wheel ruts. 'What do you make of those?'

'Looks like a quad bike.'

'That's what I thought. And from the depth of them, I'd say this track gets used quite often.'

'Are you trying to tell me something?'

I jerked a thumb back towards the Range Rover. 'Like you, Pedro there tells me we'll have no problem driving down here.'

'He's right.'

'And as soon as we do, we tell whoever drives the quad bikes that interlopers have arrived.'

'Does that matter? Once you've found the place, there's nothing they can do about it.'

I turned to the Range Rover. Paul was studiously avoiding looking at us. 'I'd rather not let Ken and Les know that I'd been here before them.'

I left Mackay to move both vehicles out of sight and went down the track with Paul. I applied rodeo technology to rig up a crude hobble, which meant that he could still move, but with a severely truncated step that dampened both his fight and flight options.

The track swung through a wide arc, passing through abandoned second-growth forest, clogged with rotted stumps and brambles. If the quad-bike tracks hadn't been so pronounced it would have been easy to imagine it as a lost place.

Paul stopped in front of a dense clump of crack willows. The track turned sharply to the right here to follow the base of a steep bank, almost a cliff, topped with Scots pine and scored with ledges of craggy turf and withered foxgloves.

'We're here.'

I could see nothing. The quad-bike ruts continued up the trail on the far side of a large puddle. 'The tracks carry on,' I observed.

He almost smiled. 'That's what you're meant to think.'

It was clever. The tracks on the far side of the puddle were a dummy trail. They used the puddle to cover the turn in through the willow clump without leaving tracks. I followed Paul, pushing in through the branches to emerge in a clearing at the foot of the bank.

The slope of the bank had been quarried here. The hut had been built against the face of it. It slumped out from the quarry, a patched-up construction of rough-sawn boards, different generations of offcuts from the Tucker family logging enterprise. The roof was a lean-to structure of rusty corrugated iron. The two salvaged windows of different sizes on either side of the slumped, slightly off-centre, corrugated-iron door worked to complete the effect of a building caught in the moment before collapse.

It looked like a dead thing.

I felt the grab on my dynamic as the drab reality of the place applied its clamp. One look told me that it had been a long, long time since this building had housed anything that didn't own claws or trail slime.

Magda wasn't here. I rounded on Paul. 'You've brought me to the wrong place.'

He just smiled again and hunched his shoulders in a constrained shrug. 'You wanted me to show you the Den. I told you we'd stopped coming.'

But someone had been coming here I reminded myself. Those quad-bike tracks were fresh.

I looked at the derelict hut again and remembered the dummy trail. *That's what you're meant to think.*

The door was padlocked. A tough-looking bronze affair with the stainless-steel lock crook still shiny. It was overkill. The hinges were rusted to shit. I could have prized the door open with a not very big stick. But I was still running with the notion that I did not want Ken and Les to know that I had been here.

Each window had been curtained with a pair of dirty sacks that had been drawn to overlap. Most of the panes of glass were cracked, but one had been replaced by a yellowed rectangle of celluloid that had been tacked into place. I used a small branch and worked at the edge of the celluloid until two of the tacks popped free. I slipped the branch in through the small gap that I had created and pulled the edge of a sack up and to the side.

The inside surprised me. It looked like the desolation had been left on the outside. The furniture was under dust covers, but from the outlines I made out three armchairs, and one sofa against the far wall. The floors were randomly scattered with worn rugs and old pieces of carpet, and a cast-iron wood stove stood in the corner, with a healthy pile of cut firewood beside it. A solitary bucket was placed on the floor. To catch the drips from a leak in the roof? Or a blood libation?

Dust covers? A functioning stove? A floor that wasn't heaped with rat shit? Perhaps I was wrong. Perhaps this place did harbour life? Or had recently.

'What girls did you used to bring up here?' I asked.

He shook his head. 'I told you. It was cider and fags and air rifles.'

'And wanking, I'll bet.' He looked away. Had I actually embarrassed him, or struck a deeper chord? 'Come on, Paul,' I pursued. 'You're not going to tell me that a bunch of young guys are not going to use a place like this to make out with girls.'

He shook his head.

'Why did you get invited in, Paul?'

He looked puzzled. 'What?'

'The group. You're quite a bit younger. How did you get to hook up with them?'

He frowned, thinking about it. 'They liked the way I played rugby,' he said, almost making it a question.

'It wasn't Wendy?'

'What the fuck has Wendy got to do with anything?' His voice cracked down into low and ominous.

'Why did Wendy run away with Boon's father?'

'We don't talk about her any more. She's not part of the family.'

'Why?' I pressed.

'Because she was a fucking little slut,' he snarled.

'And who made her that way?'

'Malcolm Paterson took advantage of her.'

'Surely he was just picking up the pieces?'

He looked at me as if I was crazy. This wasn't acting. The guy didn't know.

He didn't know. Paul Evans had not deliberately pimped his sister.

Had I got this completely wrong? My brain raced for a lever. Something that would switch the tracks back towards the possible. 'You brought her up here though, didn't you? You brought your sister to them?'

'She wanted to come with her friend Donna. I just helped out with a lift from time to time.' He smirked. 'Les couldn't exactly give them a lift, considering.'

'Considering that he was fucking Donna? Two-timing his fiancée?'

'They weren't engaged then. And Les was a mate.'

'What about Ken? Didn't you find it creepy that he was fucking around with your sister?'

His eyes flared angrily. 'He wasn't doing anything like that. They messed about, but it was just in fun. They knew she was my sister. She only turned into a slut when she ran off with that bastard Paterson.'

I watched his face. He believed this.

'Anyway, it was Donna we were all fucking,' he announced smugly.

'All?'

He smirked. 'That's right.'

'Les let you fuck his girlfriend?' I asked, playing up the disbelief.

'We all did her one night. They showed me the proof.'

I felt the tickle in my kidneys. I tried to remain impassive. 'What proof?'

He blushed. 'They showed me a photograph of me on the job.'

I kept my voice gentle. *Lead him calmly*, I instructed myself. 'Why would you need to see a photograph to know that, Paul?'

'We all took some pills that Les had. Whatever they were, they wiped me out.'

Now I saw it.

'Just one photograph?'

'We're not fucking perverts!' he blazed.

They only showed him the one. The one that made him their buddy. The rest of the set they kept to themselves. And Wendy. Oh yes, they shared them with Wendy. The tool that they had used to lock her into their lives.

'Tell me, Paul, did the photo show you taking Donna from behind?'

He scowled, reddening. 'How the fuck did you know that?'

Should I protect him?

Fuck no . . . He had been the instrument of Wendy's suffering.

'Paul, you fucked your sister.'

14

I asked Mackay for two favours. The loan of the Range Rover, and to take Paul home to Herefordshire with him. I needed him removed. I needed Ken and Les to get edgy. I wanted them wondering why Paul had disappeared.

Paul hadn't believed me. The initial shock of my accusation split his face for a moment, but his defences wouldn't allow it through. His imagination conspired with his psyche to convince him that I was playing a dirty trick on him. It didn't surprise me. The kind of manipulation and betrayal that used incest as a tool didn't belong in the Dinas that Paul inhabited.

But Wendy had not been given the choice. She would have been shown the full frontals in widescreen and Technicolor. A set of images that would have left her in no doubt that she had been buttfucked by her own brother. The pictures that Ken and Les threatened to show her parents unless she demonstrated full compliance. Okay, she probably hadn't been anywhere close to virginal. She had gone there voluntarily with Donna. She must have been aware what her friend was up to with Les. But this she didn't deserve. Now they had her anchored, riveted to their cause.

What pills had they been given? Rohypnol, most probably. Then again, as a farmer, Ken had connections with vets, so maybe ketamine. Whatever pharmaceutical it was, it didn't matter now. Long past traceability. The damage done. Paul and Wendy would both have been so out of it that they wouldn't have known what happened. Until they were shown the pictures. I winced, thinking about it. Trying to put myself into Wendy's position. The horror. I wondered whether the callous bastards had even considered the risk of this thing kicking her over so badly that she could have topped herself?

I had another thought then. The description of Paul's condition that night in the hut in the forest. The sight of him in the morning, coming down off the hill, wasted, Trevor Vaughan and Les Tucker propping him up. Were they still feeding him dope? For their amusement, or to keep him out of their affairs?

I drove the Range Rover off the track into a thicket of brush to hide it, and retraced my steps back to the Den. The light was starting to die, a wind picking up, catching the tops of the trees. I was in for a long cold wait if my hunch proved wrong.

This place was important to them. I was convinced of it. The quad-bike tracks were recent, and the ruts deep enough to show that they kept coming here. But the place was empty. Could Magda have been and gone?

I climbed the bank, up to a shelf that was large enough to accommodate me, with enough vegetation to hide behind. I made a gap in the bracken to give me a view of the approach to the hut over the clump of willows that screened it from the track, and settled down to wait.

I was pinning my hopes on Paul's mother. Her Sunday routine had been sideswiped. Her huge son had missed his Sunday lunch. She would start to be concerned. She would call his mobile phone. But, as we now controlled that, she would not get a reply. So she would start in on his friends. Ken and Les would both get a call.

And they in turn would not be able to raise Paul. So, would they get edgy? Start wondering if Paul had worked himself into a funk, and come up here for refuge? Or would they want to check out that this place was still safe?

I didn't care about the motivation. I just wanted them here. I wanted to see them open that box. I wanted to know if it really was empty. Or was there magic involved?

I felt like a hunter with only hope and the force of will to bait the trapline.

The day eased out. The light went into deep grey, the chill seeped in, and I lost all sense of time. The wind and the dampening effect of the surrounding trees chopped up all other night sounds. Even throttled down, the engines, when I first heard them, sounded like crop-duster planes. A squadron of them. The perception of distance was warped. The engines sounded as though they were getting closer, but I could see no lights.

I started to stand, hoping to increase my visual range, and caught it out there on a bend on the track. Nothing solid, just an impression of movement, a flitting of something momentarily darker than the blue-grey backdrop. I ducked back down, hoping that I hadn't sky-lined myself.

They were driving without lights. Two distinct engine notes were identifiable now. Coming slowly, using the tramlines on the tracks to navigate.

The bank's shadow deepened the darkness in the clearing in front of the den. They came through the willow screen as crude and unrefined shapes. Even when they stopped and dismounted there was not enough definition to make out which one was which.

They went to the door without talking. The padlock clattered against the corrugated iron when they unlocked it, and the buckled door opened with a screech. The door protested again as they closed it behind them, and an incandescent white light flared up as a gas mantle was lit inside.

And nothing more happened.

I waited them out. I forced myself to use my watch to stop my imagination telling me that too much time had passed. The gas light continued to flare in front of the sack curtain, and nothing passed between it to cast a shadow. I had to resist the urge to climb down and creep up in front of a window. It was too risky. I would make too much noise getting down off the bank.

What were they doing in there?

They startled me when they barrelled out of the hut flashing torches. The hairs on the back of my neck went up, and the skin around my scrotum tightened in a fear reflex. Then I realized that they weren't looking for me. The torch beams were aimed on the ground. They were arcing in front of the hut, crossing each other's trails, their torch beams swinging like erratic pendulums.

By the time they started shining the torches up on the bank, I had composed myself. The movements were perfunctory, they were just going through the motions. Whatever it was that they were looking for, they didn't expect to find it up here. There was an uncoordinated vibrancy about their actions. They were spooked.

Very carefully I checked my watch again. They

had been inside the hut for just under ten minutes. In a space that small, what could have taken them all this time?

With an almost insect affinity they came to an unspoken decision, turning back to the hut. They shut the gas light down, levered the sticking door closed, and padlocked it. This time they put their headlights on. They went through the willow screen in single file, and then branched off, each taking a different direction along the track. Both in a hurry.

I remained on my platform until the wash from the headlights disappeared, and then forced myself to stay put long enough to establish that they weren't going to double-back to sucker me. I climbed down into the clearing. The anticipation that had sparked when they first arrived had turned hollow. I had learned nothing. I still had an empty hut.

I walked to the far side where the willows clustered in. The smell of diesel from their quad bikes still hung in the damp air here.

I stopped, hammered to the spot when it came to me.

The quad bikes had petrol engines.

*   *   *

I ran through the possibilities and kept turning up the same result. I was smelling the residual fumes from a diesel generator's exhaust outlet. I risked shining my torch into the willows that crowded the base of the bank in front of me. But there was too much shadow involvement in the tangle of branches to make anything out.

I took a deep breath, shut my eyes, and

concentrated on listening. Catching the wind soughing through the trees on the bank above me, and that sense of suspension, as if all the wild things in the vicinity were holding themselves in bated stillness until my attention wandered again. Nothing mechanical.

I stood in front of the Den and went back through Ken and Les's arrival. The light that they'd turned on had had the unmistakable white incandescence of a gas lantern. At no point had I heard a generator start up.

I already knew where this was taking me. But, for the sake of professionalism and procedures, I had to argue with myself. By breaking into the Den, I would be putting a future case in jeopardy by making any evidence I found inadmissible. They would probably overlook the transgression if I discovered a body. But I didn't want to find a body.

How could I just walk away, though? Especially when there was a possibility that Magda's orbit had at last come into conjunction with mine.

I did some ethical juggling. Forcing an entry would be a Bad Thing because I did not have a search warrant, and it would corrupt any evidence that I might find. Covering up a forced entry would not turn it into a Good Thing, but, if I found anything vibrant in there to screw Ken and Les with, I was pretty sure that I could shoulder that moral burden.

The door had slumped on a mismatched set of hinges nailed to a raw pine post that was now rotted and spongy. I jiggled the door, working it towards me. The nails in the bottom hinge came out, and the door dropped and skewed with a painful screech of twisting iron. Now it was only supported by the top hinge and the padlock hasp. I slipped into the nearest shadow and practised rigid attention while I strained to hear if there were going to be any consequences arising from the banshee noise that I had just ripped the night with.

I gave a spider enough time to anchor half a web to my right ear before I crept out again. I gauged the door's list. By pulling the bottom corner away there would be just enough room for me to crawl in.

It was a tight squeeze, like trying to limbo dance into a crushed car. Inside the hut the enfolding darkness and the difficulty of the access made me feel trapped. I fought down the panic possibility that Ken and Les could return at any time. I couldn't risk turning their light on. I was going to have to rely on my torch, keeping it masked as much as possible.

The interior gave off a damp reek of burned butane gas and mildew. No sound of a generator, no smell of diesel fumes in here.

I swung the torch round slowly, concentrating on the rear wall, which was built up against the bank. This, like the rest of the interior, was lined with vertical timber planks. There was no visible door in the wall, and the only thing that could have disguised one was an old wardrobe, the walnut veneer peeling off. *The Lion, the Witch and the Wardrobe*? I resisted the temptation to open it and discover the portal to an enchanted land. Instead, I rocked it away from the wall. I didn't have to move it far. The back was solid, and the quantity of cobwebs and general crud behind it told me that it hadn't been shifted in a long time. Very carefully I moved it back to where I had found it.

I had an art teacher once who had almost inspired me. Mr Hawkins. He had a saying that he used to drill into us: *Things may not always be in the form that you expect to find them.* For him it had been about a way of relating to and experiencing abstract art; for me it became a useful exercise in keeping perception fluid.

Doors don't have to be door shaped.

I tested the floorboards with a flamenco dancer's foot stomp. Hollowness. There was a void under the floor. I got down on my knees and worked systematically across the room, moving the furniture piece by piece and replacing it in exactly the same spot as I had found it. I had a couple of false alarms but, on close inspection, they turned out to be just replacements for the original boards. There was no trapdoor.

My back ached when I stood up again. The doubt pills started to work. An instinct was nagging at me to get out of there. Had I been mistaken about the smell of diesel? Could I have misinterpreted some tricky olfactory esters produced by the decomposition of leaf mould because I had not wanted to accept that the game stopped here?

Doors don't have to be door shaped.

I used the mantra to damp down my internal panic, and looked around again. But I had already searched everywhere. The three external walls could be discounted, unless an entirely new dimension in the space/time continuum was involved, and I didn't have the physics to cope with that. I had checked behind the wardrobe. I had moved the sofa bed away from the wall. I went back to that thought and qualified it. I had moved the sofa bed when I had been looking for a trapdoor in

266

the floor.

I shifted it again, getting in close and concentrating on the wall this time. There was a horizontal seam in the vertical planking, low down, about seventy-five centimetres off the floor. It looked like a repair job, a replacement for some rotten boards. But then, they would want it to look like a repair job. Something that would pass a cursory inspection.

The panel was completely flush, and roughly square. I ran my fingers around the perimeter joint carefully, wary of wood splinters or deliberately planted needles. I missed it on the first circuit. A clever little spring-loaded catch that popped the top of the panel out when pressure was applied. I pulled it away. Behind the revealed opening was another, heavier, hatch set into a wall of dense concrete blockwork and secured with two heavy deadbolts.

I imagined Lord Carnarvon entering the tomb of Tutankhamen as I drew the bolts and pushed the hatch open. How fast-acting would the curse be in this place?

The hatch swung into silence and blackness. I crawled in, fighting the reaction that I was extruding myself into somewhere terrible. The air smelt stale, with a trace overlay of something mildly perfumed, a vague memory of the vicinity of a spinster aunt's dressing table.

I stood up out of my crouch, put a hand out behind me to steady myself, and recoiled. My fingers had just encountered a too busy geometry. I shone my torch. The inside of the wall was lined with egg boxes.

It took a moment for me to make sense of it.

They were using the dimpled boxes as acoustic baffles. Sound insulation. Back-up for the thick blockwork wall, to help to keep inside noise from travelling.

The torch picked up an old Bakelite light switch, and, instinctively, I flicked it. I heard a mechanical clunk, and the lights stuttered on. It was a demand switch to activate the generator. The clunk had been the flywheel kicking in. The noise dropped down to a muted chugging off behind some panelling to my right.

I had found the Rumpus Room.

The space was dominated by a contraption. A crude amalgamation of a barber's and a dentist's chair. The worn brown leather padded seat and back were raked at an acute angle. A range of leather securing straps was attached to the grey steel frame. A magnifying shaving mirror on a pivoting arm was fixed to one of the arm rests, and a full-length mirror was screwed horizontally to the ceiling above it.

I moved in closer, wondering why the thing gave off such a sense of clumsiness. Then I realized it was the welds. All over the frame, looking like metal scar tissue. Whatever this thing had been in the outside world, they had had to deconstruct its component parts to get it through the hatch, and had put it together without any reference to craft or beauty.

What kind of creepy experiments had been concocted on that thing?

I dropped the thought. Before my imagination could kick Ken and Les into action, I dragged my attention away.

The place was grim. It had the feel of being not

quite abandoned, as if despair had been distilled in here and allowed to seep into the fabric.

The other walls were plank-lined; the one to my right had been creosoted some time in the past. To damp-proof it, I supposed. Once I got my head around the shape I realized that the space was like a truncated wedge. The ceiling sloped down, and the walls appeared to taper in. It made sense. I was probably inside the quarry that the Den had been constructed in front of.

The floor was roughly tamped concrete. Two self-assembly single beds with air mattresses were placed on either side of a small, cheap, chest of drawers. I knew before I slid them open that the drawers would be empty.

The kitchen arrangement was basic. A two-ring gas burner on a wide plywood shelf supported on a pair of old kitchen cabinets. I opened them. Cans of beans and tomatoes mainly, dry pasta and rice in rusty biscuit tins to keep the mice and rats away.

The bathroom was a partition made from two old pine doors. Behind it there was a chemical toilet and a yellow plastic basin on another plywood shelf. The scum on the bar of soap was not quite dry. Two hairs on it. Too long to be either Ken or Les's. I didn't let myself get excited.

I went over to the two-drawer filing cabinet that I had been saving until last. I closed my eyes and unlocked it mentally before I tried the top drawer. It opened in real life too. A dish-drying cloth that was fooling no one covered a laptop computer with a mains lead coiled beside it. I cradled it out carefully on to the top of the cabinet, memorizing the position of everything that I was moving.

I checked the bottom drawer while I waited for

269

the computer to load. I almost gagged on the smell of lubricant and semen-soiled leather that time and damp had played around with. The drawer was a jumble of straps, dildos, vibrators, a metal curry comb, pliers, and a small, locked, black, precision-made box that made me think of surgical instruments.

The computer sang out its opening riff. It was prompting me to enter a password. Magda was in there somewhere, I was certain of it. Did it go back far enough to include Wendy and Donna? Colette?

I winced in frustration. How smart were those two likely to be?

I typed in *password* and hit the enter key. Smarter than that, the computer informed me. And I was running out of time. My nerves were telling me that I was stretching my luck. If I fought the flight impulse I knew that I would start making mistakes. I had no option but to put everything back, to try to leave the place in the exact same condition that I had found it.

I backed up to the hatch, making one last visual sweep to make sure that I hadn't left my mark behind before I switched off the light. The generator died and I fought down panic as the dark crushed in on me with the illusion that the room had just collapsed. I shuffled backwards into the greyness of the outer room feeling my world expand again. I bolted the inner hatch and turned round, flicking my torch on to see where I had left the outer hatch.

The torch beam picked up a patch of deeper darkness underneath the sofa bed. The thought that it could be a rat or a squirrel curtailed my reflex to reach under for it. I gingerly tilted the sofa bed up, and shone the torch again. The thing didn't move. It was dusty and had been flattened by the sofa bed, a crumpled bundle of some kind of fabric.

I tilted the sofa bed over completely to free up the space. Professional instinct warned me not to move this. I used my gloved forefinger to carefully unravel the bundle, fold by random fold, until it started to take on a recognizable form. A sweatshirt. A couple more moves turned it into a hooded sweatshirt.

Belonging to Magda?

I was trembling. This operation was too delicate and precise for an interloper who could be caught in flagrante delicto at any moment. My nerves were shrieking at me to just grab the thing and get the fuck out of there pronto. It was tempting. But I reminded myself that I was already involved in an illegal entry. If this thing was evidence, it had to stay here to be found as evidence.

I continued unfolding the sweatshirt until I was able to make out the logo on the front: S.W.A.T. in big block letters. But it wasn't that that was grabbing my attention. It was the rust-brown stain under the logo, roughly the shape of the continent of Australia.

I had been around enough victims to recognize the colour of dried blood under torchlight.

*   *   *

I was wired. I had to call Sally. I used the drive down out of the forest in search of a mobile-phone signal to try to analyse the event.

Had they simply been careless? It happened when people were in a panic. So often it was the way we got our breaks.

The body must have been wrapped somehow. There had been no sign of blood being scrubbed off that concrete floor. Probably naked, otherwise the clothes wouldn't have been loose. They would have been scrabbling out through that hatch with a body and a bundle of clothes, working against fear and high anxiety. As a result, they're not methodical. They don't think it through, don't consider that two trips might be required. They're too intent on getting out of there and disposing of this thing as fast and as soon as possible. Appalled by the weight and the awkwardness of it, they just want to be safe again.

So, somehow, the sweatshirt comes adrift. Gets lodged underneath the sofa as they struggle to get out and lock the place up behind them. The clothes are just something else to get rid of. They don't sort through them. They never realize, *Oh fuck, there's something missing.*

I had left everything the way I had found it. I had even hammered the dislodged nails back into the bottom hinge of the door with the heel of my shoe. When I went back in there, with company, I wanted the place to look virginal. Unmolested. I wanted to be able to play it as surprised as anyone.

But first I had to set up a reason to get back in there. Which was making me jumpy. Ken and Les could return at any time and find what they had missed before.

I pulled over as soon as the signal bar on my phone twitched into life. Sally came on the line at the Sychnant Nursing Home. 'What's this about, Glyn? Couldn't you sleep?' Her voice chirpy and curious.

I clenched my eyes shut for a moment, wishing that this could just be about flirting. 'Sally, please don't read anything into this, but I'd like you to try to remember what Boon was wearing the last time you saw him.'

Her voice dropped off the happy shelf. 'What do you mean, don't read anything into it?'

'Believe me, this is just routine,' I lied soothingly.

'What's happened, Glyn?'

'Nothing's happened. Someone answering Boon's description was seen in Holyhead.' I fed her the story I had prepared. For her own good, I told myself. 'We just need to check it out.'

'You mean someone saw a young black guy?' I heard her relax.

'It probably passes for excitement in Holyhead. What can you remember, Sally?'

She went quiet. Thinking back on it. 'He was up early. He had the trip to London for the rugby. Which is why I saw him when I got in from work. Normally, we're ships in the night. I made him a sandwich for the journey.' She went quiet again. 'Nike trainers and olive-drab cargo pants. Drooped, the way they wear them now, showing the top of his underpants. God, it used to drive me spare, that. He always wore Nikes.' I could tell from her voice that she was thinking ahead, using the description to ride into the memory. 'I remember telling him to dress warm. More than just a T-shirt and a sweatshirt. He said his parka would keep him plenty warm enough. I didn't argue, it was a good one, he bought it in Germany. Beige coloured,' she added, remembering I was trying to fit a description.

'What about the sweatshirt?' I asked casually.

'It was grey. The dreaded hood,' she added with

273

a laugh, 'with some sort of logo.'

I forced myself not to prompt her.

'S.W.A.T., I think. Whatever that means.'

'That's pretty comprehensive, thanks, Sally.'

'Is that a match?'

'I'll have to get back to our people in Holyhead.'

'If they confirm it, can we assume that he did go to Ireland?'

'It would look like it.'

'Is Graham staying with you?'

It took me a moment to get her slant. To remember that she was still in the world of romance and possibility. 'No, I can come out and play again.'

'When's that going to be?'

'I'll call you later, after we've both had our beauty sleep.'

Oh Jesus, I thought, after we had shut down the connection, what kind of news am I going to have for her then?

*   *   *

I was itching to go for Ken McGuire. But, as the Den was in Les Tucker's demesne, the only route that could work went through him.

Sara answered the door in her dressing gown. She looked surprised to see me, but not sleepy.

'Go away,' she said, without preamble.

I had already been to Les's home address. A ratty bungalow beside the family timber yard. A couple of dogs had barked in the house when I drew up, but the lights stayed off. I drove back into Dinas. Sara's place was a neat little Victorian villa. The lights were out here too, but Les's pickup was parked in the street.

'I need to speak to Leslie Thomas Tucker,' I announced, hoping that the sonorous formality would stop her shutting the door in my face.

'He has nothing to say to you.'

'Who is it, babe?' Les's voice called out from behind her.

'Go away,' she hissed again.

She started to close the door, but I put my hand on it, and crowded up on her. 'Les Tucker,' I called out over her head.

He came to the door. I moved back on to the top of the small flight of stone steps that led up from the street. He glowered when he saw me. He was wearing a vest over his trousers and no shoes. Even as young as he was he had a face that you would have described as craggy. Pocked and fissured from adolescent acne. Short, wiry brown hair above a receded hairline that gave him a huge expanse of forehead, and a nose that was waiting for ravage to give it its full glory.

But he looked powerful. The guy worked in the woods every day, I reminded myself.

'You're trespassing,' he told me.

'Paul Evans told me all about the Den.'

'Paul told you fuck-all.'

'Where do you think he's been all day?' I asked, and caught the tiny flicker of uncertainty.

'What's he talking about?' Sara asked, also picking up on that small change in Les.

'Fuck off,' he spat out at me.

'Does Sara know what you did to Wendy?'

The door slammed shut in my face. I counted it off mentally, trying to imagine what was happening on the other side of it. It opened again when I reached fifteen. I braced myself.

The advantage that I had always had here was that I knew that he was going to try to hit me. I just couldn't be sure when. That uncertainty disappeared as soon as I saw him in the doorway again.

He was hampered by rage. He wanted to shut me up. He was assuming that we were both equally surprised at this development. He flung a right at me, and followed through with a body charge, aiming to take me down the steps.

I wasn't quite quick enough to avoid the fist, which caught the top of my left shoulder as I was turning away from it. I sidestepped the body charge and tripped him as he went past, so that he launched into the air, executing a clumsy parabola, before hitting the paving slabs at the foot of the steps.

He landed on his side. The air went out of him with a gasp of shock and pain. I kicked him surreptitiously in the belly to drop him on to his face, and straddled his back, pulling out my handcuffs.

'Leslie Thomas Tucker, I am arresting you for assaulting a police officer.' I had the cuff snapped on to one of his wrists when Sara landed on my back. She wrapped a forearm round my throat, using it for balance and purchase, while she dug her other hand into my hair and wrenched my head back. She was drenching me with spittle as she screamed something so close to my ear as to make it unintelligible. At least with her mouth open, I remember thinking, she can't bite me.

I blocked the pain long enough to snap the free end of the handcuffs on to the wrought-iron garden gate. I was sensing Les coming back to life under me and I didn't want two of them free and seething. Sara had wrenched my head back as far as she could, but her grip on my throat was getting stronger. I summoned the gods and stood up, staggering under the burden like an overextended weightlifter. Sara clung to my back, her knees straddling my hips for better grip. To an onlooker this must have looked like weird rodeo.

I was being seriously throttled. Starting to get light-headed as the air supply shut down. I made a feint of grabbing for the hand that was wrapped into my hair to distract her. It worked. I felt the twist in her body as she moved her defences, and I let myself drop backwards.

She went down on to a small rosebush, with my deadweight following through on top. The breath went out of her before her synapses could relay the pain from the rose thorns. She loosened her grip on my throat as her body realized that this was doing nothing to help its cause. I squirmed round on top of her to keep her pinned down. Her dressing gown had come loose, and I realized that I was holding her down with one hand on a naked breast. Fuck the niceties, I thought, this lady is dangerous. 'For Christ's sake, Sara,' I yelled down at her, 'I'm not the problem—you're protecting a fucking child molester.'

She spat up at me.

I turned away and caught the flashing light bar as Emrys Hughes's car turned the corner. Pointing a warning finger at her, I climbed off warily. She glared at me balefully, pulled her dressing gown closed, and sat up slowly, arching her back against the pain, her eyes closed, wincing. Les hadn't quite made it past the groaning stage yet.

'What the hell's happening here?' Emrys yelled sternly.

'I'm arresting these two for assault.'

Emrys looked around, desperately hoping that I might be talking about someone else. He had caught the tail end of the melee, and knew that, despite his loyalties, he had to acknowledge that I was the good guy. 'Are you all right?' he asked Sara.

She stared up at him, hurting and sulky. 'He tried to feel me up,' she said, nodding at me.

Emrys looked at me.

I shook my head. 'I want these two in the holding cell at the police house. You'd better get a doctor in.' I leaned in close so that I could whisper. 'If I hear that Ken McGuire finds out about this tonight, I'm blaming you.'

'What's this all about?' he pleaded.

'You took your time getting here.'

He frowned. Only just thinking about it. 'You said there was a disturbance.'

'There was. You just witnessed it.'

'But you said you were at the scene of a disturbance when you called it in. How could you have known?'

I grinned at him. 'Psychic powers.'

15

'I'm woken up in the middle of the night because you have arrested some village boho for apparently demonstrating profound good sense by taking a swing at you?'

I was speaking to Jack Galbraith from the small office in Emrys Hughes's police house. Bryn Jones had set up a conference call between the three of us.

'I need a search warrant, sir.'

'So Bryn informed me. Now persuade me.'

'Les Tucker has a hut in the forest. He uses it with Ken McGuire. We're going to find evidence in there that has a direct bearing on the disappearance of Boon Paterson.'

'Who is your informant?'

'I don't have a direct informant, sir. I do have access to Paul Evans, who I'm sure will turn friendly when the evidence becomes incontrovertible.'

'I hope that there's no element of coercion in this?' Bryn asked warningly.

'None. He's staying with a friend of mine in Herefordshire on a purely voluntary basis.'

Jack Galbraith growled. 'But in the meantime we're meant to put our professional reputations on the line for one of your hunches?'

'It's more than a hunch, sir.'

The line went quiet. Jack Galbraith and Bryn had cut me off while they talked among themselves.

'Capaldi, if I am going to wake up a magistrate who owes me a favour, what guarantees do I have that all due procedures have been followed?'

Did he know? Had he guessed? 'Do you want me to put something in writing, sir?'

He groaned audibly. 'No, I do not want you to put anything in writing. I do not want to know about something before we've fucking found it. I do not want to be called into an office and asked to explain the startling prescience of one of my officers.'

'Due to Tucker's violent reaction when confronted, I have reason to believe that there could be quantities of illegal substances on the premises.'

'That's better.'

'What was he actually confronted with, Glyn?' Bryn cut in to ask.

'He hit me before I could get to it, sir.'

'Good point though, Bryn,' Jack Galbraith acknowledged. 'We won't be specific, just go broad spectrum about grounds for suspecting illegal activity. And we had better get that warrant to cover his house and workplace as well. We don't want any suspicions aroused by our pinpoint accuracy.'

*   *   *

We drove out to the Den in a Land Rover personnel carrier. I sat up front directing the driver, with Jack Galbraith and Bryn behind me. Les, in the company of Emrys Hughes and two big uniforms from Carmarthen, was in the rear compartment behind a heavy-duty wire-mesh screen. We had taken the handcuffs off. A shackled man behaves like a trapped man. We wanted Les flowing, we wanted to see his natural mindset, we wanted him to think that he could still use guile and cunning.

He played it affronted and disgruntled. Emrys tried to calm him down. The rest of us ignored him. But I was listening. Trying to catch his strategy. He couldn't have known about the sweatshirt or it wouldn't have been there for me to find. He had to be bluffing it out, running with the hope that we

280

were not going to uncover the inner sanctum.

We drove right up to the Den, not having to worry now about leaving visible tracks. The Land Rover was fitted with big spots, which illuminated the place like a film set.

'Isn't this taking things a bit too far?' Les protested, aggrieved, arms spread like a disgruntled Christ in his sterile suit.

'It's for your own protection, Mr Tucker,' Bryn volunteered, his reassuring smile covering the fact that he hadn't actually explained anything.

'What do you expect to find in there, a nuclear reactor?' Les asked, a thin dry crack in his voice under the sarcasm.

'I don't know, Mr Tucker. Is there any information you would like to volunteer before we proceed inside?' Jack Galbraith asked pleasantly.

Les flashed a glance at me. How much, he would be wondering, had Paul Evans revealed? He shook his head. 'No. There's nothing in there.'

'Are you going to open the door for us, Mr Tucker?' Bryn asked.

I saw a flicker of raw hope spark in Les, before it dawned on him that this was just a courtesy. Saying no wasn't going to stop this happening.

He tried anyway. 'This isn't just my place—a lot of people come here,' he protested.

'We'd like a list of names at some stage,' Bryn informed him.

'I'm not responsible for the things that get done in there.'

'You are responsible for me getting fucking cold out here, Mr Tucker.'

There is something about Jack Galbraith's voice that cuts through the shit. Les glowered at him, but stepped forward and unlocked the padlock.

The door screeched as it dropped even lower on to the bottom hinge that I had weakened. I had an anxious moment when Les glanced down at it. But it didn't hold his attention. He was obviously used to the periodic collapse of the place. And he had other things on his mind.

'There's nothing to find in here,' he announced truculently. The big spots were being trained into the hut while the portable lights were being set up. The additional light added to the sense of the room's decrepitude.

'What do you use this place for, Mr Tucker?' Jack Galbraith asked casually, running his torch and gaze slowly over the rear wall.

'It's just a shelter. Somewhere for a brew-up, if we're up this way shooting.'

I watched him obliquely, the same way that Jack Galbraith and Bryn were playing at not watching him. Looking for his troubled spots. The way his eyes pointedly refused to travel in the direction of the sofa. He thought that he was cleverly drawing our attention away from the hatch.

'Move that—' Jack Galbraith instructed, painting the sofa with his flashlight beam.

The two big uniforms took an end each and lifted it effortlessly away from the wall. Jack Galbraith's and Bryn's flashlight beams intersected on the flattened, crumpled bundle.

'Is that yours?' Jack Galbraith asked.

'I don't know.' Les was genuinely surprised, but not yet devastated. 'I didn't know it was there.' He was moving slowly, circling the bundle, making for the rear wall, trying not to draw attention to his journey. Not realizing that I knew exactly where he was going.

The portable lights came on, flooding the interior. 'Photograph it and grid its position,' Jack Galbraith instructed. 'Shift the rest of the stuff, I want to see under and behind everything.'

Les took up his position on the rear wall in front of the hatch, spreading his legs casually so that they covered the vertical seams, stooping slightly to keep the horizontal join obscured. He watched curious as the bundle was photographed. He sculpted a frown, as if he were trying to work out who among the boys could have left it there. The inherent damage in it still hadn't struck him.

The photographs and the offset measurements taken, Jack Galbraith nodded to Bryn, who dropped down beside the bundle. Slowly, and very carefully, using the shaft of a pen, he started to unfold it, making sure that Les, Jack Galbraith and the photographer always had full sight of every stage of the reverse origami.

I watched Les. Picking up the precise moment when he recognized what was unfolding in front of him. His jaw dropped fractionally, and the faintest tremor went through him, before he brought it back under control. He overplayed intense concentration now, coupled with nice-guy bewilderment. I saw the dynamic tension at work, the strain in his body as it struggled between remaining sentinel, and getting closer to the sweatshirt.

'Do you recognize it, Mr Tucker?' Jack Galbraith asked.

Les shook his head ponderously, making a show of deliberating. 'No . . . I don't think so . . . It's not one of mine. It could have been under there for years.' He tried to share a grin with us. 'The girls

283

don't get to come up here. So not too much cleaning gets done.'

'What girls are those, Mr Tucker?' I asked.

'Sara, and Sheila and Zoë,' he came back at me without blinking.

'Don't you want to get a closer look, see if you can identify it?'

'I can see it from here.'

Jack Galbraith glanced at me, and picked up my intention. 'Would you mind stepping away from the wall please, Mr Tucker.'

Les stared through him. I had seen the look before, in interview rooms, the furious concentration as the suspect searched for an act of magic, or of pure and implacable will, to get them out of there.

'That is not a request, Mr Tucker.'

*   *   *

I was delegated to stay behind to wait for the SOCO team. Since the discovery of the Rumpus Room, Les had turned mute and antsy. Jack Galbraith wanted him out of the big wide woods and into a confined place where they could start to question him formally. They also needed to get the sweatshirt and the laptop from the filing cabinet into the labs for analysis.

'I'm worried about Ken McGuire doing a runner,' I said. By this time, I had given them the tailored gist of my concerns and suspicions. The edited version. There were certain veerings on the way to this point where my trail could have been construed as having laid down slime.

'He's a farmer, he won't be going anywhere.

284

Those guys grow fucking taproots,' Jack Galbraith argued.

'He'll go if the consequences are bad enough, sir.'

Jack Galbraith frowned. 'I don't want to chance lifting him until we've got a definite on the sweatshirt. Or the laptop has started to tell tales. These people are solid-citizen category, their supporters can generate a lot of howl.'

'Do we bring Paterson's mother in to identify the sweatshirt?' Bryn suggested.

I didn't let them catch my reaction. I owed Sally this. If bad news was arriving, I was the one who was going to have to deliver it. 'Couldn't we have the blood type tested first, just to make sure that there is a match, before we put her through that?'

'We still need her. We have to establish the blood type.'

'The Army will have a record of that.'

Jack Galbraith nodded. 'He's got a point, Bryn. Let's keep citizens out of this for as long as we can.'

'Okay, I'll get on to the military as soon as we're out of here.' He gave me a knowing smile. Bryn had a memory that netted and retained lots of little details.

They walked to the Land Rover. Les was already locked in the back with Emrys Hughes. Emrys didn't realize that he was being used as Traitor Monkey, in the vague hope that Les might just treat him as a confessor. It wasn't working. They both looked like they were auditioning for the part of the last survivor on earth.

I experienced a sudden panic when I realized that the question of geography had not been discussed. 'Sir,' I yelled.

They both half turned round.

'Where are you taking him?'

Jack Galbraith dipped his head, tossing it to Bryn.

'I won't know that until I can get communications working, and start seeing what's available. Somewhere with the resources to hold the four of them, if it comes to it.'

Jack Galbraith grinned. 'Don't worry, Capaldi, we'll try to keep it on your patch.'

'Thank you, sir,' I said gratefully. For him it was a big concession. Staying in the boondocks.

I couldn't bring myself to wait in the Den. My imagination insisted on drawing my attention to the hatch, now seeing it as shaped for a coffin's exit. Or a crematorium oven. It was just too redolent of the possibility of bad discoveries. Instead, I waited outside in the cold bruise-blue night, while the breeze puffed a resin-tinged suspension of moisture into my face.

It was well into the small hours before the SOCO team arrived. They were a grumpy bunch, roused from their beds and shipped out to the operational equivalent of a leper colony. I soon got tired of shadowing them, waiting for someone to erupt into a gasp of significance. They didn't do exuberance or excitement; instead, they dusted and taped for prints, picked up fibres with tweezers, took lots of intensely close-up photographs, and grumbled quietly amongst themselves about the mess we had made stumbling all over the scene.

While they tackled the minutiae, I occupied myself with the surfaces. The floor of the Rumpus Room was old concrete, pocked and dusty, with no evidence of any section ever having been dug up and replaced. The same with the walls. They all sounded hollow, but then they were lining what was essentially an irregular cave. There were no indications of any sections of panelling having been replaced recently, and all the nail heads had the same rust patina. The wall that had been creosoted had faded uniformly. I stood on a chair to get a closer look at the ceiling, but that too appeared not to have been disturbed.

A dirty grey light was edging in from the east over the top of the bank by the time I was relieved. My eyes felt gritty and my mouth tasted like I had been snacking on fuller's earth. I drove out of the forest, the car's window fully open to stop the yawns fusing together into sleep.

I came awake with a sudden flash on Monica Trent. I fingered the scars that were healing on my cheek. I hadn't promised anything, but she had kept up her end, she had directed me to Alexandrina.

I got the answering machine. It suited me. I needed to keep this cryptic and nonattributable. Just in case somebody had a feed into her line. 'Monica, the farm boys have folded.'

I drove the rest of the way on automatic pilot and had stopped outside Unit 13 before I noticed the car. It was a dark blue Ford Fiesta, parked in the aisle between the caravans. Blanketed in tree shade and the dusky murk of early morning. It looked empty. I left my lights on and the engine running, and got out quietly without closing the door. My arrival had already been announced, I couldn't change that, but anyone inside my caravan didn't need to know that I was now out of the car.

I sidled past the Fiesta, intending to slide along the side of the caravan and check out the windows.

I stopped in mid-sidle and turned back, realizing that something had been wrong. It took me a moment to place it. The car had not only appeared empty, but it had had no driver's seat.

I stepped closer and saw my mistake. The seat had been fully reclined. The body on it stirred, sensing my presence.

She sat up slowly, rising out of the shadow of the well, looking puffy, sleepy, and bewildered.

But beautiful.

I had been allowed the grace to see the nascent Sally Paterson.

*   *   *

'I left work early.' She blinked and shivered as she stepped out into the cold early-morning air. I saw the pink nylon Sychnant Nursing Home housecoat crumpled on the back seat. She was wearing jeans, a T-shirt and a light wool cardigan that wasn't adequate for the season.

'Why didn't you go home?' I draped my coat around her shoulders.

She tried to shrug it off. 'Let's go inside; I'll be all right then.'

'No, you won't, it's just as cold in there.'

She gave in and let me settle the coat on her. I unlocked the door and followed her into the living area. She slumped down on to a seat, her shoulders bent forward in a posture of exhaustion. 'I had to see you.'

I looked up from lighting the gas fire. 'I'm flattered,' I quipped, trying to keep it light, but feeling the doom settling into the pit of my stomach.

'I thought about what you said. About Boon being spotted in Holyhead. Asking me about his sweatshirt. And the more I thought about it, the more I came to realize that it was bullshit. Bullshit, right?' Her eyes were red-rimmed. She had been crying. But the look was questioning and steady.

'We really don't know anything yet, Sally.'

'It's winter, Glyn. It's cold. Even Boon would have had his coat fastened. No one would be able to see a sweatshirt.'

'He might have been inside.'

She tightened her face to pinch in the tears. 'Don't dig yourself in any deeper. Please . . .' She shook her head and held out her hand. 'Be my friend . . .'

I hunched down in front of her and took her hand. What could I tell her? I raced through the permutations. How could I keep distress out of this? 'We've found a sweatshirt. It matches the one you said Boon was wearing.'

Her grip on my hand tightened. 'Where?'

'A hut in the forest that Les Tucker owns.'

She digested this. I saw her searching for significances. She shook her head. 'Why didn't you tell me?'

'We've only just found it. I didn't want to upset you.'

She stared at me. 'There's more, isn't there? If it was just the sweatshirt, you would have told me. That would have been a clue. Part of his trail. You would have, wouldn't you? To reassure me.'

I nodded. 'We think there's blood on it.'

Her face twisted. 'Oh God . . .'

I moved in closer. On my knees I was level with her. I put my free arm around her and pulled her

289

into me. Her head sank on to my shoulder. Her body felt like an overtightened drum. I could sense the embryonic sobs like a demonic pulse, waiting to surface. 'There's nothing to know yet, Sally. That's why I didn't tell you. We have to run tests.'

She gave a piteous wail, something raised out of, and voiced from, a deep-set archetype, and the tears welled. I held her tightly, trying to project comfort through the sobs and the shaking.

'What's happened to him?'

It was a question I couldn't answer, so I just continued to hold her as she rocked on the seat.

Gradually, her tension eased. She slowed the rocking. I loosened my clasp before she could sense it as constrictive, found a clean paper tissue and put it into her hand. She brought it up to her bowed head. When she looked up, her eyes were raw, tear runnels staining her cheeks. But she managed a small, sheepish smile. 'I'd better go home.'

I helped her stand up. 'No, you're staying here tonight. Or what's left of it.'

She started to shake her head, but gave up. We had gone beyond etiquette. I led her to the bathroom. 'Do what you have to do; I'll find you something to wear.' She nodded lumpishly, whacked by emotion and exhaustion.

When she came into the bedroom, I had dug out an old T-shirt that Gina had brought me back from Lanzarote. It was blue, faded and had a César Manrique print on the front, but it was clean and large enough to act as a nightshirt on her. 'This okay?' I asked.

She nodded, hardly glancing at it, and sat down on the bed.

'Want a cup of tea?'

She nodded again. Then looked up me, her face suddenly very young and frightened. 'I don't know what to do,' she whispered.

'First tea, then sleep, then we take it from there,' I said, hearing myself sound like a fully qualified grandmother. I slipped out before she could question my credentials.

When I returned, her clothes were half-heartedly folded on the floor, and she was in bed, lying on her back, her eyes closed. I went in quietly and put the tea on the bedside table. She opened her eyes. 'Please don't leave me alone tonight.' She drew down the side of the duvet nearest me and shifted over on the bed. 'Please . . . Just for comfort.'

*   *   *

We started off tense and chaste beside each other. Each worrying that the other might construe intent out of the simplest movement. So we stayed cocooned and rigid. And fell asleep like that.

I woke with the warmth of her pressed against me. Her face tucked into my collarbone. We had moved in our sleep to accommodate each other. I felt her breath, warm and lightly moist through the fabric of my T-shirt.

Then the sound that I had managed to insinuate into the backdrop intruded. It was the beep of the answering machine. A missed call that we had both slept through. At the same moment I realized that Sally's eyes were open. She was listening to it too. 'Don't go just yet,' she whispered. 'Don't spoil this.'

As she said it, she slipped up the bed. I turned into her. The kiss bypassed hesitation, our mouths and tongues met and functioned as if the fit had been engineered. Through the blood surge, I felt her nipples graze my chest, and my cock turned to concrete. I lifted my T-shirt to get the true feel of her. She broke the kiss, keeping the rhythm of it in her pelvis against me, to pull her T-shirt over her head. She came back to my mouth again, her hand slipping down to grab my cock. I licked the flat of my hand and circled it over a nipple, teasing the nub of it even harder. She arched her back. I was so spoiled for choice. So much to savour. I left the breast and travelled south, her weight shifting and her legs opening as she anticipated me.

She moved on to her side, raising her leg to lead me into her, cupping my balls as I drove in, pressing our chests together, clutching for as much contact as we could achieve. I felt myself come, a huge, pent-up surge that I didn't want to be ready for. Too soon. I had wanted to take her with me.

Sensing my disappointment, she whispered, 'It's all right,' Her hand stroking me down from the small of my back to the coccyx.

'I think I just spoiled it,' I whispered, full of postcoital failing and chagrin.

'No, you didn't. We have to start somewhere. That's what's important.' She kissed me. 'We've started.'

Sex had postponed the real world. We both shuddered involuntarily as the beep of the answering machine brought it back into our lives. 'What's going to happen?' she asked softly.

There were too many paths forking ahead, each with its own branches and blank trails. Too many variable causes producing too many variable effects.

'I don't know, Sally.'

'Give me a good lie then.'

292

'What about a better truth?'

'Try me.'

'I want to take care of you.'

She looked at me steadily, holding her question back. 'For how long?'

'To see you through this. At least. A step at a time.'

She leaned across and kissed me gently. 'Deal.'

I wrapped a towel around my waist and pulled a sweater on. Checked the clock. It was between midday and one o'clock. I felt my stomach clamp, it was as if I had girded tension on again with the towel. How much movement had we already slept through?

The call was from Bryn. The message had been left shortly after eleven o'clock.

'Where are you?' I asked, when they patched me through to him.

'Rhayader. We've managed to set up a facility. It's not perfect, but the phones and the computers work.' He gave me my instructions.

When I turned round I expected Sally to be in the doorway. I just hadn't expected her to be dressed. I buried my disappointment. 'We've got a positive match with Boon's blood type,' I said, answering the question in her pose.

She squeezed her eyes shut momentarily, holding control. 'What do we do now?'

'They've been trying to call you. I'm meant to find you and bring you in to formally identify the sweatshirt.'

She managed a weak smile. 'Okay. It has to be done.'

I went over and swept her up into a big hug. She buried her face into my chest. I spoke softly into her ear. 'Take all the time you need. And just remember what I said about seeing you through this.'

*   *   *

The facility was on the outskirts of town and, if you overlooked the razor-wire compound, it appeared to be a small, innocuous industrial shed. It contained a cluster of holding cells and interview rooms. The place had been set up when the top brass realized there were potential terrorist targets in the locality—numerous wind farms, the Elan Valley dams—and nowhere secure in this low-crime area to hold any terrorists they might come across.

A woman PC took Sally off my hands. She played her part well, saying goodbye and thanking me like an amicable stranger.

They took me to Bryn and Jack Galbraith. I should have remembered their habits. I forgot to suck in some good clean air before I went into the room. Their cigarette fug had achieved the density of a screen laid down by a pocket battleship running for cover. But as a milieu it seemed to be working. They both looked happy.

Jack Galbraith, his chair tilted back under the NO SMOKING sign, feet up on the desk, made a show of checking his watch. 'You keeping California time, Capaldi?'

'Did you manage to locate Mrs Paterson?' Bryn asked, before I could respond. His voice betrayed no hint of irony or suggestion.

'Yes, sir. She's being shown the sweatshirt as we speak.'

As if on cue, the phone on the desk rang. Bryn

listened with a chopped involuntary nod, and replaced the receiver. 'It's positive. She's fairly certain that it's what he was wearing to go to London.'

I winced internally. Poor Sally. She had told me that she had been prepared for the worst. I just hoped that that had included seeing her son's dried blood on his sweatshirt.

'Can we bring Ken McGuire in now?' I asked.

'We're way ahead of you there.' Jack Galbraith beamed.

'We brought both McGuire brothers in for questioning this morning,' Bryn explained.

'What changed?'

Jack Galbraith laughed at my surprise. 'The Cardiff hooker retracted her statement. She walked in this morning. Voluntarily.' He gave me a crafty look. 'Almost as if she was connected to a psychic link into the boondocks.'

'Did you talk to Mackay?' I asked Bryn.

'Yes, he has very kindly delivered Paul Evans to our Hereford friends.'

'Are we going to bring him up here?'

Jack Galbraith shook his head. 'No, we're going to leave him with the amigos there for the time being. Use the distance. He can be our control. If there's a change-of-story virus running amok up here, I want to make sure that he doesn't catch it.'

'What about the laptop?' I asked.

'It's not singing yet. The Tech boys are still delving and diving.'

'We can hold them on suspicion with the sweatshirt. And with Monica Trent's retraction, we've got enough to charge them with something inventive. So we're not short on time for some

295

careful sifting,' Bryn told me happily.

'What are they saying?' I asked.

'It's like one of those fucking gizmos with callipers and pencils that can copy the same signature.' Jack Galbraith scored crosses in the air with his forefinger to demonstrate. 'They're all telling the same story. Even after we floored them with the hooker's retraction, they just picked themselves up and launched into the next identical version.'

'Even Paul Evans in Hereford,' Bryn explained, 'when he was told that Monica Trent had pulled their alibi.'

'Now they're actually admitting that they did pick up your East European lady at the filling station.' Jack Galbraith inclined his head at me. It was all I was going to get in the way of apology or approbation. 'The reason they're giving for the hooker version is that it was to give Boon Paterson time to get to Ireland with the hitchhiker. Seems that he had a sudden road-to-Damascus moment and decided to leave the Army and take off with her. His plan, supposedly, was to make for Amsterdam via Dublin. And his loyal buddies aided and abetted him by coming up with the hooker-and-pimp obfuscation.'

This was essentially the tale that Trevor Vaughan had given me. 'How do they explain the sweatshirt? And the blood on it?'

'They're stonewalling. Pleading total ignorance,' Bryn explained. 'My guess is that they're surprised that it's surfaced. They're having to stall because they haven't been able to get together to work out how the sweatshirt got overlooked.'

'What's your take on it, sir?' I asked Jack

296

Galbraith.

He steepled his fingers. 'It's the fallback story. If it follows the usual pattern, we can suppose that there are elements of truth in it. We assume that there was an argument that they are not telling us about. So, best case, did Boon Paterson get to Ireland with the girl but with a bloody nose, and minus his sweatshirt? Or, worst case, did only the girl get there?'

'What if neither of them got there?'

He shrugged. 'Don't complicate things, Capaldi. Let's just say that, at this stage, the only blood on the tracks appears to belong to Boon Paterson.'

Ireland . . .

What was it that was niggling me about Ireland?

And then I remembered. My first meeting with Zoë McGuire.

'Sir, can I speak to Gordon McGuire?'

He picked up the urgency in my voice and flashed Bryn a glance. 'Why him in particular?'

'Because he's got the most to lose.'

16

I watched Gordon McGuire through the mirrored glass. He was sitting in the interview room with his solicitor. The audio feed was on. If he was nervous, he wasn't showing it. Or sounding it. He was telling the solicitor about a big pheasant shoot in Lincolnshire that he had been invited to.

His bluff auctioneer's manner darkened when I walked in. He let me see the scowl. 'I hope you're coming to tell me that we can leave.'

'That's not up to me, I'm afraid, Mr McGuire,' I replied soothingly, and proceeded to formally set up the interview. Bryn had already advised me that the solicitor wasn't a threat; a country practitioner who was way out of his depth.

Gordon turned his professional charm back on. 'We tried to help a friend out, Sergeant. Okay, technically, we may have done something borderline illegal. But isn't all of this—' he barked a short laugh and spread his hands, taking in the recording machinery and personnel in the room '—just a little bit over-elaborate for a misdemeanour?'

'Where is Boon Paterson, Mr McGuire?'

He glanced at his solicitor and sighed wearily. 'We've been through all this. Okay, we told some fibs, and maybe, unintentionally, we've wasted some police time, but we were just trying to help Boon.' He gave me his good-fellow stare, about to pitch the sell. 'We were drunk. Wales had beaten England. We'd had a great day out together. Possibly, under other circumstances, we wouldn't even have considered doing what we did. But, once we had, we were committed to it for our friend's sake.'

'You haven't answered my question, Mr McGuire.'

'Okay, to answer your question, I would imagine that he should be in Holland by now.'

I made a show of studying the notes in front of me. 'You didn't actually see him go, did you?'

'No, I stayed at the hut.'

'So, how do you know that they got to the station at Devil's Bridge?'

'They didn't go to the station at Devil's Bridge,

they went to Ponterwyd to catch the bus.'

I glanced at my mythical notes again. 'Isn't the train from Devil's Bridge the obvious way to get to Aberystwyth?'

'It would be, if the trains were running at this time of year.' He smirked, pleased with himself at sidestepping what he thought was my attempt at a trap. He didn't realize that I wanted him cocky. It would make the prospect at the cliff's edge that much more abrupt when I led him to it.

'How do you know they actually got to Ponterwyd?'

'Ken and Les told me when they got back to the hut.'

'And you believed them?'

He smiled at me condescendingly. 'My brother and my best friend, Sergeant? Of course I did.'

'Let me see if I've got this right . . .' I said, pretending to read from my notebook. 'They drove Boon and the girl back to his house to pick up his passport and pack some stuff. Then they drove to Ponterwyd, where they dropped them off. Then it's back to Les's to pick up a quad bike. The quad bike follows the minibus to the drop-off point. Then they both return to the hut on the quad bike. That about it?'

He nodded. 'More or less. They hid the quad bike and walked the last bit. We didn't want you lot finding it and spoiling Boon's chances.'

I pulled a puzzled frown. 'We're hearing a lot about Boon's chances. But not about why his bloodied sweatshirt was found in Les's hut.'

He smiled bemusedly. 'No, none of us can explain that either.'

'Mr McGuire, why did you tell your wife that she

wouldn't be going to the rugby international in Dublin with you this year?'

'What?' The question had come at him out of the sun.

'You told your wives and partners that they wouldn't be accompanying you to Dublin. Breaking a tradition, weren't you?'

'What has this got to do with anything?' he blustered, his smug crust starting to crumble, looking to his solicitor for support.

'I think you know exactly what we're talking about.'

'It's no business of yours what arrangements I make with my wife.'

'I don't see that there's any relevance in this line of questioning, Sergeant,' his solicitor came in, belatedly sensing Gordon's concern.

I gave him a terror stare and shifted back to Gordon. 'That's how you persuaded the girl to stay, isn't it? Told her that you would get her safely to Dublin when you all went over for the international. Safety in numbers, was that the line you used?'

'She went with Boon.'

'No, she didn't, Gordon. She was locked up in the Den. She was turned into a sex toy. Just like you did with Wendy Evans, and Donna Gallagher, and Collette Fletcher, and God knows what other ones you managed to haul into your net.'

'Sergeant, please . . .' the solicitor protested.

I leaned in across the table at Gordon, shutting the solicitor out of my vision. 'Did Boon try to save her? Is that what happened, Gordon? Did Boon get in the way?'

'No.' He leaned across to meet me, angry now. 'Boon was our friend. Can't you understand that, you bastard? Can't you understand friendship?'

'Did Boon try to protect her?'

'There was nothing to protect her from. It was her free choice. She wanted to stay, for Christ's sake . . .' He slammed his eyes shut, realizing his admission.

I gave him time. I put the flat of my hand in front of the solicitor's face to shut him up. I didn't want Gordon distracted now.

He shook his head, pissed at himself. But there was a new note in his tone, almost relief. 'Her work permit had expired, she was an illegal immigrant. She was afraid of the police. What was going to happen when she tried to get on to the ferry. And there was a gangmaster chasing her.' He stared at me. 'Does this have to come out into the open?'

'That depends. Why?'

'Sheila and Sara. You see, it wasn't Boon that she wanted to protect her, it was Ken and Les. She wanted Ken and Les to get her safely over to Ireland. She wanted to travel in a crowd. Boon was too distinctive to go with. Boon went on his own. She was happy to stay behind and wait.'

*   *   *

'Where is she, Mr McGuire?' Bryn asked affably. I sat beside him in the interview room across the desk from Ken and his solicitor, a slightly more senior version of the one who had sat in with Gordon. Bryn had opted to play the part of the Soft Cop. That suited me.

Jack Galbraith was currently in another room bracing Les Tucker with a young DC from Carmarthen that he was grooming. He would be

301

playing both the Tough Cop and Soft Cop roles, she was there merely to observe and admire.

Ken folded his arms in a gesture of weary patience. 'If you're talking about the woman that we gave a lift to, we've already told you that. The last time we saw her was when we left her in Ponterwyd with Boon, on their way to Dublin via Holyhead.'

'Are you very sure about that, Mr McGuire?' Bryn asked kindly.

'We've explained it enough times.'

'You're lying again, Ken,' I cut in. 'How many layers of shit are we going to peel off this time?'

'Sergeant . . .' Bryn remonstrated, smiling apologetically at Ken and the solicitor. But they were focused on me now, waiting for the next spout of malice. They didn't see him slip the photograph from a folder out on to the desk, face down.

'This is, chronologically, the first image that we have found on the laptop computer that was taken from Mr Tucker's hut for analysis . . .'

That grabbed their attention. Their eyes whipped round on him, Bryn's fingers splayed out on the back of the photograph as if trying to stop it from turning itself over.

'Want to tell us about it, Ken?' I probed mischievously.

He ignored me. Kept his expression impassive.

Bryn flipped the photograph over. The effect was anticlimactic. The image was blurred and incomprehensible.

Ken faked ignorance, only the solicitor was truly puzzled.

'It's a beaver shot,' I explained to him.

He frowned, even more clueless.

Bryn obliged him by turning over another photograph. 'This is from the same series.'

The solicitor gasped and visibly blanched. This time it was unmistakable. The camera was focused now, and the unseen woman had been persuaded to use her index fingers to stretch the lips of her labia, exposing the pink folds through the dark mat of pubic hair.

'Whose snatch was that, Ken?' I asked conversationally. 'Monica Trent or Alexandrina? Or were you using random prostitutes in those days as well?'

Ken shook his head. 'I know nothing about these, and I know nothing about the computer you say they came from.'

Bryn already had the next photograph prepared. 'Perhaps this will jog your memory, Mr McGuire,' he said as he turned it over.

'Oh my God . . .' the solicitor groaned, averting his head.

A young, naked girl was on her stomach straddling the contraption in the Rumpus Room. She was plump, and I didn't recognize her from the photographs of Donna and Colette that Joan Harvey had shown me at the Sychnant Nursing Home. But in those, neither girl had been wearing that faraway fish look people take on when they are concentrating on working their mouth around an erect penis. This one belonged to Les Tucker. Ken, skinny and naked, behind her, had inserted himself into an orifice. The camera had been set on an automatic trip, and both men were grinning at it, cheekily triumphant, anticipating the countdown. But what, irrationally, infuriated me the most, was the fact that they both still had their shoes and socks on. They had not even had the sliver of grace to share the poor girl's nudity.

'Donna or Colette?' I asked. We knew from the chronology that it couldn't be Magda. And Emrys Hughes, who had had to be ordered to continue looking at the images, had eliminated Wendy Evans by identifying her in other shots. Interestingly, we had also found images of Kylie, one of Sara's current employees.

'She was a consenting adult.'

'Who?' I insisted.

'Donna Gallagher.'

'Where is she now?'

'I have no idea. She wasn't around here for very long. She moved away, and that was the end of the story. There is nothing illegal in what we did.' He gave his solicitor a challenging look.

'Wendy Evans was fifteen,' I corrected him.

'Not when she volunteered to play with us,' he shot back. 'She was over the age of consent then.'

'It's not exactly normal behaviour is it though, Mr McGuire?' Bryn cut in, trying to sound like a sympathetic but slightly concerned uncle.

Ken gave a small, deprecatory shrug. 'It is what it is. I admit, seeing it laid out on the table like that, out of context, makes it look a bit disturbing. But, essentially, it was just a piece of fun. It didn't hurt anyone. And I'm fairly sure that the ladies enjoyed it.'

Bryn signalled me to keep control. He pulled a curious face. 'But why?' he asked gently. 'By all accounts, you're a happily married man.'

Ken responded to the softness with a conspiratorial smile. 'Because you're not going to do those sorts of things to your wife, are you,

Inspector?'

I could have hit him. I felt Bryn's shoe straddle my toes, amplifying his previous signal to stay backed-off.

Ken sensed my fury and helplessness. He cocked his head and gave me a look of concern that we both knew was pure twisted irony.

Bryn pulled out another photograph. Magda. Sitting on one of the twin beds in the Rumpus Room, wearing a T-shirt and jeans, smiling into the camera. I read bravery built into the smile. A tourist with her new friends.

He tapped the photograph and fixed Ken with a penetrating stare that moved the game up another level from his previous polite friendliness. 'This is the young woman who was captured on the filling station's CCTV camera getting into your minibus.'

Ken pretended to study the picture. He had to have known that this was coming. He had already had time to rehearse this. They must have realized that we had the resources to unlock the laptop's secrets.

'This isn't Ireland, Ken,' I pointed out, clawing back a little bit of self-satisfaction.

'That's very observant of you,' he snapped, and then let his voice relax. 'In fact, I'm sure you know that this was taken in the back room of the Den.'

'So, you don't deny that she was there?' Bryn prompted.

'Can we give her a name?' I asked. We already knew, Gordon had told us. I just wanted to hear what Ken did to the sound of it.

'Marta,' Ken said, no emotion. 'Her surname was unpronounceable. We took that photograph when we all went back to the Den to pick up the quad bike. This was after we'd been to Dinas to get Boon's things.'

Something was wrong. We should have been smelling fear coming off him. He was too confident.

'Of course—' He didn't quite snap his fingers, but he used his eyes and raised his inflexion to let us share his eureka moment. 'That's what I had forgotten . . . That's where the blood came from!' He smiled at us. It was meant to be apologetic, but he couldn't quite hide the tip of a small cone of triumph. 'I'd had a bit too much to drink that night. We all had. But it's coming back to me now. Boon had a nosebleed. It dripped on to his sweatshirt. I think I even remember him taking it off. Somehow it must have got crumpled under the sofa. It was lucky that we'd already picked up his things, so he had another sweatshirt to wear.'

'What caused the nosebleed?' Bryn asked.

'A violent sneeze, I think.'

'And Mr Tucker can verify this?'

Ken smiled helpfully. 'He will when he's reminded. He was even further gone than me.' He raised his hands playfully, enjoying himself now, shooting his solicitor a look of mock shame. 'Not that either of us can remember who drove the minibus that night.'

'And Marta was there when this happened?' Bryn asked.

'Sure. She'll confirm it. If you can track her down in Ireland.'

I leaned forward across the desk to get closer to Ken. 'I don't think that Marta ever got to the Den that night.'

He laughed into my face. 'You've just shown us the photograph, Sergeant. It's your own evidence, for God's sake.'

'Your computer gives that photograph a later date,' Bryn pointed out.

'That was the date that it went on the computer. Not the date it was taken.'

'I'm not saying that Marta wasn't ever at the Den . . .' I expanded cheerily.

He frowned momentarily, wondering where I was going with this. 'That was the only night she could have been there. She went on to Ireland with Boon,' he elaborated patiently.

I shook my head. Held his stare for a beat. 'The minibus was never driven there. You took her somewhere else that night.'

'I don't know what you mean.' He looked to Bryn for an explanation.

I tracked two fingers along the desktop. 'The only vehicles that were ever driven down to the Den were quad bikes. The minibus would have left tyre tracks. There were no such tracks. I think you dropped her off somewhere else. Perhaps you risked using Les's bungalow for that first night. Before you brought her to the Den.'

'Rubbish . . .' he exploded, shaking his head vehemently.

'But Boon went back to the Den with you. That's why his sweatshirt was there.'

He shook his head. You get used to seeing people's thought processes in interview rooms. His were quick. 'We all went to the Den. We parked the minibus and walked.'

'You seem to be packing a lot of activity into this night, Mr McGuire,' Bryn observed dubiously.

'Ken, it was a filthy night,' I all but shrieked, 'no one would have chosen to be out there in that weather.'

He nodded. 'That's right, the track was muddy, we didn't want the minibus to get stuck.'

'And I suppose Boon lugged a suitcase with him, in the freezing rain, wading through the mud, just in case he got a nosebleed and would have to change his sweatshirt?'

He flashed me scorn. 'He changed when we got back to the minibus.'

'I think you're full of bullshit, Ken.'

'It's Mr McGuire to you. And I believe you have to prove that . . .' He started to smile at his solicitor, and then I watched his eyes move to the small tape recorder that Bryn had just produced.

'*You see, it wasn't Boon that she wanted to protect her, it was Ken and Les. She wanted Ken and Les to get her safely over to Ireland. She wanted to travel in a crowd. Boon was too distinctive to go with. Boon went on his own. She was happy to stay behind and wait.*'

Bryn switched Gordon McGuire's voice off. We both watched Ken. He just stared at the tape recorder.

'What really happed with Boon, Mr McGuire?' Bryn asked gently.

'Where did you move Marta to?' I asked, trying to match his tone. 'Where are you keeping her now?'

'Was there an accident?' Bryn soothed. 'Is that what you're trying to cover up? We appreciate that accidents can happen. We are aware of panic reactions. I promise you, we are capable of understanding.'

Ken's head snapped up to face us. He smiled. We had hoped that he would crumble before he realized our fatal flaw. But he had seen it. 'Why don't you ask Gordon?' He threw it at us as a challenge. It was up and bobbing on top of the fountain now. The knowledge that Gordon had not been a party to the events that rolled out after they had left the hut in the minibus that night.

The interview was over.

*   *   *

We strengthened the SOCO team and split it into two. Jack Galbraith took one half to trawl Les Tucker's timber yard, and Bryn took the other to do the same with his house. We had Ken McGuire's farmhouse and outbuildings already secured to perform the same exercise.

Neither of them invited me along.

Jack Galbraith was angry and frustrated. Despite his Nobel Prize-winning skills in intimidation, he had not managed to get Les Tucker to veer from their story. He denied any knowledge of the sweatshirt in the Den, swore blind that he couldn't remember any of the girls in the photographs, despite the fact that his erect penis featured in the mouth of one of them. When Gordon's tape was played, he listened intently, looked up, and asked, 'Who was that?' Jack Galbraith's fury was compounded by the fact that the stand-off had occurred in front of his current acolyte.

Les would have been acting under instructions. To play dumb and deny everything. Ken would look for the loopholes. We couldn't keep them apart for ever; sooner or later he would be able to smuggle the new strategies out to Les.

I drove back up to the Den. I should have been catching up with the backlog on the day job, which would be piling up like faggots around a martyr's pyre, but it was too mundane. I wouldn't have been able to concentrate. I was hyped up, back in the land of sex and death that I had once inhabited, and I was hanging on to that territory.

Had we missed anything here?

I stood in the middle of the Rumpus Room, shutting the Contraption out of my imagination, trying to concentrate on anomalies. There was no evidence of any excavations or replaced boards. The blue-light scanner had revealed no concealed bloodstains, apart from some old residues of menstrual fluids on the Contraption's leather and one of the mattresses. Plenty of hair and fibre samples. A cornucopia of them. But, even if we found a match to Marta or Boon, it wouldn't help: Ken's new line of defence was the admission that they had both been here before they were driven to their rendezvous with Ireland.

Marta had been here. I closed my eyes. Tried to smell her. But all I was picking up were mould spores and concrete dust.

I was looking for anomalies. I pictured the space in my head, and shifted my stance before I opened my eyes. So that I was looking at the creosoted wall.

An anomaly?

Why would they creosote an internal wall?

Because it was getting damp? The walls were built to square off the inside of a cave or quarry. Caves are damp. Creosote preserves the timber.

But why just the one wall? If the place was suffering from damp, why hadn't they treated the other walls and the ceiling?

What else does creosote do?

I placed my palms flat against the planking. The

creosote was streaked and faded, long-dried and soaked into the timber. This had been applied years ago. I asked myself again, feeling the dread-tinged excitement rising: what else does creosote do?

It smells. It smells fucking terrible. It smells of tar distillation and poison. It covers other smells. Those other smells would have to be so bad that the smell of creosote was preferable.

I grazed my spine in my hurry to get under the hatch and out to my car. By the time I got back to the Rumpus Room with the crowbar it was hurting, and I could feel a slow trickle of warm blood making its way down to my waist. I blocked it out.

I could be wrong, I warned myself. This could turn into the wilful damage of private property.

I wedged the flat end of the crowbar into a seam in the planking. I levered the bar forward, and almost fell flat on my face from my own momentum as a section of timber broke away with neither resistance nor sound, just a big puff of dead wood dust. I worked more wood free until I had a hole big enough to shine my torch into. I peered in but could see only blackness.

Gingerly, I put my hand in. *There is nothing in there*, I told myself. Nothing is going to grab my hand. There is nothing that has been lurking in there, waiting for this moment to slither up and sink teeth or mandibles into my fingers.

I was so psyched up that even if I had encountered cotton wool I would have jerked my hand out. What I touched momentarily was cold, smooth and clammy.

Reptilian skin?

Black plastic sheet, I discovered when I enlarged the hole. Nailed to the top rails of the frame that supported the planking, and hanging like a curtain behind it. A damp-proof membrane. So why had they needed the creosote?

The plastic sheet bulged away from the wall when I pushed at it. There was a void behind. I used my Swiss Army knife to make a slit in the sheet. Plenty of bad smells lived back there. Damp, mineral and foetid, and that tight clot that takes you in the back of the throat and has as much to do with the imagination as it has with the olfactory system.

I shone the torch in through the hole in the sheet. The beam picked up the haphazard planes of a rock face. Fissured and erratically vertical, the depth of the gap fluctuating between thirty centimetres and a metre. I tilted the beam down. The floor of the void was strewn with a haphazard collection of green-brown rocks that must have fallen off the face. There was something about the shape of them though that didn't quite seem to work with the strata that they had been dislodged from.

I focused the beam on a rounded boulder. To make sense of it my mind tried to tell me that it was sprouting a tangle of mycelium. A harmless but relentless fungal operation working silently in the dark. I wasn't fooled for long. The realization made my stomach heave, and I had to draw back into the Rumpus Room for a charge of relatively fresh air.

It wasn't mycelium. It was hair. Hair still attached to a skull. The stones on the floor were bones. But nothing was whole, the skeleton had been broken and scattered haphazardly. A documentary about Tibetan sky burials came back to me. Bodies laid out on flat slabs of rock being hacked into small pieces and fed to vultures that circled and hobbled in to catch the thrown offerings.

I made myself shine the torch carefully over the bone debris, trying to assess the volume. It was a difficult calculation, but I didn't think that there was more than one body here.

And it had probably been rats. Rats and the other small mammals that make their way into caves and regard a dead human body as a bonanza. Once the soft tissue had been consumed, they would have gnawed through the bones to get at the marrow, severing and scattering them.

I forced myself to look at the skull again. The facial sockets were turned away from the beam. Algae, damp and oxidation had turned the surface of the bone green-brown. I could have been looking at a prehistoric find. But I wasn't. I knew enough to call her she.

But which *she*?

*   *   *

'Donna Gallagher or Colette Fletcher? Or someone we don't yet know?' Bryn asked the questions. The photographs of the remains as we found them after the wall was dismantled were fanned out on the desk in front of him.

Ken McGuire focused on a point above our heads. His solicitor looked distinctly nervous. First pornography and now a corpse. This was running into savage territories, a far remove from his usual pastoral frolics in title and tenure.

'We can get DNA samples from the bones and the hair,' I explained.

Ken dropped his head and looked at us both stonily. 'It was an accident.'

'Who was she?' I asked quietly.

'Colette Fletcher.'

'What happened, Mr McGuire?' Bryn prompted.

He rolled it around, looking for the words. I took some solace from the fact that, at last, he was uncomfortable with this. 'She liked to be stimulated. This one time she took it too far.' He looked at us hopefully, but Bryn nodded for him to continue. He lowered his head; we had to strain to catch his voice. 'Sometimes she liked things to be tightened round her throat while we did . . . Things . . . She said that it heightened her pleasure.'

'What were you doing on this occasion?'

'This is awkward to describe, Inspector.'

'Please try, Mr McGuire. It's important that we understand what happened.'

'She was on the chair. One of us was . . . One of us was behind her. She had a scarf round her neck, tied to the light bracket. She wanted us to push against her, to keep the scarf tight. We were worried we might hurt her, but she told us that it made the experience more intense for her. Only this time . . .' He looked up at us. 'This time she didn't tell us when to stop.'

'She was asphyxiated?' Bryn asked.

He nodded.

'Who was fucking her, Ken?' I asked.

He looked at me sharply, as if I had just ruined the poetic delicacy of the moment. 'I don't remember.'

'I'm just curious to know why the one doing the watching didn't notice that Colette was choking to death.'

Ken flashed a look at Bryn to see whether I was allowed to be this intrusive.

'It's going to be asked at some stage, Mr McGuire,' Bryn advised him.

Ken closed his eyes. 'I was underneath her,' he whispered. 'Neither of us could see her face.'

Two in the saddle. Both of them claiming to be too engrossed in giving Colette pleasure to realize that her grunts had passed way beyond ecstasy.

Which was exactly Jack Galbraith's take on it.

'Do you know what this adds up to?' He flapped the pages of Ken McGuire's statement in the air when we met later for the war council. 'Do you know what this fucker's defence is? The poor girl dies because the sensitive bastards were trying to gratify her needs. Un-fucking-believable!' He threw the transcript down. 'I want them charged with murder, Bryn.'

'It'll end up as manslaughter, sir. They'll corroborate each other.'

'It doesn't matter how it ends up. I want them charged with something big and nasty to give me some leverage. I want to wave a murder charge in their faces and offer up the possibility of clemency if they give up the other bodies.'

'Ken McGuire's going to play it remorseful. He'll use his position in the community. Solid, responsible farmer, man of the earth. So sorry, Your Honour, but we were young and simple country boys and we panicked.'

'But they went on to degrade other young girls.'

'We can't prove that they were minors, though, sir,' Bryn pointed out. 'We can't prove any criminal behaviour.'

'Because we can't find the fucking participants,'

Jack Galbraith raged in frustration. 'Donna, Wendy, and now Marta . . .' He ticked them off with his fingers. 'And all the other ones that we don't know about. Not to mention Boon Paterson, who probably got in the way. And what have they done with them all?'

'Boarding Colette up was a panic reaction, sir,' I offered. 'They learned their lesson there when she started decomposing.'

'Which leaves us only a whole fucking forest and Ken McGuire's huge farm to explore.'

'There is a way of undermining their defence, sir,' I said.

He looked at me warily. 'Tell,' he instructed.

'The manager of the Sychnant Nursing Home told me that Colette Fletcher stole certain items of value when she ran away.'

Bryn and Jack Galbraith looked at each other and grinned simultaneously as the understanding hit. Jack Galbraith nodded, voicing it: 'And now we know that Colette didn't run away.'

'That's right, sir. But Ken and Les wanted it to look like she did. They must have used her key, after she was dead, and gone in to pack up her belongings and steal some stuff to establish her Bad Girl-runaway status.'

'Which smells more of careful planning than a panic reaction to me,' Jack Galbraith observed happily. 'Where's the remorse in burglary and character defamation?'

'Donna Fletcher is supposed to have run away from the same nursing home,' Bryn reminded us.

Jack Galbraith nodded. 'And Wendy Evans and this teacher she is supposed to have run off with . . .'

316

'Malcolm Paterson, Boon's adopted father, sir,' I contributed.

'What if he was just another poor bastard who got in the way?'

I nodded in humble recognition of my leader's sagacity. I was used to credit bypassing me.

17

I didn't tell Sally about the evolving hypothesis on the possible fate of Wendy and Malcolm. She had enough anxiety and grief to contend with. She was flitting between hope and black acceptance of the worst. I knew that I should be working on comfort and reassurance, but the only good proof that I could effectively come up with was the absence of a body. Which brought us full circle, back to the possibility of a body.

We slept together that night in her bed, but we didn't make love. She was carrying too much despair, and I was still too close to the smell of Ken and Les's antics. I did my best to console her. And I took my own comfort from her presence and this re-emerging memory of closeness.

And then I woke up.

Sally's alarm clock told me that it was after three in the morning. She was sleeping soundly beside me. I tried to pretend that it was the unfamiliar surroundings that had confused me. When that didn't work, I had to confront it. It was the vivid recall of Ken and Les that had jolted me from my dream.

The memory itself wasn't shocking. It was the

new thinking that lay behind it. Ken and Les had arrived at the Den. They had driven into the clearing on their quad bikes and I had been watching them from my ledge.

They came out of the Den and started searching. I had wondered what had taken them so long, but now knew that they had been into the Rumpus Room. They had scuttered around outside, and then they had driven off in different directions on their quad bikes.

They had been spooked. I thought at the time that they might have lost something. Now I was wondering if something that they had expected to find had gone missing.

Or someone?

Marta?

We had been assuming that they had previously moved her from the Den. That they weren't giving up her whereabouts because they thought she was still a useful card that they could play. Or that they didn't want to damn themselves even more.

I concentrated on it again.

Had that been their intention that night? Was that why they had arrived on two quad bikes? To move her on? To get her out of there in case Paul Evans cracked and gave up the Rumpus Room?

This wasn't making sense. We had Ken and Les in custody. We had Colette Fletcher's remains, their admission that they had been present when she had died, and that they had concealed the body. We were going to charge them. Why was my mind trying to mess things up?

Because we had another anomaly.

I now had to confront the real trigger of my disturbance. Ken and Les wouldn't have risked the

318

lights from the generator being seen from outside. The Den had been padlocked, the Rumpus Room would have been bolted shut, from the Den side. So, if she had been in there, how could she have got out?

I had to rephrase that. Who, apart from Ken and Les, could have let her out? Who else might have known that she was in there?

I jump-cut my memory to the discovery of Boon's sweatshirt under the sofa. I had seen it when I had been crawling out through the hatch. But both Ken and Les had crawled out through that same hatch not long before me. Why hadn't they seen it? This piece of evidence effectively damned them, and yet they managed to leave it for me to find.

And why hadn't I seen it when I first moved the sofa, when I was looking for a trapdoor? I groaned inwardly. I knew that if I ran with this I would have to consider the possibility that the sweatshirt had been placed there while I was inside the Rumpus Room.

Jesus Christ, how many layers of watchers could there have been out there that night?

*   *   *

Gordon was a definite.

Paul Evans maybe knew, but he had been in Mackay's care that night. Sara, Zoë and Sheila also made the list of people who could have known about Marta's presence in the Rumpus Room.

But who had released her? The hatch of the Rumpus Room could only have been opened by someone on the outside. And I was now fairly certain that it wasn't Ken or Les. Because their headless-chicken act that night must have been the realization that Marta had fled the coop.

So, someone had helped her escape. But out of that prison into what? This was where it got sinister again. What if the motive hadn't been altruism? If she was now free, why hadn't we seen her?

And why feed us Boon's sweatshirt? I was back to asking myself complicated questions that I couldn't answer.

I didn't tell Sally about my nocturnal struggle with Faith. She didn't need the introduction of added confusion. So breakfast was quiet without being tense. She kissed me at the door, in her dressing gown, not worrying about the neighbours, giving me a pleasant foretaste of what more settled times might hold for us.

I had to run to the car through a slanted downpour of cold rain. The cloud cover was low and moiling along slowly like a nudged and sulky thing. It was one of those mornings that you wanted to miss, because already you knew that the day wasn't going to get any better.

Jack Galbraith and Bryn were continuing their interviewing of Ken and Les. I had been pulled out of the loop, replaced by professionals from Carmarthen and Cardiff who were expert at cracking nuances apart. I wasn't upset; I had already worked out the start of my day.

Gordon had now been released, but there was no way that he would want to talk to me. Zoë might be prepared to, but not while she was sharing the same working environment as her husband. I wasn't too sure of Sheila McGuire's loyalties, but, as we were currently in the process of pulling the family farm apart, my presence might have been seen as rubbing salt into the wound.

It was a narrowing down of options that I would rather not have made.

Because in my last encounter with Sara Harris, she had been strapped to my back like a demented jockey, torn between trying to strangle me or ripping my head off.

Hoping that her attitude had mellowed in the interim, I stood outside A Cut Above long enough to let my presence be registered, and to establish that a bucket of hydrogen peroxide wasn't about to come flying out the door at me.

I walked inside to find everyone in the place staring at me. The ladies of the town in the waiting area, the two young women behind the styling chairs, and the three women lodged in the chairs. All the ladies of the town looked eager, the two stylists looked nervous.

'Good morning.' I smiled to the room. 'I'd like to speak to Sara, please.'

'She's not here,' one of the stylists replied, the other nodding in jittery confirmation.

I smiled knowingly at the unattended woman in her chair, the good detective in me having already noticed that her hair was still dripping. 'I won't be long with her,' I promised, and walked towards the rear storeroom.

'You can't go back there—' One of the stylists tried half-heartedly to block me.

'It's all right, I know the way,' I announced, sidestepping her. She shared a look of confusion with her compadre; they had obviously lost the pages of this particular part of the script.

Sara was in the storeroom. I had half expected her to have exited through the back door. She was still holding a wet comb. She glowered at me and waved it like a magic wand. 'This is private property, you're trespassing.'

'I'm allowed to, I'm a police officer pursuing a line of enquiry.'

'Fuck off,' she snarled, condensing the message.

'I need your help, Sara.'

'Why would I want to help you?'

'Because I think there's a possibility that Les isn't responsible for everything that they are going to try and throw at him.'

Her eyes narrowed suspiciously. She digested it for a moment. 'Are you saying it's all down to Ken?'

'No, this applies to both of them. But I need your help. You're going to have to answer some frank questions.'

She stared at me intently, trying to work out if I was running a con on her. 'Are you serious?' she asked eventually.

'Yes.'

She moved fast. For a moment I thought that she was going to embrace me. Instead, she hooked one hand into the crook of my elbow, opened the door with the other, and dragged me into the centre of the salon while I was still trying to work on my balance.

Our audience looked on, spellbound. The sight of me trying to fathom the steps of the reel that Sara had pulled me into told them that they were in for high drama. She now held her free hand up, as if to quiet the uproar that she was anticipating. 'Sergeant Capaldi has just told me that my Les has been arrested under false pretences for a bunch of stuff that he hasn't done.'

'Sara, that's not what I said.' My protest was

drowned out by the collective gasp from the audience.

'Tell them,' she urged, yanking at my elbow, 'tell them what you've just told me. Tell them that they've arrested Les for things that he hasn't done.'

The room went quiet, staring at me in expectation. I managed to free my elbow. 'That's not what I said, Sara.'

'Yes it is. "Les is not responsible for the things they're going to throw at him"—those were your very words.' She addressed the entranced assembly with all the guile of a sharp barrister.

'Some of the things. *Some...*' I slowed the word down for emphasis.

'They've fitted him up,' she announced triumphantly, ignoring my protest.

*   *   *

The first phone call came about an hour later, while I was staking out the offices of Payne, Dyke and Thomas in the hope of seeing Zoë emerge without Gordon in tow.

It was Sally, her voice granular with anxiety. 'Glyn, someone's just called me to say that you've said that Ken McGuire and Les Tucker have been falsely arrested.'

Hell, that was quick. The Dinas grapevine had geared up to warp-speed.

'Calm down,' I soothed.

'What's happened? I thought you said that you had evidence on them.'

'We have. They'll definitely be charged, Sally, I promise you.'

'So, why are they saying those things about you?'

323

She sounded confused, but calmer.

'Things have been taken out of context.'

'So, you're not back at the beginning again? You're making progress? Finding out what's happened to Boon?'

'It's happening as we speak.'

'But you're not there? You're not interrogating them?' She tried hard not to make it sound accusatory.

'I'm back out in the field. It's what I'm best at.'

'I'm sorry.' I heard the catch in her voice as she tried to bring herself back under control. 'I don't mean to make such a fuss. It's just . . . All this not knowing is wearing me out.'

'Believe me, I understand. And I want to do anything I can to help.'

'Can I see you tonight?' She asked it hesitantly, aware of how frayed and unstable she must be sounding.

'Of course.'

My phone rang again as soon as we had hung up. 'It'll be about seven o'clock,' I said, answering it, assuming it was Sally calling back.

'What's that, Capaldi, a train arrival, or a prediction of the Apocalypse?' Jack Galbraith asked.

'I'm sorry, sir, I thought you were someone else.'

'So, that wasn't one of your Pronouncements from the Mount?'

'I'm not with you, sir,' I replied, confused.

'Not one of your on-high declarations of innocence to the multitude?'

Oh fuck . . . I hadn't expected Jack Galbraith to be hard-wired into the Dinas rumour mill.

'That was a misunderstanding, sir.'

'Fucking right it was. And a fucking big one, too.'

'I was trying to get her to cooperate, sir.'

'I despair of you, Capaldi,' he groaned wearily. 'You take us to a point where we think that you might be creeping back into the fold. Starting to look like a sensible copper again, making some astute calls, and then you go and throw it all away by turning back into Boy Fucking Wonder.'

'I'm sorry, sir, it was just a misunderstanding.'

'The essential misunderstanding is you talking to that woman in the first place,' he observed harshly. 'You get a rumour like this started and it makes it look like we're involved in chicanery. You stay away from all of them now, Capaldi—the wives, the girlfriends, and the brothers.'

'Yes, sir.'

So when Sheila McGuire rang, I knew that I should not be taking the call.

'Sergeant Capaldi, I'd like to talk to you.'

'Okay,' I said quickly, before my career-preserving mode could cut in.

*   *   *

The rain was still in place. A couple of minibuses loaded with damp and dispirited search-team members were leaving the farmyard as I drove in. A few guys stared out at me as we passed, their looks seeming to suggest that their misery was my fault.

Sheila McGuire opened the back door. She was wearing a green sweater over a white T-shirt, tight jeans, and slipper socks bunched around her ankles. Her hair looked like it was escaping from a style, and her complexion was even more outdoor than I had remembered. She looked out over my shoulder

325

at the departing minibuses. 'They're going to have a rough day in this weather,' she observed. I could smell some form of alcohol.

'Are they getting in your way?'

'No.' She shut the door behind us. 'They've finished with the barns now, and they're being taken out to trudge the fields. Poor sods. Come into the kitchen.' She led the way. 'They're not going to find anything, you know,' she said over her shoulder. I assumed that she wasn't expecting an answer.

She gestured me to a seat at the long refectory table opposite the one with a glass of red wine and an open bottle in front of it. She took a glass out of a wall cabinet and raised it. 'Join me?'

I declined with a smile and a shake of my head. She didn't insist. She sat down and topped her glass up. Her smile was very slightly cocked, and she still wore a quizzical expression, as if she had forgotten that she had invited me here.

'You decided to stay around?' I asked. Something to break the locked moment.

'It's a farm, Sergeant, there are animals here that need caring for. I'm a farmer's daughter, even though I'm in the process of debating whether I'm still a farmer's wife.'

'You wanted to talk to me, Mrs McGuire?'

'Sheila. Please call me Sheila.' She gave me a smile that fell just short of imploring. 'At the moment I need to hear friendly voices.'

'What did you want to talk to me about, Sheila?'

'You seem to have jinxed us here . . .' She looked at me enquiringly.

'Glyn.'

She nodded. 'Glyn. That's right. I'd forgotten.

Things have not been good since you entered our lives, Glyn. Trevor Vaughan has gone from us. Ken has done these awful things. Boon is missing. And that poor girl whose body they found . . .'

'These things were in play long before I turned up,' I reminded her gently.

'I know that now, but I didn't have to confront them then. Everything was unknown and excusable. I know that it's a terrible thing to say, given all that's happened, but ignorance really is bliss.'

'There is still one young woman unaccounted for.'

She took a deep drink of her wine and nodded. 'I heard. But I know nothing about her.'

'And Boon?'

'Was it Boon you were meaning when you told Sara that Ken and Les were innocent?'

'You heard that too?'

'You opened your mouth in Dinas, Glyn.' She almost managed a grin.

'Sara made a point of misunderstanding me.'

'I wondered.' She took another drink and held the glass reflectively in front of her face for a moment. 'That's what I wanted to talk to you about.'

'Sara?'

She shook her head dismissively. 'Boon.' She put the glass on the table. 'Whatever else he's done, Ken wouldn't have hurt Boon.'

'They were all very drunk that night.'

'It doesn't matter. I can't answer for Les Tucker, but I know for a fact that Ken wouldn't have harmed Boon. And besides, Ken is a very controlled drunk. Ken always makes sure that he knows exactly what he's doing.' She let me hear the

327

bitterness that drifted into that last statement.

'I thought that Boon was Gordon's friend?'

'That's how it started. That's how Ken came to accept him in the first place. His young brother's friend. A black boy was strange around here, especially for someone as conventional as Ken, but he got used to him. Got to like him, even.

'And then Gordon and Les got involved with the rugby club. They started drifting away from Boon then.'

'Didn't Boon join too?'

'I don't know the story behind it. Nothing ever came to the surface. Let's just say that Boon was never invited to join. Ken looked after Boon at that point, kept him in the group, stopped him feeling isolated. Paul Evans came on to the scene through the rugby club connection. Ken made sure that they didn't cut Boon out, that if they wanted to associate with him and Trevor, Boon was part of the deal, he had to be included.'

'Did Gordon hold any sort of grudge for that?'

She shrugged. 'Who knows? I think Gordon might always have been a bit pissed off that Boon managed to go out with Zoë before he did.'

'When was this?' I didn't let her see my mental notebook highlighting the entry.

'They were young, a teenage thing. It was a long time ago.' She poured the remainder of the bottle into her glass, drank it and stood up. I caught her momentary tussle with gravity. 'Are you sure you won't join me?' she asked, taking another bottle from the wine rack.

I shook my head. 'Don't you think a cup of coffee would be more sensible?'

She grinned. 'Probably.' She held the bottle up to

me before she opened it and poured another glass. 'But I'm oiling the decision-making process. I just wanted you to know. About Boon. There are not many good things that I can think of to say about my husband at the moment, but that was one that I thought I should share with you.'

'Did you ever suspect?'

She knew exactly what I was talking about, but she chose to hold a thoughtful frown in place. Eventually, she shook her head. 'I've been looking back. Searching for any clues that I might have missed. And the answer is no. I thought that we were normal. Boringly so, when it came to sex.' She looked me in the face, a faintly worried smile creasing her lips. 'We are friends at the moment, aren't we? You don't mind me talking frankly?'

'No. As long as you're comfortable with it.'

'Comfortable isn't quite the word I'd choose . . .' She shook her head sharply, dismissing the thought as a sideline. She had made some sort of a decision and she was sticking to it. 'He never gave me even the remotest idea that he was interested in . . . Let's call it the seamier side.' She looked at me appealingly. 'You would have thought that if things like that turned him on, he would have tried to instigate them. Or drop clues. Hints. Make some attempt to see whether I could be interested too. We were meant to be a couple. Couples are supposed to share things.' Her mind went off on a journey. 'I even tried once.'

'Tried?'

'To get him interested in branching out. We hadn't been long married. We were still getting to grips with the bedroom side of things. Although I was already getting the impression that he wasn't

329

into experimentation. So I thought that perhaps he wanted me to take the lead. Anyway, one night I decided to . . .' She smiled sheepishly. 'How to put this delicately? I tried to move down south on him.' Her head lurched slightly sideways and she pinned me with a fuzzy expression, looking for a reaction.

'He didn't want to play?'

'He positively leapt away from me. You would have thought that I had been trying to bite the thing off, from the reaction it provoked. He moved so fast that he hit me hard on the face with his elbow. He said it was an accident, and I gave him the benefit of the doubt at the time.' The face she pulled told me that she was no longer quite so sure. 'And now I find out that he was getting his pleasure from sticking the bloody thing here, there and everywhere.'

'He didn't want to involve you in that aspect.'

'Why not?'

I tried to recall the psychologist's profile. 'Because that was his dirty side. It was a compulsion, but he was deeply ashamed of it. That self-loathing was transferred to the women who indulged him. They became sluts by definition. He couldn't respect a woman who was prepared to be degraded. But you were his wife, he needed to be able to respect you, and so he had to keep you pure.'

She looked pained and puzzled. 'But poor Wendy Evans . . . I don't know about the others . . . But didn't they groom Wendy? She wasn't degraded until they got their hands on her.'

'They conveniently managed to overlook the finer points. Probably, in their books, a truly virtuous woman would be genetically programmed not to succumb to Rohypnol.'

She nodded. 'So he put me on a pedestal. Without even asking my permission.' She looked at me anxiously. There was something so raw in the look that I knew we had hit the root of what she was drinking to cover. She spoke with a quiet intensity. 'Do you think that's what could have created those needs? By turning me into something that couldn't be sullied, did he have to go to the opposite extreme to work out those urges?'

'That side of him was in place long before you came along. If anything, you helped him. You gave him a rounded, three-dimensional woman who was more than just a sexual object.'

'But it didn't stop when I came along.'

'It was embedded pretty deep by then.'

She looked at me candidly. The flush had spread on her face. 'That poor girl who died. I looked it up on the Internet: it's called autoerotic asphyxiation. People do die sometimes. It's dangerous. Do you think it was an accident?'

'I can't talk about it, Sheila,' I said apologetically.

'I know.' She nodded and took another hit on her wine. 'Do you think I could be?' she asked in almost a whisper, a rasp in her voice.

'Could be what?'

'Sullied?'

I smiled, playing it lightly. 'I couldn't possibly answer that.'

'Do you know what the worrying thing is, Glyn?'

I shook my head neutrally.

'I can't answer it myself.'

'It's not something that needs answering.'

She frowned and waved a hand, dismissing my attempt at reassurance. 'I think it is. I think it's something that I need to know. Or I'll always be wondering if it was me who drove him to it. Putting up some unconscious barrier that he could sense, giving off a whiff of revulsion.'

'He started long before he met you, Sheila.'

'But he didn't stop.' It came out almost as a wail, despair cracking her voice. She closed her eyes, bringing herself under control, and then opened them to stare as levelly at me as the booze would allow. 'I need to know, Glyn.'

I shook my head, starting to get the understanding of something. 'This is the drink speaking.'

She held up her glass. 'I need it to help me get through this. But it's only a tool. I made the decision when I was stone-cold sober.'

'I can't help you, Sheila.'

She pulled a face and smiled wryly. 'That's a real pity. Because I am going to do this anyway. If you won't help me, I will go to Cardiff or Hereford or Newport, anywhere, and find some stranger in a bar who will let me do it to them.'

'You don't mean that.'

She flared, defiance cutting through the booze flush. 'I've promised myself. I am not going to have that bastard leaving me twisted with guilt that I could have prevented all this. I mean it, Glyn. I am totally sincere. If you won't help me here, I'll find a total stranger to do it with.'

I believed her. 'Why me?'

She managed a weak smile. 'Because I don't know any other mildly attractive policemen that I can trust to be absolutely discreet.'

'You're asking the impossible, Sheila.'

She scowled. 'That bastard put me on a pedestal.

I didn't ask for that. I wanted a normal, healthy sex life. I think that I probably wanted the dirty bits that went with it as well, Glyn. Eroticism, at least. But I didn't push; he was my husband. If he was timid where sex was concerned, fine, it was no big deal, I could live with that.' She closed her eyes, taking a deep breath. 'And now I'm going to get the blame. The whispers are going to follow me around. "Ken McGuire was driven to do those terrible things because his wife was frigid."'

'They won't say that, Sheila,' I said soothingly.

'They will . . . So now I want to prove to myself that I'm not frigid. I want to do this, Glyn. I've been drinking to get the courage.' She pushed her glass away symbolically. 'But I don't need it. If I was afraid, if I was repulsed, the booze wouldn't be able to mask it. But I want it . . .' She threw her hand across the table on top of mine. Her face flushed blotchily. 'Glyn, thinking about it, talking about it has made me wet . . . I'm so aroused . . . I want to taste you . . .'

Oh Jesus . . . She was an attractive woman. She was offering me a blow job. No strings attached. Absolute discretion. A male myth. My cock was already erect.

I covered the hand that was covering mine. 'I can't, Sheila,' I said softly.

She stared at me fixedly. She breathed in deeply through her nose. She pulled her hand away. Still staring. I couldn't tell which way her psyche was about to swing.

I noticed then that her eyes were tightly closed, as if she was praying. I stood and moved quietly around the table towards the door on the balls of my feet. And then I felt a wave of pity go out towards this woman. I tiptoed up behind her, put my hands gently on her shoulder and then leant down to kiss her on the side of the cheek. 'You'll come through this, I promise you. You're a strong and attractive woman, and one day you'll be glad that you found out that you were with the wrong man before it was all too late.'

She was quiet and still for a moment. 'Thank you,' she whispered, and then began to nod. 'I'm going to tell him anyway.'

'Tell who what, Sheila?' I asked gently.

She raised her head to look round at me. 'I'm going to tell that bastard that we've just done that thing.'

I let myself out.

*　　　　*　　　　*

Sex, even nobly spurned sex, casts a mushy spell. It wasn't until I was driving home that I began to wonder if I had just been bamboozled. Had Sheila McGuire deliberately led me around by the balls to divert me from asking about Marta? Or Boon? Could she have effected Marta's release?

I shook my head to clear it.

Mush. It was all still mush.

But soon I had something more tangible to worry about. The Beast had been let out of its cage.

It was in the caravan's mailbox. A cheap Manila envelope addressed to *The Occupier*. No big deal, obviously some sort of unsolicited flyer for cheap car insurance or plastic fascia boards. Except that I had an explicit agreement with the postman not to deliver any of this crap.

Instinct made me wait until I was inside before I

opened it. Shaking the contents out on to the table. My gut tightening as I recognized the images. From the depth of field they had to have used a telescopic lens. Three shots of me with the ends of my belt dangling, in a borrowed pair of abattoir boots, looking like I was attempting to re-awaken sexual interest in a stone-dead heifer.

I shook the envelope out over the table. It was empty. But there was something on the back of the second image that I turned over. The same printer font as on the envelope.

Far enough . . .

Far enough? What was someone trying to tell me?

I called Sally to explain that I was going to be late.

How far out into the world had these travelled? I called Bryn Jones to test the waters. 'Any new developments your end, sir?' I asked breezily.

'Potentially,' he said, and I let myself go limp with relief as I realized that I was not about to face an order to come in and explain myself. 'One of the dogs sniffed out the broken chain from a chainsaw buried under a pile of sawdust at Les Tucker's yard. It was wrapped in an old rag. It's in for analysis, but there are possible blood and cloth fibres on it.'

'It's a messy way to dispose of a body.'

'Not if you've got a forest that you can call your own.'

I got off the phone as quickly as I politely could. I had only called to make sure that I was still perceived as one of the good guys. I didn't want to find myself volunteered to lead a party of amateur rangers out into the wild woods to look for scenes of carnage.

The rain was still with us, working now to mute and thicken the night. It suited me. It covered my approach on foot down Tony Griffiths's muddy drive, which was bordered with the shadow forms of junked cars.

I kept going over it in my head. The stupidity of what I had done. I had let the moment drive the occasion. Tony Griffiths hadn't needed the insurance that I had so naïvely provided. There was no way that I could have proven that he had been trucking poached venison. I should have realized it was a set-up when he let me take his phone away from him so easily. He had orchestrated the venue and the event. For someone else to capture.

I had been suckered.

Far enough . . .

I stopped and crouched into cover when I came into sight of the small bungalow blocked out against the night, the light in one of the front windows punching through the gap in the home-made curtains. In the gap I could make out part of a television screen flickering abstract colour changes.

I dialled the number and heard the phone start to ring in the house as well as through my handset. It was a weird sense of double connectivity.

'Hello?'

'Tony Griffiths?'

'That's right.'

'This is Detective Sergeant Capaldi. Do you remember me?'

'How could I forget?' I heard the grin in his voice.

'I warned you, Tony.'

'Warned me about what?' he asked, his tone textured with puzzled innocence.

'The consequences of what would happen if those pictures ever showed up.'

'Hey, hey, hey, Sergeant, hold up,' he protested. 'You took my phone away from me, remember?'

'I've stuck to my side of the deal, Tony.'

'You took the phone,' he wailed, aggrieved.

'I'm pulling together a few friends here. Brother officers who are very upset about the way you've insulted me and the force. We're coming to pay you a visit, Tony. Probable cause, no search warrant necessary. And unless you have information for me about who took those photographs, I am predicting, in your very near future, a case of injuries received in the course of resisting arrest.' I cut the connection, counted off ten seconds, and called his number again. And got the engaged tone.

A short time later I heard the motorbike start up. I ducked deeper into cover and Tony went past me, the bike slithering, its wheels kicking up arching clots of mud. He was in a rabid hurry to get away.

So, why had he used some of that precious time to make a phone call?

18

I messed up Tony's back door, making it look like a whole bunch of vengeful and rampaging cop buddies had kicked it in. Why they stopped their destructive surge after they crossed the threshold was something he would probably always puzzle over.

I found the telephone in the hall. It was a clunky, old-fashioned handset with no caller display screen.

I lifted the receiver and took a deep breath to calm myself down before I pushed the redial button. It began to ring out. I prayed that I would recognize the voice.

And I did.

One is not at home . . . A recorded parody of the Queen's voice. A fucking answering machine.

It had backfired.

I had deliberately let Tony skedaddle in order to find out who he had called. Now, not only didn't I have that information, but I didn't have him to lean on either.

Had he called for salvation? Or warning?

I paddled over to the plus side. Hopefully, he had told whoever he had just called that I was holding him responsible for the emergence of the photographs. They would assume that I thought he was trying to run a simple coercion job on me. That I hadn't seen past that to the bigger picture. Which kept the photographs viable as leverage material. It would not be in their best interest to put them out into the public domain yet. How much of this was analysis, and how much wishful thinking, I didn't want to put on the scales to test.

Now all I had to do was identify the bigger picture.

I made a cursory search of the bungalow, already knowing that I wasn't going to find anything more incriminating than bachelor crud and bad odours. Tony was a spear-carrier, not a player.

I got back to my car and started asking myself hard questions.

Why had Tony let himself be recruited? What did he get out of it? It now looked like the whole simulated bovine sex episode had been a set-up. So,

338

even at that early stage they had started to work me into the procedures. Preparing me for the patsy fall if it was ever required.

Far enough . . .

What else had they set me up for?

Stop . . . I checked myself. I was asking the wrong question. Forget about me. I wasn't important in this. I was purely a reactive force. The checks and balances had only been instigated when they saw the opportunity to weave me into the story.

Take it back to the stage before that.

What else had Tony been contracted to do? Before he was instructed to meet me and fit me up.

To deliver Marta?

But there was a big flaw in that. He left her at the filling station two hours before the minibus arrived. That timeline worked with the random, chance encounter version of the story. A hitchhiker is dropped off. It's a bad spot and a lousy time of night, family traffic mainly, going the wrong way. So it takes two hours before another lift comes along in the shape of the minibus.

Which is what we had accepted until now. But what throws it out of kilter is that I now know that Tony is not the innocent hayseed that I had taken him to be. He was not just the random lift provider.

Oh Jesus . . . Why hadn't I checked?

I scrabbled for my phone. It was so first principles, and I had neglected to follow it through.

I listened to the recorded timetables, checking the numbers in my head. I let it spool past me twice. To be certain.

The train that the group had taken from London had been approximately one and a half hours late arriving in Shrewsbury.

*   *   *

So, what did I have?

I had Tony delivering Marta for a rendezvous with the minibus. He would deny it, and until we had Marta to corroborate it, we could prove nothing.

An East European girl. Probably recruited from the seasonal student fruit-picking community. A girl who had stayed on after the season had finished, probably on an expired permit. What had she been offered? A free trip to her boyfriend in Ireland? But, the really big question, did she know what would be expected of her when she got into that minibus?

And who in that minibus knew what was happening when Marta turned up? I was about to dismiss Ken and Les from that equation, but then I shifted laterally. Could they have arranged it as a treat for themselves? Was this something that they had done before? Had I missed the obvious? Was this a process? After Wendy fled, and the children's home supply dried up, had they been using Tony Griffiths to procure new product?

I had an image then of Ken and Les helping her to climb inside. Spider grins fixed. Already salivating over the prospect. Fresh meat.

Did Boon fuck up the plan by wanting to go to Ireland with her? Or did he just get himself fucked by trying to protect her?

Far enough . . .

Had I got close somehow, without realizing it, to discovering what they had really done with Boon and Marta? Was that the warning that they were sending me? Telling me to back off? The Rumpus Room had given up its secrets; they would have to deal with those consequences, but they didn't want things getting even murkier.

They were going to have to contact me again. The delivery of the photographs had been the first shot across the bow. Next would come the ultimatum. Which would be what . . .? Full compliance or they contact my superiors/the press/ the RSPCA?

Whatever they had in mind, it was unlikely they'd be using Tony Griffiths again. They would need a more refined tool for the next piece of this business. Besides, they couldn't take the risk that I might crack him.

I drove back to Sally's feeling damp and dolorous. And nervous. Now that I had the notion that I had been choreographed, I couldn't shake the feeling that someone was keeping watch on all my movements.

My phone rang. Sally's number came up on the display. 'Hi,' I said, answering it.

'Where are you?' I picked up distress. Had someone told her about the chainsaw the dogs had sniffed out?

'I'm on my way,' I said cheerily.

'Why is no one else here yet?'

I tensed. Something dark had slipped into the picture. 'Sally, where are you?' I asked, trying to keep my voice as normal as possible.

'Where I was told to meet you. I've had to walk up the hill a bit though, to get a signal for the phone.'

'What hill? Please, can you be more specific?'

'The place where the minibus was found. I was

told that you and Chief Superintendent Galbraith were waiting for me up here.'

'Who told you that?' I asked, feeling the chill drawing in.

She heard the change in my tone. 'The man from your Operations Room. What's wrong, Glyn? Why aren't you here?'

'I'm on my way. I'll be there as soon as I can. What else did he say?'

'He said that there was nothing to be anxious about, but that you needed me to come up here and identify something that had been found.'

'Have you seen any other cars? Any kind of light?'

'No. It's dark up here . . . and it's wet and cold.' She paused. I could imagine her looking around. 'Glyn, I'm scared . . .' I heard the tremor in her voice.

'There's no need to be. I'm on my way. I'll be with you before you know it.' I thought hard. 'I want you to get back down to your car. Come down the mountain road and I'll . . . No . . .' I realized that she would be more vulnerable on that road. 'No, forget that, Sally. Just go back to your car and lock the doors. Remember that we're on our way. You're soon going to see headlights, and they'll be ours.'

'Who's done this, Glyn?' she asked anxiously.

'Don't worry about that. That's for us to sort out. I just want you to get back down to your car and out of the rain. Please, Sally, do it for me.'

'Okay, boss,' she said, making a joke of it, trying to be brave. I felt the ache of not being there to protect her.

I slammed the car into a three-point turn. I was

the wrong side of Dinas for the mountain road. I activated my blue lights, and put my foot down hard.

Now I didn't have to wait for the next approach. They had just demonstrated that they had other ways of manipulating me.

I called Emrys Hughes. 'I don't see the problem,' he said laconically when I had described the situation.

'She's up there and she's scared,' I explained, biting down on my impatience.

'She drove up there okay, let her drive back down.'

'She was lured up there by someone impersonating a police officer. God knows what could happen if she tries to negotiate those bends with some madman tearing after her.'

'Where did this madman suddenly appear from?'

'Emrys, for fuck's sake,' I screamed, losing my temper, 'can you get a car up there or not?'

'Okay, okay, watch the language,' he drawled sulkily. 'I'll see what I can do.'

*   *   *

Relief flared out the worst of the tension as soon as I saw the blue flashing light. It was a beat patrol car, parked behind Sally's. The uniform cop got out as I pulled up, his raincoat on, averting his eyes from my headlights. I recognized him. He was the one Emrys Hughes had dispatched as an emissary that first day up here, when the minibus had been found.

I nodded at him as I approached. 'I'll take Mrs Paterson back down in my car . . .' I stopped dead.

343

Both cars were empty. I wheeled on him, the question etched into my expression.

'There was no one here, Sergeant,' he explained nervously. 'The car was locked and empty when I got here.'

I closed my eyes and took a deep breath to impose control before I took my shock out on this poor bastard. I exhaled. 'You saw nothing?'

'No, Sergeant, just the car parked here, like . . .'

'Don't call me sergeant, it wastes time,' I interrupted. I took out my flashlight and started slowly panning the ground around Sally's car. 'Have you been anywhere near this?' I asked, holding the beam on the soft ground outside the driver's door.

'No, I remembered what you said the last time.'

There were footprints. Messed up, but compatible with someone swivelling their feet to get into or out of the car. The road's tarmac surface started immediately adjacent to the softer ground, giving no indication of where those feet had gone to, or whether they had been joined by any others.

I spread the beam wider. Sally had said that she had moved up the hill to get reception for her phone. A bad thought struck me. Had she ever got back down again? I scanned the ground by the driver's door again, but there was no way of telling whether those prints were two-way, or just exit.

'Bring your torch,' I instructed, leading him to the edge of the road where the hill started to rise away. I pointed. 'You take that direction. Walk along the verge, take it slowly. You're looking for any sign of someone leaving the road.' I moved away from him, torch beam trained on the verge, trying to read through the shadows the harsh illumination cast on the grass.

'Sergeant . . .'

He held his torch beam on a patch in the heather, where Sally's foot had disturbed the rain's surface sheen. The drizzle was re-establishing the patina, but not fast enough to cover her traces leading erratically up the hill. It was a definite one-way trail.

'Get on the radio. I want DCI Jones apprised of this.'

'Don't you want me to help you look?'

'No.' I shook my head to reinforce it. If I was going to find Sally up there, I wanted to be alone with it.

My shoes and trouser cuffs were soon soaked through. I followed in Sally's step pattern. It disrupted my normal gait, but it felt important to be retracing her exact steps. I kept my torch beam shining ahead. I was tensed, ready for an alien outline to show itself mounded above the low shrub cover.

I reached a trampled patch of heather. This must have been where she had performed the cell-phone pavane while she made the call to me. Squatting down, I realized why her trail had only led one way. I had highlighted a perfect imprint of her shoe in the black, peaty mulch. Pointing downhill. She had found and used a sheep track to get back down to the road.

My relief was brief and laced with frustration, before another wave of anxiety took over. She had returned to the car. And then locked it and left it. In the wet, in the dark, in the middle of a wilderness. Why, for Christ's sake?

*   *   *

345

Bryn Jones arrived with some of the investigating team. Other groups, police and civilian, were on their way to augment the search party.

I told him about the call Sally had received requesting her to come up here and meet with Jack Galbraith and me.

'What's your take on it?' he asked me, staring off towards the dark mass of the forest that loomed away to the south.

I shook my head. 'I don't know. It doesn't make sense. There are no signs of violence. They must have used some sort of persuasive force to get her to go with them.'

'An abduction?'

'I think so, sir.'

'Who would gain from it, Glyn?'

I had already thought about that. 'Maybe Gordon McGuire? To take the heat off his brother?'

He shook his head. 'He's got a reputation to worry about; he's already busy putting distance in.'

'Is Paul Evans still being held in Hereford?'

'We had nothing to hold him on. He was let out on the recognizance that he stayed with your friend Graham Mackay until we deem it fit for him to come back here.'

It was a big surprise, I tried not to show it.

'It's a very tidy scene, Glyn. Car neatly parked. Locked. You know yourself, there's usually a frenetic side to these things.'

'What are you trying to say, sir?' I asked, already knowing.

'It might be exactly what it seems,' he said softly. 'She's decided to go off for a long walk in the woods.'

'She's not the suicidal type.'

'I'm not saying she is. She may just be trying to take stock.' He shook his head slowly. 'Grief screws things up,' he said, as if reliving a particular memory of his own.

'She had that phone call, sir.'

He looked at me for a moment. 'Did she?' he asked carefully.

'Why would she make it up?' I retorted, trying to shake his scepticism.

'Maybe when she found herself up here, she had to find a reason for it?'

'She was scared. She wasn't deluding herself, sir.'

For a moment I debated whether to come clean. To show him the blackmail photographs. Tell him about my suspicions concerning Tony Griffiths. Establish that there were other forces at work that could have engineered Sally's disappearance. But what did I have? I had no demands from anyone, apart from the cryptic phrase, *far enough.* And I had no guarantee that, following the revelation, I would still be a part of the posse. Bryn, good cop and good Christian that he was, would most likely suspend me on the spot.

And he was right, there was nothing up here to indicate that Sally had been forced to do anything against her will.

'Something else you want to tell me about, Glyn?' he asked, picking up on some of the disturbed waves in my deliberating.

'I have a key, sir.'

'Meaning?'

'To Sally Paterson's house. Perhaps there will be some way of telling whether she really did receive that call?'

He smiled. 'I think we owe her that much.'

I went off at a trot, heading for my car. He called after me. 'Don't worry, Glyn, we'll find her. We've got some good people up here.'

*   *   *

I needed more reassurance than that. So I resorted to magical practices as I drove, using the force of will and despair to project Sally back into her house. The image I conjured was blurred, but I think I managed to get her into an apron. Trying to root her in place, going for settled and contented domesticity. I didn't ride my luck, and kept sex projections out of the immediate future.

It didn't work. Although I did experience an initial surge of spooky expectation when I saw that the lights were on in the front porch and the kitchen. But the place was empty. Filled with that hollow resonance that people's absences charge their houses with.

She hadn't left a note. Which wasn't surprising, since she had thought that she was going to be meeting me.

I checked the telephone. The display showed that she had been called just over two hours previously, but the caller had withheld their number. I tried last-number redial, and experienced a small shock when my mobile phone started vibrating in my pocket. She must have tried to call me after she had got that message. But I had turned my phone off while I was staking out Tony Griffiths. The thought made me feel even guiltier.

I used my own phone to call Mackay.

'Why didn't anyone tell me that Paul Evans was with you?' I tried not to sound angry.

'He was still gunning for you. Your bosses didn't want all that uncontained aggression crashing round up there, so they asked me if I minded carrying on with the baby-sitting for a bit.'

'I thought that you were his enemy too?'

He chuckled. 'Paul and I are cool now.'

'Stockholm syndrome?'

'No, we had our big breakthrough on the climbing wall.'

'You got Paul Evans up the climbing wall?' I couldn't hide my astonishment.

'Not quite. I took him up the easy way and gave him the options. I pointed out that there were only two ways down, and that we had already walked up one of them.' His tone shifted, sensing the tension coming off me. 'Why the concern with Paul Evans now?'

'Sally's been abducted.'

His voice turned grim. 'I'm on my way.'

'No. It would be more useful if you could get your new buddy to tell you if Ken and Les had anyone else up here they could have trusted to do this.'

I put the phone down. 'Where are you, Sally?' I intoned silently with my eyes closed, part rhetorical, part an attempt to get the crash-cart back on to the magic.

In the absence of an answer, I allowed myself to drift into Boon's room.

Sally had shown me in here the second time that I had visited. Then I had been looking for any significant links between Boon and the group. What had surprised me at that time had been the absence

349

of any. No record of them, either assembled or as individuals, in the photographs, snapshots and souvenir scraps of paper that were pinned to the corkboard above his cheap computer desk.

I looked at the images again. Boon in uniform with fellow soldiers. Boon in mufti with a variety of companions, male and female. Sally was in a couple of them, and, in one case, Boon was bending, grinning into shot in front of a puzzled llama behind a wire-mesh fence.

Images from happier times. Telling me that Boon was a normal, attractive, gregarious young man. Could they tell me anything else?

I went round the corkboard again slowly. One young woman recurred. I took down a picture of her with Boon, both of them smiling self-consciously into the camera in front of a grey stone Gothic church. The careful block printing on the back read *SOPH—LUNENBURG*.

She had fine, light brown hair, high Slavic cheekbones, a sharp nose and thin lips, but a confident and engaging smile that she wove into her whole face, which veered her over the border into loveliness.

I took down another one of the two of them. A beach shot. Boon in a pair of swimming trunks looking muscled and fit, Soph in a green bikini that didn't quite work on her, one hand trying to hold back the hair that the breeze was playing with. *LIMASSOL* on the back in the same block printing.

I went to pin it back and noticed the photograph that it had been partially covering. A small black-and-white studio portrait. An old one, judging by the curled corners and the crazing on the surface sheen. A young black woman smiling out into the world, the photographer just catching her on the verge of uncertain laughter.

I turned it over. The message was in pencil, crabbed and unsteady handwriting, much faded. I took it over to the desk lamp and had to peer hard to decipher it.

Please let my baby keep this . . .

I went over it again and took my time to make sure that I was reading the name correctly. I sat down on the bed. It was trying to tell me something. Or rather something lodged in my memory was trying to flag my attention.

When it came back to me I had to dampen it with the rider that it could be a total coincidence.

I stood up carefully, not taking my eyes from the chicken-claw scrawl on the back of the picture. Not wanting to lose the moment. This was too slow-burning for a revelation. And it lacked the certainty. But it was still gut-churning stuff, the dawning realization that there was a possibility that I now knew why Sally had locked her car and walked off into the night.

And, at that moment, that possibility was all I cared about.

I palmed my phone and scrolled down through the contacts. I found the number that was singing to me. I took a deep, steadying breath and pressed call. It started ringing out.

One is not at home, please leave your name and number and one will return your call when one has dispensed with the affairs of state.

I cut the connection.

My phone rang. It startled me. I stared at it for a moment, unable to answer it. I was overcome with a sense of dread, a feeling that if I took the call I

351

would be talking to a dead man.

'Glyn?'

'Mac . . .' It was only when I released my breath that I realized how long I had been holding it for.

'Paul says that there is no one he knows that Ken and Les would trust.'

'It doesn't matter, Mac.'

And it didn't. Not now. I knew where I was going.

*　　　*　　　*

It was a strange sensation, standing deep in the night shadow, intensified by the wellingtonia tree, watching the front of the house. A perverse kind of high. An exhilaration composed of tension, dread and anticipation. But I forced myself to be patient, trying to get the feel and pattern of the place. A light shone in the hall and the sitting room. On a couple of occasions a light had gone on in one of the upstairs bedrooms, where the curtains had already been closed. This was where I needed Mackay. So that I could stand back here for the overview, and watch what happened to the pattern when the doorbell was rung. But I was on my own and stuck with it.

I called the number again and let Her Majesty cut in on the answering machine before hanging up. I wanted him to know that I was trying to reach him. He would wonder why I was calling, but he would also assume that a telephone call implied distance and separation.

I psyched myself up for it and set off down the front path under the low rumble cover of a big plane high up in the North Atlantic corridor. I used

352

slow, deliberate strides, planting each footfall with the delicacy required to avoid the gravel turning into an auditory land mine. I wanted him to stay surprised. I stood dead still when I reached the porch, adjusting to the closeness. My heart was thrumming like a rogue piece of biology.

I used the door knocker rather than the bell to re-connect myself to the world of solid things. Nothing exploded. It seemed to take longer than it should for a blurred figure to frame itself in the door's obscure glass. The porch light came on.

'Who is it?' The voice on the other side of the door was guarded.

'Detective Sergeant Capaldi.'

The front door opened with the shocking squeal of a piece of trapped gravel on the quarry tile floor.

I nodded at him. 'Mr Ferguson.'

He looked down at me from the top step, his face showing that the surprise was not a happy one. He recovered his composure. 'It's very late.'

'Can I come inside, Mr Ferguson?' I asked, ignoring his observation.

He couldn't help the reflex. The momentary glance behind, before he caught himself. 'What do you need to talk to me about?'

'Coincidences.'

'What coincidences?'

I held up the photograph that I had brought from Boon's room. He came down off of the step and peered at it under the weak porch light. He looked at me quizzically. 'Am I meant to know something about this?'

'Rose Marie Ferguson.'

He nodded slowly, aware that something was changing. 'Ferguson is a fairly common name.'

I smiled at him. 'Tell me, is there any deep-veined psychological significance in re-naming yourself after your son's birth mother? Or was it just laziness?'

'Have you got a warrant?'

I slipped past him and in through the open door, turning on the threshold to look back at him still standing in the porch. 'I don't need a warrant, you invited me in.' I took a step into the hall, listening for sounds of occupancy. Just a radio from the living room. I was aware of him moving into the space behind me.

'I could call Constable Davies and tell him that you're trespassing.'

I turned round, shaking my head. 'Huw Davies is a friend of mine. We protect rare birds together.'

He waited. He wanted to know where I was driving this.

'Where is she, Malcolm?'

He drew in a slow breath, wondering whether to issue a formal denial. He closed the door behind him. 'Back in Jamaica. We didn't keep in touch. We left that up to Boon. When we thought that he was old enough we gave him that photograph and explained about his mother.'

I nodded, acknowledging that we had managed to punch through one layer of bullshit. 'I meant Marta. Or should I say Soph?'

He used a blank smile as a screen while he ran through the permutations. Was this a bluff? How much did I really know?

'Sophia—Boon's ex-girlfriend,' I amplified. 'Where is she now?'

'In Germany. I was on the phone to her yesterday, trying to reassure her as best I could

354

about Boon. As far as the other girl is concerned . . .' He stopped, frowning, when he saw me pick up the hall phone.

'Call her,' I instructed, holding out the receiver.

He shook his head and backed away from me.

I gave him the rueful smile of a disappointed headmaster. 'Malcolm Paterson, it's time to tell me what the fuck you have set in motion here.'

He closed his eyes, his head drooped and he shook it. 'It's all gone sour. It's all gone terribly wrong.' He dropped down to sit on the stairs, head still shaking. I waited him out. He looked up at me.

'It wasn't meant to happen like this. Nothing bad was meant to happen to Boon or Sophia.'

'Sophia was Marta?'

He nodded.

'Who you just called in Germany?'

He shook his head. 'I was just trying to put you off. I didn't want you to know that this had been organized.'

'Start from the beginning, Malcolm.'

His head dropped again. 'Wendy . . .' he said the name so softly that I almost didn't catch it. 'Wendy tried to commit suicide for the third time.' His voice strengthened. 'I had learned to keep the sharp stuff away from her. This time she broke my razor apart. Tried to use those thin strips of blades on her wrists. She cut her fingers to shreds in the process.' He looked up at me, a blaze of rage crossing his face. 'All because of those bastards. She still has to suffer. I've had to have her committed to a psychiatric unit in Cyprus.'

'So this is all about revenge?' I asked quietly.

He nodded. 'I wanted to take something back to Wendy. I wanted her to know that they were now

355

suffering. That they hadn't got away with it.' He looked at me, a pained expression on his face, as if I was working on a misunderstanding that hadn't been aired. 'Boon wasn't involved. Not in the beginning. This was my fight. Mine and Wendy's.'

He burst into tears. 'Why did it go so wrong? She was the victim. We should have had right on our side.'

*   *   *

I went to the kitchen for a glass of water. It gave me the opportunity to survey the ground floor. There was no evidence of anyone else living here. One single mug with tea dregs by the sink, any other dishes and cutlery washed and stacked away. No signs of any excess foodstuffs in the cupboards.

He drank the water gratefully, slowing down as he composed himself. 'I got the job here. Just far enough from Dinas. Then I had to think of a way to make contact with Trevor Vaughan. I got lucky: he brought his mother to that concert I told you about. I thought luck was with me then. That was the plan you see: to use Trevor to get at them.'

I shook my head, not getting it. 'Surely he recognized you? You're his friend's father, for God's sake, a teacher at the local school. You went off with another friend's sister. Didn't he run a mile?'

'He didn't know me. Not at first.' He allowed himself the ghost of a smile. 'I've inverted myself. From the neck up. I used to have longish hair and sideburns, now I've got more hair on my chin than my head. And I wear contact lenses instead of Clark Kent glasses. And I had a Cyprus sun tan. He

356

may have thought that there was a resemblance, but what you have to remember is that he wasn't looking to find Malcolm Paterson. What he thought he'd found was an interesting older man who understood music.'

'But he did find out who you really were?'

'I told him. It was the whole point in me coming here.'

'And he didn't run a mile?'

'Not when I told him about Wendy's condition. What those bastards had done to her.'

'He didn't know?'

'He said he didn't. Maybe he just wanted to be able to pretend that he didn't.'

I nodded, letting him know that I was keeping up with the train so far. 'What did you expect from him?'

'It was more about hope. That he would back me up. Go to the police and corroborate the systematic abuse that McGuire and Tucker had inflicted on Wendy. And the other girls they messed up.'

'But he wouldn't?'

He shook his head. 'Not that far. He sympathized, he was genuinely morally torn, but in the end his loyalty to his warped friends won out.'

'So you activated Plan B?'

'Plan B?'

'Boon and Marta, aka Sophia.'

His expression shifted back to doleful. 'It backfired. We only intended to persuade Trevor that they were still capable of terrible things. Not that terrible things could really happen.' He looked up at me. 'Remember, we didn't know then that they had actually killed that poor girl.'

'What was meant to happen?'

'Boon was meant to convince them that he was going to quit the Army that night. Sophia was the bait. She was going to offer to stay with McGuire and Tucker after they'd helped Boon on his way. I was going to pick up Boon in Aberystwyth, and then work on Trevor to persuade him that McGuire and Tucker were up to their old tricks again.'

'You deliberately let Sophia go off alone into the night with them? Christ, man, you of all people should know what they're capable of.'

'Sophia's tough. And Boon was going to be monitoring her.' He looked up at me plaintively, a rasp in his voice. 'But Boon never showed up in Aberystwyth. I don't know what's happened to either of them. I don't know what they've done to them, and I don't know what to do.'

I let the silence expand for dramatic purpose before I shouted, 'Bullshit!'

It had the desired effect. He was so startled his bum almost lifted off the stairs.

I leaned in close to his face. 'There never was a Plan B.'

He squirmed away from me, shaking his head, working on puzzled and injured.

'Wendy was over sixteen. She was legal. They did terrible things, but there was no offence committed that could be proven, so there was nothing for Trevor to go to the police about. Not until you tried to con him into thinking that Boon had been disposed of, and that Marta had been abducted. Boon and Sophia were part of Plan A right from the start.'

He shook his head more vigorously. 'I told you . . . It's all gone wrong . . . I don't know what's happened to them.'

358

'Then why haven't you come to us to report them missing?' I answered for him: 'Because you're quite happy with the way things are panning out. You've hit the bonus with the discovery of poor old Colette. That was unexpected. But it serves to concentrate the mind even more on the still unaccounted for Boon and Marta.'

He stared up at me. 'God, you are a cold and unfeeling bastard, aren't you?'

I grinned. 'Nice try, Malcolm. But I was there the night that Ken and Les came to get Sophia out of the Den. I saw their reaction when they realized that she wasn't there. And who, I wonder, let her out? Because it wasn't the Good Fucking Fairy, was it?'

He studied me warily, trying to calculate where I was going with this.

'Ken and Les will be put away for what they did to Colette. You've got your revenge to take back to Wendy. It's time to call Boon and Sophia back into the fold.'

He shook his head so slowly that I wasn't sure whether he was refusing or still calculating.

'And why did you need to bring Sally into this?' I let him hear my real anger. 'I couldn't figure it out. She was frightened, she was in a cold and wild place. What would make her get out and leave her car?' I held up the photograph of Rose Marie Ferguson again. 'And then I made the connection. God, what would have gone through her mind when she saw you walking up out of the gloom? She probably thought she was hallucinating. What did it take to make you solid to her? A rap on the window? An old, familiar, cracked smile? Because you knew that she would have to respond. No matter how bitter, betrayed and damaged she felt, you still had Boon linking you. And Boon was in danger.'

'It wasn't me.' He said it quietly, head down, not looking at me.

'Who else could it be?'

Something in the air changed. I sensed the movement at the top of the stairs. Before I heard the voice.

'What about her son?'

19

Boon Paterson looked down at me, smiling, amused by my surprise. He looked healthy. Dressed in tight black jeans and a grey, baggy sweatshirt.

'Is Sophia up there?' I asked.

'Why?'

'It's time for you both to come in. It's time to stop this.'

He came down the stairs, taking them slowly, rolling a sway into his steps. Even with the loose-fitting sweatshirt, I could tell that he was powerfully built. I hoped that this wasn't going to turn into something that I was going to regret.

'Soph isn't here.' The same studied swagger in his voice as in his gait.

Malcolm got up to let him join us at the foot of the stairs. I had the height, but he was stacked with youth and energy. And no fear.

'Where is she?'

'That's what you people are trying to find out in the woods.' He laughed. 'Along with poor busted-up old me. Isn't that where everyone thinks we are? Chopped up and buried by those two sick fucks?'

'We've got them for Colette, you don't need to take this any further.'

He shook his head. 'It isn't enough.'

I realized then that he had brought his own agenda into this. He had embraced new histories and cultural possibilities and was now looking back on his past with venom. He was possessed of a confused rage that Malcolm had been able to channel.

'They'll deal it down to manslaughter,' Malcolm protested.

'We can't charge them if we don't find the bodies,' I reasoned.

'But you can fuck up the rest of their lives with the insinuation,' Malcolm said gleefully.

'If we're never found, they'll carry the blame around with them for ever.'

I turned to Boon. 'You can't just disappear for ever.'

He grinned. 'Wanna bet? Believe me, people disappear all the time. I've taken advice from enough of them before I started this.'

'I've seen you.'

He scowled. 'So?'

'I now have a responsibility to take you in.'

'The fuck you will,' he growled. I saw the muscle cords in his neck tense.

Malcolm eased in to keep us separated. 'It's okay, Boon, let him.'

Boon and I looked at him, equally surprised.

He smiled snidely. 'If Boon goes in with you, he's going to testify that he went to Ireland. He's only just managed to make it back after he heard about poor Marta's disappearance.'

It took me a moment to see the path his game had taken. The bastard had just used Boon to check me. If I took Boon in as a live one, he would swear on oath that the last time he saw Marta she was going off in the company of Ken and Les. Off into the sunrise with demonstrable sexual deviants and killers. And she had never been seen since. We would have to redouble our efforts to find her. And I would know, but could not prove, that there was nothing to find.

I realized then that there was another way out.

'Okay,' I played up my reluctance, defeat in my tone, 'I'm going to walk away. I'm going to leave the doubt diluted.'

Malcolm nodded. 'Either way, it works for us, Sergeant.' He dug into a pocket and produced a small plastic case, and proffered it, trying not to grin too hugely. 'There's something on this that you might want to keep private.'

It was a digital memory card. *Far enough . . .* It ratcheted into place. 'Tony Griffiths's truck? You took those photographs?'

He nodded smugly.

I pocketed the case. 'Why me?'

'You were the only one who took an interest.'

'Where does Tony Griffiths fit into this?'

'I used to score weed off of him in the old days,' Boon answered. 'He's a useful, minor local outlaw.'

I turned to Malcolm. 'You paid him to deliver Marta. The rendezvous was a set-up. Boon was the only one in on it. He was the one who persuaded Ken and Les to come up with the fable of the Cardiff hooker. It had nothing to do with loyalty or friendship, he was trading in his girlfriend. He pimped Soph to them.'

Malcolm put up a hand to quiet Boon's angry reaction.

I shook my head angrily. 'She was the tethered goat. Jesus, you were playing it close to the wire. What if it had gone wrong?'

'It didn't go wrong. Boon was watching over her the whole time.'

'You think we didn't have safety checks in place?' Boon snorted angrily. 'We knew from Wendy exactly how the Den worked. How to get in and out. And Soph had a short-range pager, just in case she needed a panic button.'

'But we knew that wasn't ever going to be necessary,' Malcolm expanded, 'because Ken and Les were still in the soft, nurturing, gift-bearing stage of the grooming process. And they had to stay high-profile model citizens following their escapade.' He grinned. 'And now it's going to haunt them for the rest of their lives.'

I stared at him coldly for a moment, and then did my wondering right out loud. 'How far would you have gone?'

He shrugged.

'Reassure me, Malcolm.'

He smiled at Boon before he replied. 'We've killed no one, Sergeant Capaldi.'

I let his self-satisfaction roll around us for a moment.

'Yes you have.'

Surprise kicked the smugness off his face.

'You killed Trevor Vaughan.'

'Whoa . . . Whoa . . . Whoa . . .' He held up a hand and shook his head slowly and firmly, wanting to impress his words on to me before he spoke them. 'Trevor Vaughan killed himself.'

'He may have tied the rope, climbed that ladder, and launched himself off into the great by and by, but you were the motor that powered him.'

He shook his head contemptuously.

'All the way over here tonight, I've been trying to figure it out. Why you took the chance? Why you made contact with me, pretending you wanted to know about the funeral arrangements. My first thought was that it was because you were a risk junkie. You were getting off on the danger. It worked with your arrogance, your sense that you were in control of this thing.'

He smiled patronizingly. 'Whatever you think, Sergeant.'

'There was probably an element of that. But essentially you wanted to feed me. You wanted to make sure that I was on the right track. What was it you told me? Something about his inner conflicts, the line between betrayal and duty? You just wanted to make sure that I was pointed in the right direction.'

He flashed Boon a supercilious smile.

'Because I was always part of this, wasn't I?'

He shook his head, not understanding.

'You built me in. When it was just Emrys Hughes and Inspector Morgan, you didn't have a hope in hell of anyone taking this seriously. But when you heard that I was in place, a new rogue kid on the block, suddenly it all became possible. Someone prepared to spit in the old guards' faces.' Another tumbler connected. 'You impersonated the dispatcher. You told me where to find the minibus.'

He grinned. 'I was actually calling as a concerned

citizen. It was you who mistook me for the dispatcher. I didn't correct you. And we did get you there in the end,' he observed with a smirk.

'Did you flirt with him, Malcolm?'

He shook his head. 'I'm not going to dignify that with a reply.'

'Trevor Vaughan was terrified of his sexuality. Is that the wire you played him out on?'

'He knew I was Boon's father.'

'But, as you said, he also knew you as an interesting older man with an understanding of the finer things in life. Did you charm him with your urbanity? Did you weave the spell of a possibility, Malcolm? Knowing that Trevor couldn't allow himself to fall for a man. Wouldn't dare to; there was too much turmoil and self-loathing in that direction.'

'We never intended that Trevor take his own life,' Boon said, a note in his voice that sounded almost close to regret.

'No, it may not have been your intention—but it still worked for you, didn't it?'

'And what was our intention?' Malcolm challenged.

'You already told me. You wanted to get him to turn informant, tell the world what Ken and Les were really like. He was good people, a cast-iron, solid citizen. He would be listened to. If he were to point the finger at them as sex fiends after Marta and Boon disappear, then it's not too much of a connective leap for the world to make . . .' I paused, looking at each of them in turn. 'But he couldn't do it, could he?'

Malcolm shook his head. 'He came very close.'

'But he couldn't take it as far as direct betrayal.

365

Even with you threatening to expose him as a homosexual.'

Boon shook his head angrily. 'We wouldn't have done that.'

'I know. You couldn't have—it would have meant revealing yourselves in order to do it. But he didn't know that. He was a gentle, tortured bastard, who believed what people told him. That threat, and with it the betrayal of his first real sexual possibility, was enough to destroy him.'

'I never let him believe that I was a sexual possibility,' Malcolm protested.

'You don't know what you built him up to believe.' I stared at him for a moment, wondering. 'Or do you?' I let that hang there. 'You gave him Wendy's panties. What was he supposed to tell us? That he had found these years ago, along with other evidence of Ken and Les's behaviour? He had only kept quiet about it up until now to protect them?'

I saw from the look that they exchanged that I was close to the mark.

'You bastards drove him into that awful corner.'

'You're not entirely blameless yourself,' Malcolm sneered. 'You were hounding him too.'

'Right, but I was floundering. I was after answers.' I turned to Boon. 'I thought that I was trying to save you and your fucking girlfriend. You were cold-bloodedly directing him, leaving him with no options.' I shook my head disconsolately. 'I can't forgive you for that.'

'Is that meant to be a threat?' Malcolm asked.

I suppressed my anger. I flashed them both one bitter last look before I walked out the door.

I had to leave. I didn't dare betray the fact that I was about to attempt to cut them off at the knees.

366

Bryn called me to tell me that Sally had been found near Dinas, and that the search had been called off. I heard it in his voice that he was pleased to be passing this news on to me. I had been expecting it, but I managed to play it surprised and relieved. I still had an empty feeling, knowing that I was the only one among the good guys with the understanding that we were being directed. Sally was going to save us, but I had to wonder dismally how far she had been pulled into their game?

I drove past her empty house, parked a little way down the street, and waited in the dark. I watched the complicated physics of amalgamating raindrops on the windscreen, and kept attempting to tuck Malcolm's parting smile of triumph away for ever.

She arrived in a squad car. A uniformed cop got out and opened the rear door for her, and I watched the mime as she declined an escort. They waited until she was inside. I waited until they had driven off.

I didn't use my key. I rang the doorbell. She opened the door with a half-prepared smile, expecting to find one of the cops who had driven her home. 'Glyn . . .' Her face collapsed with the complication of having to deal with my being there. She clutched me, and I felt her head on my cheek, straddling my shoulder. 'Oh God, Glyn . . . I'm so sorry to have caused all this fuss.' I returned the embrace. But I couldn't hold back the uncharitable thought that she didn't want me to see the mechanics at work as she struggled to find a place to pitch her control.

We walked through to the kitchen, a silent double bundle of nervous smiles. I watched her take her coat off. 'Are you okay?' I asked.

She managed a chastened smile. 'I feel very foolish.'

'What happened?' I asked, sitting down at the table.

She shook her head, grimacing self-reproachfully. 'I couldn't get the car started. I know I should have stayed put, like you told me, but I was getting a bit scared. I felt I had to move. To do something. And you had told me not to drive. So I walked. It was only when a car stopped to see if I was all right that I realized that I had been going in completely the wrong direction.' She experimented on taking her smile slightly out of chastened.

She had rehearsed the story. And Bryn would have bought it. He probably didn't believe it, but he would only have assumed that she was trying to cover up her lapse into fugue.

I nodded understandingly. 'It was Boon wasn't it?'

The smile that had started to grow slipped, and her mouth fell open. For a moment she thought seriously and hard about protesting, continuing the lie. Instead, she slumped. 'Who saw me?' It came out as a hard-drawn whisper.

'No one. I worked it out. Although at first I thought it was Malcolm you saw up there.'

'You know?' She brought the knuckles of her right hand to her mouth.

'I've seen them both.'

She shook her head, her eyes wide. I felt so sorry for her. She had been through so much turmoil already tonight. But I couldn't let up.

'Was Soph with Boon when you saw him?' I asked, trying to keep my voice as gentle as possible.

'No.' It came out as a choked whisper.

'Did he say anything about her?'

'Only that she's okay. Waiting for him in a safe place.'

'He didn't say where that place was?'

'No.' She seemed close to tears. 'I didn't want to lie to you Glyn. But I didn't think you knew. DCI Jones didn't say anything.'

'No one else knows, Sally.'

She looked gaunt. 'I only cared that Boon was all right.'

'I know.' I reached across and took her hand away from her mouth and held it. Stroking the back with my thumb. 'You know that this is all about Wendy Evans getting her revenge.'

'They did terrible things to her.'

'I know, but that doesn't excuse what they've done here. Or what they've done to you. What they've put you through, the way they're using you.'

She shook her head weakly. 'They're not using me for anything.'

I let that ride for the moment. 'Did Boon ever tell you that he and Soph had hooked up with Malcolm and Wendy in Cyprus?'

'No.' She screwed her eyes closed. She had already been through this pain once tonight.

'Who is Boon doing it for, Sally? Who rates all this love and sacrifice? Malcolm or Wendy?'

She closed her eyes again. 'Please, Glyn—don't.'

She tried to pull her hand away, but I held on. 'I'm not being deliberately cruel. I just want you to be aware how callous and calculating these people are. Where they've positioned you. Keeping you

369

out of the loop until you were needed.'

'Boon didn't have to come back here to let me know that he was safe.'

'Yes he did.' I stood up, held her shoulders across the table, and made her face me to emphasize how seriously I wanted her to take this. 'Sally, they knew that I was going to tell you. They had to get in there first. They didn't know how much I knew, only that sooner or later I was going to be able to tell you that Boon was not in a hole in the ground somewhere in the forest. They were buying your silence so that this can go on playing itself out. This hunt for bodies that don't exist, just to mire Ken and Les deeper in it. But it's not a game, Sally. I don't give a shit about Ken or Les, but I do care about what happened to Trevor Vaughan. And I care about our people wasting time, resources and worry on a bullshit investigation.'

She looked away and shook her head hopelessly. 'You could tell them.'

'With what? I have no concrete evidence to back me up. Even if I go public about seeing Boon and Malcolm, that won't count—I'm not an impartial witness. They're relying on that, and now they're relying on you to keep this vicious farce rolling. They're playing you for a patsy. Don't you see the awful irony of it? You are the one who is propping up Wendy's sweet revenge.'

'She deserves something for what they did to her,' she said stubbornly.

'She got your husband Sally. They got their life in the sun. You got Mid Wales and the night shift at the Sychnant Nursing Home. She now has the satisfaction of seeing Ken and Les going down for

Colette Fletcher. That's enough. She doesn't need or deserve any more than that.'

She dropped her head and sobbed. I felt my heart wrench. I walked round the table and pulled her close and wrapped myself around her, feeling the spasms of anguish racking her like physical jolts. 'Oh God, Glyn, what am I going to do?' She pulled her breathing together, shook her head, searching for the words. 'My first reaction was total relief . . . Knowing that Boon was okay . . . Then he told me that I wouldn't be able to see or contact him again until this was all forgotten. That could be years. Boon can never come back here.'

I kissed the top of her head. 'Bring him back to life, Sally.' I gave it time for the worm of the thought to wriggle in before I whispered again. 'If he isn't dead, he doesn't have to stay hidden.'

She shook her head. 'I promised,' she blurted, not looking up.

'Wendy and Malcolm have got enough out of this. You don't need to bleed too.'

'I don't think I would ever want to be with Malcolm again,' she announced quietly, as if she had only just surprised herself with the realization.

I felt a small plug of latent anxiety vanish. 'I'll be here with you. I'll help you. All you have to do is call DCI Jones and tell him that you've seen Boon. That he and the girl are okay.'

She twisted her head round to look up at me. 'It would be betraying a trust.'

Yes, to a cheating bastard of an ex-husband, and a dumbfuck adopted son who cannot work within the normal extremes of loyalty and friendship. But I didn't say it. 'You'll be freeing-up Boon's life,' I said instead. 'He'll thank you for it later, when whatever kind of a mission he feels he's on has worked its way through his system.'

I could see that she was tempted.

'Do you want to go to bed?' I whispered, trying to pitch the prospect of comfort rather than lust.

'Yes please,' she whispered back with a long sigh. 'I would like nothing more than to close my eyes and curl up with you holding me, and forget all about this . . .'

I sensed the 'but' poised, ready to intrude.

'But I can't forget about it. I'm sorry, Glyn, but I need the time alone to think things through. Try to think about what's best for Boon—'

'And what's best for you,' I interrupted.

She smiled weakly. 'And that too.'

'If it helps with your thought process and decision making, I am unfettered and unencumbered. As a cop, I have to stay here. They'll make sure that no one else will have me. But I don't have to stay as a cop.'

'Thanks, Glyn. That helps me.' She reached down, took my hand and squeezed it, lifted it and kissed the back of my fingers. I knew that it was the signal to release her.

I left happy.

Shame that it wasn't going to last.

*   *   *

I went to sleep alone that night in my own bed with the conviction that Sally was going to come through. She would see sense and make that call to Bryn, and the bullshit investigation would be called off. And we could all, barring Ken and Les, live happily ever after.

The morning brought a joyless film of wet snow that was already morphing to slush. The sky was the grey of weathered zinc, and the birds seemed to have abandoned the planet. When the phone rang, I got out of bed with the duvet wrapped round me to postpone the shock of the cold.

'Glyn . . .' Her voice was shaky.

'How are you this morning?' I asked solicitously.

'We need to talk.' I could hear the fatigue in her voice.

I saw it in her eyes too when she opened her front door. And something more. Something hard and set below the pillow-mussed hair that she hadn't bothered to brush.

'What's wrong?' I asked, concerned, following her through to the kitchen.

She spoke without turning. 'There was an envelope in the hall when I came down early this morning. Someone must have put it through the letterbox.' She wheeled round to look at me, no smile, her eyes deep-set and dark-rimmed from lack of sleep.

'And . . .?' I felt something hard and heavy drop into my stomach.

'Someone has sent me a photograph of you.'

The bastards . . .

I winced inwardly. I should have realized what they were capable of and prepared for this. They must have made copies of the images on the memory card before they had given it to me.

'It's a fake, Sally.'

'It looked real enough to me.'

'It was a simulation. Malcolm and Boon set it up.'

'Stop blaming my son for everything,' she

snapped angrily, simultaneously lifting a magazine off the table to reveal the photograph that was lying there, face-up.

Oh fuck . . .

I closed my eyes and prayed that when I opened them again the world would have been reinvented as a kinder place.

It didn't work. The photograph was still there. It was a bad shot. It was a terrible shot. Dark and fuzzy, taken from outside without a flash, reliant on the low level of ambient light in the kitchen. But the grainy image only served to make the scene more intimate.

There I was, leaning over Sheila McGuire, head bent coming down into a kiss. No caption saying that this was a pure act of consolation. No way of telling that the trajectory was only aimed at her cheek. And, more damning than that, in the lost shadows it would have been easy to make the mistake of thinking that I had one hand down cupping her breast.

'This wasn't the picture I meant . . .' I stammered without thinking.

She shuddered. 'I don't want to know about any more.'

'Sally, I can explain . . .' I pleaded.

And then, just at the high point of the very worst time it could ever happen, my phone rang. Sally stared at me impassively. I checked caller ID: Bryn Jones. I knew instinctively that I had to answer it.

'Hello?' I said, turning my back on her.

'Glyn, something's come up, we need you to get up into the forest.'

I cupped the phone in my hand and turned to Sally. 'It's DCI Jones, will you speak to him?' I

374

entreated.

She shook her head. And all the despair and the finality of it hit me then. They were going to win.

'Glyn, are you there?' Bryn was shouting.

'Sorry, sir . . .' I stared at Sally, letting her see my anguish under the semblance of the normal tone that I was keeping up for Bryn, 'What's so important up in the forest?'

'We've had a call. A male, wouldn't give his name, but he thinks that he might have witnessed something suspicious that night near the hut.'

'Probably a crank, sir.' I felt my stomach tighten even more as I realized that they had just ratcheted the game to another level.

'He said he saw a group of men digging. We can't ignore it, Glyn. You know your way around that place; get up there and wait for us to arrive with the search team and the dogs.'

'Yes, sir.'

I shut down the phone. I looked at Sally across the room. She looked back at me. 'I was trying to give Sheila McGuire some comfort, Sally.'

'Good for you, Glyn,' she said, deadpan.

I pointed to the table. 'Think who benefits from that picture.' I looked at her despairingly. 'Please, Sally . . .'

'Just leave.'

If she had slammed the front door behind me, I might have thought that there was some hope.

*   *   *

I drove like a madman. I did it partly to scare the shit out of myself and block the recall of the hurt and contempt on Sally's face as she had closed the door on me. But I also wanted to buy time. I had a new agenda, and I needed to get up there before the search party arrived to spoil it.

Because I had now worked out the secret of why the hole that they had dug in the forest had been empty.

They had always intended it to be part of the evidence trail. Drunk as they all were that night, it wouldn't have been hard for Boon to persuade them to join him in some kind of sentimental ritual. *Hey guys, let's bury something up here, let's symbolically sever my connection to the Army.* It would have been something loaded with his DNA. So that, when the hole was conveniently found after he became a missing person, it would read as an attempt to conceal incriminating evidence.

But Trevor followed them out of the hut. He didn't see what they were up to, but Soph, who had followed him, didn't know that. The plan appeared to be compromised. Gordon's presence they could handle, because his testimony would always be seen as slanted. But add Trevor's corroboration that he had witnessed a celebration, and they were fucked. Where was the black intent? It was hardly sinister any more, the last sighting of Boon and he's horsing around with the guys who were supposed to have topped him.

So they removed whatever had been buried, and left the hole empty.

Except now they must have re-seeded it. With Trevor out of the way, and not knowing that he had shown it to me, it had obviously been deemed safe to re-plant the evidence.

But I was going to screw them.

I had dug that hole up once before and found it

376

empty. Now I intended digging it up again and making it empty.

I had to slow down after spinning the car on the snow that was still a fixture on the tracks higher into the forest. But at least it would also delay the cavalry. As another precaution, I left my car so that it blocked the access to the track that led down to the hole.

I had worried about finding the exact spot again, but the snow cover actually helped me pinpoint it. The ground had been excavated so many times now that the snow crust had slumped, showing a perfect outline.

But the snow soon posed another problem. As I dug, the ground around the excavation turned muddy, runny-shit caramel, in stark contrast to the surrounding virginal whiteness. There was no way that I was going to be able to dig this up and fill it back in again without it being obvious that the ground had only just been disturbed.

I carried on. I had to at least find out what they had left in here.

I had guessed that I might find a beret, but it was a cap. A baseball cap, not a military one. It was sodden and muddy. It could have been a larger twin to the one at the lay-by. I could make out the initials *BP* on the sweatband. And it would be swarming, I knew, with Boon's DNA. It was too wet to tell if they had augmented it with blood traces.

I had no moral or professional qualms. I was not tampering with evidence but disappearing a corrupt signpost. Fuck it, I was Excelsior, lighting the way back up to the truth. I was on the side of the angels. Despite what Sally now thought of me.

Except that it was going to require a trade-off.

Jack Galbraith was not going to buy an empty hole.

I took the cap back to the car and stashed it in the boot well, under the spare wheel. I would burn it later at Hen Felin, along with the one that Soph had left for me to find. I returned to the hole and placed the one thing that I had to offer as trade goods in the bottom, and started filling it in. I didn't put too much effort into it. It was only going to be dug back up.

As I had hoped, when the cavalry arrived, they assumed that I was in the process of digging out, not filling in.

Jack Galbraith and Bryn, both in borrowed Wellington boots, led the procession. The dogs had been left in the vans. I was glad, I didn't want them sniffing out evasion.

'What the fuck are you doing, Capaldi?' Jack Galbraith shouted, striding towards me. 'We told you to look around, not start mining for fucking gold.'

'There was an obvious depression in the snow, sir. And this has been excavated recently. I did check for footprints before I started. And I've been very careful while digging.'

'I can see that,' Jack Galbraith observed, making a meal of surveying the muddy penumbra that I had created around the hole. He nodded for Bryn to take over the organization and management.

I stood back with the rest of the executive branch while two uniforms painstakingly continued with the excavating. No one spoke. There was an anticipatory tension in the air. I was sharing it, although for different reasons.

'I think we've found something.' One of the

uniforms relayed the message to Emrys Hughes.

Instinctively, we all drew in closer. Emrys knelt down and held out a clear plastic evidence wallet. The uniform picked the object up gingerly between a latex-gloved thumb and forefinger and dropped it into the wallet.

Emrys stood up holding the wallet skyward like something about to explode.

'Let me see that,' Jack Galbraith instructed.

Emrys swung it towards him. 'Shall I get this down the hill to the technical boys, sir?'

I coughed.

Bryn Jones and Jack Galbraith looked at me enquiringly.

'Shepherdess,' I said.

Bryn frowned, puzzled. Jack Galbraith started to nod, a pained smile tilting the corner of his mouth. Without turning towards Emrys Hughes, he took the wallet from his hands. 'I think we'll be taking this straight down to Carmarthen with us.' He dangled the wallet containing the memory card case in front my eyes. 'What do you say, Capaldi?'

I nodded. 'I think that that would be a very wise move, sir.'

THE END OF THE AFFAIR

I told them everything.

Well, that is, everything to do with the bluff that I had invented as I had waited by the hole for them to arrive. I had considered the truth as an option, but I didn't linger long there.

Yes, I had seen these images before. No, I had not been aware at the time that photographs had been taken when I had stopped a truck to check for poached venison carcases. Only when they had been sent to me with an anonymous note advising me that it would be in my best interests to back off from asking any more questions about McGuire and Tucker. Now that Ken and Les had been arrested, I assumed that the memory card had been planted to capitalize on the earlier threat.

Jack Galbraith had looked at me then with an almost fatherly concern. 'Did you ever want to be a vet, Capaldi?'

'Not particularly, sir.'

'I only ask that because it seems to me that this is the only profession that should be showing such a particular and close-range interest in an obviously dead cow.'

'Yes, sir.'

'And why are your trousers undone?'

'With respect, sir, they're not, it's just the way the photograph was taken.'

'Why didn't you tell us about this?' Bryn asked.

'I was embarrassed, sir.' I nodded towards the computer screen. 'That could so easily be misinterpreted.'

Jack Galbraith nodded. 'It could, couldn't it?'

They didn't believe a word of it. But what were they going to do? Abandon me to the wolves and have Jack Galbraith's hand-picked Man in the Wilderness publicly accused of bestiality with a necrophilia dressing?

And it would have been even worse PR while we still had an ongoing investigation into the disappearance of Boon and Marta eating up manpower, morale and resources.

I was not popular. I was officially removed from the investigation, and dispatched back to the boondocks while they considered what action to take. I wasn't concerned about being taken off the case as I knew it was only a tree of smoke, but I did have fears for my so-called career. After all, there was nowhere further downhill for me to slip.

It was the day that I was burning Boon's and Soph's caps that I came up with the answer.

Mackay was reluctant at first, until I reminded him that together we constituted the Brotherhood of the Dumped.

I scanned it in and emailed it as an attachment to Bryn Jones.

He called me as soon as he received it. 'What is this?'

'You remember my friend Mackay who helped us out with Paul Evans?'

'Of course.'

'He put out the word to friends he still has in Special Forces.'

'What word?'

'They've come back with this. They were on an exercise in Cyprus when they took it. But it has to be nonattributable. We can't go public with it:

Special Forces training is sensitive.'

'When was this taken?'

'Two days ago. There are enough people who will be able to confirm that that is Boon. And all of the men who were on the minibus will be able to identify the girl as Marta.'

'This was taken on a beach, Glyn. It's the middle of winter.'

'Not in Cyprus. And there is a wind, if you look at the way her hair is moving,' I offered, looking at the photograph on the screen, which bore a remarkable resemblance to the one that I had removed from Boon's room at the same time as I had taken his birth mother's picture to confront Malcolm with.

As anticipated, it didn't take long for Jack Galbraith to call me.

'If this fucking backfires, Capaldi . . .'

'It can't, sir.'

'Why so certain?'

'They can't exactly call anyone up and say, "Hey, we really are dead, you know."'

He was silent for a moment. 'So we have closure?'

'I think so, sir.'

'And what do you want out of it, Capaldi?'

'Would headquarters be too much to ask, sir?'

'Fucking right it would . . .' But at least he put the phone down with a chuckle.

I called Sally, ostensibly to report the happy news that Boon and Soph had been resurrected. She heard me out. I waited, ready to gauge her response. She just told me that she was leaving Dinas. Nothing more personal in it than if she was cancelling the milk. Permanently.

I never did find out whether the news that Malcolm Paterson took back to Cyprus had a recuperative effect on Wendy.

But he had been right about Ken and Les. Their lawyers managed to talk the charges down to manslaughter. They are currently out on bail awaiting the results of psychiatric reports before sentencing. And I am glad to report that both they and their respective partners are avoiding me. And each other.

And I had been wrong about Donna Gallagher, the other girl from the children's home who had disappeared from the Sychnant Nursing Home.

When we eventually traced her, she was living in Scunthorpe and working as a beauty therapist. And she had called her child Danni, not Dwayne or Britney.

And the Brotherhood of the Dumped? Against my advice, Mackay followed Gina and her Australian to Queensland. Using Special Forces techniques, he arranged a seemingly casual encounter as she was snorkelling off the Great Barrier Reef.

He emerged from the sea. I like to picture him with a dagger between his teeth, but that would have made it difficult for him to tell her that he still loved her.

Gina laughed, he told me, shook her head and told him that history had just repeated itself. When she had left me, she thought she had got rid of the only pathetic bastard in her life.

To Mackay, this cemented us even closer.

When he visits, the crazy bastard still makes a point of walking up *through* the river. And so far, touch wood, the albatrosses are staying on the wing.

CHIVERS
LARGE
PRINT
-direct-

If you have enjoyed this Large Print book and would like to build up your own collection of Large Print books, please contact

Chivers Large Print Direct

Chivers Large Print Direct offers you a full service:

• Prompt mail order service

• Easy-to-read type

• The very best authors

• Special low prices

For further details either call Customer Services on (01225) 336552 or write to us at Chivers Large Print Direct, **FREEPOST**, Bath BA1 3ZZ

Telephone Orders: **FREEPHONE** 08081 72 74 75